HENRY IN PIECES

HENRY IN PIECES

A NOVEL

To Marian,
As a professional you
must tell me what
you thought of Henry
Keith

KEITH CHATER

Library of Congress Control Number: 2010905438
ISBN: Hardcover   978-1-4500-8612-7
                 Softcover   978-1-4500-8611-0
                 Ebook   978-1-4500-8613-4

To order additional copies of this book, contact:
Xlibris Corporation
1-888-795-4274
www.Xlibris.com
Orders@Xlibris.com
79526

For my wife Sonia

And in memory
of
My Dad
Philip Raymond Chater
who never heard my voice

*   *   *

"The grand essentials in this life are something to do,
something to love, and something to hope for."

Joseph Addison

1

Henry peered at the clock. Light was beginning to come in under the curtain but he still needed to squint at the numbers on its face. 6:32 a.m. Time to get up. If he didn't move shortly, Leah would shove him in the small of the back and tell him to get going. She didn't need an alarm clock. She always knew the time: when to get up; when to eat; when to leave the party. Well, he was about to leave the party. He rubbed his index finger along the crease of his eye to get the sleep out, and, cautiously, raised his right hand until his whole arm was standing upright in the cool of the room. Leah kept the window open at night and, of course, she had turned the heat down. She did that every night of their lives from the middle of October to the beginning of May. After that, it went off.

Gravity permitted his pyjama sleeve to slide slowly down his arm and he looked at the thin white appendage in the gloom. It was a long time since he had seen his arm like this and he twisted it round to get a view of the whole thing. Not much muscle tone, and he seemed to remember more hair. The veins on the inside of his wrist stood out, two almost parallel purple lines, and he wondered what the effect of a razor would be. He knew there would be hell to pay if he got blood on the sheets, and, in any case, he didn't think there was a suitable razor in the house. These days everything was either disposable or electric. Still, it was an interesting thought.

In the brightening murk of the morning, Henry turned the arm round. He could see what his parents had called liver spots on the back of his hand. He had always had freckles but these were different. There were similar marks on his face, plains of light brown on pale skin. Bringing his hand down, he rubbed at the biggest mark with a moistened finger. His fingers were like twigs on a bush in winter. His wedding ring glinted, mocking him. Just the other day, he had spent fifteen minutes in the bathroom trying to ease it off with spit and soap and a bottle of Vim from under the sink. It wouldn't move. The knuckle was too big and the ring too tight. Thirty-some years it had been there and it wasn't about to budge now. He used his thumbnail, absently trying to flick it off, but Henry knew the thing was there to stay. A life sentence. Now there's irony for you. He smiled at the thought.

She moved.

He held his breath. His arms were still outside the warmth of the sheets, waving surrender in the morning air. Then, he turned his hands so that he could see his palms. No stigmata in the dawn's early light. He wondered what it would be like to throttle her. Put one thumb in the crevice of her larynx under the chin, except that she didn't have much of a chin, never had had. Less with age. Unless he was careful the thumb would skid up inside a nostril or dig an eye out. She'd be furious at that, so he'd have to be careful. Thumbs in place, fingers edging round her neck, yes, that's it, steady now. Squeeze. Gently does it.

She pushed him. 'Henry, it's time to get up.'

Did he really hear the words or did he just anticipate what she always said?

'Yes, dear, just going to.'

Pavlov's dog.

Sitting on the side of the bed rubbing his face, he felt Anna Karenina against his legs and he reached down to stroke her arching back. He could feel her purr.

'Tea?' he asked.

He posed the same question each morning. He never waited for a reply. If she didn't reply, well, no harm done. On the other hand, if she said 'yes', he would know about it later; how she lay there and the tea never came and he was the most unreasonable man. She might even call him at work to whine about how hard done by she was, how hard put upon. Or she might wait until he came home, was in the hall taking off his overshoes. 'Henry, is that you? I'm still waiting for my tea!' And she would be. And who else did she think would be coming in the front door at that time of day? Jack the Ripper? Ted Bundy? Crippen? He should be so lucky.

A small rectangular sign on the notice board at the supermarket read, "Woman in house alone. Front door ajar four o'clock. Make tea while you smash her brains in with electric kettle or garrotte her with cord of same. No reasonable offer refused."

After today it would all be moot. If she phoned him at work, she wouldn't get him and he wouldn't be coming home either. Not if things went as planned. Although they rarely did.

Henry moved over the bare tile floor of the bathroom and turned on the light above the washbasin. It was a neon light, vaguely lilac, and it washed what little colour his skin had down the drain. Anna Karenina pushed herself against the front of his shins and collapsed at his ankles, presenting her belly to be rubbed. She waved her paws at him. He nudged her aside, not without affection but firmly enough that she stalked away. She should have known better. She might have meowed but surely experience had taught her by now that it wouldn't help. Henry examined himself in the mirror. He wanted to see the image he presented to the world, to see what he looked like, one last time. Then he turned away.

What did it matter? He was presentable enough. Small children didn't run away screaming when he come into the room. He was clean and tidy. She saw to that. 'Henry, did you shower today? You'll smell! I honestly don't understand you how you English only bathe once or twice a week, its awful!' or 'Henry, I'm not going out with you in that shirt. It's wrinkled. You're hopeless.' She hadn't said that for a long time. He had learned to iron his shirts himself, had become an expert at it and could have got a job at a Chinese laundry. Shoes: it was shoes now. 'Henry, shine those shoes before we leave. They're a disgrace.' If she was not in the room, he would take a cushion off the couch and rub it across his uppers. 'Yes, dear, just doing it now.'

The basin overflowed. Water began to run down the front of his pyjamas and he pulled the plug. Undoing the cord of his pyjamas, he stood in front of the basin naked and damp from the waist down. Leah had put his shaving cream away as she did every day and he got down on his haunches to look for it under the sink. 'This will be the last time I use you, can,' he thought, shaking it vigourously back and forward in his hand. 'I'd much rather shake her than you. I'd really like to see little bits of white frothing out of her,' he said, dabbing small mounds of foam at the edges of his mouth. He opened his mouth wide in a silent 'aaargh', and stuck out his tongue. 'Let it loll.' That was the word, wasn't it? Then, grinning, he began to lather his chin.

Suddenly, the bathroom door opened and she was standing there. She was pointing at the lavatory bowl, patently yelling something about wanting to use the facilities.

'I've been calling out to you forever.' She swept past him. 'I won't be a minute.'

This meant 'Get out' in Leahspeak. Henry left the room all foamy-faced, razor in hand, and sat at the top of the stairs. Anna Karenina flopped at this side baring her belly once more, all forgiven. The cold of the house was beginning to turn Henry's backside mauve. He had had enough. He stalked back into the bathroom waving the razor.

'If I don't get shaved, I'm going to be late,' he said. 'You've had all night to use the bloody loo.'

She opened her mouth to speak but he was reasonably certain that she didn't say anything. It might have been the shock of his answering her back but, more likely, she had caught sight of the penis dangling under his pyjama jacket. She hadn't seen that for quite a while. Even when they had sex. Not that that was a regular event. She swept by him, slamming the door. Ever the lady, she flushed the toilet as she went. The bedroom door crashed closed. He felt it shake. He was shaking slightly himself, but he began to shave anyway. What would a few nicks here and there matter? He'd have nicks aplenty before this day was done. And he smiled at the thought, breaking his promise not to look at himself again.

Perhaps she'd trip on the rug at the foot of the bed and break her fool neck.

Henry kept his clothes in the guest bedroom. He had put out his best three-piece suit the night before. It lay flat on the bed and Anna Karenina had slept on it so there was a furring of orange on the jacket. The room was still dark. He had closed the blinds to keep the heat in. The cat jumped up and sat on his trousers. She rolled on her back and pawed the air. He could see that she was meowing, wanting him to get downstairs and give her breakfast so that she could begin her day. Whatever he intended to do with his. Henry pulled the trousers out from underneath her. She rolled off the bed and fled, leaving a scorch mark of marmalade across the crotch of the trousers. 'Damn you, Anna,' said Henry, but he didn't mean it. Anna Karenina was his ally. She gave him the only warmth that he seemed to get these days. He'd give her a mound of food this morning, well laced with the soft treats she adored. He'd have to make sure that he left enough for a day or so, at least enough until one of his daughters remembered and took pity on her.

They went downstairs together. Henry had often thought that one day she would get under his feet and he'd go head first, crashing into the coat-stand at the bottom, but it hadn't happened yet and he had no great hope that it would this morning. In the hall, he stood in front of the mirror straightening his tie, moving the knot from side to side. Tightening it. Could a person choke doing this? Hmm, it didn't seem likely — so he proceeded into the kitchen. It was to be his last day on earth and there was a great deal to be done. It wouldn't do to waste a moment.

*

It had rained during the night but in the last hours before dawn the temperature had dropped, leaving a patina of ice on the outdoor carpet of the front steps. Opening the screen door onto what appeared to be a skating-rink gave Henry pause, but when Anna Karenina wove between his legs, sniffed the early April air and ventured daintily down the steps, he wasn't about to change his mind and stay at home. Even if he hadn't a whole agenda of things he had to do, even if this wasn't the designated day, he wouldn't have stayed home. But this is the day the Lord hath made, he thought. And the Lord and a few others were going to a get a shock before it was over. He moved gingerly forward. Should he sprinkle salt in case his beloved slipped and broke something when she went shopping? 'Get thee behind me Satan,' he said, lips mouthing the words, and he picked up the heavy plastic container of salt, moving it to the front of the porch just out of reach. 'Let's give the ice a fair chance.'

He could see it now.

She would lie there in the remains of last year's herbaceous border until their next door neighbour returned from his shift at the plant. They'd find her frigid. He had, often enough.

'Was that your wife?' the ambulance driver asked when Henry appeared, called home from the office.

'Well, there is some resemblance. As cold as ever, but I don't remember her being quite so blue. Pessimistic, yes, but not that precise shade of blue.'

'So you can't be sure then, sir, because, if it is, we have a nice clean gurney, but if not, it'll be a couple of these hefty garbage bags.'

'The bags, I think,' said Henry. 'Yes, definitely the bags.'

He nodded his head slowly and shut the door behind him.

Gingerly negotiating his way along the driveway Henry looked up the incline of the street. The bus stop was on the main road, itself a bitch to cross at the best of times, about a quarter of a mile away. A brisk walk usually, but a teetering trudge this morning. As he moved hesitantly forward, he began a conversation. With God. A monologue, really. God didn't seem to be speaking to him much lately, or if He was, Henry hadn't heard Him. Not that that would be strange. He hadn't heard much of anything for a long time now and what he did hear hadn't been good, heaven knew.

'Okay God,' he said, 'listen up. Whatever you do, don't let me fall and break my blithering neck today. Unless I do it literally, of course. Not today. All I ask is, get me up the street, onto the bus and into the subway and we'll call it George. We'll be even for all the other things you haven't been doing for me for the past twenty years.'

One testing foot in front of the other, Henry went stiff-legged up the little hill.

'None of that miracle on the road to Damascus business either. I've got a plan and if you, or any other member of that Trinity thing you're in, decide to do the omniscient thing, you'll hear my mouth when I do get up there.'

He skidded on an unharvested piece of dog dirt.

'Shit!' he yelped, flinging his arms around. 'Damn it to hell!'

His heart pumped violently and a pulse activated itself above his left eye. It was not so much the skid that frightened him, but the realization that if he was so apprehensive about falling and doing himself an injury, it didn't bode well for the rest of what he was aiming to do.

He prayed again.

'You just get me safely up to civilization and you can go back about your own business and leave me to get on with mine.'

He searched for an angle, a negotiating point. What might the Almighty want?

'Get me to the bus or I'll turn around, go home and smother her with one of her own crocheted pillowcases. Then You'll have to deal with her through all eternity and I'll be sitting home next to a nice warm fire.'

Gotcha God.

He looked up from his firmly planted feet. A van was coming towards him. Inexorably, and also sideways, skidding on the ice. Henry was about to be sideswiped by a florist's truck.

'Yes!' he called out exultantly, lifting his arms skyward, 'Alleluia!!'

He could see the driver of the van spinning the steering wheel as the vehicle floated towards him. The man appeared to be screaming, he also was perhaps calling on the name of the Lord. Their eyes locked momentarily before Henry closed his, waiting for the thud that would toss him through the morning air into an exquisite eternity. He was elated that he felt no fear, only an effervescence of anticipation.

Eternity? Thou pleasing, dreadful thought! Then another thought intruded: that this was not the way it was supposed to be, not how he had planned it. He had had no control over coming into this life but he had intended to have it over his going out. On the other hand, what if the moment was finally here?

The van hit the curb, ricocheted across the road and bounced off a large oak tree on the far side. The driver regained control of the steering wheel and pounded on the horn as the van slithered to a shuddering halt. Henry, it missed completely. It was a few moments before he realized this and then he could only shrug his shoulders, sigh out loud and begin to edge his way up the street once more. He hadn't heard a thing. Perhaps, to be entirely accurate, he did hear something. Perhaps he imagined it was the drone of an out of season bee or the hum of a washing machine at the end of the spin cycle far off in a basement somewhere, but it didn't register. He had other things on his mind, but there was another reason as well.

Henry was deaf.

2

Out on the main road at last, Henry looked first to the left, then to the right and then to the left again, just as he had been taught to do as a child. Of course, that had been in England and he had never been sure, even after all this time in a country where the cars drove on the other side of the road, whether he was supposed to look right first and then left and finally right again. Over the years, he had had long conversations with law enforcement officers, logicians and even the occasional technical expert from NASA trying to determine which was the correct way to do it.

One time he thought he had the right answer, but the lady to whom he was speaking, a representative in the legislature of one of the islands, Barbados perhaps it was, had pointed out that she could not really be considered reliable since they drove on the other side of the road there, too. And, as she said, what did a figment of his imagination know about such things anyway? She had faded to black in the colour photography of his mind and his dilemma remained unresolved.

Traffic was coming towards him from both directions at once. He looked across the road. A dozen people were waiting outside the bus shelter and he moved steadily towards them. A bit like walking on water, he thought. Hands waved at him, clearly ordering him to stop. One woman covered her eyes; another put a fist in front of her mouth. He was reminded of long ago: a little girl killed in traffic. It was as vivid to him as if he had seen it yesterday and he struggled to put her out of his mind. A Volvo passed in front of him. A good car, the Volvo, good brakes. The little girl faded. One of the men waiting for the bus plunged off the sidewalk, grabbed him by the sleeve, yelling — something — at him, and dragged him to safety.

Interfering so and so.

'Thanks,' said Henry, 'forgot to turn my hearing aid on and couldn't hear a word you were saying!' A gloved finger pointed to the tiny device that nestled, hardly visible, in his ear. 'So sorry!'

He laughed. But he didn't turn the hearing aid on. Didn't turn either one of them on.

The man shrugged and retreated, shaking his head. Henry was alone on the curb. He wanted to say something to the people, that they didn't know the half of it, that they didn't know anything about him, but he could feel their animosity. He knew he had scared them; they didn't need this at seven forty-five on a Friday morning. He smiled to himself. If he told them what he was intending to do later in the day, they would have had him taken away in the back of a police car.

'Yes, officer, that's the man. Standing there, he was. Not doing a thing to get out of the way of the Volvo.'

'Was he drunk, you ask? No. Not drunk. Deaf! They really shouldn't let people like that out.'

'Don't they have dogs for people like him?'

'You mean to bite them?'

'No, no, of course not! To lead them around and keep them out of trouble.'

'Only for the blind, eh? Well, you would think they'd have something for these people, too. I mean, you can see the blind.'

The villagers were sharpening their axes, hefting their brightly burning torches aloft.

Mutter, mutter.

'I agree. You can't see the deaf ones. They could be anywhere!'

'Who knows what they're up to!'

To the castle! To the castle!

They were right of course. Henry acknowledged the fact in his head. But he also nodded at just how invisible the real Henry was to the general population. He climbed on the bus when it came to a stop in front of him.

'Just one, this time, folks! Another will be along in a minute!'

He dropped his token into the container and the bus edged out into the rush hour crush. As he always did, he tucked a transfer inside his pocket for safe keeping, in memoriam. He wasn't sure where he was going to go first, but it might be needed eventually. Should he brave the mob and journey downtown now?

No one would know. No one would care: he acknowledged a truth. Today was to be a great day for the truth, so he might as well begin early.

North. What about North? To the end of the line!

Now that's an appropriate turn of phrase. The end of the line. There's a mall there and I can have a bite to eat if I want, perhaps even splurge on a cinnamon bun, and keep warm until it's time to go.

He frowned. Words played tricks. He could go any time, any time at all, but before he went he had specific places to visit, things to do and once he got through them, only then would it be time to go.

A decision. He would go North in the morning and downtown for his meeting later in the day. He would tell them what to do with their pension and he had to be out of there before five. Out of there and out of here. He smiled at the thought and twisted the tight gold wedding ring on his left hand.

'Before that,' he said aloud to the bus, 'let's get rid of this.'

*

When Henry arrived at the mall half an hour later, he found that the jewellery repair shop was still closed. He tapped on the glass door, but no one was there, so he wandered around looking in display windows, not seeing much, not focusing on anything at all really. He played with the ring, rubbing it with his thumb. The action reminded him of his mother playing with her engagement ring, hiding the stones — opals and diamonds they were, he could see them vividly even now — twisting it so that only the gold band was visible. It was a habit she had.

'Give over. Don't fiddle with it, woman,' his Dad would say. 'You'll wear the blooming thing out.'

Her response was to rub the ring, and the wedding ring next to it, against her breast, a playful Mona Lisa look on her face.

'They're mine! I'll do what I like!'

'I know that,' his Dad would reply, shaking his head, getting into the spirit of the thing. 'To my cost!'

Henry smiled at the memory.

*

He and his father were rolling the carpet up in the dining room. Actually, his father was doing the rolling, not trusting ten-year-old Henry to get it tight enough. He wanted a cylindrical pipe of Axminster, is what he wanted, and was squatting crab-like over the middle of it while Henry hovered behind him. His Dad had a bald spot about the size of a half-crown and Henry couldn't take his eyes off it.

'Here, lad,' said his Dad, 'don't just stand there. Take an end. Get it tight!'

Henry was bending over when his mother came into the room. From all those years in the future, Henry checked himself. What rubbish! Mam never just 'came' anywhere, or 'went' anywhere either. She trotted. Really, it was more of a gambolling skip. When she was tired, she shuffled.

And there she was.

'Our Henry,' she said, in a worried voice, 'have you seen my rings?'

'What rings?' he asked.

'My engagement ring. How many rings do I have? And my wedding ring. I put them at the back of the draining board and now they're not there.'

Henry considered the matter. 'I didn't see them when I was peeling the potatoes for dinner. When did you put them there?'

His mother peered through her glasses back at her morning.

'I don't know!' She laughed. 'I don't even know if that is where I put them. I do know they're not where they're supposed to be. On my finger.'

She wiggled her fingers at him, behind his Dad's back.

'Hey up, our Henry, you're supposed to be helping me, not chatting away with your mother. Mother, leave the lad be! Can't you see he's trying to help. Or he would be, if he ever got his finger out!'

'Philip, don't you talk like that!'

She pushed her husband roughly against his shoulder, a playful push that sent him with a bump onto the linoleum covered floor.

'Come on woman, give over I tell you! I don't have all day to get this done.'

'Don't you tell your Dad!' his Mam said to Henry. 'When you get a chance, come into the kitchen and have a look with me.'

She tapped her husband on the shoulder, a tap to get his attention.

'What now?' he sighed, miming exaggerated frustration. His Dad was one of the great actors. Gelguid, Olivier, Richardson, all rolled up into one, a fair dollop of Finlay Currie added to the mix for majesty on occasion, every bit in his own proud north-country accent, completely unafraid of the grand gesture.

Henry's mother looked directly at her husband and shaped her lips. She spoke clearly and precisely, articulating correctly as she had had to for most of her married life. Henry often thought she must have strong lips, all that careful enunciation over the years. He wondered if he and his brother, Edward, did too. Sometimes, he found himself flexing his lips into pursed rosebud 'oohs' and letterbox teeth baring 'aahs'. Practising. A son in training. His Dad was deaf. What, in those days, they called stone deaf. So deaf, the experts said, peering into their Petri dishes and shaking their heads, that no hearing aid would have helped.

'How long are you going to be, before it's done?'

Dad looked up at Henry's Mam.

'Well, all of it won't be done today, lass.'

'I know that, but how long before you get the hole made and the dust settles.'

'The what made?'

'The hole.'

'How long before we get the carpet rolled?'

'The hole!' Slightly less patience this time. 'The hole!' She pointed at the wall.

'Oh, the hole, love!' He nodded. 'How do I know! As it is, the two of you are more of a hindrance than a help, so get off with both of you!'

He had regained the equilibrium of his haunches. She pushed him again.

'Out of the way, now! Bugger off both of you!' he said. 'Out!'

'Come on, our Henry, help me find my rings.' She turned towards the door, gunning for a quick start. 'He'll be in here for a fair while, I can see that.'

Once again, she tapped her husband on the shoulder.

'Now what?' Genuine annoyance came through this time.

'Don't you make too much mess with that thing.'

She pointed at the sledge hammer he had brought home from work. It lay inert but threatening against the wall. Henry didn't think his Dad heard. He was already disappearing down the rabbit hole into his own private world. Henry sometimes envied his Dad this separate, secret world, but, later, as a man, with access to his own terrible version of it, the memory of it would make him want to weep for both of them.

His Dad leaned over the carpet and began to roll it again. He pursed his lips and began to puff, his public puff to prove that exertion was in progress. He paid no more mind to either of them.

'I'm off, then,' Henry said to his father nevertheless.

The words ricocheted round the room. His Dad hadn't heard them. His Dad never heard anything that Henry said.

Never had.

Never would.

*

Henry and his Mam were peering down the kitchen sink when his Dad brought the sledgehammer down on the wall between the dining room and the kitchen. His Dad was making a hatch through which he and Henry's Mam would be able to see each other, speak and pass the food. If he couldn't afford a maid, he could at least ease the work that his beloved Edith had to do. The first step was to make the hole, two feet by two feet in the wall.

The entire house buckled.

Next door — it was a semi-detached — old Mrs. Blenkinsop soiled herself sitting on the couch drinking tea with the curate and had to be sedated.

'Eeee, our Dad!' shrieked Henry's Mam.

The glasses fell off the end of her nose, shaking themselves down into the sink. China cups slithered off the draining board to join them. Milk curdled on the pantry floor and Mam's best silver tarnished in its velvet sleeves. The kitchen door, closed in case his Dad came in, flew open and the top end jumped off its hinge.

Henry stared at the wall. Nothing. Not a chip. His Mam was peering at the same spot, swallowing repetitively.

'Go and tell him to stop,' she said, starting to giggle, somewhere between a wholly genuine amusement and the beginnings of hysteria. 'He'll kill us all yet!'

Before she could say more, they felt another almighty blow. Richter himself would have been hard pressed to measure it. Henry spread his toes inside his slippers to make sure he kept a good purchase on the floor and his mother, dementedly energized by the detonation, grinned. 'He's done it this time! He's mad! Wait till I get my hands on him!' She said this through tears of the most inappropriate laughter as a third hullabaloo rocked the house. 'Go, Henry, go!'

Henry had hardly moved, however, when a crack began to appear in the wall. It began roughly half way up and, as he and his Mam stared, it spread upwards towards the ceiling and downwards towards the skirting board. They heard his Dad call out, 'Anything yet?' which even Henry thought funny. His Mam was mewling into her handkerchief, hopelessly, asthmatically, engulfed by hilarity. Then his Dad struck the fourth blow.

Plaster flew off the wall, attacking them shard by shard. Whole bricks jumped out, flinging themselves across the room like kamikaze pilots. Cabbage rose patterned wallpaper waved at them and petals of it began to make merry circles in the vibrating air. Henry and his Mam were blinded by shavings of cement and particles of dust that spread like an atomic cloud through the whole room. Mam grabbed Henry's arm and held on tight. Henry wondered if the house might not collapse on top of them, except that his mother was still having a fit into her apron. Henry could hear her giggling.

It was several minutes before the air cleared enough to see what remained of the kitchen. Gradually, they made out the fatal wall, just eight feet away. His Dad had made a hole alright. You could have pushed a small pony through. On the other side, he was peering at them peering at him. He stood there, cradling the sledgehammer in the crook of his elbow like some enormous infant.

'Well,' he said, 'don't just stand there, lass. Make us a cup of tea and we'll do a bit of cleaning up.'

He began to sing: 'Ah, Sweet mystery of life, at last I've found you . . .'

His mother moved the apron away from her face.

She beamed at Henry, 'Eee, our Henry, well I never! They were in my apron pocket the whole time,' she said.

3

Henry was thirsty. Just for something to slide by his epiglottis and tip down his gullet. Not for life. He thought of coffee and shrugged. No more coffee. It would only agitate him and he didn't need that. He already felt more frangible than a reed in a rainstorm. Tea wouldn't do it either. He'd never had much truck with tea since Edward and he, long ago in the days of rationing after W W 2, had come to an agreement that they wouldn't drink it. Their Mam could have it. 'Just put on the kettle, love, and we'll all have a lovely cup of tea.' It was her mantra, the universal panacea. Henry smiled; well, she'd have needed a couple of gallons of the stuff to get through today. He decided on root beer. He'd always had a liking for the medicinal, slightly off-putting taste that he'd had first heard about when he got off the boat so many years before. He wandered over to the convenience store and got an icy can from the cooler.

He had to go back for a straw. He forgot to pick one up the first time when a little dollop of a woman stopped him near the cashier and said, 'Good morning, Mr. Earl.' Being recognized out there in the mall so early in the morning was a shock. Only then did he remember there was a branch of his bank here, and hadn't he audited it, oh, years ago? Surely she hadn't been here then! Henry really had no idea where he had seen her before and he slurped up his soda in a frustration of not knowing. He had accepted that his ears were defunct, but it nagged at him when he suspected that his brain might be following suit.

He turned his hearing aids off so it wouldn't happen again, but then he turned them back on. Sometimes, between the crackling and the background noise, they made him think more cogently, as though the batteries gave out tiny ohms that revitalized his not quite golden-aged grey matter.

'Hello there, Earl.' Another voice was hurled at him. Christ! 'How are you?'

Henry jumped. It was like an attack of mosquitoes. This one was male and quite definitely a banker.

Henry waved his hand vaguely and tried a smile. He was not sure how it came out so he added, 'Fine, thank you. So, you're up here now, are you?' A question, he knew immediately, was the wrong thing. He had no interest in the man and none in any conceivable answer that might be provided and, who knew, the man might have questions of his own. He might even have heard. He might stand there offering sympathy or, worse, the hearty best wishes of someone who had escaped a similar fate. So far. Henry had had enough of that on Wednesday and he squirmed in his seat.

The man sighed. 'Okay, I guess. Nearly the half-year end and they just cut my staff by two. Again.'

Jesus, thought Henry, and he wants sympathy from me!

'Where are you these days?' the man asked. 'Still downtown?'

So he hadn't heard.

Henry shrugged. 'For my sins,' he said, with the hint of a laugh.

Soon I'll be all over the newspapers. And you'll remember this conversation well enough.

The man had a thought. 'You're not still in Inspection are you?' Probably the last thing he wanted was an audit.

'No, no. Not at all. I'm at Head Office now. A desk jockey these days!' False hearty. Definitely not Henry.

The man's relief was palpable. Had he been fiddling the books? Dipping into his Suspense Account? Turning a blind eye to kiting?

They had nothing more to say to each other. Both nodded and the man moved away.

Henry had no idea how he knew him. In over thirty years in the trenches of banking, he had met many people. He had a fine network of acquaintances. Even, he nodded slowly to himself thinking about it, a network of fine acquaintances. He knew people from the branches where he had started out, from the management councils to which he had progressed, and from the branches he had later audited. He knew scads of people from the seminars he had attended at the bank's Staff College, and from focus groups and product launches across the city. More recently, his position involved sitting around in meeting after meeting.

Oops, Henry old boy, that's a past position!

Recently past, but past nevertheless.

He caught his reflection in a plate glass window and saw the wry smile that twisted itself round the straw. Past and last.

He turned so that his back was facing anyone who might walk by. It was a dangerous thing in the banking business to turn your back on people, they might slide the knife in, right in there between the third and fourth vertebrae, little blood and not much twitching, but he couldn't face anyone else. Not quite yet.

*

A woman sitting opposite was taking a croissant out of a brown paper bag. He watched her. It was greasy and unpleasant looking and he got a whiff of that slightly nauseating smell that France's answer to good old English white bread always seemed to have. They'd be making whole-wheat and rye croissants next and it would be the end of civilization as we know it. He cheered himself up with the epiphany that he wouldn't be around to see it.

Croissant. Crouton. Cruet. Crayon.

He liked to do this sometimes, the word thing. To see where a locution led him, where he would end up. He let the syllables roll off his tongue.

Crustacean.

Could he put them together in a single sentence? Possibly. Although with crayon in there it might be a stretch. And what exactly was a cruet?

The woman flicked at the edges of her lips with a serviette. She looked like she was a smoker in a hurry to get outside and fill her lungs with the swirling, sweet fumes of a cigarette. Henry knew how she must feel. He had been a smoker himself once until Leah had given him an ultimatum, 'Stop or I'll leave you.' He should have taken door number two but he had gone meekly off to an acupuncturist who stuck needles into the back of his hands and into his forehead until he looked like a porcupine in extremis.

He never smoked again. He often wanted to though. Wanted to draw the wonderful smoke deep down into his flushed-clean lungs and push it back out through the nostrils of his slightly aquiline nose. Instead, he had made a pact with himself. As soon as they closed her coffin, he would light up. He'd rest the palm of his left hand on the lid in case she tried to get out and hold his king-sized Rothmans' right-handed. He'd puff away nonchalantly, talking loudly to muffle any banging from the inside, scattering the ash in front of him until the filter burnt his fingers. The thumping would diminish and it would become quiet. Post coital ennui.

Henry walked over towards the bank. The doors were open but the entrance was hidden by a row of automated teller machines. It was all planned, of course. The last thing a bank wanted these days was for customers, actual people, to go inside. He peered in but the long banking hall he could vaguely recall no longer existed. In its place was a series of little cubicles, each one empty now, each with a sign saying 'Here Is Your Banking Rep'. The days when rows of polite tellers gave personal service were long gone. Everyone was a client now. Hookers' johns. They didn't want you in the place if you had less than a couple of hundred thousand on deposit. You had to have at least that to get anyone to speak to you and even then it was difficult. For the hoi polloi it was The Phone Bank — they had trademarked the silly name — or nothing. The mucky-mucks pretended it provided electronic efficiency and faster service, but at the end of the day gutting the teller line had been a cost cutting measure and thousands of people had been thrown out of work, people who actually liked their customers and knew them and were knowledgeable about banking. What a concept, Henry thought!

These days you picked up the phone and dialled. Or you got nothing done. If you had the bank on speed dial, you waited for the first ring and then began pressing and repressing 'One' to avoid having to listen to an anodyne voice that intoned,

'For service in English press 'One' now'. Henry knew for a fact that no-one above the level of General Manager had ever heard these words. They had Administrative Assistants (erstwhile secretaries until the name was deemed too mundane for a majestic VP to be associated with) to do their banking for them.

The other alternative was Internet Banking. If the bloody system wasn't down. The computer had erased thousands of jobs and no one even expected good service from it. The mucky-mucks couldn't have used it if they wanted to: they were too busy emailing one another with their blackberries to learn how to manipulate a whole PC.

*

Henry remembered the day of his interview to join the bank, all those years ago. It was the day after Labour Day. He hadn't really wanted to go into a bank but he had been wafting around wondering what to do with his life for long enough, working at lots of little things without a great deal of direction — or success, if he was honest about it — and Leah was pushing him towards OISE, teachers' college for crying out loud, which would have done him in completely. It seemed like his choices were other people's kids, working for his in-laws or fiduciary fastidiousness. He knew that the first two would have driven him insane before the leaves left the trees.

He had always envied teachers their vacations — not to mention their union — but he knew that he would not have been able to hack it. Leah was already a teacher, only a librarian mind you, and the thought of all those cosy fireside chats in the long winter evenings comparing notes about their problem kids and the PTA was almost enough to deliver him over to her father for indenture. Almost, but not quite. He couldn't see himself selling insurance either.

'Yes, Mrs. Luckinbill, we need to top you up on your term. You've plenty of life, but I've been recalculating the amount of your annuities.'

'No, no! When Mr. Luckinbill went he was unfortunately without double indemnity, so you lost out there. Else I'd have married you myself.'

'What do you mean you'd have wanted a 'suicide included' clause added if you had known? I'm not sure First Allotment has those.'

So he was left with the big bad bank.

And it, it appeared, was left with him.

At the end of his interview, he was asked if he had any questions or concerns for the interviewer and, with trepidation, had asked, 'Is there job security in banking?' The interviewer thought he was making a joke. He nudged Henry's knee, and replied, 'As long as you keep your fingers out of the till, it's as secure as Fort Knox.' Wink, wink. Henry had forborne to tell him that he might be mixing his metaphors, but the answer seemed clear enough.

It had been with a certain malicious satisfaction that he had seen the fellow's name a few years ago in an email that reported the names of people who had euphemistically taken 'early retirement' or had otherwise 'chosen to pursue career initiatives outside of the organization'. These days, of course, even that kind of public attention wasn't given. The bank had learned from the statistical manipulations of Chernobyl how to keep people in the dark. Henry's own little Wednesday massacre might be very small potatoes in the overall scheme of things and it would be communicated only by rumour.

Fifty-seven deceased and the rest, a hundred odd, walking wounded.

4

Everyone in his Division knew that the axe was coming. They had been sharpening the bloody thing for months, grinding it down so that its steel blade shone silver where it rested on the Senior Vice President's desk, alongside her little Japanese sand garden. Just before Christmas — the woman always had a fine sense of timing — right before the happy holiday, they brought in time and motion people to re-evaluate the FTEs — Full Time Equivalents to the unaware. FTEs had to balance the Division's ROE — Return on Equity, or Rowena's Orgasm Evermore, as Henry privately called it. Rowena was the SVP. She sat thirty feet away from Henry and occasionally, if he was standing up and she had to pass the opening to his cubicle, she had been known to nod, 'Hiya, Henry.' Since he made it a firm practice not to turn his hearing aids on until he had read his morning mail, both E and actual, he hadn't heard a casual word from the woman in nearly two years.

It was no great loss. She had been brought in from out West to shake things up and she had succeeded better than a good bartender with a dry martini. Even her looks were cause for comment: she dressed like a bounty-hunter, although lypo would have been needed before she could have handled the chaps. If she had not had her two offspring framed in teak on the outer wall of her office, people might have been less than believing of her femininity. But about a year ago her belly started to burgeon and Rowena began to waddle. She grew to an enormous size: the office wits said that the poor kid couldn't find its way out. Then one day she disappeared and her assistant came round asking for contributions to a gift for the 'wee bairn'. Most people gave out of sympathy for the baby. For fear of retaliation, of course.

To no one's surprise, Rowena reappeared three weeks later, a Divisional email thanked everyone for the gift and very little more was said. Henry's assistant was instructed to scan, upload and circulate a picture of Rowena and her family. Two small infants with what seemed to be cloven hooves, the suckling babe looking slightly scared and a male who appeared absolutely petrified, posed alongside the boss. The tendrils of the bank's grapevine, a communication channel lusty enough for Tarzan to swing from, reported that her partner was a house husband. He was never allowed out socially and was currently under a physician's care for postnatal depression. It was a wonder to Henry that he didn't kill the lot of them.

Henry's immediate boss called a meeting with Henry the morning after the Christmas party. Llewellyn Bonnet was one of those unfortunately pear-shaped people the Anglo-Welsh marches seemed to specialize in and which Great Britain was understandably desirous to export. He had the quintessential grammar school ruddy complexion and a rosebud upper lip to match. Henry suspected that he turned his personality on and off just like a light bulb. Not too bright, perhaps twenty-five watts. The switch was located half way up Boney's bum.

Mr. Bonnet was sweating.

'I want you to make a list of everything you fellows do, all the tasks you carry out, the time each takes and assign percentages to them.'

Holding the boss's hand: 25%

'Our Division is going to be the guinea-pig for the whole bank. We're going first. We'll lead the way!' He clearly did not know whether to celebrate or gnash his teeth.

Wiping boss's arse: 15%

'We have to improve ROE and the pooh bahs have decided to assess FTEs as a starting point.'

Mr. Bonnet used words like pooh bahs when he was being chummy. He was chummy only when he was scared.

Picking up after boss: 20%

'The whole exercise, divisionally, will take about three months. Hymen, Gladys and Funk will carry out the statistical work, analyse the findings and make all the determinations on staffing.' Having HGF, the Bank's chartered accountants, make the decisions about whose noggins were to be topped, whose testicles were to be handed them in a brown paper bag, might just save Rowena from being vivisected in the executive lavatory — if, that is, the entire staff had been recruited from Grade Six. Since they were not, it was pretty well recognized that she was merely covering her own well upholstered rear end.

Feeding boss pabulum: 20%

'I don't think we have anything to worry about,' said the false prophet. 'Rowena is pleased with our work. She was telling me so only yesterday.' Self-adulation would cause him to explode in a moment. 'But we've got to wrestle with everything that affects the bottom line.' The inefficiencies of the institution had recently led it to the announcement of a billion dollar net profit. For the third year in a row. 'So write down everything you do. Justify yourself.'

Actual work: 20%

Boney — so called by Henry because he was short and Napoleonic — left the meeting leaving behind an unusual odour of Welsh fear and cheap cologne, adjourning to the Executive loo to which Rowena had given him his own personal key. He kept it in a plastic container behind the pens in his shirt pocket, next to his heart. It was rumoured, however, that, although he had been keyed, she would not allow him to use her toilet paper. Henry himself had whispered into the better ears that he had seen Boney sashaying along the corridor, toothbrush in hand, a bulge under his woollie cardigan.

Henry completed a spreadsheet, three pages, everything single spaced, detailing his workload, and passed it on. Boney returned the hardcopy, having severely cut everything by percentage and time spent, and taking unto himself several of the more important and onerous tasks that he could not have carried out to avoid exile on Elba. Mr. Bonnet, in fact, had three functions, and they were well known. First, he edited Henry's work. Nothing escaped him. If, in a superbly written and well-argued report, Henry made an unfortunate use of the indefinite article, the whole thing would be handed back with the offending word circled, its designated replacement inked into the margin in red. Second, he laughed, and frequently, at Rowena's jokes. This, Henry would have been the first to admit, was no easy task. They were small and often very difficult to discern. Third, he kept the riffraff off her shores. Boney would have been the ideal Minister of Immigration for a small, virginal nation consumed by xenophobia. No one would get in. Boney had the keys to the kingdom (as well as to the toilet) and he wielded them as though they were the keys to her chastity belt.

After an initial fluster of concern in the New Year, the Division settled down to work. Since no one was ever paid overtime — thus did the bank break several federal statutes — people were too busy trying to get out of the place at a reasonable hour to think very far ahead. Henry, however, had no place to go but home.

*

It was the middle of February when Boney called his entire fiefdom together for a top-level meeting in one of the ill-ventilated, cell-like chambers that doubled as meeting rooms. It was a very finite fief. In attendance was the boss himself, still sweating that strange faintly leek-like effluvium that Henry loathed; a subdued Henry; Olaf, the person who worked for Henry, a louche Lithuanian techie who spoke interminably, and to Henry unintelligibly, about dialectical materialism; and Bettina, Boney's Administrative Assistant. Bettina, an enormously breasted lady from one of the smaller islands in the Caribbean, lacked more than a passing acquaintance with grammar or any form of the written word. The divisional enigma, no one knew what she did for a living and hardly anyone could understand anything that came out of her mouth.

'Ras, mon, eye 'ave sooch ha dye coomin dis Satchurdee, ham not likely tuh be year hon Mondee.'

Everyone agreed that Bettina had some sort of hold over Boney. It was generally acknowledged that this was not likely to be sexual, but its exact nature remained exasperatingly unknown.

'Well,' said Mr. Bonnet, calling the troops to order. He was awash in his own perspiration. 'Word has come down that we're substantially overstaffed. They're going to make,' he paused to swallow the saliva that threatened to drown his uvula, 'deep cuts.'

The part of him that was English began to slip away. Henry half expected him to don a miner's lamp and burst into song.

'Look you,' he continued, 'we have to be ready for whatever happens.'

He ran a hand across his forehead and placed it on the table where it left a perfect, damp, palm print.

'I, of course, will do my best for you but there can be no promises. Deep cuts is what I hear, boyos.'

Bettina looked at him as though calculating at what time it would be necessary to change him.

Olaf stared out from hooded eyes as if to say, 'This is what defeated the forces of Marx and Lenin? This is the entity that will determine my fate? May Mao protect me.'

Henry said, he wanted to rub it in, 'I thought you told us you would be able to protect us.'

The others said afterwards that Boney flinched.

'Who said that? I never said that. No, no, not that I said!'

He was beginning to hyperventilate.

Henry pondered pressing the issue. If the department were to be reduced by, say, 25% through the unexpected, though fortuitous, demise of one of its members, that itself might be the solution.

I'll hold a bag over his nose. Bettina. You pull his tie tight to keep in as much air as possible. Olaf, stop inveighing against capitalism and insert your index fingers into his eyes. Yank 'em out the sockets. There's plenty of time. We have the room until three-thirty. Steady on now. Don't panic. Boney, old chap, can you still hear us? Nod once for yes and twice for no . . . . Oh, you can, eh! Pull the tie tighter, Betty girl, I'll double-bag him.

'They say that for our current work load, the work the four of us do now,' Boney could hardly control his tongue well enough to utter the words, 'only two point three FTEs are required.' He hurried on. 'It will be very hard for Rowena. She says she doesn't know what she will do without a full complement.' Boney was usually a natural tenor but the more anxious be became, the more he edged towards falsetto. He was currently a boy soprano. 'Of course, we shall all stick together and I'll keep everyone up to date.'

From that day on, however, he was mute on the subject. Henry was able to calm Olaf, who went deep into a proletarian funk, by pointing out that his job was as safe as houses since he was the only one of the four who had any computer skills whatsoever. Henry knew Word and PowerPoint but Excel defeated him. Zipping files belonged higher along the evolutionary grid than he had so far reached. Boney himself had trouble even turning his PC on in the morning and Bettina long ago had insisted on having a typewriter — the only one in the Division, people came from other floors just to look at it — on which to write any absolutely unavoidable correspondence.

In his heart, Henry was sure that it was he himself, and himself only, who was for the boot. He was the perfect candidate for the firing squad, the preternatural Judas goat for the poisoned apple. Whichever way he looked at it, it was unavoidable. He was male, he was white and he was over fifty. Off with his head! They could pay someone half his age half his salary to do his job, in twice the time, half as well.

*

Henry had a friend the bank fired after twenty years service. Lola and he had met on the audit. She taught him just about everything he knew about inspection. They travelled together from the Niagara Escarpment to the wilds of Northern Ontario going from branch to branch spreading terror before them as they went. The hours were long and onerous, but those were the days when banking was fun, and they shared the work and the burden of it lightly, falling exhausted into the bad beds of cheap per diem motels night after night. A couple of nights they had almost fallen into the same bed — auditors were notorious for it — but Lola was a moral woman and they never quite reached the sticking point. The spectre of Leah somehow finding out about it was enough to cool the most tumescent of Henry's fantasies, anyway. Be still, oh my heart!

After their audit stint, both of them moved on to other things and they lost touch. Lola, he heard, was in statistical analysis; he found a niche in projects. Then one evening, she telephoned to tell him she had been given the shaft. They had poked her hard up the ass, rewarded her with the usual aren't-we-generous educational grant and held out the golden handshake. Sent her on her none too merry way.

The joke was that thirty-two days later, the absolute legal minimum to be rehired, she received an urgent telephone call asking if she was available to work on contract, fifty bucks an hour for three months. Doing her old job. The Human Resources newt on the other end of the line — one who had risen slightly above the ooze from whence her ilk was generally spawned — then, unfortunately, added, 'and perhaps you could also teach someone to fill the position.'

Lola had gone quietly apoplectic, but since revenge, as they say, is a dish best served cold, she asked for time to consider the offer. When she called back, it was to say that, given her financial obligations, she could not consider anything less than sixty per, she could only work at home due to her aged father requiring nursing care (which would have surprised him), and she would not be able to teach anyone anything since she had already enlisted at the university and was currently upgrading her own skills for the future. The amphibian did not blink. Henry's friend reported to her old department the following Monday morning.

Met by the person who had performed the hysterectomy on her career only five weeks earlier, Lola was shown to the same desk she had occupied for, lo, the past several years. It was awash with papers where someone — Lola never did find out who — had tried to figure out how to do her job. She downloaded all the files she required, carried everything she would need home in a taxi — she made sure she got a chit — and did her work as superbly as ever while keeping an eye on the progress of the soaps she previously had had to record. She did not return to the office.

She and Henry, in the meantime, rekindled their friendship. They met for long lunches well away from Head Office, swapped war stories and compared notes.

'Henry,' said Lola, shaking her head over a large G and T, 'whatever you do, don't trust 'em. They'll hang you out to dry like nappies in a tornado when it suits them.'

Henry giggled into his third half pint. (He had to get back to the office for an all afternoon seminar and it wouldn't do to be totally shit-faced) 'They're not that bad. You had an unfortunate experience, is all. The wrong place at the wrong time, that was you. It couldn't happen to me.'

As Henry said this, the last loop of a pretzel scraped against the back of his throat and he started to choke. Lola pounded him on the back, his eyes flooded with water and his ploughman's lunch lurched upwards towards his oesophagus.

She sighed. 'If you really believe that, you're nuts, Henry. Almonds and Macadamias. Mixed'

At the end of the three months, Lola's contract was extended. At the end of six months, she phoned her boss to say that she had been offered a job elsewhere and was not going to renew the contract. She was told by a departmental spy — management never seemed to twig that the serfs form friendships as they slave away — that the General Manager had a bit of a weep when she heard this, but the long and the short of it was that Lola was jumped two pay grades, all benefits were restored retroactively, and she continued to work at home several days a week.

Three years later, she was declared redundant again.

*

Henry had other problems in addition to waiting for HGF's report.

His hearing was failing at a tremendous rate. Both ears seemed to have given up the ghost. He was reminded of the Titanic and how quickly it went down at the end. No longer sure that his heart could go on, he was beginning to panic. One afternoon after he had been shouted at in a meeting for half an hour, he retired to the washroom, where he sat in a stall and cried. Then he became anxious that people might come in — and he wouldn't hear them. It was all too much. Henry pulled up his pants and went back to his desk. Luckily, for the next month or so, the two worries seemed to cancel themselves out, although Henry could fret with the best of them. You can only worry for so long before your mind begins to dribble back to the safety of its daily routine.

He continued to do his work until, in the last week of March, Boney began to appear at the gap of his cubicle asking for updates on each of his various projects. Since normally Boney could not have cared less, Henry knew something was up. On All Fool's Day, for example, Boney, hawking phlegm from the back of his throat, had asked if the two of them could have a one-on-one on the Main-Talbot Proposal as there were a couple of things in it he wanted to clarify.

I'll bet, thought Henry, like who the hell is Main and what a Talbot is. Even for Henry, the project included rather more that was arcane than the bank usually tried to get its collective head around.

'Oh, and while I think of it,' Boney added, trying to be offhand and coming across like someone with an advanced case of palsy, 'where do you keep the files?'

It was at this point that Henry contemplated crashing the computer system — he had managed to do it once before by accident — but it would only mean that some poor schmuck, probably Olaf, would have to restore it and everyone else would have to do all of their work over again. Besides, his was good work. Even if it was likely to be his legacy. So he had his one-on-one, was careful to make everything appear even more complex than it really was, and waited. Patiently. Sufficient unto the day, as the Bible says. He began to take long lunches, always leaving after Rowena stomped her way out and managing to return just before she galumphed back in.

During that first week of April, Boney appeared to be chained to his desk. Henry received small flurries of emails asking specific questions on this, that and the other thing. He answered each question accurately and promptly in language that even a small child would understand, always managing to imply, however, that said small child should not have had to ask. He was never impolite, and he invariably finished with a postscript to the effect that if Mr. Bonnet required further clarification, he should not be afraid to ask for it. He designated his replies High Priority and blind-copied Rowena.

5

Three days ago, Boney had appeared, wraithlike, on the other side of the partition asking what was on Henry's calendar for the coming day.

'Well, I have a Main-Talbot meeting in the afternoon. Offsite. Uptown. It's been arranged for quite a while.'

'Could you cancel it?' asked Boney, dithering.

The room swam before Henry's eyes.

There's a cliché for you: the very thought that it was a cliché even crossed his mind, but it was gone in an instant. He closed his eyes the better to absorb the palpitations in the cavity of his chest. It felt like his Dad was wielding the sledgehammer all over again. This was it! He knew it! He wanted his father to be with him in the here and now, but his Dad was long gone. Six feet under. Toes up.

Swimming with the fishes. Like the room.

Swim, swum, swan.

What a beautiful creature a koi is! Graceful. Elegant. Colourful.

Not like Boney.

Boney's a minnow.

Let's see if he can swim away from this.

'There'll be some very high level people there, you know. Discussions are moving on apace and we are reaching a critical juncture,' Henry spoke thoughtfully. A tad of pomposity worked wonders when conversing with Boney about business.

'Well,' hummed Boney, 'I ah I,' he hawed, 'would like you to attend a meeting for me. Here. Downtown. I won't be able to go myself and would like you to sit in. It's very important.'

Henry shrugged, 'Of course, if you don't think Main-Talbot is important . . .'

He had an idea.

'Perhaps, if you're in the neighbourhood, you could drop in yourself for a few minutes.'

There was the suggestion of a question in the thought.

'You'd be able to explain anything that they might want to have clarified.'

Some hope.

'No, er, I'll be with Rowena all afternoon, it looks like. I doubt I'd be able to tackle that as well.'

'What a pity,' sighed Henry, 'the team might have been intrigued by your vision.'

Henry took the small, flat box from his pocket. There was a cough lozenge logo on its lid. He kept his bait in it.

He opened it with bated breath.

The pounding in his chest was abating.

Perhaps it was something he ate.

From a plate.

Wait! My head on Boney's plate.

That's a platter, not a plate.

'So, men,' he said, peering down at his collection of captive platyhelminthes. 'which one of you is going to help me hook old Boney? He's wriggling just as much as each one of you is!'

'Why does it have to be one of us?' A chorus of objections blossomed upwards.

'Don't get any ideas above your station,' Henry retorted, slightly affronted. 'That's what I bought you for. Suck it up!'

He really couldn't blame the spineless, soft-bellied little creatures though. He wouldn't want to be ingested either, but in their case there was also Boney's family resemblance to be considered. Hooking Boney would be vaguely incestuous and far from tasty. Nevertheless, Henry did not pause. Reaching into the box, he squeezed one of the more fractious fellows in two. One half went onto the end of his hook; the other was tossed back into the box for future duty.

Turning towards the bigger Boney, Henry contemplated making his own verbal assault as well.

He wanted to shout, 'May the worm of conscience still gnaw your soul'.

The line was certainly appropriate, but would he be able to declaim it as resoundingly as he wanted? His Dad would have relished the task, bellowing out each syllable at the top of his practised and powerful lungs, but Henry was not sure he could manage it.

Shakespeare would have been lost on the little cretin anyway.

He said instead, 'You'll remember that I'm down to give a presentation. Of course, Fred Fallow will want me to take minutes as well.' Fallow, known to all as Shallow Fallow, was an Executive Vice President, said to be destined for great things. Henry paused. 'Someone should represent us.'

Boney's Adam's Apple bobbed up and down. His profile was probably the sharpest thing about him. He swallowed.

'Help me, help me,' cried the hooked worm as it disappeared down Boney's throat. 'What did I ever do to you, Henry Earl?'

Henry was relentless. He began to reel Boney in.

'Perhaps you'd better phone Fred. Let him know you don't want me to go,' he said, handing Boney his telephone, 'I know his number.'

Boney was masticating and it looked like he didn't much enjoy the taste.

'No, um, ah, I, uh, I, uh, don't have time.'

Henry let him dangle, the rod high above of the water. Just a moment more.

'Well, I could send him an email, I suppose,' he said quietly.

Henry would have loved to yank out the hook and stomp Boney's head against the filing cabinets until he stopped wriggling, but slippery beggar that Boney was, he was already squirming away, jumping back into the oily waters, his natural habitat now he was out of Wales.

'Oh,' he whined, adding as though he had just thought of it, 'we should get together beforehand and I'll brief you for the meeting. Eleven o'clock. I've already booked a room.'

This came out in a rush and, having said it, he began to sidle away.

Henry couldn't resist one more tug on the line.

'What shall I wear?' he called out.

Boney looked at him blankly over his shoulder.

'Wear?' asked Boney.

The worms in the bait-box ducked to get out of the way.

'Yes, wear!' said Henry, as innocently as he was able, 'You said I was to take your place at a meeting. Will there be anyone important there? Anyone who requires a white shirt and tie? I mean, should I dress?'

'Wear what you like,' breathed the boss, flip-flopping on the edge of the gunwale.

'Hmm,' mused Henry as Boney swam off sweating, 'I wonder what one wears to a beheading.'

*

Alone in his cubicle, Henry began to shake. It started with his fingers but soon it seemed that his whole being was beginning to tremble. His ribcage palpitated xylophonically — he was outside of himself standing next to his body when he noticed this — and it appeared to be connected to a throat that twitched erratically, at twice the beat of his heart. He was a science experiment, and he turned his wrist soft side up to check for a pulse. He couldn't find one at first and shoved his index finger into the pliant white flesh. Still unable to locate it, but aware now that his left eye had a new, spasming life of its own, he laughed out loud. The point of Boney's head rose like a U Boat periscope above the rim of the partition and then disappeared almost immediately, evidently thinking better of visibility. He wasn't the type to ask what the joke was.

*

Henry reached into the inside pocket of his coat as it hung on the back of his chair, feeling for the thin cylinder of paper he kept there. He smoothed it on the top of his desk. It was his list. He had started it the first day of January and considered it his new year's resolution, although he realized that resolutions were intended to assist one to improve. His list was to help him complete. When he began it, he had known that it required a title, so he wrote down the first one that came into his head: 'Things To Do Before I Die'.

Looking at the words, however — he had written them in a notebook in block capitals — they seemed, well, rather pretentious. Arrogant, somehow. So he had ripped the page out. A better title might be 'A List'. This was nicely anonymous and he adopted it. He began to add bullet-points, but soon found he was using the list to remember things he had to buy, like razor blades, that had only a peripheral possibility of being part of the subject at hand. Then — he had worked with Boney too long not to consider it — he changed the 'A' to 'The', but he found that even more highfaluting than his first choice.

'Watkins. Bring me 'The List'.'

'Yes, my Lord! Should I bring it into the library or would my Lord prefer it in The Gun Room with the port?

'Oh, I dunno, wherever her ladyship is not, I think.'

A word to the wise. 'Yes, of course, my Lord.'

Over time, Henry had reverted to the original title. It was accurate and it kept him honest about what to put on it. If he had been called upon, Henry could have told his co-workers, his family (had they been interested, of course) and all the sundry passers-by of his life, the myriad things he had to do before he embraced the blessed blankness of the final state. He knew who he was going to write to, and, implicitly, who he was not. He knew which bills he would pay, and those he purposefully would leave outstanding. He had listed the people he wanted to see, and, in a series of parentheses, what he was going to say to them.

There weren't many. Why waste time and effort?

He even knew what he would be wearing when he became deceased. Not only that it was a suit with white shirt and tie, but the more niggling stuff as well, like making sure his underclothes were fresh and clean. His Mam would have been appalled if they took him to the hospital and stripped him down to find dirty underwear. Among the items he wrote down were such things as 'take family photographs out of wallet' and 'read Three Men In A Boat again'. The former was there because he didn't want anyone to get the wrong impression, and the second, quite simply, because, God knew, he needed a laugh.

Of course, sometimes he changed his mind or he carried out a task, and he had already inked through certain lines. 'Eat steak and kidney pie' had been happily achieved after he and his wife had a huge row when Leah had asked him what he wanted for dinner — a surprise in itself. She told him kidney wasn't an option. He had gone out and cooked the bloody stuff himself, relishing it, fondling it against the roof of his mouth, embracing it with an almost erotic enjoyment. Not that he had had much of that lately! 'Buy a Geoffrey Beene sports' shirt' he had reluctantly crossed off when he decided that Mr. Beene would be too casual for the event. Not sartorially compatible with the tie that had been designated as The Suicide Tie. Not likely to be white even.

Looking at it after his meeting with Boney, the list seemed complete enough. Several items caught his eye that he could accomplish and then quickly erase, now that he was sure the bank was about to wield the axe. Almost sure, anyway. The bullet-points energized him and he decided to get a start on at least one of his must-dos that very afternoon. He considered a couple of items before his eye caught on the line 'Visit Morganthau', but immediately he ticked it.

'Yes,' he thought, 'I'd like to do that. Even if it turns out to be a false alarm, I wouldn't mind dropping in.'

6

Inez Morganthau was Henry's audiologist. It was she who had monitored his deafness over the years and chartered its advance. He always thought it remarkable that he should have ended up going to her. Her basement office was next to a fruit market and for years he had bought tomatoes and onions within feet of her equipment not ever realizing she was there. Then his doctor had referred him and he had entered her doors for the first time, swallowed up whole into the cold, grey world of the officially hearing impaired.

The first time he went in, his mood had been buoyant. Surrounded by so much deafness all his life, he was not the least afraid of it, and pretty sure that his was a minor case, easily remedied by some kind of listening device. He was proved correct and much of that first consultation revolved around whether he should try to do without artificial auditory assistance — the alliteration amused him — for a further year. He was, as Ms. Morganthau said, on the cusp. He had done without.

By his second visit, he was more apprehensive. Either everyone in his acquaintance had started to whisper or something was amiss. It had not taken long for Inez to confirm this. Really, she didn't even have to tell him. In his heart, Henry already knew, and he certainly botched the tests. Enclosed in the soundproofed room, looking at her through the window, he found himself trying to read her lips to supplement the distant words that he was supposed to hear and repeat. He was not too bad with the explosive consonants, the buhs and the guhs, and he easily got the lisping esses, though she didn't give him too many of those, but there were far too many words that seemed to drain away into the void before they ever reached his ear and he had never realized how many words depended on their seemingly innocuous vowels for comprehension.

He began to sweat although the room was cool and he was only partly relieved when he did much better with the other ear. He caught a look of concern on Inez's face and sensed an insincere lightness when she appeared at the door, fixed a small contraption over the right ear and said that she was going to play him some sounds. She put a little buzzer into his hand and instructed him to press it whenever he heard a noise. The exercise went swimmingly, however. He heard high-pitched beeps and low mournful ones and everything in between. He heard them when they were loud and he heard them when she softened them and even when she held them back, delaying them and sneaking them in, with no kind of rhythm to prompt him.

When she came in to switch the equipment to the other ear, Henry was feeling quite chipper and he did not realize that she was particularly quiet and businesslike. She did what she had to do and left, closing the door behind her without a single word. It was only afterwards, when he reconstructed the events of the afternoon in his mind — Henry always went over the events of his day, picking at them, weighing them — that he remembered she had patted him on his shoulder and squeezed it quite firmly before she left the room.

That second part of the test, the testing of the left ear, was a disaster. It began well enough when Inez transmitted a long shrieking beep that made him jump, but that was about it. Sometimes he thought he heard a beep and he pressed the buzzer, but he couldn't be quite sure. Sometimes there seemed to be a long silence and he didn't know what to do so he pressed the buzzer anyway, not quite rationally, not perhaps even intentionally. It just got pressed. He turned his head to the right so that his left ear could see Inez through the glass, be nearer to the origin of the sound, as it were, and he closed his eyes to concentrate. Occasionally, he would discern the low rumble of a beep and he would press the buzzer eagerly, several times. He felt like a child wanting to please the teacher.

Then he heard her voice, a long way away, 'Relax. Very good, Henry. I'll be with you in a minute.'

It was several minutes, however, before she came into the booth and released him from the equipment, leading him back to her office, seating him in front of her, knee to knee. She was quite blunt.

'It's not good, Henry. The right ear is just about the same as before, still on the edge, but there has been a significant deterioration in the left.' She looked at him sternly, 'You must have noticed it.'

'Well, yes, I guess I did,' he replied, 'Perhaps I just haven't been willing to acknowledge it.'

Inez must have felt that she had been too abrupt. 'Actually, you may not have noticed it that much. It will have happened gradually during the year and you might have become used to the decline and compensated for it.'

Henry nodded.

He looked at her.

Her eyes were moist and for a moment he wondered if she had a cold. Then, intuitively, he knew that the moisture was for him. Inez was responding to his loss. He was suddenly alarmed. All his life he had known that someday someone would tell him what he had just been told, but he had always shrugged his shoulders at the thought. If his Dad could cope with it, he could too. Henry had never felt sorry about his Dad's hearing, but here was someone feeling sorry for him. Inez turned away to wipe her eye, nonchalantly hiding the gesture, but her doing so made him more frightened. He could scarcely breathe. He held out a hand in front of him, the palm facing toward Inez. It looked as though he was warning her off, but she clasped the hand in sympathy.

'No!' said Henry, 'No!'

'No, no,' replied Inez, 'It won't be so bad. We'll take an impression of your ear and fix you up. Right now!'

She misunderstood.

Henry opened his mouth to tell her so, but the words would not come. He sucked in a breath and began to sob, huge heaving sobs that scared both of them. Inez clearly did not know what to do. She stood up, took his head between her hands and pressed it against the top of her stomach. Henry pulled away roughly.

'It's not me! It's not for me!' he said, trying to explain. 'It's my father.'

He strove to catch his breath. His throat was constricted by unassuageable regret. He had never realized before, not in his most vivid imaginings, how much his father must have suffered. His father had always coped so well, he had been sure of it! But was he wrong? Was he? He had glanced into Inez's eyes and what flickered back at him for the merest tick of time was, yes, a compassion and a professional condolence but also, not quite able to be hidden, pity.

Henry had never realized.

He had never known until now that his Dad must have seen such looks every day of his adult life.

*

Edward and Henry had been fighting in front of the fire, fooling around, calling each other names, and Henry, giggling wildly, out of control, slid off the sofa onto the floor just as Dad came into the room. Bump. Edward, four years older and more than a bit more mature (he always claimed), pushed his face into a cushion, snorting in his laughter.

From out of nowhere, it seemed, their father had roared, 'Talking about me, are you? Making fun of the old man?'

He struck the back of the door with an open hand. They heard the wood crack.

Henry and Edward stopped in their tracks. They shook their heads.

'No, no, it wasn't you!' said Edward, shaking his head. A look of concern Henry had never seen before spread across his brother's face.

Henry, younger, denser, shook his head as well.

'Dad, it was Edward. He was playing the fool.'

He giggled again at the recollection of what it was Edward had said.

Now, so many years later, he knew that that had been another insertion of the knife. How could I have been so unaware, he wondered?

*

The doorbell rang but he took his time coming down from upstairs to answer it. By the time he reached the hall, his Dad had seen the silhouette of the caller through the bottled-glass door and opened it to see who was there. The visitor was already impatient, beginning to shout.

'Mr. Brown! Mr. Brown! Is this where he lives?'

How much more ordinary could a question be?

'What? Who?' said Henry's Dad, 'Yes. That's right. She's in the town.' Henry's Dad was a master lip-reader, but he had to know the lips and the speaker had to use them.

The visitor saw Henry coming down the stairs.

'Hey there,' he said, switching his attention and looking at Henry over his Dad's shoulder. 'I was asking him which house Daniel Brown lives at. Perhaps you can tell me.'

Henry placed his hand gently between his father's shoulder blades, not intending to move him away but to offer support, reinforcement. His father flinched. Here, now, in Inez's office, Henry realized that his Dad must have thought he was being shunted aside so that the conversation could continue unencumbered without him. Had he sighed? It was too long ago for Henry to be sure, but he seemed to remember a small sound as his father turned away towards the kitchen.

7

Family lore had it that the last noise, the last inkling of slight resonance, Henry's father heard was the whine of Hitler's bombs one night during the blitz. The fact was, however, that his Dad may have pretended he could still hear things long after everything had became completely silent, long after he had found an accommodation with the still abyss in which he found himself.

The last words, coherent sounds, he claimed to have heard was Edward VIII's radio address to the nation the day he abdicated. His Dad had put his left ear directly up against the wooden lattice work of the radio, the wireless they called it in those days, turned the knob as far to the right as it could go, tried to force it further, and hunted for the monarch's voice among the shrieks of the ether. Everyone fled. Henry's Mam went outside for a bit of a cry, but the others tried to make a joke of the bedlam, as did his Dad when the broadcast was over.

Philip Earl came from the burgher class, although over the years his disability would cause him to slip a rung or two on the social ladder. He came by his deafness honestly enough. His grandma and grandpa on his mother's side had been first cousins and everyone knows what that meant. Apart from smashing the old Church of England laws of consanguinity wide open, you were likely to give birth to the village idiot. The family avoided that fate (although, according to his Dad, there was a second cousin in West Hartlepool he wasn't too sure about) but congenital deafness came among them like a plague. All Henry's paternal uncles were deaf to some degree, more rather than less, and his Auntie Isabel ended her days both blind and deaf. Deafness ran in the family like diarrhoea of the ear his Dad always said, which, if it didn't quite make sense, had a lovely cadence to it. To the end of his life his Dad loved the sounds of words; how they could be strung together to make a point or add an effect.

Henry had never known his great grandparents but, as a little boy, he had been acquainted with their youngest daughter, Maisie. His Gran. Maisie was a sophisticated, spoilt lady of leisure who felt herself entitled to just about anything that caught her eye. She had been a beauty in her day. She had dazzled Granddad, his Dad said, until the poor chap begged for mercy and she deigned to marry him. Henry knew her only as an old woman. She was lined, arthritic and smelled of 4711 with an under scent of camphor and the latrine, husband long gone. She was — each one of her children called her this — a tartar. And as deaf as a post. The proverbial post. Henry kept out of her way. Not that either of his parents put him forward, they loved both their sons too much for that. There was one exception. Christmas Eve was a command performance. Gran called all her progeny and all of their offspring to an audience so that she might dole out largesse.

At the top of her voice.

Henry's Gran knew, to the very core of her being that the reason she could not hear people was because people did not speak up. They mumbled. They dribbled their vowels and they ate their consonants. They generally emulated the servant class from which most of them had undoubtedly sprung. So, good Christian that she knew herself to be, she lived by example and she shouted. At everyone: the butcher, the baker, the candlestick-maker and certainly at everyone in her family.

Each child got the same gift each year: an orange, which, Henry had to admit, was quite something in the days of post-war rationing, and a three penny piece, which was not. Gran would hold the coin flat between her thumb and her first finger, and drop it into his outstretched palm.

'Don't spend it on sweets, boy. Rot your teeth!'

The words were bawled into his face. Her fingers never brushed his flesh. Next came the worst part: he had to stand on tiptoe and kiss her on her lips. Except that she had no lips, just a line of dissatisfaction drawn across her face, and the close-up smell of what, years later, he realized was sherry.

'Thank you, Gran,' he said by rote before Mam whisked him off to stand safely behind her skirts until he, his brother, his male cousins and all the men were allowed to leave the room. Henry wondered what happened to Mam and the aunts who had to stay behind, what happened when they ran out of polite conversation to yell across the room at their mother-in-law. Gran always took centre stage.

'I swear to God, Edith Earl,' this to his mother, 'you don't have the sense you were born with.'

He heard this once when the maid was closing the door, shaking with relief at no longer being in her presence.

'Nasty old bat!' he heard the maid say and although he knew that females shouldn't say such things, nor young boys either, he flung his arms around her waist and give her an enormous hug.

*

As Henry grew older, he learned more about his Dad and his Gran. How his Dad had been a menopausal baby, unexpected and unwanted. He heard how, when his Dad was fourteen years old, he ran away from home and went to live with the family of his best friend, Reg. Salt-of-the-earth people they were, a bit common perhaps, but warm and loving. Mrs. Hammond, a farmer's wife, had gone to see his Gran and given her a piece of her mind, told her off for the way she treated her youngest. Dad stayed with the Hammonds, surreptitiously supported by his father, until he joined the merchant navy and went away to sea. Gran sold his clothes the day after he left.

As a man, his Dad had tried to excuse the harridan who had been so bent on ruining his childhood. Henry didn't. He did wonder, as he got older, whether it was linked to her deafness, to not being able to cope with going deaf at twenty-five when she was still the belle of the ball. It had certainly shut her off from society and perhaps she really did believe that people were talking about her, but Henry didn't hear anything that could excuse the way she was. His Dad was much more forgiving. No worm ever went inside his Dad's ear to take away his enjoyment of life or his love of Mam or his determination to see the bright side. He even saw the comic side of his own tragedy. Well, usually he did.

Henry also blamed his Dad's Dad. Gran's husband was an amiable, generous man, a gentle man, but he wanted a quiet life and she wore him down. She wore everyone down. Granddad had loved his Maisie once and he maintained the proprieties until the end, but he shouldn't have let her rule the roast to the detriment of every single one of his children. He died young. He caught influenza, went to bed, put up not the slightest fight, and died. His sons said his last breath had been a sigh of relief. One of them, the one who never married, who lived at home and became odd in his own old age, said he wished it might have been him. Gran lived on in the silence.

Of course, Henry only heard these stories, he hadn't been there and his Dad was not the most reliable of sources. He would never have dared asked his uncles, so much older than his Dad, if the stories were true. He knew that his Dad was the great exaggerator, the spinner of tall tales, retailer of the shaggiest of dog stories. Such tales set his Dad apart, their embellishments were like silken threads woven into the tapestry of the silence that surrounded him. He might not be able to hear, but he knew how to captivate his audiences, how to grab them by the scruff of their necks — his Dad was not averse to the appropriate cliché — and hold them in the palm of his hand. Yet, although the stories were invariably told with high good humour, Henry had always been aware of their underside.

*

One time, they were sitting in the backyard on the grass, his Dad had told him how, when he was himself about ten years old, he had been sauntering along the high street and he saw his mother strolling along in front of him. Coat to the ground, fox fur slung with studied nonchalance over one shoulder and a feathered hat trailing clouds of glory, he saw her spy a boy leaning on a bench. She tripped slightly when she saw the boy and had then to look right and left to see if the hesitation in her step had attracted attention. It would not do to perambulate improperly in a public place. The boy was well-dressed but his tie was askew and one of his shoelaces was undone. A likely lad, his Dad said. His Dad and the boy were about the same size and they had the same russet auburn hair. His mother put her shoulders back and drew up every inch of her five foot and a bit as high as it would go. She strode behind the boy, heels click-clacking on the sidewalk, and whacked him on the head with her furled parasol. Whap de ap bap!

It was always the details that made his Dad's tales so fascinating. And the sound effects.

'Wait until your father hears about this, boy!' she bawled, stopping the strolling citizenry in its tracks. 'No supper for you, this evening! Dreadful boy! Be off with you!'

She barked, as usual, in exclamation points.

The astonished innocent turned towards his assailant and she congealed in mid-strike, spider fingers shooting up to her throat, covering the antique cameo that, for the longest time, Henry had thought was a part of her anatomy.

When young Philip returned home that evening, he was sent to his room, nothing to eat except what the maid smuggled in when she was going off duty. He had made a fool of his mother by not being the boy she thought he had been. His father dropped by later. He sighed, shook his head, kissed his son on the forehead, and pressed two giant, sticky jawbreakers into his hand.

'Night, my boy. Chin up!' he said.

No, Henry never did summon up much sympathy for Maisie Earl. His Dad would tell him stories about her, his Dad was full of stories, and he knew he was right to hate her. It was only when he become an adult, and turned the stories over in his mind, thought about what they meant and what it must have been like to be his Dad, that they became more than the tales a father tells his son to make him giggle and squirm. He still remembered the day he realized, it was a shining bolt of illumination, that his Dad had turned his whole life into a series of funny stories just to be able to cope. He had embroidered his scars with clever words.

And they were good stories.

Henry sometimes wondered if his dear old Gran hadn't affected him as much as she had his Dad. More, in a way, because his Dad had a resilience that he knew he lacked. Also — and Henry eventually became aware of this — he himself had a more unforgiving streak, a sometimes cold stillness that would make him seek revenge when he might more easily have forgotten and gone on with his life. His Dad, Henry knew this with certainty, had been a better man than he would ever be.

8

On the other hand, there had been times when Henry could cheerfully have strangled his father. Forty years on, he was still not likely to forget his most embarrassing moment, a moment quintessentially Dad, a moment that even now made his blood run colder than the ice directly under the North Pole and which, contrarily, still had the power to turn his face redder than the most luscious, fresh tomato just thinking about it. Even his Mam had been fit to be tied that time. If she had believed in it, Henry thought — it was cold comfort — she would have sliced, diced and divorced him on the spot.

*

Every so often, Mam suffered from a wanderlust. She pined to get out of the provinces and visit the big city. She keened for the wider world and its attractions.

'Let's go somewhere,' she urged one day as the four of them sat round the dining table polishing off his Dad's dumpling stew. 'Edward, where would you like to go?'

Edward shook his head. 'Can't,' he said, 'Got skating practice, all next week.'

Henry's brother was a roller-skating fiend.

'I don't mean next week, I mean anytime. Where would you like to go?'

Edward was the practical sort. "Durham Miners' Gala is on at 'end of 'fortnight.' Edward liked to keep things simple. Dropping the article, Yorkshire style, helped.

'Our Edward,' scolded his mother, momentarily sidetracked, 'don't you speak like that. It's common.'

'What's he saying now?' Henry's Dad asked. 'Are you swearing in front of your Mam again? I'll skin you alive.'

Edward must have bridled at the 'again'. The boys never swore in front of their mother. Never swore at all really. Well, not much.

'No, no, no, you're not listening, he was . . .' Henry's Mam rolled her eyes and then shrugged. It would be a frustrating business to get the finer points of the definite article across to Dad, who had been known to drop one or two of them himself. Better to drop the discussion. She took a breath. 'I was asking him where he would like to go to for a holiday.'

His Dad was not about to be sidetracked.

'I'll sharp tell him where he'll be going to if I catch him swearing at his mother.'

Edward might as well have been invisible at this point.

'He'll be going to his room with a good clout around his ear, that's where he'll be going.'

Dad was getting up steam. Henry laid his hand on his arm.

'Mam was asking,' he explained, lips moving very precisely, 'where we would all like to go, if we went somewhere, you know, on a trip.'

Dad didn't hear him, or didn't want to. Edward had pushed his chair back and was standing. 'I wasn't swearing. You never listen. He never listens. I'm not going to say anything again. All I get is bother, when I do.' He was on the verge of tears.

'There, love, don't you take any notice of him' To Dad: 'He wasn't swearing. He was saying he wanted to go to the Gala.'

'What's he want to go there for?'

'Give me strength!' Henry's Mam turned to Edward. 'I didn't mean somewhere nearby, I meant where would you like to go to. You know, travel to. Visit. If you could go anywhere you wanted to. Anywhere at all.'

'Australia,' replied Edward.

His Mam laughed. 'Well, there's quite a difference between Australia and the Durham Miners' Gala, now isn't there?'

Henry's Dad had, somehow, caught up. Almost.

'What on earth do you want to go to Australia for, our Mam? Terrible place. Big, hot and full of convicts.'

'They don't have convicts there now,' Henry interjected, as knowledgeable as only an eleven year old could be, although a little voice in his head was already warning him: 'Our Henry, don't get him started. You're not going to win and you'll not get to go anywhere either.'

Henry's Dad liked a good argument.

''Course they have convicts. That was why it's there. 'Place is full of them.'

Not an article in sight.

'Rubbish! The country was there before the convicts.' Edward took up the fight. 'Any road, Cousin May emigrated to Sydney and she wasn't a convict.' What he lacked in logic, he was willing to make up for in vehemence.

'Aye, and she married a Welshman. See what I said! Just as I told you.'

The man couldn't carry on a logical conversation if you gave him a bucket.

He knows exactly what he is doing. He doesn't want to go anywhere, so he is going to stop us talking about where we want to go.

Well, stand up to him then. Don't let him get away with it.

Me? I can't stand up to him. No one can.

Your Mam can.

Yes, but she's had years of practice. Anyway, he'll just change the subject again.

Coward.

No, it's not being a coward. He's my Dad.

But he's like a big kid.

A sigh: Yes, but he's still my Dad.

While Henry's Dad continued to fulminate against the Welsh, Australia, convicts and travel in general, his Mam's lips were levelling into a thin line of determination. Henry knew that look. They all did. It didn't bode well for whoever caused it.

'Nevertheless,' she said — Henry had also noticed that when she was about to lay down the law, she always began with a word of three or more syllables — 'we are going to go somewhere. And soon.' Then she added, as though she'd just had a brainwave. 'I know, let's go to London.'

Henry, his brother and his Dad groaned in unison. This wasn't a brainwave: it was a great big hole in the ground, and they had fallen right into it. Whenever Mam had the chance to go anywhere, it was always London. She had London on the brain. London was Henry's Mam's favourite spot. Her pot of gold. Fortnum and Mason's. The Mall. Traipsing about all over the place. Anything at all to do with the Queen — you couldn't hold her back.

Well, you bloody well might have known that was coming.

I was hoping she'd think of somewhere else. Have a blackout or something. Forget that it existed.

Quick. Suggest somewhere else and see if you can get her mind off it.

Fat chance!

*

And so, a month later, they took the early train down to King's Cross for the day. His Dad absolutely refused to stay overnight, saying it was a waste and why anyone would want to sleep in London was completely beyond him. They had to consider the safety factor. Henry's Mam knew better than to fight that battle, she had already won the war, after all. Edward, at fourteen, was allowed to stay home. Henry was not.

'We'll come back on the last train, then. The overnight. That way we'll be able to see a show.'

His Dad moaned as if pierced through the heart by a javelin thrown with malicious and fatal intent. 'What would you want to do that for, woman? When we could find a nice comfy pub and have a couple of drinks before we set out back.'

'And what do you think we'd do with our Henry while we're sat snug in the lounge bar? Leave him tied to a post outside, I suppose.'

'Woof! Woof!' Henry raised him hands in a fair imitation of begging and stuck out a panting tongue. His Dad swatted the back of his head.

I could go for a walk in Soho.

You? You'd be lost in Soho in two twos.

Says who? I've got a good sense of direction.

You'd be sitting on the curb in five minutes bawling your eyes out, wondering where they were.

Liar!

'We're going to a show! And that's that!'

'What will I do at a show, love?'

The amount of petulance his Dad could put into his voice always amazed Henry. If he had tried it, he'd be in trouble. They'd tell him to grow up, but with his Dad it was another story.

'We'll go to a musical and you can watch them dance and see the costumes.' This clearly did not appeal, so his Mam continued, 'And I'll have a gin and tonic in the intermission. You'll be able to have your pint.'

'He could stay in the bar the whole time if he wanted,' said Henry, seeing an opportunity to stir the pot, but making sure his Dad didn't see what he was saying.

'Oh no, he won't! It'll do him good to go to the theatre. Anyway, he'd probably wander off if we gave him half a chance.'

*

Henry's Mam walked their feet off. They took the tube to Piccadilly Circus so she could trot up Shaftsbury Avenue to see what was on, then they were off along Oxford Street before taking another tube to Kensington and that Mecca of all earthly desire, Harrods. Unfortunately, every show that she and Henry suggested was pooh-poohed by his Dad and eventually they stood on a corner in the drizzle looking at a newspaper. No one's temper was very good.

'Someone called Beatrice Lillie is on at the Strand in "Auntie Mame",' he reported, the three of them hovering underneath an umbrella.

'Beatrice Lillie!' said his Mam turning to his Dad, 'you like Beatrice Lillie.'

It was always amazing to Henry how much his Dad could take in when he wanted to. Who would have thought he would be able to get his head around such a name, out of the blue, just like that.

'Lady Peel? I thought she was dead.'

Henry's Mam mouthed the words, lips thinning, 'Would you like to see Beatrice Lillie?'

It was not so much a question as a decision. His Dad knew it.

The show was better than Henry expected. His Dad had told him about the actress, and the story intrigued him. He was a little bit in awe of London policemen.

Of course, she was quite old, but she was very funny. The first act made him laugh out loud. The trouble began in the intermission. His Dad started it.

'Now we have to leave here no later than ten thirty,' he said, waving his pint for emphasis.

'What if it isn't finished?' Henry asked his Mam. There didn't seem much point asking his Dad.

She passed the question on, 'What if it isn't finished by ten thirty?'

'Now look! It'll take an hour to get to King's Cross. So that's when we'll have to leave.'

'An hour! It couldn't take an hour to get to King's Cross if we walked it.'

'Barefoot!'

The response burst from Henry before he could stop it.

If his Dad's look could kill . . .

Aarggh! He got me, sir. I saw it coming, but couldn't get out of the way in time. Right through the breast bone, it went.

Don't move, lad. Messy! We'll have the medic over here in two shakes of the cat's tail, see if we don't.

Ohhh, it hurts so bad. I think I'm a goner. Anyway, the cat's a Manx.

Henry drained into the plush red carpet. He hardly made a mark at all.

'Our Philip, surely we don't need a whole hour.' Henry's Mam looked doubtful.

'What if the tube breaks down? What'll we do then?' Trump.

'Why would the tube break down?'

'How do I know?' And trick.

It's only four stops.

Don't tell me, tell him. Tell your Mam.

Wouldn't do any good.

Baby.

Who? Him or me?

'Well, it should be alright. It's sure to be over by ten thirty.' Henry's Mam sounded doubtful, but she going to pursue the matter in such a public place. North country accents stood out in the dress circle as it was, and his Dad, as usual, wasn't even attempting to keep it down. People had been staring. Henry concentrated on his orangeade and pulled up his socks.

*

Henry had been glancing at his watch every five minutes, but eventually he became absorbed and forgot about the deadline. At ten twenty-nine, the whole cast was on stage and a party was in progress. All eyes were on Auntie Mame. She was about to speak directly to the audience and the audience was hanging, to coin a phrase, on her every word. Turning sideways to intercept a waiter who filled her long-necked glass to the brim with champagne, she took a puff from her cigarette and waved it and its long holder in the air. Head back, laughing, she faced the orchestra stalls and opened her mouth to speak. The theatre was hushed. Miss Lillie milked the silence like the professional she was.

'Come on then! It's ten thirty! We have to get off!'

A drill sergeant could not have said it better. Or more definitively. Or louder.

Henry's Dad stood up, turned to the startled woman sitting on his right and said, this time in a sotto voce whisper that must have reached the back row of the gods, ''Scuse me, love, we've got to catch a train. Let us out, then.' And glancing back over his shoulder at Henry and his Mam, he added, 'Come on you two,' effectively foiling any small chance of their pretending they were not with the man and had never set eyes on him before in their entire lives.

Henry retained a pristinely clear memory of all that happened next. It was indelibly tattooed on the inside of his cranium.

He hauled himself out of his seat, slunk down the row, and asked, begged, to be excused by each of the persons who had to stand up to let him past. There were seven of them: two men, four women and a girl in glasses about the same age as himself, who smirked. Since both he and his Mam were carrying parcels, it was neither a quick nor a quiet exit. They were in the centre of the second row. Everyone in the dress circle was staring at them. Beatrice Lillie was staring as well. It still curled Henry's toes to remember how she had stopped what she was doing on the stage and peered up into the balcony, cigaretted-hand shading her eyes so that she could see the cause of the commotion. She was waiting for them to leave. She didn't say a word.

Henry's Mam didn't say a word either. She did not say a word for the next three hundred miles and she did not say a word for the next three days. Their arrival at the railway station in a fast fifteen minutes cooked his Dad's goose completely, and standing there on the cold platform for an hour and a quarter (the train was late) was like basting it with bacon fat. His Dad blustered, but no one was listening.

He looks as though someone shot him.

I would like to shoot him myself.

Your Mam would like to, too. From the look of her, she could use her bare hands on him.

We should have thrown him over the balcony on the way out.

Heave and thud.

I could just see their faces if we did that.

I wonder if he'd have bounced?

You know, I was just thinking . . .

You would!

Well, if you do think about it, it must have been hard for him. I mean he couldn't hear a word of what was going on. All he could see was people all round him laughing their heads off.

Hard cheese!

And then he doesn't know the sound of his own voice. You know that.

I know that he behaved like a spoiled kid. You know it as well.

But he's my Dad!

He won't be much longer if your Mam gets her hands on him. And now the train is late.

She looks like she'd like to push him under it when it comes into the station.

Henry sighed. I wouldn't mind doing that myself sometimes.

9

When Henry arrived at Inez's office on that last Tuesday afternoon of his life, he found it bright and bustling. While her practice was mainly for adults and seniors, her partner specialized in children and there was usually a couple of four year olds there, waiting with the impatience of the very young. A small boy was sitting on the floor playing with a toy that involved moving blocks up, along and over wavy plastic wires. Playing, Henry saw, was the wrong word. The boy was absorbed, as only a child can be absorbed, in stacking all the blocks at one end of the wires. He was a blond haired lad, with a glorious rosy complexion. His cowlick stood up and his mouth looped open in concentration. Above and behind him, on the very edge of her seat, sat his mother. Tweedily dressed, she was groomed to perfection. Henry, however, had the impression that she probably didn't know what she was wearing, and cared even less. She turned when Henry sat down, two seats over, and smiled briefly. Her attention was on the little boy. She seemed to hover over him, febrilely tense.

The boy wore glasses and, in his concentration, he reached up, an ancient gesture in one so young, to touch their bridge, pushing them back up his nose. Attached to the pale beige, cumbersome spectacles, Henry saw a hearing-aid. A port wine stain. A prosthesis. A haemangioma.

The boy's mother held out her hand to calm his cowlick, patting the delinquent hair into place. He paid no attention. If her world was him, his was the brightly coloured toy and its stack of blocks. Oblivious now to Henry and even to where they were perhaps, the woman reached out her hand once more, and held it inches from the side of her son's head. Henry held his breath. He knew what she was going to do. She was going to flick her fingers. She wanted to learn, in her mothering way, what she was here to find out scientifically. She must have done this countless times at home, he thought. She must have made a noise, different noises, experimenting, pleading with the gods, hoping that her wee angel would react, would turn, inquire. Would hear!

Before the woman could move her fingers however, the boy turned — for reassurance perhaps, to tell her of his love, surely. A blazing smile lit his face and then, satisfied, the frown of concentration beginning again before he even looked away, he returned to his task. He did not see the fingers suspended so closely behind him. His mother withdrew them, as if ashamed, but when he was at his play again, she moved her hand forward yet again. An emerald ring, confident and at home on her hand, green twinkling in the neon light, sat next to a rich gold wedding band. She tucked her thick, healthy blonde hair behind her ear with her other hand, and made up her mind.

She flicked her fingers.

The sound ricocheted around the room, a castanet of hopelessness. Both the woman and Henry flinched. He wanted to take the woman into his arms, to croon softly into her ear. He could smell Givenchy on the nape of her neck, but it was mixed with the sour sweat of sadness. Cut off from the world, like her son in front of her, she sat still, straight-backed, silent.

The little boy remained steadfastly at his task.

The door of Inez's office opened.

'Henry,' she said smiling, 'what are you doing here?'

'I just dropped in. My hearing aid has been making some buzzing sounds. I wondered if you have time to look at it.'

Inez frowned. 'Can you wait a few minutes and I'll try to fit you in.'

She smiled at the little boy's mother. 'Laurie will be with you shortly.'

Bending down in front of the boy, she cupped his chin in the palm of her hand, lifting it up to get his attention, so that he was looking at her.

'Hello there, young man. How are you today?'

She smiled, enunciating each word as she said it, and smiled at the arrangement of the blocks.

'My! Aren't you a clever boy!'

The boy smiled back at her and turned towards his mother. The warmth of his smile caused the temperature in the room to rise. Henry felt himself bobbing along in its wake enchanted. No longer was it bare April. It had become a glorious summer day.

Then the boy spoke: 'Ooork, Maarm-ah.' The voice of a troglodyte.

In an instance, Henry was becalmed. Inez, professional smile firmly in place, rose stiffly and repetitively smoothed the front of her skirt.

'Just a few minutes, Henry.' she said, looking at the floor.

*

Inside her office, Henry took the hearing aid from his left ear and Inez hooked it up to a machine. She worked in silence for a few minutes and, in his own silence, Henry watched her. When she was done, she fitted the hearing aid back into his ear and carried out further tests, monitoring the results on a screen behind him.

'Everything seems to be fine,' she said.

Henry had always found Inez quiet spoken and the irony that he could hardly hear his audiologist amused him. It seemed inappropriate somehow to ask her, of all people, to speak up. He liked her. He liked her small Spanish stature. He liked her thin immaculate fingers, and, most of all, he liked her kindness.

'Okay, then. I just thought I'd check,' he said.

'What about the other one? Would you like me to have a look at that one, too?'

'No,' Henry replied, 'it seems to be alright at the moment.'

'You sure? It won't take long. I wouldn't like anything to go wrong with that one.' Inez smiled. Her smile and a slight emphasis on the 'that' was her complicit acknowledgement that Henry's right ear had its own story to tell, and that, when it came to stories, Henry too knew how to tell them.

*

It had been almost five years since Inez told Henry he needed a second hearing aid. That he could wait no longer. That he needed it now. For many years that good right ear had carried the other one, eked out words that it missed. The left ear, buoyed by this assistance, had toiled mightily but, like a man overboard in a fast current, it was drowning, less and less able to even bob about in the wake of the boat. Inez said it flatly: the right ear required attention. Immediately. It could not swim by itself anymore. It required its own life-raft: Henry, awash in quasi nautical metaphors, had agreed, but he still decided to wait another year.

It was not that he had a horror of people seeing he was wearing hearing aids in both ears. That was not Henry's vanity. Rather, it was that there was, even then, less and less that he wanted to hear. Music? Yes, some. Classical anyway. Movies? A few. These days most of them played better silent. Work? Well, he could always tell them to shout. Family? Heaven forefend! In any case, he could imagine what Leah would say when he told her that he would be dipping into the bank account for another hearing aid with the last of the girls still in college.

A year later, at his annual check-up, Inez read him the riot act. He could wait no longer. His right ear had declined exponentially. So determined were her words that Henry had visions of it coming loose and having to be scotch-taped back in place.

What if it fell off completely?

'Excuse me, sir, could you move your foot a little? You're standing on my ear. Thank you so much. Don't worry about it! I can wipe it off.'

Perhaps he could keep it in the little purse that he used for his replacement batteries, alongside the tiny brush and the other cleaning equipment.

'Excuse me just a minute,' he might say when a meeting was called to order, 'while I put my ear on.'

Laying his head, right side up, on the table to staple it in place would ensure everyone's complete attention.

Or perhaps double sided Velcro.

'Ah, there we are. Oops, not quite straight! Boney, do they look properly aligned to you? Come round the other side and compare the two.'

'Not bad, not bad,' responded Boney, judiciously. 'Pull on the lobe just a bit. That'll give a better balance, look you.'

'Very good,' interjected Rowena. 'Have you ever thought of earrings?'

'Yes,' replied Henry, 'but I can never decide whether to go with clip-ons or to get them pierced. Of course, pierced could lead to hepatitis.'

'Oh, I'd get mine pierced in a flash, but I can't stand the sight of blood,' said Boney, 'Especially my own.'

Henry had been about to tell Inez to begin the process, but he was unsure how much it would all cost. The government would kick in a percentage but Henry was uncertain whether the bank would. It was only two and a bit years since he had had a new hearing aid for his left ear and he knew that there were only so many dollars in so many years. He had a suspicion that all his dollars had been used up. He told Inez that he would have to get in touch with the bank's staff Insurance Division and come back to her.

*

He had been waiting on the telephone for fifteen minutes. All the lines were in use, due, as the disembodied voice kept reassuring him, to a heavier than usual concentration of calls. He had always been taught that only trains were supposed to be due, and those into stations. Henry could be — as even he would have admitted — a bit of a pedant himself.

He found it difficult to write while holding the telephone, but having punched in his employee number, it was unwise to hang up. You never knew if they might make a note in your personnel file about your lack of endurance. You could be tagged as someone who failed to follow through, someone who was, that horror of the banking community, flighty. He had a cramp across his shoulder blades by the time the music ceased and he was connected.

'Hello. Your insurance team-mate, Shirley, speaking.'

'Good afternoon, team-mate of mine,' he replied. 'My name is Earl, Henry Earl, and I have an inquiry about my benefits.'

'Hello, Henry, how may I help you?'

'Ah yes, Miss Speaking, you have the advantage of me. I can't remember ever having met you, but it's wonderful to talk to you again.'

'My name is Shirley. I'm sorry, did you say we have met?'

'Well, yes, Miss Speaking, I thought you indicated that we had, but you would have to tell me where it was.'

Rattled. 'My name is Shirley. I said I was speaking, Henry.'

'Oh, ah. I see! Perhaps we crossed paths in a branch somewhere.'

Firmly. 'We have never met, Henry!'

'But you keep calling me by my first name!'

Silence.

'How can I help you?'

'I'm calling about my coverage. I would like to hear about my hearing coverage.'

'Yes, Hen.' She swallowed the word. 'Let me bring your file up on my screen.'

'How clever of you,' replied Henry and, as succinctly as he could, he recounted the details of his hearing history.

'That's correct. You have used your entitlement and will not be eligible for a further aid or for treatment for the next two years and, let me see, five months. The eighth of August.'

This was as Henry had supposed, although he had not been sure of the details. He laid his trump card on the table with a flourish.

'Ah, yes, but that was the left ear. I am calling to inquire about my right.'

'Your rights? Well, Hen . . .' She hurried on, 'you do, of course, have all the rights that belong to you legally, along with your benefits. That you are covered for.'

'No, no,' he said. He was beginning to enjoy himself. 'Not my rights,' he hissed the ess into the mouthpiece. 'My right. My ear. My right ear. I think that your sturdy screen will indicate that I also have a right ear and that this right ear,' a slight emphasis on the adjective was intended both as a clarifying assistance and a sorrowful rebuke. 'this right ear is, unsullied benefit-wise. In fact,' he added pedagogically, 'In fact, I think I can *assure* you of that. Your screen will be able to *ensure* that this is true. So my *insurance* must still be in place.' The emphasis on the first syllable of each of the words was unmistakably playful. In Henry's mind.

Had he not been hard of hearing, Henry might have commented that the silence on the other end of the line was deafening. He waited for Shirley to process his thought. Instead, he heard her clear her throat.

'Well,' she said, hesitantly, 'No. You have, as I have indicated, used your entire entitlement at this time.'

Henry knew what was coming. It would be as he had supposed, but he needed to hear her say it and he repeated what he had said before. 'I am inquiring about a disability vis a vis my right ear. I fully understand the position regarding the left.'

'Mr. Earl,' replied Shirley, suddenly formal, ready with the royal flush, 'We go by the head!'

Even as she spoke the words, Shirley must have noted the strangeness of what she heard coming out of her mouth. Common sense demanded that she did.

Henry knew he had her. He slammed the trap shut.

'You go by the head, eh?' he repeated, as though processing how this could be. 'But I have two ears! You know the old expression, "Ear, Ear"?'

He heard a rustle of paper at the other end of the line. Shirley was paging through her manual.

'One is on the left side of my head, and the other on the right. I should mention that the one cannot see the other. They listen, I am fairly certain, separately. In so far as they hear at all of course, which is why I require these devices!'

'I'm sorry.' Shirley interrupted hurriedly, 'I could check with my supervisor, but I'm quite certain that,' she paused, 'we, uh, go by the head.'

A further short silence ensued.

Henry could not believe his luck.

'So let me understand this correctly, Miss Speaking.' He took a deep breath and said, endeavouring to unravel a great mystery, 'The allowance is for one ear per head. My right ear is, for all intents and purposes, uninsured. Umm. I can assure you that this was not my intention. Nor do I recall designating a particular or specific ear on the questionnaire accompanying the application. Could you check that it was the left ear I chose.'

'No, no! You didn't choose an ear. It's just that you used all of your entitlement on the one, the one ear!'

'Oh dear! So let me get this right! Perhaps I should say, 'correct' given the thrust of our conversation. Could we try a hypothetical? Suppose,' he paused for a moment, 'suppose I had a wooden leg. Was born with it. Well, not quite born with it, of course, too uncomfortable in the womb for my dear mother, but came to this glorious institution with it.'

'. . .'

Shirley was a cautious soul.

'Well, suppose I broke it, oh say, skiing. And it had to be replaced and I got one of those expensive plastic jobs. The kind that would permit me to genuflect before my betters in the organization.'

'Yes . . . ?' said Shirley.

There was a smidgen of a chuckle in her voice. He felt she was beginning to understand where he might be going with this, and, being a functionary in the trenches herself, the bond among the villagers was perhaps beginning to come into play.

'Well, and just suppose, Shirley, that coming to work one fine morning I caught my leg, my other leg in one of the express elevators — the good one, the leg that is, not the elevator — and it was so mangled that they had no other alternative but to amputate . . .'

'. . .'

'Do you mean to tell me,' Henry was all astonishment and put-upon disbelief, 'that that leg, or to be precise, that want of a leg, would not be covered? That that, should I say, void would be uncovered? Trouserless?

Henry could feel his insurance teammate's desire to laugh, but she would be a brave woman to do so. Conversations are monitored for quality control.

'What would the bank in its infinite, altruistic wisdom expect me to do then?'

A pause to ponder.

'Hop?'

Disbelief.

'Until two August the eighth's from now?'

Shirley couldn't help it: she laughed anyway.

'I really don't know, but they'd probably make an accommodation if you appealed the case. A leg would be different.'

Henry stopped the laughter short.

'Not if you are deaf, my dear,' he said, 'Not if you are deaf.'

Somewhere in the conversation they had established a bond. Henry could not leave her like this.

'Another hypothetical,' he said. 'What about eyes? What if I was born with a glass eye?'

Henry heard Shirley stifle a whoop on the other end of the line.

Before they ended the conversation, Shirley advised him to put his case in writing and see what happened. She didn't sound very hopeful but she said, 'What harm can it do? And Henry, a word of advice,' she whispered this, 'don't mention anything about a wooden leg!'

*

He did pursue his case to the highest level in the bank. Four months later, he received a response from a Senior Teammate in which his appeal was denied. The letter began with a declaration that was calculated to drive him at a high speed into a concrete abutment: 'We regret that this reply could not have been more favourable . . .' His, he was informed in the mellifluous prose of high finance, was neither a catastrophic nor a life threatening situation. He had not, it was noted, cited financial hardship in his letter.

He thought about writing again to point out that the hard of hearing are regularly mowed down in traffic and that large objects have been known to fall on them from tall buildings even as onlookers failed lamentably to warn of their approach. In the end, he could not be bothered. The result, he knew, would be the same. A lawyer friend suggested that it might be illegal for the bank to factor into its decision any considerations of either his affluence or his relative poverty, but earlier rumours of coming cutbacks were already beginning to wash over the Division like waves of dirty dishwater. He did precisely what the bank hoped he would do. Nothing.

Henry did have his revenge, however. He began to tell. He told the story of the head. A little embroidery here: an embellishment or two there. He quoted the letter. Verbatim. Not to Boney, of course, and certainly not to Rowena, but to his peers, his acquaintance. To people he sat next to at meetings, chums from other banks, passers-by on the way home. He told people at church, the mailman and the man at the pet shop who sold him Anna Karenina's cat food. He even thought of telling his wife, but he couldn't see the upside.

When he told Inez, they laughed together. The audiologist, squeezed his hand and said, 'I'll do it for you as inexpensively as I can, Henry.'

And so she had gone to work on his right ear. He paid for the work himself. The hearing aid helped for a little while, he noticed the improvement and was positively giddy with the information he was able to pick up at meetings. He supposed the little device was still toiling away. It was the ear itself that wasn't.

10

Henry had finished his root beer and was shredding the straw with a long fingernail when he noticed that the lights were on in the little jewellery shop. He should have cut his nails a week ago but he had been holding off in case he needed one or more of them to pry open a bottle of pills or hold on to a balustrade somewhere before launching himself into a void. He had been keeping his options open.

Finally, he thought to himself, now we can get this show on the road.

He walked into the store, going straight to the cluttered counter at the back where a little Chinese repairman sat, hunched and taut, working at his trade.

'Good morning,' said Henry, 'I wonder if you could help me. I want to remove this ring.'

He held his left hand up, fingers slightly splayed so that the ring, and how tight it was, was visible.

'I can't get it off.'

The little repairman peered at the ring and then up at Henry. His look clearly demanded more of an explanation and Henry, not often inclined to converse with the help these days, felt constrained to offer one.

'I've been putting on weight recently. Too much, actually. Some of it in my fingers.' He wiggled them as proof of what he was saying and, in truth, they felt like eight pale Oscar Meyer wieners waggling in front of his face. God knew what the thumbs resembled.

'Wiffee not dead then?' the repairman asked.

Henry blinked. No. Alas! he thought, but he smiled and said, 'Indeed not! She's, um, quite concerned about it.'

'Ah! So den you wa new ling awso.'

'Um, oh, I suppose so,' replied Henry, thinking quickly, 'but my wife is going to buy it.'

'Good ling here! I give good deer on ling.' The words, more than a little aggressive, erupted out of the repairman. He took hold of Henry's hand and began to examine the finger. He twisted the ring round, and turned the hand over to see it from the other side. His movements were abrupt but Henry felt them to be strangely gentle at the same time. The two men stood facing each other, hand in hand. Henry wondered when he and Leah had last stood like this. Then the little man gave the ring a precipitous tug and Henry followed its momentum forward, almost tumbling into the shopkeeper's arms across the workspace.

'I tried that,' he said. The ring received another tug and Henry was pulled forward again, spilling himself against the counter and dislodging some of its contents. Innards of watches cascaded onto the floor.

'Eeeyah,' said the repairman, letting go of Henry's hand. He turned to a cupboard behind him extracting a vial full of yellow liquid. 'We tly oin.'

'Umm,' said Henry, 'I've tried that too. And soap with hot water. Also a piece of string twirled around.' He did not quite know how to describe what he had done with the string, and he certainly wasn't about to tell the little man about winding dental floss round the finger, like a corset it looked, trying to make it thinner and the knuckle less bulky. He wasn't sure where the idea had come from, and it hadn't worked.

The little man took no notice and slathered the buttery liquid over Henry's fingers, the two of them shaking hands as he did so. Then came the tug. For a small man it was considerable. Henry felt his knuckle crack.

'Couldn't you just cut it off?

The repairman looked startled. 'Finger?'

'No, of course not the finger!'

'Spoir ling so,' the repairman said. He shook his head. It wobbled.

'Well,' laughed Henry, 'its either the ring or the finger and I'm rather attached to the finger.' He held it up, rather beginning to wish it had been the middle finger, but he added jocularly, 'Let's get on with it.'

The little Chinaman squinged up his eyes. 'Take off jacket. Rorr up sreeve. May be brud.'

'Ah so!' said Henry and found that he had bowed to the repairman. He wanted to giggle. He was beginning to feel as though he was in a bad amateur production of The Mikado.

Wait a minute though, surely the Mikado was Japanese?

Henry could be punctilious sometimes.

'You! You come in back.'

Henry felt he was entering another world, a world of clocks tick-tocking, little cabinets black-labelled in a foreign hand, and strange implements possibly for torture or mayhem. The repairman pulled out an instrument resembling a pair of pliers, six inches long with sharp teeth. It was abruptly thrown back in favour of a larger, more lethal looking pair.

'Not good. Not good.' The repairman shook his head again, raking through the drawer like a cat in a litter box. 'Yes, now. Heh!' he said finally, taking out a delicate pair of secateurs and dragging Henry's whole hand towards him. The rest of Henry followed not quite willingly. The man inserted one blade under the curve of the ring and pressed the handles together. As he pressed, his lips made little popping sounds. Henry would have preferred the radio. An intense pain shot up his arm as the little man stood on his toes to get more purchase on the shears. Henry yelped aloud.

'You cause trubba wid this ling,' the repairman said, and he moved off further into the back of the store where Henry could hear him rummaging around.

Everything about this ring had caused trouble. The thickness of the band and the yellowness of the gold had disturbed Henry from the moment he first set eyes on it. It was part of a matched set and Leah made up her mind that these were the ones she wanted as soon as her eyes swooped down on them. She had taken him, almost dragged him in fact, into the jewellers to see if they could get what she demurely termed an "upgrade" on her engagement ring, a larger stone would be prettier she said, not twenty-four hours after accepting it faster than the speed of light.

*

'Will you . . .' he began.

'Yes,' she replied. 'Oh yes!'

Henry's neck pivoted as she gazelled past him out through the lounge door. He heard it crack. His neck. On one knee, wanting to the job right, his body went out of whack and the velocity of her departure spun him off kilter.

'Mommy, Poppie! Henry asked me to marry him!' Almost.

Some people wait years before beginning to doubt their uxorial choice, Henry waited rather less than two minutes.

Her mother, a wide-end receiver for the Packers, charged into the room to find Henry sprawled on his backside. She grinned down at him, that peculiar, slightly loopy grin that his intended had inherited and which had fascinated Henry when they first met. He had thought it mysterious, perhaps even exotic, until his best man pointed out — too late — that the word 'vacuous' was possibly more accurate. Of course, Henry had been loathe to admit his creeping agreement. Except alone in a rowboat in the middle of a bottomless lake somewhere.

'Welcome to the family,' her mother said and leaned right over to kiss Henry in that dreadful way, right on the lips. He could see right down the front of her blouse and the sight was not encouraging.

'Thank you, Mrs Barrington,' he stuttered.

She snorted. He hadn't realized until that moment that there was an element of hysteria playing at the edge of Mrs. Barrington's laughter, and he could hear something similar down the hall. Henry wanted to laugh too, and it wouldn't have been at the edge of hysteria either. It would have been in the dead centre. He felt as if someone was hammering nails into his skull.

'Call me Mommy,' said the woman in front of him, middle-aged bosoms, mere inches away, swaying not quite seductively.

Henry was opening his mouth to reply when Poppie appeared in the open doorway. Leah was peering over his shoulder, beaming. The look on her father's face caused Henry's heart to flutter. The look: scorn? relief? pity mixed with unbelief?

'You did it,' said Mr. Barrington. 'You . . . actually . . . did it.'

'Of course he did it!' Mrs. Barrington turned to her spouse. 'Get out the sherry. It's an occasion for sherry!' It was almost a snarl.

Henry would have preferred something longer and stronger. Ninety proof in a large bottle. He would have pulled the cork out with his teeth to get at it. He had indeed come there that evening to ask her to marry him, it was true, but for the life of him he could no longer immediately remember why. When Mr. Barrington left the room to fetch the sherry — they kept the liquor in the kitchen above the sink — his affianced bride skipped into the room and deposited herself beside him.

'Oh Henry,' she sighed, 'just like you not to give me any warning. Oh, Mommy, when will we have the wedding? June, don't you think? A June wedding.' Rapture. She clapped her hands together. He flushed and flinched. 'Oh, a lovely white wedding!'

Henry thought somewhat bitterly that she certainly possessed the prime qualification for that. He had the suspicion that her thighs were permanently welded together. Scylla and Charybdis he had named her knees, inaccurately perhaps — not many sailors would ever be washed up anywhere near them — but what a danger zone they represented. Crafty experimentation taught him that they might be loosened if he exhibited a degree, a high degree, of petulance and did not answer her telephone calls for a couple of days. She would then rail at him but she might also allow a certain degree of breeziness (both small and temporary) to flow between those legs of hers. Nothing else, however. She made that clear.

'No Henry! It's just not right! We'll wait.'

He had always thought that this assumed too much, but he never called her on it. Perhaps if she had not invariably followed it with an 'I want to be pure for my hero' he might have behaved differently but, at first, he had been intrigued with the idea of being someone's hero. By the tenth time he heard it, he was no longer listening, so intent was he of dreaming up ways, metaphors totally muddled, to ford the moat, lower the drawbridge and storm the keep. Perhaps if he had not been a Taurean, stubborn as a mule his Mam said he was, he might have given up, but he continued his assault even when he was bleeding and bowed. When he did finally breach the ramparts and unlock the vault on their wedding night, he was such a quivering mess of indignant frustration he scarcely remembered what all the fuss had been about in the first place.

'No brud, no brud! Not cut finger!' The little Chinaman was fretful as he reached into the drawer of a cabinet behind him. He withdrew a small saw and held the thin blade across the palms of both hands. He bowed slightly to it. Henry wondered whether he might lean forward and kiss it.

'This lemove ling!' said the shopkeeper.

11

'Oh Henry, I'll never take it off!' Leah was holding up her hand so that the engagement ring could catch the light. Her mother was beaming from a straight-backed chair opposite, legs splayed wide. Mr. Barrington doled out thimbles of sherry, blowing into each glass to remove the dust that had accumulated there since they were used last, before pouring. Leah's christening in all probability.

'You got it at Glybourne's. You naughty man!' Arch. 'Poppie knows Mr. Glybourne. If you'd told him beforehand he would have got you a bigger stone. At the same price. But this is darling! I just love it! A single diamond is so . . .' she searched for a word, 'chaste.'

Henry felt a great weight pressing down on him from above and, unfortunately, it was not his hat. God must be really displeased, he thought, and I can't say I blame him. His colour was returning and the palpitations had stopped, but that enabled him to take some deep breaths and these caused him to inhale her scent and the dregs of what was probably a feminine underarm deodorant. He was becoming nauseous instead.

Mommy clapped her hands. 'Oh yes! Poppie will phone Seth Glybourne and tell him who you are, Henry, and then you can go down and get a . . .' she had the grace to stumble, ' . . . to upgrade the diamond.' She shook a finger at her daughter to admonish her, 'Just the diamond, of course. I love the simplicity of the setting. Don't you, Poppie?'

Poppie opened his mouth and took a sip of sherry.

So it was that Henry and his beloved found themselves poring over rings. Her eyes soon glommed onto matched wedding bands of thick, yellow gold. Henry thought they looked like brass curtain rings.

'Don't you think it will kind of overpower your engagement ring?' he asked. If she had been listening, she might have heard a soupçon of half-hidden truculence but, as he was in the process of finding out, Leah rarely listened.

'Oh, Henry, we'll just have to get a thicker band on the engagement ring. Silly! The bigger diamond will need it anyway! Don't you think so, Mr. Glybourne?'

Who winked.

Henry suddenly had the impression that his Dad was standing behind him poking a finger into the small of his back: 'Ee lad, you're as daft as a brush, you are! Get out. Be gone with you! Now!' but Henry slipped the wedding ring onto his finger nevertheless.

'That's not a ring, that's a limpet. You'll never get the thing off.' The voice of doom just behind his left ear.

Mr. Glybourne snorted, rubbing his hands. 'Very nice,' he said, 'Classy.'

Tears welled in everyone's eyes.

The crowd was on its feet. Dressed from neck to knee in sequins — what did Henry know about such things? — the matador essayed a slightly vacant smile. 'Ole!' they yelled as Poppie the picador opened the gate to let the animal in. It had been a bull once, but it was lumbering now, rheumy eyed and confused. Defeated. Deballed from the look of it. Through its nose, covered in slaver, Henry could see his wedding ring, dull and dangling. 'Kill the effing bull!' bawled Mommy from the stands. The matador turned to look towards Henry and he knew it was his bride, in mufti. She slowly slid the sword into the nape of the old bull's neck. They stared into each other's eyes until Henry could dare no more. He toppled over onto his side and the crowd chanted, 'Ole, upgrade! Upgrade ole!'

The little Chinaman inserted the double-sided saw between Henry's skin and the ring, teeth parallel to the finger, in the direction of Henry's palm. It was a snug fit and the saw was sharp. It nicked soft flesh as it edged forward. Drops of bright red blood bloomed.

'Aaayye' muttered the little man, 'Why you move so much?'

Henry hadn't moved at all. He was fascinated.

Perhaps he could abscond with the saw and draw it slowly across his throat ear to ear. He hadn't even felt the breaking of the skin. Tiny needle-like teeth seemed to beckon him. Just a gentle pull, no pressure necessary. Take your tie off first. Don't worry about the shirt. She'll throw it out afterwards anyway.

'Keep hand stin! Stin, Stin, Stin! You hee me!'

Henry closed his eyes. He was drifting. A dress rehearsal. 'Take your time,' he said. 'Take your time.'

He was uncertain that he had heard the minister correctly.

'Do you take this woman to be your awful dreaded wife?'

He had noticed before that he had sometimes heard words incorrectly, but, in those days, he never connected it with deafness. He worried rather that he was not concentrating. Perhaps he was losing his mind. Leah would often tell him to pay attention just before she gave him a genteel shove with her elbow.

He couldn't hear anything but he was too busy digging his way out of the stalag to think about it. The air didn't help: the air in the little hole was dank, rank with sweat, and the hopelessness of his captivity.

'Captain Glybourne, sir! Corporal Earl reporting, sir! The men dug three feet this afternoon, sir. We reckon we are just about beneath the Kraut latrine, sir. Can't come up now, sir, or we'll be flush in the bogs, sir.'

'Jolly good, chappie!'

'Yes, sir. Several casualties, I'm afraid, sir. Three of the lads broke their fingernails prying the dirt loose and had to be sent to the manicurist for treatment. They won't be able to report for duty for a week. Oh, and, Sir, Poppie, Sir. He didn't make it. Tried to swallow the dirt instead of packing it down his trousers. He choked on one of the larger lumps. They would pull him out but they have to wait until Mommy's not using the loo.'

'Poor sod! Keep up the good work, Earl. We'll be home with our nearest and dearest by Christmas if we can keep up the pace.'

'Yes, sir. Thank you sir.'

Henry crawled away to dig some more.

'Do you promise to love and cherish her?'

Well, no, I'm not sure.

'In sickness and in health?'

Whose sickness, whose health?

'As long as you have money to give?'

The little repairman tried to establish a rhythm and was popping off key. Through the smeared blood, Henry could see that his finger was half way to freedom, but the teeth of the saw kept getting caught the more the gold split. His palm was bleeding too, although the repairman strove mightily to keep the hungry teeth away from his skin.

'Keep hand stin!' shouted the Chinaman. 'Open wide.' He looked sternly at Henry. 'Why you not co-operate?'

'I'm sorry. I didn't hear what you said,' said Henry.

Not a sound could be heard in the church. The minister stared at him.

'I'm sorry. I didn't hear the question,' he repeated.

La Belle Dame Sans Merci was looking at him with narrowed eyes and he peered down at the thin, scarlet nailed hand held in his. It was turning into a claw before his eyes.

This was as far as he dared go. Further resistance would be futile. Mom and Dad were here from England and Edward and his wife and the baby as well. All the arrangements for the honeymoon had been made. A security deposit put on an apartment. Just two blocks from Mommy, she had exclaimed exultantly as if she hadn't realized. The napkins, peacock origami he had been informed, were folded for the reception and non-alcoholic champagne was on ice.

Henry cleared his throat. The air in the tunnel was foul with sweat. They worked in shifts, day and night, week after week, even on statutory holidays, digging their way to freedom. Digging their way into Germany more like, but at least out of this hellhole.

He saw the bride's side frowning at him. The groom's side seemed even less sympathetic, but it may just have been that they knew it was going to be a dry wedding and they were already parched.

He opened his mouth to whet his lips. His upper lip quivered, no longer hidden by the moustache that she had begged him, threatened really, to get rid of before the ceremony. Had he had it, he might have had more guts, but there was nothing there to hide behind.

"A horse! A horse!" He remembered the play from school but he couldn't remember who said the words and he didn't have time to think.

'I say, jolly good show, old boy,' said the Captain.

'Ayeeah! Ormost off.' The saw stuttered the last sixteenth of an inch, spraying gold dust and the finest of claret across the front of his shirt.

'Perhaps I should repeat the words?' The minister, a righteous man, appeared to be in a quandary.

'Say it, Henry!' Teeth clenched Leah. Nothing vacuous about her at the moment.

Henry took a shallow gulp and burbled his response,

'I must,' he said.

*

When the repairman finally pried the ring free, Henry flexed his fingers and lifted his arm to see whether his hand felt lighter unencumbered by this outward sign of his matrimony. Hand be damned, he felt less constricted in his very soul.

'How much do I owe you?' he asked. He was aware that he was grinning like a fool. He took all of his money out from his wallet, spreading it across the counter in the shape of a fan as if to say take your pick. 'And I would like to buy the saw from you. A souvenir,' he said.

The little Chinaman looked at him, narrowing already narrow eyes. 'Naw,' he said, 'can't serr saw. Need saw. What for you want saw?'

Henry shrugged. 'Just a reminder of how difficult it was to get the ring off.'

'You have ling!' He thrust the ring into Henry's hand, and grabbed a twenty and two fives. 'Now you go. I busy,' he said, waving Henry away and turning his attention to the clock on which he had been working when Henry came in.

Henry walked back to the food court. He sat at an empty table, turning the ring over and over. He was still grinning, and he guffawed whenever he tried to stop. He inserted his thumbnail in the space where the saw had severed the perfect circle and tried to pry the two sides apart. This damaged his nail slightly, but he continued to worry the ring long after it was apparent that the metal was not about to give way more than a little. He leaned over and opened his briefcase on the floor beside him. He took out a sheet of foolscap and a felt pen, spending some time thinking about what it was he wanted to write and he was still hesitant when he penned the words. Then he rolled the paper so that it could fit inside the ring and repeated aloud what he had written.

'Beware!' he said, 'I wore this ring too long. God help you, if you wear it at all. He never did help me.'

He rose slowly into the cold night air. The others were still behind him in the tunnel. It was after Christmas by two long dusty months. His limbs were aching from crawling crablike though the narrow fissure in the icy earth. Behind him, he could see the stockade fence with its barbed wire loops strung along the top. The moon was pale lemon in the sky.

'Move it, Earl, for Christ's sake.' An impatient voice from beneath his feet hissed up at him.

He began to run forward in the darkness, but suddenly a searchlight lit the ground ahead of him, blinding him so completely that he fell to his knees. The man behind him stumbled into him and fell forward onto his shoulders. Henry collapsed full length in the mud and the sirens began. He had reached the end of the line.

He wiped the blood from his hand with a Kleenex. The worst cut had been the first, underneath where the ring had been. He thought of buying a band-aid to cover it but in the end he let the blood dry by itself, licking the residue off with his tongue. No one would be able to say, when they found him, 'Well, look at this, he had a band-aid where his wedding ring used to be.' With a bit of luck, no-one would even notice the pale circle of skin where it had been.

12

If someone had dragged Henry into a room, shone a light into his eyes and pummelled him in the solar plexus, he could probably have been brought to admit that the period of his betrothal was not really as bad as he sometimes remembered it. The fright of his engagement, for example, was diluted by a perfervid anticipation of coital bliss. Niggling doubt was whitewashed by Leah's unwonted hints of coming expansiveness. Disagreements about the honeymoon caused a frisson of apprehension, it was true, and in retrospect he should, perhaps, have paid more attention to what they signified, but ecstatic anticipation about the activity on the honeymoon — well, Hallelujah! — it diverted him.

He had always assumed that his honeymoon would be spent on a beach in a warm climate. His last minute getaway to Ocho Rios with college friends was fondly remembered. He had fallen in love with the three esses: sun, sand and sea. Not so unconsciously, he thought that his honeymoon would add the fourth ess to such delights, but he was to be quickly disabused.

'Oh no, Henry, it'll be too hot! You know how blotchy my skin gets in the heat.'
He did indeed.

'But Leah, love,' Henry reasoned, 'everything is air-conditioned and there's always a breeze coming off the sea.'

She looked at him sternly. 'Henry, you know very well there are sharks.'

He had not expected this, and he felt a first whisper of panic in the pit of his stomach.

'Well, my dear, I don't think either one of us will be so far out in the sea that they'd be interested in us. They don't come in beyond the breakers.'

The word was out before he could stop it.

'Breakers?! Oh Henry, I shouldn't want to go anywhere where the sea is rough.'
Henry back-peddled.

'No, no, they're not exactly breakers. More like ripples. You have to see them at dusk, love, with the sun setting behind the palm trees and the sky red and orange and . . .

'I have seen them, Henry! In your photographs. And they definitely looked like breakers to me. I'd be so afraid.'

She snuggled against his chest and batted her eyelashes.

'Couldn't we go up North for a nice week in Wasaga? Poppy can arrange with Uncle Joel to rent his cottage. They could drive up to visit.'

'Oh, joy!' thought Henry.

Jamaica suddenly felt a long way off.

'But Leah, my sweet, I want you to see Jamaica. The scenery, the vegetation, Fern Gully . . .'

His voice was somewhere between a wheedle and a whine, and he didn't like it, but this was important.

'We could drive over to Rose Hall, have dinner on the terrace and walk in the gardens in the moonlight.'

She snorted. Actually snorted. 'Not me, Henry, not me. Walking on the grass outside — in the tropics? Think of the mosquitoes, and the reptiles. The wild animals. The snakes!'

He was so taken aback by her vehemence that he completely forgot there are no snakes in Jamaica, and thus lost a major selling point. Without realizing it, he began his retreat.

'But Wasaga! For our honeymoon?'

'Why Henry Earl, I do believe you are a snob.' The pot accused the kettle. 'What's wrong with Wasaga? In any case, we wouldn't be outside often, would we?' She ran her finger along his inseam. 'Umm?'

'It doesn't have to be Jamaica,' Henry was aware that he sounded like an apology for a hominid. 'How about Mexico?'

'Mexico? They don't even speak English there! And, Henry. You know my tummy.' She took his hand and placed it just below her belly-button. 'That wouldn't be what we want on our honeymoon, would it?'

The question was rhetorical.

*

Why he had ever married the woman was a question for which Henry never found a satisfactory answer. If he had lost a pound for every night he stayed awake searching for one, her next to him breathing harder asleep than he could ever manage to get her to breathe while she was awake, he would have been a textbook specimen of terminal anorexia, but he had only begun to ponder this conundrum after the ink had dried on the marriage certificate. A reasonable man — perhaps that was one of his faults — Henry had to admit that being married had its advantages: cooked food, a clean house, the occasional civilized conversation. For a man who was cosseted and comforted by his own imagination, he had to admit that having someone around, someone to go home to, was for quite a long time after the honeymoon a fact that could cheer him at the end of a working day.

Henry wasn't exactly gregarious, but he wasn't a hermit either and you could be companionable without being close. Silences don't have to be filled with animosity. You can break a silence by saying that you were going to have a cup of tea before going to bed and would you like one, and it will be friendly and civilized and workable. And for a while it was. It was when Leah began to fill their silence with complaints — all kinds of complaints — that things started to fall apart. An offhand inquiry about whether you changed the electric light bulb in the basement became, over time, an accusation that you didn't change the electric light bulb in the basement, did you, I'll break my neck one of these days when I'm down there doing the laundry. It wouldn't have done to respond to the second part of that exchange, either. Henry was no fool. He knew they were in trouble when he found that he didn't mind staying that extra hour at work to finish off a report or to clean up after someone else's mistakes. He knew they were in trouble when most of his comments of an evening were made safely under his breath rather than said aloud, when his response to not changing the light bulb was to jump up then and there, at ten o'clock at night if need be, and to disappear down into the basement — nearly breaking his own neck on the stairs in the process — to putter around there long after he had completed such a mundane task, just to get out of the room and be beyond the sound of her voice.

*

It was, however, when the children began to arrive that Henry's marriage really began to go South. Henry and Leah never did. Both of them wanted children and Henry was quite content to go to bat getting his wife pregnant. His inning was a short one, though. She was, it turned out, remarkably fecund: fucking fecund in fact. As soon as she was sure he had hit a home run, however, the game was called and the pitcher's mound covered. With a tarp. Still and all, it had been nice while it lasted and if he got a baby out of it, well, he could live with that. He'd have to. His complacence did not last long. His father-in-law plainly did not like the idea that his baby girl had been violated, and his own father, whose growing animosity towards his daughter-in-law was equalled only by hers for him, put his foot in it during the transatlantic telephone call Henry made to give his parents the news.

Henry's Dad could not hear what was said over the telephone, but he insisted on taking the instrument from Henry's Mam when she told him the news.

'Congratulations, my son,' he bawled into the instrument, 'let's hope it takes after you!'

Unfortunately, Henry had handed the telephone to Leah so that she and her mother-in-law could talk baby, and she heard every word. He could not even pretend that she had somehow got it wrong: his Dad had shouted so loudly everyone in the room heard every syllable from three thousand miles away. Henry apologized so often for what his Dad had said, that he began to resent it. Exactly what he resented, however, changed over time. It was difficult to maintain a grudge against the man he adored, and the more he looked at his wife, plaintively begging her forgiveness for something he had not done in the first place, the more he came to consider that his Dad had a measure of truth on his side.

It didn't help that Leah gained an enormous amount of weight during the pregnancy. She joked that she was eating for two, but even her best friends must have wondered what kind of two she was talking about — elephants, hippopotami, sumo wrestlers? When the child did finally appear, she was the image of her mother, and, not to put too fine a point on it, as plain as the nose on Leah's face.

At one of the several baby showers in that last long month of pregnancy, Mommy gave Leah a book on Madonnas. It was a large coffee table book, with reproductions from the old masters in all their chiaroscuro magnificence. Everything from Georges de la Tour up to and beyond the pre-Raphaelites. Even a few grotesque Picassos were to be found at the end of the book. Leah and Mrs. Barrington took the concept to heart. He would come into a room and find them posed like — what else? — mother and child. He found them seated in sunbeams; he found them lit by candles, soot slowly wending its way to the ceiling. Worse, Leah began to think of herself as a Madonna. He became convinced that she was edging towards the doctrine of the virgin birth. Not for this child of course, but certainly for any other that they might think of having. He practically had to tie her down to incubate their second, and bham dammit, it only took the once. After the third — he crept up on her one cold winter's night — she declared that three were enough and 'no more'. Henry was unsure exactly what the 'no more' referred to, but he had his suspicions.

He learned to live a largely celibate life. What he was unwilling to live as, however, was a man who had only daughters. He wanted a son. Just like his Dad had sons. He would settle for one, but, oh, how he wanted that one. Being the father of girls turned out not all it was cracked up to be.

Male friends at work commiserated with him that he only had girls and seemed to go out of their way to tell him what they were up to with their boys: hockey, fishing, baseball. Men things. It didn't matter that he had never played hockey and that he couldn't, in fact, skate. Or that fishing — the few times he had tried it with his own Dad — bored him silly. It must be said in his defence, though, that he was equally inept when it came to the girly things that Leah led her daughters towards. It remained a puzzle to him why girls had ringlets, why they wore organdie, why they all liked to congregate around Barbie. Yet he tried to be a good father. He played house, sipped imaginary tea from minute pieces of real china, and he read Nancy Drew so often he could recite it from memory.

Even so, over the years, the girls gravitated increasingly to their mother. She had infinite amounts of time, patience and Henry's hard earned cash to spend on them. By the time the last of them hit puberty Henry was beginning to feel like a guest in his own home. He loved his daughters, but it was an unexcited, dutiful sort of love. He was surrounded by everything female. Piles of what his mother would have called 'unmentionables', hung on the shower curtain. If he reached under the bathroom sink, he was as liable to put his hand on Tampax as the toilet roll he was looking for, and he became horrendously aware that the female of the species squeals when it is excited. And it is excited a lot.

His daughters discovered boys. Unfortunately, boys took a little longer to discover them. As an unbiased and discerning bystander, Henry had to admit that his girls were not what would generally have been termed the pick of the litter. The passage of time and the application of lotions and potions helped. Diets should have. Every diet book in print seemed to have been bought, annotated, emulated and ultimately dispensed with by the four females in Henry's kingdom. The trouble was that each one of them loved dessert. Over the years, Henry — and he alone — passed on everything from pavlovas to profiteroles, from crème brulet to coconut cream pie and back again. He remained whippet thin to the ire of his offspring, and it was only when it turned out that Leah was incipiently diabetic, that dessert ceased to be a staple and the pounds began to peel off.

Then, at last, the boys found them. They began to sniff around Henry's front door like the young pups they were. Except, as Henry looked at them, not many of them could have been expected to win Best In Show. For months, his eldest clung like lint to a youth who had more spots than a Dalmatian, only dropping him when a lanky fellow with adenoids and duck toes appeared to take his place. His second daughter went for the strong silent type. Henry found it off-putting to be seated opposite two hundred and twenty pounds of sixteen year old silence in his own living room. Then, in the fullness of puberty, his youngest introduced him to a slim, blemish-free individual who hit Henry up for a loan as soon as she left the room to bring her sweetheart a snack.

'It would help with the entertaining, man' said the youth. 'Can't be expected to cough up for everything, you know!' Callow did not begin to describe him — lummox, possibly. Henry was caught between admiration and annoyance but it would have been better if he hadn't told the lad to take himself off, because that was what he immediately did. This led to a fine demonstration of teenage hysteria when his daughter returned with the requested coke and chips. She spent the next month peering from behind the front curtains in the vain hope that he would return, and blaming Henry when he did not.

Ambivalence was Henry's main emotion when it came to the boys who shuffled through his house in these years. Sometimes he thought it might be paternal affection that caused him to want to warn them away, but, later on, when his brood began to reach their twenties, he forced himself to recognize that, in all likelihood, it was economics, and the price of three possible weddings. He was still in hock over college fees, first cars, and those occasional jaunts to Puerto Vallarta. His daughters, at least, had no objection to sun, sand and sea and none, he suspected, to participation in that other ess word either — that word which fathers do not like to use in any sentence that also contains the word daughter.

When the weddings did begin, however, Henry became more sanguine. During the nuptials of his eldest, he kept repeating the words, 'One gone'. At those of the second, it was, 'One more to go'. He didn't feel the slightest bit guilty. Just so much lighter in the pocketbook.

13

To be scrupulously honest about it, Henry was always grateful that, apart from the big things — the engagement rings, three fully catered matrimonial events, cream cake (before the advent of insulin), Virgin and Child knockoffs — Leah wasn't that much of a spender. There was one exception to this, however, one further chink in Leah's chain mail, one more Achilles' heel that Henry had had to learn to live with. Well, not exactly live with. Perhaps among would be a better word, although, not to put a fine point on it, there were usually several of those. Points, that is: sticking out. Somewhere along the way, Leah became a devotee of rattan.

To be accurate, it began with wicker and burgeoned at a later date. They had been given a wedding present — from one of her aunts if he remembered correctly — of a wicker garden set. Four chairs, one of which bit the bottom of anyone who sat in it, and a table that was so wobbly you couldn't stand anything on it. Henry thought the set clunky and preposterously brown, but Leah adored it. She had even initiated sex in it, one time. What a disaster that had been! Over the years, the set had been varnished and repainted until it became a death trap. Little shards of wood stuck out and attacked anyone who came within striking distance. It particularly went after the backs of legs and the smalls of backs, and it liked large female posteriors and cellulite thighs. Heaven knows the family had enough of those.

In time, wicker invaded the house. It began with letter racks and end tables, and culminated in a huge coffee table that Henry thought could have had religious significance in an earlier age. It didn't help that Leah liked to spread bunches of (fake) grapes on one end of it. 'God, our Henry,' his Dad had said when he first saw it in a photograph, 'is that where you sacrifice the virgins?' Henry had laughed aloud, but it was a scary thought. The girls had loved to sprawl all over it when they reached puberty.

Then, one day, Leah moved up market. Rattan appeared. Henry came home from work to find the living room completely changed. The walls were still white, dead white (the colour, he always thought, of corpses — she would brook no pastel in her parlour), but the old furniture, even the old coffee table, was gone. Henry blinked. Everything was rattan. Two high back armchairs, a small loveseat (you should excuse the expression), another coffee table, end tables, side tables, a rack for keeping the TV Guide, a unit that held the TV itself, and — Henry had to lean against the wall when he first saw it — an enormous four-seater settee. Who would make such a thing, he wondered?

'Isn't it darling?' she asked. Leah stood in the middle of the room, hands clasped to her bosom, ecstatic.

And it was white. Every single bit of it was white. Painted to match the walls. The carpet was white, too. ('Don't come in here until you take your shoes off, Henry!') White and fluffy. A shag. The profusion of purple grapes had survived the putsch, and the cushions on all the chairs were floral. Tendrils of flowery leaves. On a white background, of course. Henry had been appalled, but more amazed than anything else. The room reminded him of a rustic morgue. Bucolic but frigid. Where could she have located such stuff? And how had she pulled the changeover off? She must have had men moving things out and in as soon as he left for work.

'Sit!' she said.

'Where?' he asked. It didn't look like the kind of furniture people would want to sit on, could sit on.

'Anywhere you like,' she said. Unplumbed expansiveness.

Henry's mind was reeling. She must be out of her mind, he thought. Anywhere you like! He waited for the qualifying clause. Never had she spoken such words to him. Even when they were engaged, she would qualify things.

'You can go to second base, Henry, but I can't allow you anywhere near third.'

'That's nice, Henry. Keep your hand right there. No, not lower!'

Henry sat down on one of the armchairs. On it, not in it. The cushion was harder than a rock. When he leaned back, the thing creaked.

'Umm. Its not very, umm, comfortable.' He said it more to himself than to her.

'Of course, it is,' she said, 'and anyway, it's not supposed to be comfortable, it's rattan.' Rapture.

Henry got up and moved to the loveseat. She came and sat next to him.

'Love it. Love it,' she said.

He rose and moved over to the couch.

'I like to lie on the couch,' he said wistfully. She didn't allow it, of course, but there was no way he could lie on this one anyway. It would be like reclining on an operating table.

'Well, you shouldn't sprawl on the furniture anyway,' she said, 'Sit up! And relax.'

It was then Henry noticed how deep the seats were. If he sat with his spine against the back, his legs stuck straight out. If he sat with his knees on the edge of the seat, he couldn't touch the back. If he forced the issue, his spine curved and he had to tuck his chin up into his neck, resting it on the top of his chest.

'I don't think I can sit like this,' he offered.

'You'll get used to it,' she replied gaily, 'Just sit up!' It was an instruction in a sex manual. Do this, and you will achieve release.

When she left the room, Henry went from seat to seat looking for a comfortable place. He didn't find one. He never found one. Anna Karenina, very young in those days, came into the room and looked up at him reproachfully. Henry never saw her in there again. He went upstairs and changed his clothes, shaking his head, sitting gingerly on the side of the bed wondering whether the changes would extend to their sleeping quarters.

Thus began the reign of rattan.

It became one of Henry's little home pleasures to welcome visitors and to listen to their comments.

'Why . . . ! I've never seen a room like this!' You betcha.

'It's so . . . charming.' Almost a question.

'Where did you get all this?' Henry never did find out.

'It's like a fairy tale, isn't it?' Just before the ogre appears.

Best of all were the tradesmen. The meter reader, repairmen, the cable man, people from Bell. Most of them were immigrants and Henry's living room was beyond their comprehension, out of their universe.

'Oh mih God, wha yuh do 'ere?' asked a plumber from the islands. He stumbled at the door in passing and couldn't get traction to move on.

A Greek giggled.

A Ghanaian guffawed.

'Hola!' grunted a Hispanic, in what sounded suspiciously like fright.

14

Maximilian Earl was conceived in a fit of largesse on his wife's part some seven years after their third daughter was born. Without telling Henry, she had had her tubes tied before leaving the hospital. He had learnt about this diversion of her nether plumbing long afterwards during a somewhat threatening conversation about vasectomies at a church picnic.

'Oh,' Leah said airily, 'you can't rely on a man having a vasectomy. They don't always work. I had my tubes tied when Melanie was born.'

Henry had nearly choked on his ginger ale. He wasn't even absolutely sure what she meant. He had visions of two — why two? — balloons being knotted in her lower intestine, the idea being to keep the air out and the eggs in. It sounded neither comfortable nor certain, and it turned out to be far from the latter.

The day Leah found out she was pregnant, she phoned him at work.

'It can't be, Henry! It just can't be! I can't be, I'm pregnant, Henry.' It was an accusation. 'What did you do, Henry?'

'Me?!' he replied. 'I didn't do anything.'

'Well, you must have done something.'

'What? What did I do? You're the one who had your tubes tied. One of them must have come undone!' Not being quite certain what he was talking about, he added hurriedly, 'Or something.' Feeling that more was required of him, he added, 'Have you asked for a second opinion?'

A mighty roar of despair assaulted his ear.

'I don't need a second opinion, I'm preh heh heh gnant!'

Leah's tears disturbed Henry more than her ire and he left work early to see what he could do. Abortion was quickly ruled out on the grounds that someone might hear about it, only to be reconsidered when it was learned that the baby she was carrying was a boy. This aspect of the situation cheered Henry considerably, however. The thought of a son was wonderful. Unfortunately, Leah was of a different opinion.

'I don't want a boy!' she shook her head, enraged. 'I only wanted girls!' she moaned. 'Boys! You don't know where they've been!'

The trouble was that by then everyone knew she was going to have a baby. Plus, there was something about trimesters — he understood these even less than he did tubes — and the danger so late on.

Henry Earl was thrilled, however, and he remained that way all through Max's short life. It was the last time anyone could have looked at him and said that here was a man who enjoyed his life. And he did. He preened when he showed the baby to people: he goo-gooed and he ga-gaaed at him in his bassinet; he showed the infant's photographs without mercy to everyone at work. He loved. He adored. Leah, for her part, was an efficient mother, but increasingly Henry was reminded of his Gran, Maisie, and how cold and distant she had been to his beloved Dad. Was Leah the same? If she was, he became a countervailing force to her disinterest. But he had only so much love to give and his love for his daughters seemed to wane proportionately. Subconsciously, and perhaps it wasn't so very subconscious, sides were being drawn — Max for him, Leah for them. It didn't help Max's cause that he came to have his Granddad's beautiful auburn hair. What an affront to the girls' mousy brown! What a symbol of all that wasn't wanted.

Nevertheless, Max's life was a happy one. Henry was content to put his career on hold. It had been percolating well off the boil, but he was content during these years to let it cool. Do the work and sign out. He hurried home as early as he could. He looked after the baby, did the batheing, took him for walks and played with him endlessly. His first word was 'Dad'. His second was 'car'. His third, 'worker guy'. None of them particularly endeared him to Leah. Max himself turned aside all attempts the girls and his mother made to prettify him, to make him less of a boy. As soon as he could walk, he ploughed through the house turning it upside down. Jumping on the wicker, romping with the rattan. His favourite toy was a pot he used as a drum. He banged away on it for hours. Leah became more and more content to leave him to Henry — except for Sunday mornings when he was to be dressed, combed and shone for church, ready to be displayed to the congregation. Max didn't mind. He knew that after lunch he and his Dad would be off to play in the snow in winter, to kick ball in the spring and to splash in the community pool in the summer. To ride the subway any old time.

But Max died.

*

The child stood high on a hill throwing a balloon into the air to catch the breeze. But there was no helium in the balloon, only puff and an accumulation of spit to send it skyward. It remained exasperatingly earthbound and, before long, he scraped it purposefully against a jagged rock and the balloon went pop.

The first time Henry had this dream — it was a long time ago — he had thought nothing of it, had not viewed it as a cataclysmic metaphor for what his life might become and what course it could take. He didn't think like that. He lacked the philosophical turn of mind even now. If he had, he might have committed suicide years before. And why not, he wondered. No reason at all. It's a choice, after all. Something a person can do. If he wants. If he doesn't want to do anything else.

Why not, indeed?

It never crossed Henry's mind that his question was always why not. It was never why?

*

David lived a few houses down the street, although Henry had never been in his yard. When they played together, it was always at Henry's house. Henry liked David because he was one of the few who went along with the intricacies of Henry's games, who was willing to follow the convoluted machinations of his plots, who could match him, imagination for imagination, on the carpet, farm and fort before them. He was a boy with specs and sallow skin he seemed to keep hidden from the sun. Smart, studious, diffident and, as Henry was to discover, private. They would walk to grammar school together, duffle-coated, rather demure among the bustle of their fellows. Then, gradually, they grew apart. No reason: the exigencies of adolescence.

Then, one day in their final year, David — the smartest of all of them, Oxford bound — went out into his garage, threw a rope over a wooden beam and hanged himself. Only then did Henry hear the talk, the reason. David's parents, neither of them, ever left the house. They relied on their son for everything: buying the groceries, paying the bills, representing the family. It seemed unbelievable. He took the talk to his mother, barely noticing how subdued his father was that day. He had been sitting on the same hardback chair for hours, not saying a word.

'Is it true?' Henry asked, ready to accept a prompt denial, 'I heard that they were both, both of them, deaf and dumb.'

His mother nodded. 'They were mutes,' she said.

She glanced over at his Dad, edging towards him with worried eyes. Tears dabbed the corners of her eyes, Henry saw them but he did not understand.

'Why didn't you tell me?' he asked.

'It wasn't for us to tell you,' she replied. 'It was for David.'

'You should have told me,' he insisted.

'Shhh,' she said, 'you'll upset your father.'

For a long time afterwards, years afterwards, Henry hated his friend. Hated him for leaving. Hated how he had not told him, hated him for his solitariness, for his plight, for his subterfuge. Henry had told David about his Dad. In the way of boys, he had embroidered fun tales about how hard it was to live with a deaf person, 'a deafie' — what it was like to have such a volatile, eruptive parent. He made jokes at his Dad's expense and when, we are talking several years later here, he finally realized that David had never more than smiled at the best of them, he felt betrayed and furious and ashamed. Yet, somewhere in the passage of years, his affection for his friend grew again and his understanding with it, until one night, he was in bed, he felt as though his heart would break. He turned onto his side and sobbed into his pillow, wanting to see his friend again, wanting to keep him close.

It was also that night that he knew, in the lassitude of its early morning light, that someday, he might do it too.

*

The image of the balloon would not let him go.

If I were truly a balloon, what colour would I want to be?

Well, certainly not a red one!

Nothing so vivid, so jolly.

Perhaps they make grey ones.

He closed his eyes to concentrate.

I'd be perfectly round, blue, sky-blue, a foot in diameter. One of those balloons whose skin is so taut you can't pinch it and it squeaks when your fingers rub against its surface. One of those that awe small children and they find hard to grasp in their pudgy little hands. And it must have writing on it. It wouldn't matter what the writing said as long as it said something, had a message to tell, a point of view.

Not likely, he responded, shaking his head. You, you'd be more like the balloon that's found behind the sofa two months after the party, not quite flattened but almost empty of air, wrinkled and exhausted.

Cheerful, aren't you? A real bundle of fun.

15

Settling his shoulders back into his overcoat, knowing he had been sitting in the food court too long, Henry stood. He went over to the money machine outside the bank and took twenty dollars from his account, and then forty more for good measure. The condemned man, so the saying went, ate a hearty breakfast, but his last meal would be lunch — before he went to the office one final time. He needed to pull himself together, get his act together ready to take it on the road, and not allow himself to deflate further. Nothing must — he couldn't grasp the word — betray him, deflect him, something like that — from his appointed task.

He was awash in a sea of clichés. His Dad wouldn't have minded, but impending mortality should make the language fresh again. He shook his head at the unlikelihood of this and wondered if it wasn't tiredness, the closing off of his emotional responses, that made him spew forth such trite patter, such time molested phrases. Wouldn't it be wonderful to come up with a phrase, an image, a metaphor, of such exquisite originality that saying it would itself drain the last liquid lifeblood from him and he would be immortalized by it, wherever it was repeated, always with awe, for the rest of recorded time?

The subject of his immortality had taunted Henry for a long time. He had seen a movie once, Godard he thought it was, in which a journalist asked someone famous what his ambition was. The answer, 'to become immortal and then die', had impressed Henry and he repeated the words over and over in his mind. He liked their cleverness, their pith, and he had been neither mature nor experienced enough to see how shallow and portentous they really were. That came later. What he did want however, still wanted, he felt it in his gut, was to be remembered.

Realistically, his main claim to remembrance was anchored in three still slightly overweight daughters, none of whom ever evidenced much interest in becoming his avenue for posterity. They no longer even carried his name. He had nothing to leave behind. He wasn't a writer, and he couldn't paint, sing or dance. Even his friends would soon forget about him, although he hoped he meant more to them than most of them did to him.

'Henry! Dead?'

'He did what?'

'When? How?'

'Jesus!'

This would be the initial reaction. Shock and unbelief folded into a shudder of delicious surprise that they knew someone who had done what he was about to do.

Did you know him well, sir?

The microphones would be thrust into their faces while the TV cameras zoomed in. Local channels only.

I was his best friend, ten people would say. And shaking their heads, one hand cupping an elbow, another stroking a carefully razored chin, they would add, Well, we knew he had been having a difficult time recently, what with the massacre at the bank and, between you and me, he couldn't have been too content at home — I mean, look at the woman — but we never thought it would come to this.

They didn't know the half of it.

Tears might even be spilled, although he couldn't quite picture exactly whose.

What kind of man was he, your friend?

Why was it that in death the most reprehensible of bastards became plaster saints, praised to the heavens they hadn't a hope in hell of ascending to? He had once attended the funeral of a miserable old biddy whose only saving grace was an acerbic sense of humour, her better nature a cross between a pit bull in heat and a sufferer from Tourette's. The eulogist so polished the statuary of her memory that more warmth emanated from it than from the place in which, if there were any justice at all in the world, the old bag would ultimately reside. 'Tomfoolery!' she would have called it all.

Henry was reasonably sure that the precipitous nature of his departure to the hereafter would staunch both the amount said about him and the fulsomeness of its content. Even so, a still unacceptable degree of palaver would be hurled at the assembled multitude, if only for propriety's sake. Leah would see to that. She might sulk and she might seethe, but she would see to it. Somewhere down the road she might take her revenge, but for the nonce she would play the bereft and it would be an award winning performance.

'Yes,' she would say to the eulogist afterwards at the reception, holding his arm with a gentle claw, 'you caught him just right! You captured the essence of Henry!'

Sob.

Could I blame her for wanting revenge? I'm going to rock her world — another cliché, I know — I'm going to overset the underpinning of her assumptions, I'm going to take her so far aback she'll bleat like a sacrificial ewe.

What a pity he would not be around to see it.

Here, of course, was his dilemma, one to which Henry had given much thought ever since he had determined his proposed course of action. How could he have his cake and eat it as well? Part of the fun would be in being there, watching the reactions, giggling at the grief, smirking at the sadness. It had taken him some time to realize it wasn't cake that he should be thinking about. It was blood and guts and sinew. His. It was permanence, not petulance. He was embarking on the everlasting. Suicide was not some alkaline battery that could be replaced by spending a few dollars and turning back on the switch.

Yet he needed to be there! To observe, to gloat. It had taken time to accept the fact that although he would, indeed, be present, he would be inert, deafer than he was now, blind, dumb, nothing able to percolate, nothing that would or could resonate, nothing that felt. Probably, stitched together again from perhaps scads of uneven pieces. Just his blooming luck.

                                      *

A man bumped into him from behind as he stood there, still wrapped up in himself.

'Move out of the way, you stupid old man,' the man muttered.

Henry bristled. I'm not old.

And then: I'm never going to be older than I am now.

He pirouetted on the spot and laughed out loud.

I'm all set. I've shined my shoes. I'm dressed for the dance.

Who will remember you in six months?

Leah will. She'll stew, she'll congeal and she'll think of me in the long cold night of her soul. And then erect a monument for public consumption.

But others?

For a while it will be, Do you remember that time when Henry . . . ? Or, How could old Henry have done it? And, That Henry was a card! But he had no false expectations. This time next year it would be, When was it that Henry killed himself? And, What was it Earl used to say about . . . ? Before two springs had passed they'd wonder, Who was that guy, the one who used to work for the bank and offed himself? What was his name?

But he didn't change his mind.

Tally ho! said the fox. Ooops, I really shouldn't use their war cry but we foxes have had to run so fast we've never had time to come up with one of our own. I can hear all those dumb dyslexic hounds baying in the distance and the johnnie-one-note bugles, closing in. All those chinless upper class twits, they're going to get me, it won't be long now. I'm tired of running, being chased and I never wanted to be chaste. They don't know, they don't care, who I am. So I rumple a few feathers and kill a few chickens, so what! That's my nature. I can no more help it than I can hide my big bushy red tail between my legs, or mate with one of those pretty little layers. Why am I here if not to be a fowl killer? Explain that to me. Or give me a better reason.

The first hound, a breathless bitch, rounded through the undergrowth, gleefully launching herself onto foxey's back, knifing sharpened jaws into the soft skin between his shoulder-blades. Yum, she drooled.

He tried to remember how many years it had been since the first of the hounds had sunk its teeth into his all too tender flesh?

16

Henry was still remembering when he heard the first pop. Then there was another. And another. Three of them. They came from the far side of the mall, where he had been. He was certain what they were and, placing his hand over his heart like an American pledging allegiance, he swallowed great gulps of warm mall air. Gunfire! Had to be! He knew it as certainly as he knew there was a robbery in progress at the bank. He knew, just knew, that the man who had bumped into him was the robber, too eager by half to get on with the job to watch where he was going or to offer apologies to anyone he maimed on his way. He had that kind of face, that demeanour. Henry would bank on it. He was a banker himself, after all.

*

It had been a series of robberies that initiated the ruination of Henry's career. True, there had also been the time he took Leah to the Christmas ball and she told Barclay Clark, a Senior Vice-president, his senior VP, to watch where he was going, standing on her heel like that in the crowded elevator.

'See you Monday, Earl,' was all Clark, one of the cleanest, most antiseptic men Henry had ever set eyes on, his starched eyebrows raised, said as he stepped round her to get out.

She had called after him, 'Who do you think you are?'

Clark, known across the bank as Kotex Clark — something to do with his reputation for tinkering with the secretarial staff — turned round and said, 'Ask your husband.'

Henry saw his career begin to seep into the carpet in front of him. Even then he hadn't known how to shut her up.

Still, he might have survived if he himself hadn't been tagged 'Heist Henry' because of the number of times his branches managed to get themselves robbed. Statistics suggest that most bank managers have a career that never sees a single robbery. Maybe one over thirty years. Well, how about fucking six? Henry stabbed the air thinking about it. They weren't normal robberies either. Oh no! Henry was haunted by the odd, the out of the ordinary. No doubt about it!

*

There was the time, mere weeks after his first appointment as a manager, that a robber came behind the counter and seeing a man in uniform emerge from the vault, obviously thought him some kind of security official. He was an off-duty Transit Inspector who had been in his safety deposit box taking out his late wife's engagement ring to give to a new and highly nubile fiancé. The robber threw the man down the basement stairs, tossed him there bodily, breaking his leg in three painful places and, worse from Head Office's point of view, using his head to put a hole clear through the plaster wall when he landed in a heap at the bottom. Henry's Dad would have been envious. The head went all the way through to the ladies' washroom and scared Henry's Accountant half to death in the process. The felon fled penniless. His largely female staff wanted to use the facilities rather more often in the aftermath of the incident and they were uncomfortable with their new visibility and the accompanying draught but Henry was taken to task for immediately hiring a local plasterer to put the wall back together again without permission. He had not followed procedures.

Head Office told Henry to negotiate a settlement with the injured party. He was not — it had been his first conversation with Kotex — to admit culpability on behalf of the institution, but rather to offer his own personal sympathies and, only if he deemed it absolutely necessary, one thousand dollars as recompense. Still green in the ways of his chosen profession, still a believer, Henry was appalled. He considered doubling the amount from his own pocket. He sent flowers and a card but was still ruminating on his employer's ethics, when the injured man's brother-in-law — a lawyer alas — asked to see where the incident had taken place so that he could take pictures. Henry didn't feel he could refuse. When Kotex heard about it, Henry was practically keelhauled.

'You did what?'

'He wanted to take a couple of snaps.'

Henry became more English when rattled.

'Snaps? What the fucking hell are snaps?'

The telephone crackled in Henry's hand and he held the receiver away from his ear.

'You moron!'

'They wanted photos for his insurance,' Henry tried to explain.

'They wanted photos — your shitty 'snaps' — to sue us. Idiot!'

Henry drew himself up in his chair, taut as a violin string, quivering with rage. He opened his mouth to speak.

'Think of the bank, man,' Kotex continued, shouting into Henry's ear. 'Think of the shareholders. It's the fucking shareholders that count and you're going to be taking the bread out of their mouths if you go around helping every Tom, Dick or Harry who wants to fucking sue us. Christ!'

Henry was in the process of finding out that bankers are largely heathen persons. They have no God but Mammon, however much they call on the name of the firstborn Son. He took a deep breath and not for the last time in his working life swallowed his pride.

'Yes, sir,' he said. The words came out in a gruelly whisper. 'Do you still want me to make him an offer?'

Kotex spluttered his ire. 'Don't fucking bother! You're out of there!'

And so he was. In its infinite wisdom, Head Office transferred Henry to a branch known, far and wide, as Robbery Central.

Flash forward.

17

Two years later, on a bright fall morning, Henry was seated at his desk staring at the mounds of paperwork. 'We are outstanding,' they chided. His files mocked him. 'Do your duty. Complete us in quadruplicate. Move us into your out tray'. Pounds of paper, too thick for staples, were held together by painful clips that jumped at him, scorpion-like, discouraging perusal and — these were loan applications — decision. Scratching his scalp through the precisely placed strands of hair that bisected his skull from right to left, he sighed. 'When will it end?' he wondered. He had, he thought, had it up to here.

It was a normal work day.

On entering the branch that morning, before he could remove his overcoat, he had been assaulted by a female who poked at him in the general direction of his private parts with a furled umbrella as she fulminated against service charges, lost cheques and the amount of time she had been kept waiting. Worse yet, he had been ogled by Glynis, a new teller whose gambit at her wicket with anything remotely male, was to deposit her bosoms on the counter like twin sacks of coin, kittenishly inquiring in what way she might be of assistance. Then he had been informed by his Accountant — he still had his coat on — that Kotex had called to say that yes, they were aware that he was five staff members short from everything from pre-menstrual-cramps to jury duty, but, no, they were unable to provide assistance. It was Head Office Sports' Day.

Coat off at last, his secretary told him that she had set up an appointment for Mr. Benson, whose first action after sitting down would be to remove his false teeth, placing them, grinning, on the desk between them.

Henry shuddered.

There occurred next, in rapid succession, loud thumps as of people hitting the ground, screams, shrill post-religious age voices calling on the Lord, and one very rough, determined, yet slightly unsteady bark commanding, 'Alright everybody! Down on the floor. This is a stickup!' Henry listened to the vocals, but he couldn't see anything. Having finally made it through his door, he had closed himself off from the customer area, shutting it firmly behind him. Banker's hours were a figment of the public's imagination. The paperwork had at least to be skimmed before he could implement the open door policy demanded by those who were now undoubtedly stripping for the three-legged race.

Henry's initial reaction was that two of the miscreants' three exclamations were surely redundant. His second was to groan with something like despair. He was not afraid: repetition tends to dull fear and they were evidently about to undergo the fourth robbery since his appointment. If his branch was notorious, he, its innocuous manager, the 'heist man' to his peers, was not far behind. He had heard the nickname retailed between employees in the vault one day: it was unfair, it was an embarrassment, and it was only the slightest comfort that no one had said it to his face.

Yet.

He crouched on the floor, half under and half out of his desk. His chief emotion was fury: fury that one did not require an account to get cash out of his branch; fury at the necessity of having, yet again, to inform Kotex when it was all over; and fury, fine and fully fledged, that he could not see the perpetrator and from this position it was unlikely he ever would. If nothing else, he wanted to be able to give a description of the individual who was helping to submerge his career in a swamp of risibility. Moreover, he honestly felt that he should be on the front line with his troops. His nose should not be caressing the carpet out of sight while they stood exposed like so many skittles.

He was not hopeful that this could be achieved, however. Normally, a robbery is straightforward. Robbers are not known to be big on originality. A man at a teller's wicket passes over a note demanding funds, usually in unmarked twenties, which are to be stuffed into a sandwich bag. This done, pleasantries are exchanged and the man leaves. Only then does the teller sag against the counter, crying, 'I've been robbed'. The constabulary is then called.

Henry's robberies, unfortunately, tended to the unpredictable.

*

No one knew that Henry's first robbery at Robbery Central had even occurred until five hours after it was all over. The teller, her intelligence a comment on Darwin and the dimwit who hired her — actually Henry himself but he didn't like to admit it — simply did not tell anyone until she was balancing her cash after closing. She informed the police that she had harboured vague hopes remorse would smite the man and lure him back into the institution to make retribution. Indeed, she had taken a short lunch so as not to miss him when he did. Only, he didn't. She then reasoned, she said, that the Manager, our Henry, might be upset if she told him. So she didn't. Instead, she implemented the novel scheme of giving a little too little cash to anyone making a withdrawal in an attempt to even everything out. Only, it hadn't.

What Henry came to refer to as the Robbing Hood School of Banking still left the girl several hundred short at the end of the day. When she announced that she was, in the parlance of the trade, 'out', her supervisor offered to check her cash. This lady, a largely pregnant career banker who had raced her biological clock to the last tock, practically went into cardiac arrest when told the facts of the case, and she did go smoothly from hysterics into labour. Later, she was to suffer extreme postpartum depression and attempt suicide. Henry, in more recent times, had thought to consult her on possible methodologies.

The next robbery, a scant eight business days after the first, quickly descended into chaos. Percy, another teller, a fey young colt with blond highlights and wrists so limp they appeared to be perpetually in need of splints, refused to hand over so much as one thin dime. This surprised both himself and the robber, but not so much as what happened next. Percy reached across his wicket and slapped the robber, almost a caress, on the cheek. This was followed by a fine display of girlishly shrill ear-shattering epithets. These, in turn, ignited several old ladies standing in line. They had come to look upon Percy as a surrogate grandson — although they would neither have endorsed nor understood his night-time proclivities — and they were more than willing to sally forth in his defence. The robber found himself attacked from behind. There is little more lethal than grandma, interrupted in the encashment of her social security, defending her young. Percy, all aquiver, was screaming bloody murder when the robber, searching for a quick exit, any exit, tripped over the walker Mrs. Jardine, an ancient in the advanced stages of arterial-osteoporosis, thrust in his path.
    'Villain,' she hissed.

Henry might have accrued to himself a modicum of glory in the third robbery — if, that is, he had been on the premises. As fate would have it, and fate, as we have seen, was rarely kind to Henry, he had been called down to Head Office to discuss improvements to branch security. The unfortunate thief, known in the trade as a jumper, high on adrenalin and possibly something more pharmaceutical, stretched his luck by vaulting a counter four foot six inches high. For a man five four, enough should have been enough, but he still had to escape. His outward leap to freedom was Olympian but he was now weighed down by cold, hard cash.
    He caught his heel on the far edge of the counter and collapsed with an almighty din both on top of the teller line stanchions and a prone off-duty policeman who had already begun to contemplate the ignominy implicit in his situation. The felon was taken away before Henry returned. The talk of the day was of Glynis who, irate, most likely, that the robber had not given so much as a glance at her superstructure, had, when they stood him up, promptly knocked him flat again. It was only left for Henry to put the whole business into correspondence with Head Office, and to complete forms in triplicate regarding the hurt to Glynis's fist

and a requisition, in quadruplicate, for a new counter where the wood had been shattered.

He had been present on the occasion of the fourth robbery, not that being there did him any good at all. Total confusion had reigned. Just before closing, one woman and four smartly dressed men from the Inspection Department of the Bank entered the branch to begin their annual audit of its books. While the female gave a letter of introduction to Henry and the males dropped their large black bags on the desks of his ledger keepers, the whole staff was thrown into a state of subdued panic as it strove to remember rules that were only enforced when the Inspection team was on the premises.

No one, and certainly not Henry, noticed that they had been preceded behind the counter by another individual who, also in a three piece suit and carrying a briefcase, approached the nearest teller, pointed what might have been a gun at her ribs and told her to hand over or else. Else being of no interest and perhaps even some considerable distaste, she had done just that, politely telling the startled customer at her wicket that she would be with her in a moment. Transaction complete, the robber expressed heartfelt appreciation for the teller's co-operation, turned, walked back out into the customer area and made his exit through the door which, it now being closing time, Henry's Accountant obligingly locked behind him. The teller's announcement that she had been robbed shocked everyone, but as staff blamed Audit and Audit blamed staff, the police remained uninformed for several vital minutes. What the robber thought never came to light, but as one wag put it, he must have laughed all the way from the bank. Henry's previously singed goose was now cooked.

*

Here he was again!

Thirty seconds had elapsed. Henry was determined. He would be a man of action, seen to share in the danger of his staff, seen to care. Lowering his rump and lifting his nose, he began to elbow his way towards the door of his office. It led directly to the work area and the banking hall. At its portals he would see all. It flashed through his mind that he would have made a mean marine, but he was also aware that, inch by inch as he went, thin elbows and knobbly knees can cause excruciating pain. With three feet to go, he could hear the man demanding that everyone keep calm and hand over all the cash and what the hell were they taking so long for.

Recalling the award given for Glynis's estrogen enhanced bravery, and how Kotex had insisted on making the presentation personally, even taking her to lunch at a local bistro, Henry felt himself spurred on. He was mere inches from the door when his junior ledger keeper bolted into his office exhorting the deity. Marlene was a member of one of the noisier evangelical churches. Her pious chanting accelerated greatly when she beheld the unexpected sight of her boss blocking her path, crawling, pate first, towards the action. Henry's office represented sanctuary, and if getting into it meant leaping the length of his wriggling body, so be it. She shot into the air, a mare at the water jump, landing spike-heeled between his legs threatening his crotch and what little sex life, even in those days, he had left.

Unaware of being nearly neutered from behind, Henry put a hand out in front of him and pressed proverbially on. He was almost there. The hand, however, was immediately, and painfully, trampled on by a wide, brown foot. Mrs. Maraj, saried and hennaed, was in the habit of taking over a safety deposit box booth while choosing her jewellery for the weekend. Perhaps forgetting that she was hidden from view in the booth, she suddenly materialized, fist grasping a handful of baubles, and sallied forth, as fast as her bulk and raiment would permit. When asked about it by the police afterwards, she said that she had been in search of Henry. Authority would protect her! The robber may have been startled both by the vision in pink, shedding bangles and other valuables as it passed by. Henry certainly was. He inhaled a mixture of sandalwood and curry, uttered a strangulated yelp of pain and banged his forehead on the floor in bewilderment.

When he was able to raise it, it was his remembrance of times past that propelled him forward. He dragged himself through the door and all unfurled, visible before him. Unfortunately, Henry had become visible as well. There, not five feet away, dressed from top to toe in blue denim, stood the felon. From Henry's angle, he was an extremely large felon. The upper portion of his face was hidden beneath a stocking mask and one hand clasped a shopping bag into which the Accountant was packing bills from the Head Teller's drawer. In his other hand, aimed in no particular direction but generally pointing at Henry's head, was a large sawed-off shotgun. Henry blanched. Had he been capable of movement, he would have embarked on a backward scuttle, but like a rabbit in front of the headlight, or himself closeted with Kotex, he could only blink.

The robber wrote it all down in his statement at the police station and the police retailed the information (with an unwonted, not to say unprofessional, amount of snickering Henry thought) to Henry the next day. They explained that the robber had imbibed a significant amount of liquor to bring his courage to the sticking post, liquor that had been followed by several mugs of black coffee to ensure the sobriety necessary to go through with his intent. He had been, as he stood there, in desperate need of three things: the swag to provide for his material needs; a clear avenue off the premises which the newly appeared crawling gent seemed intent on cutting off; and last, but increasingly not least, a lavatory. This third item might have appeared trivial in the overall scheme of things but it was quickly assuming an importance beyond anything imagined in his planning of the event. He was nervous, and it felt as though his back teeth were floating. Determining that no goggle-eyed fellow with a clenched red fist could stop him, the man, in search of riches and a more immediate blessed relief, though he never intended it and could never afterwards quite understand it, aimed the gun directly at Henry. And peed his pants.

So too, alas, did Henry.

18

He wasn't about to do it again, and certainly not in a public mall.

Henry took a deep breath, willed air into his lungs, commanded it down to his diaphragm via the very soles of his feet and took off running towards the branch.

'Chazzam,' he hallooed, beginning to levitate, traction on the marble floors not being necessary, 'wait till they see me this time. No more Mister Nice Guy! No more hiding behind desks. I'm gonna show them all.'

His winter coat, unbuttoned in the warmth of the mall, billowed behind him. The belt flapped like a flag in a high wind and strands of hair, pathetic remains of a once glorious mane, streamed behind. The neon lights reflected off his glistening forehead. He was flying through the air, undulating round the waste food depository, navigating through the cacophony of the morning crowd. The knot of his tie was pressed against his gullet by centrifugal force imprinting the outline of his shirt-button onto his Adam's apple like a secret sign.

'Look,' he heard people say in astonishment as he flew by, 'it's Henry, out to save the day! Go Hen! Save Friday!'

At the door of the branch, he eased his feet back to terra firma. He wiggled his toes and ground his left heel into the floor so that his overshoe — it tended to flap when he walked — did not come off. He had told Leah his size, but the ones she bought were too big. He hadn't noticed it until she told him that he walked with a suction sound, that people could hear him coming. Well, he couldn't hear it, so what did it matter.

'I'd like to suction her,' he thought, as he straightened up and peered round the doorpost to see what was going on inside the branch.

Two women were strutting about the banking hall. Both were dressed in black and boots, and they had big hair. Eighties' hair, he thought. One of them was pointing a revolver, it looked like a twenty-two, possibly a twenty-three, at the customers who were cowering against the counter.

'Shut the fuck up!' commanded the woman with the gun. 'Or you'll get yours!'

'No, no! We don't want ours,' cried the customers a cappella, in unison like a Gregorian chant. They were a bit ragged in the alto, but, hey, it was a nerve wracking situation for them. They'd be alright on the night. The other robber — was that a robbette? Henry wondered — jumped to straddle the top of the counter near the vault. She didn't look at all comfortable. Her eyes were an orgasmic red and she was yelling to someone to get the lead out, which confused Henry momentarily since she should have been more properly interested in bullion. Banknotes, at least.

He had no time to think. He bounded forward into the air again. Six inches off the ground, he went so fast that he was sure everyone must be able to see the slipstream behind him. 'Chazzam,' he bawled again, careening like a cannonball towards the first robber. 'Henry to the rescue!' And, in an aside to the cowering throng, 'Fear not. You are safe. You are safe!' He said it twice to doubly reassure them and he could see them looking up at him, wiping away the tears, gratitude and awe on their faces as they began to stumble to their feet no doubt getting ready to hug and kiss their deliverer, to shake him by the hand, to throw their arms around his thin shoulders. 'Oh Henry, you did it again! You saved us.'

Unfortunately, such effusions were premature.

'I told the lot of you to stay down. You asked for it. You got it!'

The robber began to shoot. Holes appeared in foreheads, blood spurted out of chests and limbs arced through the air. Ice cream flying. Why was he reminded of ice cream? It all happened in the blink of an eye. Customers begged and tried to hide but no mercy was shown. The woman on the counter urged her companion on as she pointed her Uzi into the vault.

'You go, girl!' she yelled.

Then she saw Henry.

'God! No!' she wailed, 'It's Henry! We've had it! But we're not going down without a fight.'

He was moving smoothly towards her, no more than ten feet away now, though his vision might have been a little blurred by a flying piece of brain that had smeared his glasses. The woman, a little long in the tooth for a bank robber and with more than a passing resemblance to his late mother-in-law, brought the Uzi round towards him and stroked the trigger.

Ack, ack ack ack ack!

He was down. He lay on the floor looking up at the ceiling. The lighting receptacles had not been cleaned and he could see dead bugs silhouetted in them. Wouldn't have happened in my day, he reassured himself, and reached down to feel warm thick plasma oozing out of his belly. He frowned. Didn't feel a thing. He poked a finger into what he was sure was a hole the size of a saucer and moved it around. Stirred it up. No pain. He blinked.

He kept very still. He could see the steaming Uzi high over him. The woman threw back her big hair and laughed. At him. He saw the carnage over on his right. A stream of blood was edging its way across the marble floor towards him. Another stream, this one coming from where he was lying, was going forth to meet it. When the two streams began to mingle, he heard music, organ music. Henry hated organ music. A massed choir, there must have been a hundred voices, joined in, pulling at the heartstrings. His heartstrings. Henry listened, but nothing vital was to be heard. No voice, no sympathy, no balm. Just blasting, vibrating Bach. He put the heel of his hand against his forehead, smearing blood that clotted in his eyelashes.

'She wasn't supposed to shoot. I'm a superhero. Superheroes don't die,' he said and, following the logic of his thought, added, 'But if I do die, then its finished. That's what I want. I won't have to do it myself. It'll have been done for me.' His mind shifted. 'Of all the bloody nerve. Here I am a hero and I get myself killed. Its not supposed to happen like this.' He sobbed. 'I even caused these people to be massacred, rushing in like that. I should have minded my own damn business.' Another thought. 'Oh Jesus, what will Leah say? She'll say that I can't do anything right.'

He closed his eyes and then opened them again. 'But is it a dream? You can't die in a dream. If you die in a dream, you really die. You never wake up!'

He was beginning to panic. He wasn't certain whether he was dying or not. He couldn't figure it out. He knew it was Friday. He thought he was in the mall. He was pretty sure that he was not in bed with Leah. To be certain, he moved his right arm sideways, feeling around to see if she was anywhere near. 'Please God, don't let me feel her. Let me be here on the floor, my life's blood draining away, bleeding out before the doctors arrive. Too late to be French-kissed by the paramedics. Too late for them to push my guts back in.'

Then he heard a voice say, 'Get out of the way! You can't just stand there in the walkway with your arm sticking out hitting people like that as they pass by. Who do you think you are? Get to hell away from here or I'll call Security.'

And Henry knew, knew with a horrible certainty, that God wasn't listening. Still.

19

Henry Earl was the kind of person who always wanted to know where he stood, literally and figuratively, in a place or in a situation; a man who knew all about his space long before the concept became popular. But sometimes he had had to face doubt. There had been other occasions in life when Henry wondered whether he was having a hallucination. Had an event occurred? Or had it somehow not? Perhaps he only dreamt it. The gradual realization that he could yank himself back to the reality of the world around him generally managed to calm him, and, eventually, he had decided that worrying about it wasn't going to help. In time, acceptance of this led to ease and he developed the comfort of not fretting, sometimes not even being aware these days.

His habit of telling himself stories, embroidering events and playing them out within a lively imagination went back to his childhood. As a small boy, he would line up his soldiers on the living room carpet in front of his fort. The fort itself would be stocked with animals from his farm, and if he placed his garage next to the moat he could drive his cars over the drawbridge when the Indians attacked. He always had a very good reason why Indians should want to attack Vauxhalls and Austins, and how Utes and Hopis were likely to have come across such modern motor cars in the first place.

His mother considered the whole elaborate set-up an eyesore.

'Pick one thing and play with it, like a good boy,' she would suggest when he began to drag his toy boxes out from the cupboard under the stairs.

'But, Mam,' he would wheedle, 'I need them all.'

'Our Henry, if you don't clean everything off that carpet before you go to bed, you'll find it all in the bin tomorrow morning,' she would say, prodding him with her slipper as he lay, cheek to the floor so that he could see the parading soldiers in proper perspective. His Mam never carried out her threat, but sometimes, if visitors were coming, he did wake up to find that she had brushed the whole lot behind the couch.

He was ten when he began to realize that his friends lacked an appreciation of the finer points of the complicated tapestries he wove into the games they played, and his toys began to become a more solitary occupation. David still liked to come by, but his quietness somehow defeated the purpose of the fun. His best friend,

Trev, liked the games but insisted on killing everyone off in a series of bangs and explosions before he went home at the end of the day. Henry worried that tossing the lead toys into the air and flattening them with a variety of dinkies would take the paint off them. In any case, he didn't see why a game should end just because it was time to go to bed. Why couldn't they begin tomorrow where they left off today? Did they really have to start all over? He still had a great time with his chums, but he began to keep the living room carpet to himself. He began to carry the hero of the moment — or a favourite vehicle or an animal — up to bed with him. He would place it on his bedside table and look at it in the twilight of an English summer, sometimes ten o'clock at night, and continue the story in his mind. Just behind his eyelids.

Now then, General, the men are worn out. They need snacks and lemonade or they won't be able to hold back the Sioux much longer. It's too hard to get to the barn across the river where all the supplies are stored.

What do you propose, Corporal Henry, my lad?

Well, we could make a night run, come round the armchair leg and outflank them. The bus would be able to get through the river.

The double decker?

No sir, the local bus. The blue one.

Give it a try, my boy, if you think it will work, but we don't want any casualties, mind.

No, sir.

And Henry would drift off into sleep, prayers forgotten, planning strategies and the ifs, ands and buts of his complicated campaigns.

*

Everything began to change when he went to the Grammar School. History became his favourite subject. He loved the Norman invasion and he soon knew all the names of the early Kings. Queen Matilda too, who he'd never heard of before. He liked geography as well, eagerly learning about contours, how valleys and rivers were formed, about the continents and why countries had borders where they did, how to chart things like lighthouses and cliffs and railway tracks.

Then, one glorious day in his second year, when he was twelve, Mr. Allan, his geography teacher announced, 'Boys, your homework for the whole of next week is to map out a country of your own. To invent a country.'

The class groaned. Henry held his breath. He wanted everyone to shut up so that he could understand what they were to do.

'Now pay attention!' Mr. Allan tapped the blackboard with his cane. 'I want you to show me what the country looks like. Roads, rivers, mountains, forests. The sea. Is it a cold country or does it have a warm climate? Remember the topography will come out of the geology and that climate has its part to play on geology.' Mr. Allan let the boys absorb this. Most seemed to be appalled at the implications of what he was saying. Henry was ecstatic. 'Tell me what the latitude and the longitude is and be sure that everything is consistent with where you place it on the surface of the globe.'

More groans. Henry's hand shot up.

'Sir,' he said, an expression approaching bliss on his face, 'can we put in towns? And' — why didn't he think of this immediately? — 'will it be alright to give the country a name?'

'It's your country, Earl! Anything you want! Boys, you have a week. I want it handed in one week from today.'

The fort was put aside. He was getting too old for it anyway. He had just got his first pair of long pants and was feeling very grown up. His Mam certainly wouldn't be letting him roll around the floor in them, wearing out the knees. He disappeared into his room and scarcely came out the whole week. His Dad had rolls of brown paper in the shed. Henry scissored off a piece four by four and put it under his bedside mat to get it nice and flat. He went to work on scrap paper doodling coastlines, adding harbours, plotting where the mountains might be and how the rivers ran to the sea. On Sunday night, he had a brainwave and skeltered to school the next morning to stand outside the staff room waiting for Mr. Allan to arrive.

'Sir! Sir!' said Henry. He held on to his teacher's sleeve to make sure he had his full attention. 'Can the country be part of a continent, with other countries — like enemies and such like — next to it, or does it have to be an island?'

It seemed to take Mr. Allan a moment to realize what he was being asked. He was busy rearranging his cuffs. Then he laughed.

'Anything you want, boy. As long as it all makes sense and you can explain it.'

'Yes sir,' replied Henry, grinning widely now. 'Thank you, sir.'

He ran off before anything further could be said that might diminish his vision.

*

It was a week of missed meals, Dad yelling upstairs to come and get it — not that he ever heard the response — and Henry putting his bath towel along the bottom of his bedroom door to keep the light in late at night when he should have been asleep. His country evolved: it developed a geology, a meteorology, neighbours and a history. It changed its name several times and though its people began solidly Teutonic, they became vaguely Eurasian by the time he had finished with them. They had their own language, a pidgin English with mots of second year French thrown in where Henry thought suitable. He taped the map to his wall so he could see it better but it only remained there until his Mam came in to make his bed and ripped it down. She put a tear across a peninsula on the north coast, just next to the border with his country's neighbour, its great enemy, where the mountains came right down to the sea. After those magnificent mountains, it was the sea and the navy that was his country's first line of defence. Not that there weren't passes that could be infiltrated. (Henry wasn't absolutely sure if this was the correct word, but he was pretty sure it almost was.) He had erected walled, military towns the better to be prepared.

Henry was heartbroken. He sat next to the torn map, tears spilling down his cheeks. His stomach was upset and it seemed to him that something like the end of the world was at hand as he looked at it: the end of two worlds, in fact. It was a long time before he thought to turn the brown paper over and tape the back of it so that the join wouldn't show. He decided that an earthquake, a huge gigantic enormous earthquake had struck his country right at that spot, destroying everything in its path. It was a couple of years later that he learned that seismic activity is likely to follow mountain ranges and that mountains can be indicative of fault lines in the earth's surface. He smiled to himself when he heard that.

When Henry did finally turn out the light each night, he lay awake plotting and planning, working on a more detailed history, one that went through the centuries. He planned a legend for his map — Mr. Allan was big on legends — and checked off in his mind what would be required on it, trying to think what he might have missed. He could see the map on the carpet in the moonlight, and would fall asleep with a smile of contentment looking at it, waking fresh the next morning with ideas for improvement, more detail, more more. He checked his homework diary to verify that they had been told to draw only one map, and he tried to remember if he might have heard the words "at least" in front of the word one, but he didn't think so and Mr. Allan was a stickler for something like that.

Then he had an idea. He would write his country's history in a book with details about other stuff as well, language for instance — what was the word for that, vocabulary? — and a bit about flora and fauna. He couldn't see how anyone could object to a book. Masters were always saying that boys should show their prep work, their scribbles, in the margin so that they could refer to it later on. There wasn't a hope in Hades, as his Dad would have said, that he was going to put anything on the lovely clean borders of his map, so a book made sense. At the end of the week, it was twenty pages long and more remained in his head.

The look on Mr. Allan's face when Henry handed in his homework was not one that he soon forgot. He took it to be congratulation mixed with awe, but later, much later, he realized it was probably closer to a stunned 'what the hell is going on here?' The rest of the boys in the class clearly thought Henry was crazy and giggled at the long brown tube he had brought with him to class. When he explained what the exercise book that went with it was, Mr. Allan had to hush them. Their whoops disturbed the seniors' Physics' class next door and at recess everyone wanted to know what all the noise was about. By noon the whole school had heard about Henry and his map and wanted to see it, but by then it was in the staff room. Henry imagined the conversation there: the map spread open on the lunch table, a tea cup on each corner so the masters could get a better view, the masters themselves in various degrees of highly acceptable awe.

'The boy's a genius!' said Mr. Stringer, Sixth Form English.

'Which one is he?' asked Miss Charles, Latin.

'You know him. He was in your class last year. Brown bangs and doesn't say prunes,' clarified Henry's form master, Mr. Lewis. 'Always seemed normal enough to me. A bit shy, but well mannered. But this . . .' Mr. Lewis became uncharacteristically speechless.

'Do you think he's right in the head?' Mr. Burniston didn't think any boy was right in the head. Henry and he didn't get along. Mr. Burniston taught Math, and Henry and Math didn't much get along either. 'I mean, it's a bit . . .' The teacher was silent. He couldn't think of a word.

'Byzantine?'

'Feverish?'

'Much.' Mr. Burniston finally had his word.

'Well, I think it's too bloody wonderful,' said Mr. Stringer, who was examining some of the detail and cross-referencing it with what was in the exercise book. 'What an imagination the boy has. There's a whole world here. A whole parallel universe. That he has invented. I can't even get the Sixth to read 'Nicholas Nickelby' without whining. Congratulations, Allan, old man! What a lad, the lad is!'

Henry's reputation was made. Masters who had never spoken to him before, called out to him across the quadrangle. 'You boy,' they would say. 'Are you Earl? Come!' He would trot over to them to be congratulated or questioned or, sometimes, just examined. It was the first — and almost the last — time that he got ten out of ten on a piece of homework. In the end, the whole thing probably worked against him, however. He became known. Expectations had been put in place. Not his, but the worst possible kind: other peoples.

He continued to work on the map after it was returned, replacing it with three later versions as time passed. The history of his country became more detailed and the pages were rewritten. There were more of them, too. As his French improved (and, in the Third Form, he took a year of Ancient Greek), the natives developed significant outside influences that added to their vocabulary and to the inflections with which the language was spoken, although, truth be told, a diet of Hollywood movies gave it a certain American twang as well. Geographical changes came about when, that same year, his class began to study the Amazon basin. Later on, everything was complicated by a visit they made to the Railway Museum at York.

*

It was a good two years before the map and the exercise book finally disappeared into the back of his wardrobe, but in that time Henry had begun what would become a lifelong pattern. He developed the facility of being able to take himself off into another world, several worlds at once sometimes, whenever the current one became too heavy, too worrisome or just plain too boring. When he finished reading a book, for example, he would ruminate on what its characters would do next in their lives. He loved the multi-volumed Galsworthy, the long stories of Dickens, and books called "The Further Adventures of . . ." He hated it when the hero died, and he began to read the last three pages first, just to check on that individual's well-being at their conclusion.

It was the same with films. He would walk home from the cinema analyzing what might have happened next if they hadn't closed the curtains and turned the lights back on. He adored Saturday morning serials. His favorites shows were pirate movies. He loved the swash and the buckle and would wend his way home slashing at privet hedges. He was never sure whether he wanted to be the pirate king or to be His Majesty's Commodore of the Seas sent to the Indies to deal with the dastardly brigands, and he sometimes solved the dilemma by being both at once. You could do that if you organized your brain and divided the parts up carefully. The characters' parts, not the brain's. Of course, not the brain's parts!

His Mam called him a day-dreamer and would shake her head at the number of times that she had to call out to get his attention. That didn't trouble his Dad, though. His Dad calling someone was like an air raid siren. It could just about raise the dead, and it certainly got the attention of more people than the one or two it was designed to attract. Mrs. Blenkinsop once complained to her doctor that Henry's Dad gave her migraines. The doctor never believed her until one time he was making a house-call and he heard him loud and clear through the wall. As Mrs. B told his Mam, the doctor said it was 'positively stentorian', and advised her to have a word with the culprit. She didn't like to do that though. Preferred to speak to his missis. Henry's Mam said Mrs. Blenkinsop was one of those people who didn't know how to communicate with the deaf. She once let slip that Mrs. Blenkinsop thought Henry's Dad was a bit 'doolally', which is a North country term for daft. Henry didn't like her much after that.

The name of Henry's country changed several times before he put the map in the back of the wardrobe. The name, the first one, the one the masters saw, was ordinary and uninspired. Puny. It didn't last. The one on which he finally settled was found when he was thumbing through an old dictionary. He changed it up a bit to make it sound more like a country and he loved the sound of it. He didn't mind that the meaning might be a little off. Or perhaps, really, it wasn't! He wouldn't have told anyone what it was in any case: it was a private thing.

The name of his country was Jactatia.

20

The emphasis of Henry's imagination changed a bit when he discovered girls. He gave up on great sagas and began to concentrate on specific events. Nothing too involved or complicated, just the female of the species and he, together. Unfortunately, he didn't have too many options on whom to base the girl. He went to an all boys' school, and he was sure he would rot in Hell if he incorporated as the shortly-to-be-ravished heroine any of the girls on his street. It didn't seem right. The girls at church were of even less use. Pale, thin little things they were, and it was a bit difficult to incorporate the Bible into what he was thinking about. Fortunately, a solution was at hand. He fell madly in love with the queen of the B movies, the pirate queen herself: Yvonne de Carlo. Unfortunately, like most of the youth of his generation, he was not quite sure what to do with her. His knowledge was definitely sub par, and poring over his Third Form biology book — "Chapter VIII: Reproduction In The Human Species" — to suss out the process didn't help much. Well, it helped but it certainly wasn't the stuff that dreams were made of. Puberty, it turned out, had a detrimental effect on Henry's imaginative life. To a degree, it stunted it. At the very least, it made it less complex and certainly less time consuming. What had previously been an ongoing epic saga, with revisions, footnotes, parentheses and recapitulatory montages, became something rather shorter than a novella. A poem. Haiku even!

*

It was the voyage to Canada that revitalized Henry's ability to weave dreams. While packing for the trip, he had discovered the old map. The exercise book was nowhere to be found. Unrolling the map brought all sorts of memories flooding back. He rubbed his fingers gently over the now brittle paper as if to touch the contours of his country, to feel the tops of the trees in the forests and the rough waters of the seas that surrounded the land.

On board ship, he was alone and lonely (except for the nymphomaniac, of course), and the journey seemed to take forever, but the excitement of the adventure to come was ripe for the picking of his imagination. It began all over again. Not inventing countries, of course, he was too old for that, and there was no need to invent a country when he was going to a brand new one, but he conjured up amazing scenarios about what would happen when he got there. He began to play out the possibilities, a bit nervous perhaps, but wide open for the new adventure.

When I get there, what will I do?
Well, it will depend, won't it?
On what?
On what you find. On what happens.
Do you really think the streets will be paved with gold?
Shouldn't think so, and in any case, isn't that Los Angeles?
You're right. Canada won't be anything like that.
Too cold.
Hudson's Bay, mind.
The R.C.M.P.!
Will I like it, do you think?
Why wouldn't you like it, you clot! You're the one who wanted to come.
Yes, but . . .
No buts, it'll be great!

When it was great, Henry forgot about dreaming and got on with his life. When it wasn't, he still got on with his life, but part of him hung back, idling, playing at the edge of a better, nicer reality that was always ready to accompany him through the day and on into his recollections, even occasionally into his decision-making. At the same time, he never thought about why or how he did what he did. He never wondered why so many people had to call his name at least twice before he responded, never thought he might be strange or unusual in any way. He was just Henry.

But it was becoming a pattern, nevertheless.

21

Ironically, it was in Canada that Henry's imagination failed for the first time. Well, perhaps calling it his imagination was reaching a bit, and certainly it was a long time, years, before he came to think of it that way, but when he did and when he analysed what had happened, he had to admit that that was what it was. The failure of his imagination. For a long time he didn't like to think about it. His was a text book case of denial, and he told no one the whole story, though his college friends would have had to be blind, he knew, not to have seen some of the twists and turns, the skid marks near the end and the crash. When he finally brought himself, reluctantly, to admit that it was something in him that had been to blame — his nerve or whatever he wanted to call it — he also had to acknowledge that something else had triumphed. What would he call that? Timidity? Prejudice? Fear?

Dorcas Standish was black. There was no way of getting around that unalterable fact, and, initially, he hadn't wanted to because Dorcas Standish was also the most beautiful woman Henry had ever seen. He met her in the cafeteria two days after registration when she reached over his shoulder to take a bun from the counter. Dorcas didn't like to wait.

''Scuse me, mon,' she said flashing her eyes and grinning at him, daring him to object. Henry stared. He could no more have objected than he could have recited his two times table. Everything about her seemed lifted up, high: her cheekbones, her breasts, her waist, her spirit. Dorcas had the longest pair of legs he would ever see. 'You a frosh?' she asked. 'Well, frosh mus' give way tuh junior, yuh know.'

With a laugh, she was gone.

He caught up with her five minutes later as he stood looking around the crowd for somewhere to sit, and she called out, ''Ere, boy, yuh could sit 'ere, if yuh doh take up too much a meh space!'

Henry would have sat at her feet if she had told him to.

He had never met anyone like Dorcas Standish. She was loud, she was opinionated, she was intelligent — an engineering student — volatile, and she loved to laugh. He had to run just to keep up. She had come from Jamaica where her family was involved in politics and she was in Canada to learn how to build roads, to irrigate fields and to improve the lot of her people. And have the entire universe at her beck and call while she was doing it. She said what she thought but no one could have said that she said things without thought. Henry was bowled over. He had never met a Jamaican before and Dorcas Standish was exotic. Exotic by any standard.

It suddenly seemed to Henry that his own provincial background hadn't provided him with standards. Everyone at home had been the same. They spoke the same, looked alike, had much the same opinions, and everybody was comfortable with everybody else. It wasn't true, of course, but this took some finding out. A good chum, for example, had disappeared from his life at age eleven when he went off to a Roman Catholic high school. Henry was aware that Papists poisoned Protestants but Albert had seemed so ordinary. How was he to tell? At fifteen, he had been shocked to find out that he had been sitting next to a Jew for two terms. Heaven knew what Jews did, but when he told his Dad, his Dad had only shrugged. There were rumours that a Nigerian family lived in Harrogate Hill, but Henry had never seen them and when he finally clapped eyes on the man, a bus driver, he found himself waving. The man waved back. In the whole town, it was Henry's own Dad who stood out most.

Of course, there was always the Welsh . . .

Dorcas's colour was her own and it was difficult to describe: a kind of pitch denseness etched in with purple and mahogany, eggplant almost. 'Black as the fire back', his Dad might have said she was; 'black with no shine' was how one of the other Jamaican students described her, but he belonged to a different political party so Henry was never quite sure if there might not be an implicit insult in there somewhere; 'Sheba-black' was what Dorcas herself said she was with a toss of the head, almond eyes sparkling when the subject happened to come up.

He took a deep breath and asked her out for coffee after class. The two of them became inseparable and had a great, though initially platonic, time together. Dorcas didn't seem to mind that Henry was two years younger and shyer and less committed to ideas than she was. She taught him to dance (in so far, she said, as anyone could teach a white boy to dance), she fed him foods he had never heard of and was almost able to persuade him that he liked most of them. She fed his ego too. Her nickname for him was Killer, or The Killer, and although he knew there might be more than a hint of mockery in it, he chose only to see the real affection that was there as well. She told him stories of a place and a country that he had only seen in the movies. Jactatia seemed like a poor relation by comparison. She changed his language, too. The cadences of the Caribbean edged their way into speech patterns already confused by his arrival in Canada, and if, for example, Jamaican aitches (or the lack of them) didn't remain permanently, they were, at the time, absorbed by osmosis and proximity rather than by any conscious effort. In the end, only one echo of Dorcas's dialect would remain in Henry's speech: the word Satcherday — the first day of the weekend — was to journey on with him through to the last days of his life. It was a pronunciation that always annoyed Leah: she did not know where it came from and was consistently after Henry to be rid of it.

Then came intimacy. There, Dorcas was shyer than Henry was — he always thought his few short minutes with the nymphomaniac were a help — but only until they mounted the roller coaster and accelerated into bliss.

It was his roommate who first commented on how dark Dorcas was, said it in an implicitly negative kind of way, a way that caused Henry to pause, to reflect on it for the first time. He had always been aware that people looked at them when they were out together. The little old ladies in Murrays' stared. Grown men, in the Anglo-Saxon Toronto of those days, fidgeted and frowned at them on the subway. More than one changed his seat so that he would not have to look at them — or so it seemed to Henry. If he had had to admit it however, Henry would have had to agree that being noticed was part of the adventure, and no one threw things. To be reminded that your girlfriend is black in the middle of an earnest undergraduate discussion of life and one's plans and aspirations for it, however, and to have this pointed out as something that should be considered, was not something that Henry had expected. He may have been naive, but it brought him up short. Not even consciously at first perhaps, he began to weigh the thought and to put it into the scales of their relationship.

Dorcas, so completely of a different tribe, never seemed to consider it. It was not a subject they talked about and on Henry's side it was not a subject much understood, though there were occasional reminders. On one occasion, Dorcas received photographs from home, and, with great familial pride, showed them to Henry. Everyone was at the seaside, palms framing the background of the pictures. In one photograph, ten people were seated on the white sand, smiling into the camera. Dorcas pointed out who each one was. Her father, mother, little brother Jessamy, her two younger sisters, Auntie Lou and Uncle Magnus, cousin Nelly on her father's side, her big brother Noo-Noo (whose real name was Alexander — but he could never be called that with Bustamente, the antichrist, leading the Opposition) and his blonde girlfriend Ceci. Ten different complexions seemed to want to catch Henry's eye. They succeeded. He did not understand it. How could each one of them be so different? And Dorcas was darker than any of them except possibly Uncle Magnus who was sitting in the shade and a bit difficult to make out. Dorcas tried to explain, but it was difficult, and Henry found the picture and all these happy people unsettling. But in the protected, open society of a university what did it really matter anyway?

He remained besotted. The doubts that might have flickered through his head were overpowered by Dorcas's presence. It was only when she began to assume things that these doubts began to resurface, like mice made apprehensive when the tomcat slinks into the larder. She began to assume that he would come to

Jamaica after he graduated. That he would find a job there. That they would make their home there. That they would be there forever. He could not quite remember how it came about, but he woke up one morning to find that he had agreed, and, although he was still a sophomore, his life was being planned for him by this force of nature.

Henry's imagination — and, with it, his courage — began to falter. He began to find reasons why he could not make a decision yet (Dorcas was graduating but he still had two years to go), why he wouldn't be able to visit during the Christmas vacation (He needed to see his parents, his mother had not been well), why he couldn't have dinner with her aunt who was here on a shopping trip (He had essays due and a cold). When he did meet Auntie Lou for coffee, she proved to be as vivacious a woman as her niece, but she was also enormous, big-boned and — how could he describe it? — of all things, a yellowey kind of brown colour, reddish really. Henry had never much considered Dorcas's hair, but Lou's was tight and almost non-existent. He could hardly keep his eyes off it and her habit of rubbing the palm of a huge hand over the top of her head didn't help. Then, soon after this, the whole cast of characters arrived for Dorcas's graduation and if Henry did not know what to make of their noise and their bustle, it was apparent that they didn't know what to make of him either. He was intimidated, and it showed. Dorcas sheltered him from their good-natured stormy blast but he thought he could see a sadness in her eyes. Perhaps even she was beginning to doubt their future.

When she departed for home, everything was left open ended. Yes, he would come down after he graduated but what he would do there was not discussed, and, yes, he would visit before then, but they did not quite determine when. Dorcas remained as ever she was and she did not force the issue. Had she, on that last evening as they sat under a tree in an early Toronto summer, he might have given in — how many times in the years that followed had he wished he had — but nothing was said and something held him back. He stayed there on the cooling ground after it was time for her to join her parents at their hotel. She kissed him on the top of the head and said her goodbyes. He let the dark settle around him and pulled absently at the grass, some of it by the roots, seeing quite clearly what he had lost, knowing that it could never be replaced, that he would eventually have to settle for something less, yet failing to act, not doing the one little thing that would have put everything right.

They wrote for six months, at first almost daily. Then weekly. Then every so often. Then when there was some news to tell. Then — he wasn't even sure how it happened — not at all. Dorcas wrote twice more, but he didn't open her last letter. It sat against the back of his desk until he could bare to look at it no longer, and he flicked it with the back of his hand into his wastebasket, unopened.

He was to see her twice more.

*

Nothing about Henry's visit to Jamaica four years later was designed with Dorcas in mind. Friends suggested and organized the trip and, in any case, neither of these particular friends knew about her and Leah was already beginning to be in the picture. Kingston and Montego Bay were far apart and he shrugged away any slight itch for a meeting, but then, when he sat on the beach, he found himself looking at the local women, hoping that she might somehow appear. On the fourth day, he became palpitatingly sure that he had to contact her, and enlisted the aid of the concierge at the hotel to put through a call to her parents. An animated conversation between the concierge and whoever it was on the other end of the line produced another number to call. Henry retired to his room and stared at the telephone for a long time before he dialled.

''Ello? Oo his there?' A rough unhewn voice barked at him. This was never Dorcas.

'Hello,' he said, rather more loudly than he intended, 'may I speak to Miss Standish, please?'

'Don't got no Standish 'ere!'

'Dorcas Standish?!' He was ready to hang up.

'Ooh! Hah!' It appeared that the telephone in Kingston had dropped to the floor. 'Pardon, pardon! 'Old hon.' Then, in a voice so gigantic his Dad would have been envious: 'Mistress!! Ha man fuh yuh!'

He heard her laugh in the background and had to sit down on the edge of the bed.

'Hello?'

'Dorcas?'

'Killer? Killer!' She knew him immediately. 'Is you, nuh? Where yuh are?'

The next morning he hired a car and drove over the mountains to Kingston. Once there, it took him an hour to find his way to the Red Hills and another fifteen minutes to get up his nerve to turn the car into the long driveway to the house. She had told him she was married, but he did not expect her to be quite so magnificently pregnant. When she wrapped her arms around him, he felt the baby kicking against his stomach and when she would not let him go he had to pull his head back to be able to look at her. Still the same slightly mocking, shining eyes, just a glaze of moisture in them at the moment, the same full lips ready for laughter, the same dusty dark shining skin.

'Come!' she commanded as if they had been apart for a day, 'Come and meet Jerome. My 'usband.' This was said with a raised eyebrow and a twinkle, but she took any sting out of it when she rubbed her belly and added, 'Yuh've 'hallready met meh eldest!'

Jerome was a large, fair-skinned Jamaican man ten or more years older than Dorcas, of whom he seemed both paternal and proud. He pulled her to sit on his knee but she shoved him gently away ruffling his curly hair and plonking a kiss on the top of his head. He seemed content to serve drinks, sit in the background on the woven wooden furniture, and listen while Henry and his wife caught up. Henry could hardly bear to look at him. In any case, he couldn't take his eyes off Dorcas. She was wearing a loose tent-like dress that gathered under her breasts and accentuated them. Then, he had known the very veins of those breasts, but now he had no right. She kept her legs wide apart for comfort given the weight of the baby, and he could see only where the material of the dress made their outline visible — the outer edge of her thighs, the shape of a knee and the right shin when she hoisted up the material to swat at a dive-bombing mosquito that was admiring its target as much as Henry was. He could hardly catch a breath and he had driven all the way back to Spanish Town that evening before he was able to do so with any semblance of ease.

*

The last time they met was by accident. It was fifteen years later in Toronto, summer time, and Henry was on vacation. Leah had decided that they should take the girls to the zoo. They had been to see the elephants and were trundling along the pathway over a slight rise towards the lion house, he, his wife and three slightly overweight pre-teen girls, all of them enjoying the sun and the outing, and each one of them slurping on Popsicles in the heat of the afternoon. Strolling elegantly towards them, came Dorcas and three teenaged boys. Loose-limbed, tanned like well-oiled teak and just as handsome, the boys resembled their mother and appeared as confident. Enjoying themselves and laughing in the sunshine, they seemed to own the pathway, but they moved aside politely to let Henry and his motley crew pass by.

Dorcas saw him first. 'Killer!' she exclaimed, and held out her arms. "Hit's meh Killer!'

From there, the afternoon went downhill rather more steeply than the pathway they were standing on. Leah was obviously offended that some — foreign — woman was embracing her husband and calling him a name she had never heard of. Henry had told her nothing about Dorcas (why would he?) and although she managed to remain polite, she did not seem comfortable. Neither did the girls. Introduced to the Dorcas's boys they became tongue-tied and lumpen, at a loss to know what to say to such blinding young princes. The boys themselves, mannered and quintessentially polite, answered every question put to them with assurance, but they moved from foot to foot like young foals wanting to be off for a gallop.

Stuttering to keep the conversation going, to keep them there though he knew he would pay for it later, Henry gave Leah a highly expurgated version of his knowing Dorcas. She, in turn, glanced from Henry to Dorcas and back, saying little. Dorcas's eyes smiled. Was there, he wondered with a sudden lurch, some malice there? Or was it merely fun at the situation they were in, at what she knew and at what she thought Leah would now suspect? No one was fooled except the girls, Henry was sure. 'Yes,' he said to himself, 'I'll definitely pay for this later.' It would be worth it. To pacify Leah perhaps, Henry asked for Jerome. He had died three years before. Another lurch. Dorcas hugged her youngest son to her as she told the story, kissing him on the top of his head.

Henry had been jealous of that kiss before and, in the sunlight of that glorious afternoon, while the two families stood on the pathway halfway between the elephants and the lazy August lions, he knew, knew of an absolute certainty, the magnitude of his mistake. Dorcas was lost. The young princes could never be his, his imagination had failed and he had settled for less. Someday it might not be enough.

22

It was time to go downtown. The hours were passing, time was moving on, bringing him closer to his release — for that was how he had come to think of it. There were still things to do, of course, and perhaps, if truth be told, somewhere deep inside himself he had not quite made up his mind. For, as he walked through the mall and its burgeoning crowds on that most April of mornings, his eyes darted back and forth, surveilling, seeking. For what? A sign? A Divination, perhaps. The merest vestige of an indication — a wink would have sufficed — that he was not beyond the help of which he had so long since despaired.

The subway entrance was decorated in hospital white tile. Purple graffiti, outlined in a metallic black added a message in jagged, gothic letters. Henry stopped to look at the words, but they didn't offer much comfort: 'The World Needs Yor Help. Look for a Savier'. He shook his head. He certainly wasn't about to help the world. It hadn't done much to help him recently. He glanced at the wave of human traffic coming towards him, bumping repeatedly into him, then bouncing off and careening away to go about its business, but he couldn't see anyone who remotely resembled a Saviour.

He wondered about the person who had scrawled the message: what misplaced confidence to think that he could speak for the whole world, how vague his thinking that he didn't define the nature of the person who would provide the help. What kind of assistance was he thinking of? Free food? Cheap housing? Legalized marijuana? How about better education? Spelling lessons, at least, although, he thought, I should be able to forgive the 'Savier': it was not a word much used these days.

At the bottom of the graffiti, a signature in black acknowledged ownership, although the artist's name wasn't clear. Henry would have liked to contact him to remonstrate — not for defacing the general lavatorial effect of city property, but to ask him where he got off spreading what were essentially words of hope. He knew the writer was a young man, that he had not yet given up. The thrust of the message was that, if the world got help — yours, mine, ours — it might improve. Henry knew that this was not true. Couldn't be true. That those who answered the call, those who banded together to offer their particular iotas of assistance, would be fooling themselves and fooling everyone who relied on them for action. So he passed by. He shielded his eyes, keeping them firmly on the ground in front of him, as he descended the first level of escalators.

He was looking for sandals.

If the Saviour did come back, if a new Messiah was wandering about somewhere in the busy city, ready to proffer open arms and a new "come unto me all ye who are bowed down and heavy laden", surely he would be wearing sandals. True, it was still nippy out and his tender tootsies might suffer a bit of frostbite, but wearing sandals was what saviours did. Leather, size twelve. Jesus boots. Henry's neck craned towards the oncoming traffic and he watched warily, eyes jumping from foot to winter-shod foot. Perhaps, he mused, you won't be wearing trousers under your winter coat, and no socks of course. Just hairy legs going down into open-toed fruit boots.

He almost tripped at his next thought.

Perhaps you are a woman! Could the next Saviour be a woman? He kind of doubted it, but that was a personal opinion. There had been enough jokes about God being a female. Perhaps someone knew something he didn't. If — always an if — if there was a God, in the first place. And what kind of sandals would she be wearing, this new Emmanuelle?

Now wait a minute! Naming the new Jesus after a seventies soft-porn movie heroine wasn't right. Couldn't be. His mind hurtled on anyway. Perhaps it was just that she would look like a movie star — some pneumatic noviciate to save the world. All kinds of uplift.

'Emmanuelle!'

He said the name out loud. He said it to the person walking just beyond his right shoulder and to the next and the next as they were swept down the second escalator into the new catacombs, the elongated crypt of the modern city. He was sure it was a she! And he stumbled forward looking for a woman. In sandals. Toeless, flimsy footwear fresh from the beach.

All that passed him by were boots.

Henry looked about him for the transfer machine. It stood against a pillar, its red button beckoning him, inviting him to listen to the soft grunt when he pressed it for printed authorization to go from one form of public transportation to the next across the sprawling city. He stood in front of it, hesitating, before, gently caressing, he pressed the button twice.

23

He held the paper transfers, slightly scumpled, in his left hand and felt little fingers reach up and become lost in his big right hand. It was the game they played whenever they could. They would take the subway to the end of the line, sitting up front in the first carriage, as near to the driver as they could get. Max liked to see where they were going, although more often than not he stood, splay-legged against the movement of the train in the centre of the aisle between seats. He would stand there and ions of energy would spark through him. It was happening now. Henry loosened his suit-coat and made his tie comfortable, smiling at his son. His sun. Max's chubby little fingers moved, vibrated like a prodigy at the grand piano, and he rose to his toes with the sheer delight of being there. Glee in his face at the wonder of the adventure.

It was their adventure. Only theirs. Leah never came with them, neither did Max's sisters. They had no interest, but for Max it was the ultimate trip.

Once they reached the end of the line, like now, Henry would collect two transfers and then they would get back into the train. They didn't have to be at the front anymore. What they needed now was to be in a carriage near the transfer machine. When the train came into the next station, each subsequent next station, they would get out. Henry would stand on the platform and Max would go tearing off, as fast as only a five year old can go, to collect the transfers and bring them back to his Dad, their official custodian. Sometimes the machine would be up a flight of stairs, even just inside the turnstile at the subway entrance, but Max could be relied on to find it, punch it twice, and return as soon as the milling passengers would let him.

'Excuse me, sir!' he would yell, when someone was in his way, 'Lady, can I pass, please?!'

Oh my son, you can — but may you?

At the first stop, the adventure began in earnest. It was an open platform and the rainy slush had soaked everything in sight. Henry stamped his feet on the cold platform. Max went charging off and Henry was happy, so happy, waiting for him to return in time to catch the next train.

He sang, 'Ah, sweet mystery of life at last I've found you.' His Dad's song. His now. Was that really mystery? It couldn't possibly have been misery, could it?

114

Henry shook his head. Not with Max here.

Station by station they would go, all the way to the other end of the line.

Max was back. Henry saw his feet first, coming down the steps — all the stations were different — and Max jumped the last two of them onto the platform, grinning. He would have jumped a puddle as well, if there had been one handy. The little boy ran towards his father and came to a halt about six feet from him. Then, very formally, he walked forward, an emissary from a foreign nation, bowing, the two transfers cupped in his open palms.

'Here, Daddy,' he said.

The two of them looked at the pieces of paper. One had been slightly torn when it came out of the machine. He took it from his son as an archaeologist might take a valuable artefact from his assistant. 'Thank you, my son,' said Henry, again echoing his own dear Dad, gingerly taking hold of the transfer by a curling corner, adding it to the two already in his hand. Then he took the other one, all four together like a fan.

'Here comes the train,' he said, feeling its distant rumble through the concrete platform. 'Stand away from the edge of the platform.'

They stood three feet back, hand in hand. Max waved to the driver as he spun by, looking up at his Dad to see that he had done it correctly, grinning beneath his brown bangs in the bliss of their companionship. Henry nodded his benediction.

The ritual was performed again at each successive station. On the train, Max continued to arch his back, stand on tiptoe and let all the energy of his body be released through ecstatic fingers. This is my son, said Henry to himself. My own true son. Occasionally, he glanced sideways at the other passengers to see how amazed they were, how delighted they had to be, how enchanted the boy made them feel. He could hardly hold back the tears — but he knew that to cry would not be the manly thing to do, would not set a good example for Max, that he might not understand.

Although, of course, Max understood everything. When he put his small hand in his father's and squeezed as tight as his fingers could squeeze, Henry knew that Max knew. There was one other thing as well. Max would smile at his Dad, a closed-mouth complicit smile. His eyes would be slightly — Henry had been appalled the first time he noticed it — moist. Not tears-about-to-run-down-the-face moist, just the feeling of moisture, glinting in a ray of the sun.

Max squeezed his hand again. Something caught in Henry's throat, a blockage that he had to clear.

Why, he wondered, is Max wearing summer clothes? He must be cold. He was in short pants and the sleeveless pullover that his Grandma had sent from England for his birthday. Leah hated it, 'that terrible fawn thing' she called it, but Max loved the argyle pattern that ran across its chest, he liked to trace the diamond outline with his finger, and he wore it whenever he could. One sock hung around his ankle: the other was in a valiant but losing fight to stay up.

The subway track swung momentarily to the left. The movement of the carriage threw Max off balance. He gurgled his pleasure at trying to stay erect, standing totter-footed until, unable to maintain the position, he collapsed in a heap into Henry's outstretched arms. They hugged each other, giggling with the joy of their fun. Max rubbed his cheek against his father's, and stroked Henry's itchy chin, wanting, perhaps, to feel the slight stubble that was already there despite a firm morning shave.

Henry looked down at his son's feet. Grey socks and brown, yes, sandals. It didn't make sense. Snow was still on the leafless bushes, it would lay beneath north-facing fences for a while yet. How could she have sent him out dressed like this today? He could catch his death. No! Not Max! He knew Leah had never wanted a boy. A boy was a nuisance, what would she do with him? Boys were messy creatures, as she was always telling Henry. They played violent games. 'Hawkey'. They swore. They got dirty. Why did he have to be a boy? He had heard her say it to her mother while she was still in the hospital. It hadn't even been a hard labour, not that she could have felt much, drugged and out of it as she had demanded to be every time she gave birth. Even to her blessed girls.

The sandals!

Perhaps Max was the Saviour? His Saviour! A sweet savier. Henry grimaced, his mouth a slit of concentration following the thought into the maze of his mind. I hope not, he said, as Max righted himself, returning to stand in the centre aisle of the moving train, electrified hands churning once again in the sheer delight, the camaraderie, the adventure. God, I hope not. I don't want him to be special. Then he would belong to everyone: I want him to be mine. I want him to belong to me, and a mist of despair crossed his eyes before he could blink it away.

The train came into a station. Max leapt completely into the air.

'Daddy, we're here! Come on!' he said.

The man stood with his back to the empty platform, pleasant, ordinary looking. Late middle-aged but not unpresentable. Clothes a little out of order this morning. He seemed preoccupied, listening for something, someone, his ears cocked, head to one side, mouth slightly open in concentration. Transfer tickets were clasped in his hands. A train was coming down the track. You could feel it. The man held up the transfers, held them away from his body at waist level, and with the most delicate of movements, swanned them into the shape of a fan, before turning to face the track. Taking a step back, he looked down, to his left, put his hand out, slightly open, slightly away from his side. When the train stopped and the doors slid open, the man entered the carriage. He was smiling.

Henry chuckled. 'Heaven help us,' he said to himself. 'At this rate, it will take hours.'

His toes curled at the idea. What did he care if Leah questioned them when they got home?

'Where have you two been?' she would ask, but then she would see the transfers and she would know.

The first time they had their adventure, Max had presented the transfers to his mother, excited fists cramping them together. A gift. A bouquet of the most precious scented blossoms could not have been given more carefully. Their collection was his greatest achievement. They were for her. Henry still remembered the brittle gesture of her hand.

'What are those dirty things?' she had asked. 'Look, there's ink all over your fingers! Go and wash your hands, its time for dinner. And do a good job. I don't want black marks on my nice linen serviettes.'

She frowned at Henry.

'How could you let him get so filthy?'

After that, they didn't bother to tell her where they had been and the transfers were kept hidden in Henry's pocket until they could carry them, secretly, to Max's room.

Henry no longer noticed that their progress through the subway system was slow. Neither of them noticed it. Their delight was complete. They were underground now: the whoosh of air seemed to throw the train from side to side as it raced downtown. Henry winked at his son. Max squeezed one eye closed with his fist and tortuously squished the other. He guffawed. Henry reached out and rumpled the thick shantung thatch of auburn hair.

'Daddy!' the boy declared, mock-annoyed to be mussed.

The train came out of the tunnel, shuddering into the open air. A woman stood, moving away from the man who, out of nowhere, had wordlessly lifted his hand towards her. He seemed like a respectable enough person, but you never knew these days. She was getting off at the next stop anyway.

Her rising caused Henry to blink. He peered out of the window. The train was hardly moving. On his right, a high retaining wall blocked any view of where they were, but Henry knew. He didn't need to look. If he did, he would see it and he couldn't bear that, to see where his sweet boy was, the place he always hid his eyes from. Today, however, he had to look. Gravestones stared back at him. There was a road between. He wished it was a highway. He wished it was a whole country. He wished he had never driven along it, never seen the place, never entered its gates.

He rose slowly and walked towards the door as the train acknowledged a green light somewhere up ahead and then entered the darkness of another tunnel. It was only right that he should say goodbye to Max.

*

When Max was seven or so, he and Henry often went to play in the cemetery. It catered to the dead it was true, but, for a child it was a huge sprawling park, meandered with pathways, sheltered by trees. A wonderful place for a game of Hide and Go Seek. Tombstones of all shapes and mausoleums the size of garages held no fear for a little boy bent on making his father guess and search and wonder where he was.

'Hmm,' said Henry aloud, a very bad imitation of a scary voice. 'I wonder where that rascal is. Is he hiding behind old Mr. Hodsgon? No! Perhaps, Mrs. Laverne Prufrock? What a silly name!'

He heard Max giggle. Henry knew exactly where Max was: he had been circling the hiding place for the last five minutes.

'Okay, not there either. I know. Let me check the Ablacks!' He leaned towards a rose-coloured gravestone etched with black cherubs. He absently traced the letters of the inscription with an index finger. 'Hello there, Mr. Ablack, have you seen my son? He's here somewhere . . . . No? What about you, Miss Marlene Ablack . . . ? An untidy little ruffian with scuffed shoes and a dirty neck that will need to be washed before his mother gets hold of him . . . . Grimy paws, too.'

'Oh no, they're not!' objected Max. The words were out of his mouth before he could hold them back. 'Daddy!' he said in disgust at himself, and accusingly, 'You made me say it!'

High dudgeon!

'Me?' said Henry, all innocent. 'I was speaking to Miss Marlene Ablack, born 1927, deceased, alas, 1978. Rip! Come and see, Max. It says 'rip'!'

'Daddy!' Parents could be so hopeless. He wasn't going to be fooled by a mere parent, even his beloved Dad. 'That's not rip. That's,' a slight stammer, he wanted to get it right, 'R.I.P. It means Rest in . . .' what was the last word? 'Peace!'

Max poked his head out from one side of the Celtic cross he was hiding behind to look at Henry as if wanting to confirm the meaning.

'Gotcha,' roared Henry, lunging forward, grabbing his son by the waist. The two rolled together on the soft sweet grass, Henry tickling him so hard that they both became breathless. Max roared with love and laughter, and they lay on the damp ground staring up into the branches of the trees and beyond to the cloudy blue sky above.

Henry crossed the road after he came out of the subway and leaned a heavy arm against the cold stone wall of the cemetery. Tears sheeted his cheeks and he could not see, but there was no real need to see. He had buried his son here and he knew every stumbling step to the place where he would find him.

*

Max had been eight. He was to attend a birthday party on a lazy summer afternoon. His mother dressed him in his Sunday best and sat him in a chair until Henry came back from the supermarket to drive him to the festivities. Henry had replayed the scene over in his mind so often that the celluloid was brittle, the audio scratched.

'Sit still,' Leah admonished, 'And don't get yourself all hot and bothered or there'll be no party for you.'

She could have had no expectation that he would obey her and must have known that Henry would see that Max got to the party whatever her threats, so she was surprised when she looked in on him half an hour later and saw him, still all neat and tidy, lying on the couch. When Henry returned, he unpacked the groceries, organized the cold stuff in the freezer and put detergent into the dishwasher — they had run out — before he called to Max.

'Hey, Max. We're off!' he said.

No answer.

He put his head around the living room door.

'You sleeping? Well, get up, my lad, or those greedy friends of yours will have swiped all the ice-cream and choked on the last piece of candy before we even get there.'

Max didn't wake up. He was in a coma.

The doctors said it was cerebral meningitis, that Max felt nothing, had no pain, just went to sleep.

It didn't really matter what he died of, thought Henry now, struggling to get enough air into his lungs to be able to voice the thought.

'He just died.'

It was Leah who arranged for the gravestone. He hadn't had the energy, the heart. They quarrelled about the inscription. The stone said "Maximilian Raymond Earl September 21 1978 to August 26, 1986. He Has Gone Home To God." The words were an offence. The graffiti writer might have put them there. Such pious claptrap. Why would a boy, his bouncing energetic boy who loved life and all its mischievous opportunities, want to go home to God? And why would God want him there, so soon, so unnecessarily?

Leah went regularly to clean the grave. He had never been back. Every spring she pulled out the dandelions (how Max would have loved to puff their parachutes), and, every August, she put flowers. Across the way was a large marble slab memorializing the husband of one of the ladies of the church, a woman who Leah both admired and sought to emulate. Henry didn't think the woman was fooled. He sometimes felt guilty for not coming here, but he knew in his heart that Max didn't mind. They still played together in his imagination.

And he was here now.

He stood by the side of Max's grave.

Max. His only son. His only begotten son. In his mind.

*

Henry sat, knees drawn up to his chest, on the soft ice in front of the grave, passing handfuls of slushy snow from one hand to another. His gloves lay discarded at his side. After a minute or two, he could no longer feel what he was doing and his hands were red and numb. When the snow melted from the friction, he reached to his side and scooped another palmful of the mixture of ice and snow and began to knead and pass, and pass and knead, again. He was not thinking of anything, was perhaps incapable of thought, and he did not see either, although his eyes were open. The squawk of a blackbird intruded. He dropped the snow and brought his left hand to his ear, probing for the minute off-switch for his hearing aid. There was no feeling in his finger and he felt nothing, but he could have done this in his sleep. The finger found the place from long practice and he pressed. The bird receded. He reached up with his right hand, and brought it to his right ear. This was a different hearing aid, differently engineered. He had to use the tip of a fingernail to loosen the inserted battery so that it could disengage but, in trying to do it, he felt drops of ice water run into his ear. He flinched with the cold and, without thinking, tried to wipe the wet away, but his fingers were still too numb and the hearing aid shrieked at him, unhappy at being disturbed. In the distance, he could still hear the blackbird. Wanting quiet and solitude for this last time with his son, Henry reached, fumbling, into his ear and pulled the hearing aid away from its moorings.

It was silent at last. He looked around him, still not seeing, and closed his eyes. Then, he slid his hands out in front of him on the icy snow, so that he was on his hands and knees leaning forward. He sighed and slowly lay full length on the grave, gently resting his left ear against the frigid earth.

24

The remainder of the ride downtown was underground. Henry thought about his destination, the bank surrounded by all the other banks in the financial section of the city. It was difficult for him to differentiate between the slabs of marble in the cemetery and these other stark oblong structures that reached for the sky but which were so solidly stuck in the earth. Each gravestone one had been a person once, but these amorphous edifices of commerce had never possessed a beating heart. Tombstones spoke of God but these temples to T Bills used God only when He was convenient, casting Him off when it was not. They purloined His virtues to inflate their bottom line but they would shunt Him aside soon enough when He threatened to interfere with the pursuit of profit.

And here Henry was, once again, one last time, burrowing like a mole into the coffers of the moneylenders, into the vaults of the soulless city. He would emerge into a wilderness of subterranean granite, pink or black or speckled grey depending on which institution it was, bobbing alongside its other employees, each one of whom was never able to breathe the tart freshness of open air, and would never know the passage of the city's fair seasons. Thousands of fragile tugboats, tossed and turned by the vagaries of finance, whose job it was to prevent ocean liners of money from going aground. Henry's bank was the one with black grained marble and vaguely sickish yellow granite.

As the escalator ascended from the depths, the transfers, two dozen of them, fluttered in Henry's hands. He didn't notice them there.

He rose into a food court tightly ladled with people, bankers all, milling around having a late lunch. He had turned his hearing aids off in anticipation of the place. It was a riot of unassimilated yattering. The cacophony of a lunatic asylum. For years, complaints had been made about the lack of sound baffles or any kind of carpeting. It was rumoured the pooh-bahs didn't want them. The shareholders didn't want 'em. The stakeholders would have driven spikes into the hearts of the villagers rather than have them. Not to have them meant that few employees could bear to stay there long; the tumult quickly sent the peons back towards the thirty or forty or fifty story elevators and to the wind-swayed towers of their trade.

And Hallelujah for that, shouted the moneychangers.

Henry kept walking to the next level of escalators, still fighting to emerge from the netherworld, wanting to feel the fresh touch of a breeze or a persuasion of sunlight on his cheek, but the building was hermetically sealed against nature, against the natural. Security guards, paying lip service to eco, were alert to its intrusion. In their bottle-green blazers they resembled not the brightest of middle-aged students, prefects at his old grammar school of long ago, and they were about as useful. Props for the plenteous, he called them. The guardians of gilt.

Then Henry saw something he had never seen before.

*

Squads of people — women mainly, and a good number of them East Indian — were on their knees. Dull pewter buckets nearby, scrubbing brushes and wash cloths in their hands, they were swabbing the marble floors. They wiped the back of their forearms against their foreheads and arced half-circles in the wet in front of them. Others were dabbing at the granite of the walls. No one spoke. Everyone worked in metronomic motion, in an appointed place. When they wiped, they smeared each surface the palest pink. Henry looked into one woman's bucket and saw that the water was a deep, rusty red, a viscous colour, the colour of the operating table. The woman sank her scrubbing brush beneath the surface and lifted it out, shaking off the excess. Drops speckled his overshoes and impregnated the cuffs of his trousers.

'Watch out,' the woman said, 'Fool!'

He saw that she was a pensioner of the bank. He couldn't remember which department she had worked in but he knew that he knew her, even though she had no teeth now and lines of discontent were edged deep into a surly face. She seemed annoyed that he had interrupted her rhythm, and, worse, that he might get her into trouble. She grasped at his leg.

'Don't let them take away my free chequing,' she begged in whine of desperation.

Henry moved towards the express elevator that would take him into the sky, hoist him up to the floor where he worked. A man stood inside. Henry knew him too from somewhere, but, again, he couldn't quite remember where it was. A good fellow though, gone now. A stress coronary perhaps: Henry weighed the likelihood. There were many of those. A caring chap, he recalled, but now here he was, like everyone else, swabbing the walls, though these in the elevator were oaken with a cherry-wood inlay. All the fittings of the elevator were brass, polished each morning along with the big front door before the poo-bahs arrived to put their fingerprints where they would, spoiling the effect of a virginal cradle of commerce. Henry noticed that these walls were also speckled, and that something had dried hard and unapologetic on the panels of the mighty. The man, his three-piece pinstriped suit horse-soiled with sweat, used a long cash-counter's thumb nail to pry off slivers that jumped into the air of the elevator before falling like brittle dandruff onto the wooden floor.

'What are you doing?' Henry asked.

His voice seemed a long way off. He was still barrelling through the city underground, still cutting capers with Max, gathering transfers for their collection. Where shall we hide them? he wondered. No one must find them. They'll remain hidden all their days; our secret always.

'Hide them in my bucket if you like,' whispered the man warily, as though making sure no one was listening.

Henry looked down at the bucket. The red liquid shook with the speed of the elevator's ascent, rippling out to slop against the sides of the container. There was no sound. He turned his hearing aids back on and heard the hum of money for the first time that day: elevator music for this mountain of moulah.

Then he noticed that the man had no socks. A dark, dirty-nailed, big toe was thrust through the leather loop of a backless slipper. He peered into the man's face. Was he? Could he be? The veins in the man's eyes were red, what should have been white was yellow, and the irises coal black.

'Are you . . . ? Henry stuttered, 'Are you God?'

The man laid a trembling hand on Henry's arm.

'No, alas, I'm not God,' he replied. 'Never even got to be a VP.'

'Then what are you doing here?' Henry asked gently. 'What are you all doing here?'

'We're cleaning the blood off the walls,' the man replied. He shook his head and whispered again, 'So very many. Dead. Massacred for Mammon. Fifty-seven in one day, they say. In your Division alone. And you among them, I think.'

Henry's ascension continued.

25

Two days earlier, the Wednesday morning elevator had been crammed. Bankers like so many fat pilchards, scrubbed and suitable, on their way to gutting. By the time he reached the fifty-fifth floor, however, Henry was the sole occupant: a man alone in the tumbrel. Stepping out, he pulled out his swipe card to access the secure ozone of his Division. It was not only that the secrets of the bank had to be kept confined within these walls, there was also a tendency for anything, everything, that was not battened down to go missing. On one Friday afternoon, four computers had disappeared as staff wended their way homeward. Not laptops either: big, bulky desktop models, nineteen inch monitors and ICUs the size of refrigerators. The shit hit the fan over that and management installed cameras to screen the egress of the villagers. One of Bettina's few real jobs was to change the surveillance tapes each morning and hand them over to Boney. Bettina on a stool, bosom shaking largely, larger rump wobbling, hands flailing above her head, fiddling like a blind man with the eject button, was a sight to behold.

'Com hon, man! Wha deh arse, yer fockin ting don let go!! I go skin dis ting halive when ah get old ah hit. Ras.'

Boney, with his lower centre of gravity, a much more suitable shape to stand on a stool, would disappear into a meeting room with his morning coffee and The Financial Post for random viewing. As far as anyone knew, he never found anything. Rumour had it that he brought tapes of the soaps from home and watched those. Henry was sure that it wasn't true. Boney wasn't a soapy kind of guy, but it sounded like a good rumour when he started it, and he certainly hadn't allowed it to lie there unattended. Also, Henry knew about Boney. He knew about the pilfering. One evening when almost everyone had gone home except for a couple of techies who probably had no home to go to, Henry had been finishing up a report when he found himself caught short and had to go to the washroom. Passing by Stationery Supplies, he heard an oath of imprecation that could only have been uttered by his boss.

'She-ite, look you!!'

Henry poked his nose cautiously round the door. He had seen Boney leave, on time and with his usual alacrity at four-thirty, and it didn't seem possible that he would have come back. Perhaps, ye gods, it was a doppelganger! There however, with his back to him, was Boney in the flesh, stuffing stuff into his briefcase. Envelopes by the handful. Reams of paper. Boxes of cheap pens that only Boney would think to use — most people bought their own, ones that wouldn't leave oily blots all over the place. A large canvas LCBO bag stood on the floor behind him, and Henry saw that it contained two twelve packs of toilet paper. Single ply.

Henry paused. If he pushed the door open, Boney would probably drop dead of fright. This, indisputably, would be a good thing. He knew several people who would take him out to lunch to celebrate the event. But what if Boney only collapsed twitching on the carpet? He couldn't just leave him there, gasping like a beached whale on the staple strewn floor. He would have to give him mouth to mouth. He was reasonably sure that even Mrs. Bonnet wouldn't give Boney mouth to mouth and he didn't think he could do it either. And whom could he call? He knew there were emergency procedures, his copy was somewhere in the back of a drawer, but he had never read them. Didn't want to. Never went to fire drills either. Didn't know anyone who did. Except Boney. What is more important, he had a call of nature to attend to and it wasn't about to go away. He let the door close slowly and sped off to the loo where he thoroughly enjoyed the desperate release he fumblingly accomplished just in time, flushed, as it were, with the new secret he possessed. An almost erotic 'ahhh' erupted from the back of his throat. Whether it was from his relaxing bladder or from what he had just witnessed, he couldn't decide.

When he was quite sure that Boney had left the building, Henry returned to his cubicle. He sat in front of his computer thinking about what he had witnessed, wondering what to do with the information. In the end, he did nothing. It was enough that every time he saw Boney in the future he would know something about him that Boney didn't even suspect he knew, didn't have an inkling of. How, after all, could he ruin someone's career by reporting the theft of a gross of bad ballpoint pens, even when that person was about to ruin his for the most impersonal reason of all: cutting costs. He simply couldn't do it. The knowledge cheered him, and he began his work again, more buoyant, feeling better. Whatever he was, he wasn't them.

And he whistled.

Oo ee oo.

*

Henry had hardly put his foot out of the elevator door when he came face to face with Rowena and Fred Fallow. Rowena was breathing heavily, like a carp on the dock of the bay, as she stared rapturously upward into the face of her boss. She could suck up better than a Hoover. She had the gift. Probably a diploma as well. She didn't even see that Henry was there, she was so busy ogling Fred. From the look of her, an orgasm was not far off.

Fred had the usual polished, partially lobotomized, look of the male executive, but Fred was different, too. Someone, somewhere along the way, had taught him manners, and he had never quite forgotten them.

'Hello there, Henry. How's it going,' he said. He added, 'I got your email. Sorry you won't be at the meeting this afternoon. We'll miss you. Not even Llewellyn's expertise, eh?!'

Hearty ha!

He turned towards Rowena and jogged her arm with his elbow. 'Perhaps you can persuade Bonnet to attend his own meeting and let Henry attend mine, Rowe.'

Tone is all, and Henry knew that, whatever his faults, Fred was not in on the putsch, not on its details anyway. For one glorious moment he considered reaching out to shake Fred's hand, wishing him goodbye and a nice life, but he was holding himself together today, not wanting to come apart, not yet anyway, and he didn't think he could come up with a rational explanation, well, an explanation rationally given, that would be clearly understood when it came out of his mouth. The elevator alarm was beginning to ding and if he said anything at all there would be so many subordinate clauses, dangling participles, and adverbial phrases (not to mention brackets) that the two execs would press Escape so precipitously the cables might snap and Miss Otis would really regret.

Henry glanced at Rowena and saw that she had blanched, surely not at seeing him — she could cope with that any day — but probably at the way Fred had spoken so easily to an underling. Human to human. Wow, he even knew who Henry was! Was she wondering if she had done the right thing in consigning Henry to the fiery furnace? Not bloody likely. More likely, his unexpected appearance had interrupted her coitus.

Fred reached round Henry to stick an immaculate loafer in the closing door of the elevator. The dinging became faster. Rowena manhandled Henry sideways so that she and Fred could advance, passing him by on the other side. At the same time, she chucked Fred in the small of his back to urge him forward, and, really, Fred had done his bit. He had shown his humanity to the foot soldier in the trench. He had provided a shining example to executives everywhere on how to treat the non-coms. Time to move on. No point in just standing there. Gerry might gas the lot of them, eh what!

'Next time,' he said, over his shoulder.

Rowena had yet to say a word. Not a ''Morning' or a 'Nice suit, Henry,' or 'How's yer father?' Not even a 'Get out of the bloody way, fuh Christ's sake'.

Well, she'd get hers, later on, if everything went as he intended it to go.

*

Inside the Division's security doors, a convention of computers was at work. Air-conditioning droned and the sound of money being made was all around. Henry didn't hear it, but he knew well enough that it was there. You could almost smell it. He could also smell coffee and he walked over to his desk, nodding to Olaf who was reading The Vilnius Gazette on his computer. Henry picked up his mug and set off along the corridor towards the lunch room.

His rubber overshoes stuck to the carpet like black Velcro and his left knee clicked as he lifted his leg to slog along. He suffered with that knee and had always thought there would be a replacement in its future. He was walking like a man who had suffered a stroke, with that ungainly don't-you-dare-look-at-me step of extra deliberation, so he leaned against the wall to take a breath and pull off his scarf. He gulped down the warm dry air of the counting house, and saw that one of his rubbers had come askew on his foot again, half on and half off. He could see the empty heel, and he pulled his foot back, like a donkey pawing at the ground. The overshoe came loose. It made a lazy parabola in the air before landing right side up facing the toe of his other shoe.

Once again, Henry was reminded of ice cream. He didn't know why.

He would have bent down to pick up the overshoe but the straitjacket wouldn't let him. They had tied it too tight. It was difficult to breathe properly and bending was out of the question. What was the question? He wasn't sure. In any case, what would be the good of trying to pick the rubber up? Usually, he was quite adept with rubbers. Leah always made sure he wore one. That was their agreement. She remained on the pill well past menopause and he remained adept. Of course, their couplings had always been few and far between. Like solar eclipses.

Henry's arms were pinioned in front of him, gift-wrapped for the ease and enjoyment of the attendants. Even his fingers were battened down and immovable. He turned his head into the wall, feeling where the strap went tight between his legs — these guys were professionals — and he was aware that it was digging into his testicles. Lifting his shoulder made it worse, but he wanted to scratch his nose and he had no way to do it. No way at all. What could he do?

Think, dammit, think!

'You alright, Henry?' Someone was hovering over him, patting his shoulder, obviously concerned.

Henry sucked in an enormous sinew of air. He concentrated all his efforts on it. He tried to breathe, not breathe as he wanted to breathe but the breath of the long distance runner. The Loneliness of the Long Distance Runner. The back of his throat rattled with the effort. He could taste the nastiness of his own bile.

'Yup!' he said, keeping his eyes down, 'Stubbed my goddamned toe!'

'You sure you're okay?'

He looked up to see who was so concerned about him. She was frowning at him, concern clear in innocent eyes, and Henry was hard pressed not to reach out and touch her cheek. She would not last the day. She was on his list of probables

— everybody had a list, it was a parlour game on the floor — too innocent and non-political to survive when Rowena hustled them into the chambers and turned the spigot.

'Fine,' he said, 'You go on ahead.'

He stood still, taking control of himself, pulling himself together, calming himself down, sorting himself out, raising himself up, keeping himself in. He could do it, he knew, for he had to get through the day. Get through the day. One foot in front of another. Who said that? Had it been that? One foot? One step? Which was it?

Everything must be carefully carried out. Each action should be separate. He would do one thing and finish it. Have one thought and complete it. He would keep himself together that way and he would survive. He would conquer. He would defeat them all. It would all begin with this one step: one, each, step. One thought, one sentence. One fucking phrase if he needed to do it that way. To get there. To get through. Through the day. Minute by minute. Action by action. Twitch by twitch, if necessary.

He put his left foot forward, mildly surprised that it moved. He bent, a lovely clean from-the-waist bend like a principal dancer at the Bolshoi, sweeping up the overshoe so that it came to rest nestling next to his heart, the empty heel snug in his armpit.

He turned to leave his coat in the cloakroom. One step.

He hung his scarf on a wire coat hanger. Two.

He unzipped his overcoat. A third.

He deposited the right rubber on the floor. (It bounced again.)

Etcetera.

He heeled the left rubber next to it. And.

He shucked his coat. So.

Hung it up. Forth.

This is good comma he thought.

Everything is going according to plan period.

I can do this comma I'm sure of it comma or was that a semicolon question mark I can get through the day exclamation point.

Henry put a hand out to steady himself.

His hand collided with a row of hangers and they clanged their annoyance at being disturbed.

Bugger off, Henry.

'Stop!' he called out above the din. 'Not,' he said this aloud 'now. Not today.' He sideswiped the hangers; ten or twelve empty, thirty or forty that contained the paraphernalia of winter. They erupted.

'Jesus!' he said.

He began to laugh. Clattering the hangers was the kind of thing that his Dad would have done in one of his roaring rages, very much aware of what he was doing, scaring the civilians, a gleam of glee in his eye, playing the odds, amusing himself in his aloneness. His mother would have taken no notice and Henry and Edward, after feeling the terrible surprised thump of their hearts, would have realized what was up and want to laugh. As long as Dad didn't see. As long as they didn't spoil his effect.

So Henry did what his Dad would have done next: he raised an eyebrow at the desolation he had caused, and left the room with the smidgen of a swagger.

And he whistled.

Oo ee oo.

His Dad came from work one day, singing.

'One two three o'clock, four o'clock rock.'

Edward and Henry sat down to dinner, while their Mam passed the vegetables through the hatch.

'Four five six o'clock, seven o'clock rock.'

Dad brought the meat round through the door so the gravy wouldn't spill.

'What's he on about now?' whispered Edward, his face averted to avoid examination.

Henry shrugged his shoulders, 'Dunno. Perhaps he's gone off.'

'How could they even tell?'

Edward punched Henry's arm and grinned at him. He loved his Dad as much as Henry did.

'What are you two on about then?' asked their Dad, but he didn't wait for an answer.

'Eight nine ten o'clock, eleven o'clock rock!' His baritone took off: 'We're gonna rock around the clock tonight.'

Mam peered through the hatch.

'What have you done to him now?'

'Nothing,' said Henry.

'Who? Me?' said Edward.

'He's singing,' said Henry, a mite nervously.

'Well, I can hear that!' replied his mother.

'But he can't sing!' said Edward.

'Sure he can,' answered Henry, 'he's always singing.'

'Yeah,' said Edward, 'but he can't be singing that! It's at the top of the hit parade. He's deaf! How could he have heard it?'

Henry looked at his brother, the hairs on his forearms standing straight up like grace notes, and bawled for their mother.

She explained while their Dad chortled away in the background.

'His friends teach him songs at the pub. They write out the words and give him a starting note. Then they tell him to go up or down. Apparently they use hand signals. Reg Hammond told me it takes them hours but you know your Dad. Won't give up. He likes to sing. He used to sing in the choir. I thought you knew all about it. Don't take any notice of him and he'll stop.'

'Wow!' said Henry absolutely awed.

'You sly bastard!' said Edward, older and wiser, in a whisper almost under his breath.

26

The lunch room had been judged suitable for the 105 workers in the Division. It seated ten. Had everyone arrived at the same time, there would have been a riot. Rowena and her four V.P.s each had coffee tables in their work areas and had never been seen carrying a cup. All ten chairs were occupied and people stood against the counter near the sink waiting with their empty mugs. Those in front of them inserted loonies to get the scalding Columbian. No one smiled. No one made eye contact. The word was out. Something was going on but no one was going to speak about it. The sound of the coffee spluttering down the spout was complemented by the slurp of it being sucked up, too hot, all around the room. Like everyone else, Henry was not about to say anything, although he wanted to make a joke, to lighten the tension. Did you hear the one about the bears masquerading in the woods, he wanted to ask, but he might forget the punch line. Jokes were not his forte. Stories, yes, but not jokes.

Henry was saved, they all were, by the arrival of Rowena's Executive Assistant.

The 'executive' in Executive Assistant clearly implies that that person executes things. Rowena's Exec Ass executed people. She was Rowena's spy. The Mata Hari of the Division was what she was, although the very opposite of anything voluptuous or come hither. Priscilla Brace was just short of five foot tall. She reminded Henry of the woman in the movie Poltergeist. There was not an ounce of fat on her spare frame — not one iota of female pulchritude anywhere — and she dressed like a maiden aunt at a funeral. There was one very catholic exception to all this: Priscilla's hair was a silken chestnut. Its luxurious ends jounced and frolicked just out of reach of her bony shoulder blades; they poked and played against her skinny neck and they swayed against the ramrod stiffness of her posture. Almost every man in the Division, and not a few women, had leaned in close to smell that riotous mane of thick, touchable hair, wanting to sample its glorious excess.

Henry himself had almost toppled over one time trying to get a whiff, an actual feel, and he had had to steady himself by injudiciously putting a hand on her shoulder. Priscilla gave a little yelp and expelled a modicum of surprised air — it smelled of digestive biscuits as Henry recalled — and said, 'No, Henry!' He had the horrid suspicion that in another time and place, she might have said, 'Yes, Henry!'

or even 'Oh yes, Henry!' (there was something in her voice) but he apologized. Quickly. 'Ooops. Sorry,' he said, and they got back to work. The incident rattled him and he replayed it in his mind, apprehensive and unsure.

A few days later, Priscilla had appeared at his elbow with a china cup full of coffee.

'Just pouring one for Rowena,' she said. 'Save you the trouble of having to get up. One lump or two?'

From the corner of his eye, Henry could see Olaf throw out an arm to steady himself on his chair, and Boney stood up to look over from the other side of the partition. Henry panicked.

'Four,' he said. 'And half and half, please. Just a dollop.' His voice was an octave higher than usual. He might have got away asking for a dollop, but his next request went too far.

'Do you have any of those little muffins with the sprinkles?' he asked.

The words just came out. They lay there on the floor of the cubicle, trying to scuttle away sideways before anyone would notice them, but it was too late. Priscilla drew herself up. Her hair flounced round the nape of her neck, affronted.

'Well, I never!' she said. 'Really!'

She took herself off, but from then on she never had as much as a thin wintry smile for Henry.

Coming into the room now, however, Miss Brace caught his eye, held it steadily and pursed her lips into a line as warm as the December solstice. She nodded. 'Henry,' she said. He felt a chill that she had singled him out, but others also felt the cold spell that Priscilla generally signalled, and parted, like Moses at the Red Sea, for her to pass by on her journey to the coffee machine.

There had been enough talk for Henry to know that it wasn't only because of her proximity to Rowena that people didn't like Priscilla. The scuttlebutt was that she carried tales. Henry was convinced that that was what Executive Asses were for, their main purpose, and he wasn't alone in giving Priscilla a wide berth. You could have launched an aircraft carrier in the space most of the staff gave her.

Henry was also aware that if the staff in general disliked Priscilla, it was the Assistant Admins who actively hated her. Most of the Admin Asses were immigrants, usually of a South Asian persuasion with a few Philipinos and the very occasional black thrown into the mix (Henry considered Bettina a product of affirmative Admin Ass action). Whether there had been a secret edict to this effect or whether all VPs came to the same Kiplingesque conclusion during the hiring process, Henry did not know, but it was a generalization that he was quite certain would hold up. Perhaps, he thought, stirring the pot of his imagination, the idea was that their dusky hue would complement the paler master class or at least match the mocha furniture. Perhaps the thought was that those who had sprung from a colonial circumstance might better appreciate how fortunate they were to tote for their betters, but it was certainly true that the Admin Asses were as café au lait as the coffee they carried. It hadn't taken a great deal of observation on his part to realize that Executive Asses were another thing entirely. To a woman, they were white, generally third generation Canadian, lacking of looks, humour and the ability to perspire. Henry had sweated buckets when he realized about the perspiration. He knew that the Admin Asses might always have to part to let Priscilla pass by, but he hoped that they would turn their backs on her only when it was absolutely safe to do so.

'Big day today, eh, Priscilla?' he said.

Every eye in the place swung in her direction.

Had people, he wondered, finally woken up? He was always amazed that previous pogroms notwithstanding, a majority of the Division still refused to believe that the bank would throw them willy-nilly into the street, discounting their hard work, the long hours they had put in, and their accomplishments if it suited it. This morning, however, Henry could smell doubt in the air.

Priscilla shrugged ever so slightly. The wonderful hair bounced. She was dipping a teabag up and down in a cup of boiled water. The Royal Doulton of the executive.

'For some,' she replied.

Henry felt the ice of her eyes as their gazes met.

She blew the smoke from the end of her gun. A single puff. She put it back, licketty split, into its holster. Henry hadn't even been able to draw his, get the safety off, much less point it in her direction. It was a hit, a palpable hit.

'For some,' she repeated, looking round the room.

The townsfolk drew back, recoiled. Women hid their children behind their gingham skirts and the menfolk tried not to show fear, not to soil themselves in front of the gunslinger who had just ridden into town, just one step ahead of her boss. A castanet of spurs.

Oo ee oo.

In that one look, Henry knew he would not be the only one going toes up today, not the only one bound for Moriah Cemetery, Boot Hill for bankers, not the only one to be screwed, blewed and permanently tattooed by Rowena in her ever onward rise to the top, to be the cream of the crop, the paragon of the posse, the doyen of the dipsticks.

Writhing on the ground, he winked.

*

At nine o'clock, Henry attended the regular monthly meeting of a committee that discussed ergonomics, wellness and air-quality. There was a member from each department and the meeting was convened and chaired by Boney. Henry liked to attend although he always complained to Boney that his being there was a waste of time since they were in the same department. Boney's answer was that Henry was there to represent the people. The committee, Boney's own brainchild, was meant to show management's concern. It had accomplished nothing in two years, except to publish a semi-annual report on the dangers of smoking in the stairwells, which remained endemic anyway. Henry said little and generally took a quick nap.

As usual, Boney had arranged his papers all around him. File folders sat to his right and to his left. His laptop lay, closed, diagonally on his left at — as Henry's Dad would have said — eleven o'clock. Henry always thought that Boney strove to give the impression that he was chairing a plenary session of the General Assembly of the United Nations, with the galleries full and the peace of the world hanging on his every word. What was new today was an eight and a half by eleven envelope, about a half an inch thick, lying in front of him at two o'clock. It was not the envelope that caught Henry's attention however, but what was on top of it. Stapled to the right hand corner was a taxi chit.

Henry could not help but guffaw. The sound exploded from him before he could stop it. Everyone stared. They saw a grin of sheer delight. Dad in his devilment.

'Going somewhere, Llewellyn?' he said. 'Or sending someone somewhere, perhaps?'

Boney slid the envelope under his laptop. He had the grace to blush.

The young boy tossed the core of his rosy red apple aside and ran, full tilt, along the wooden sidewalk. His hat flew off but he kept on going until he came abreast of the saloon. Pushing his way through the swing door, he called out, 'Sheriff, come quick! They're almost here. They're coming into town right now! Don't let them get my paw.'

Oo ee oo.

27

Henry's whole body was twitchy, itchy for action. That his throat was parched and his tongue lolling exhausted on his bottom teeth, indicated the necessity of further refreshment. Spirits would have been good, but he knew he had to be sharp, honed even, for his eleven o'clock meeting with Boney, so he decided to go down to the food court and splurge on a cup of the better java.

Perhaps a muffin, too.

Those great greasy things that look like grenades with raisins? What do you want one of those for?

Let him have one, for pity sake. The condemned man and all that jazz!

Won't do his midriff much good, will it?

Much anybody would care, any road.

Henry closed his eyes and contemplated the possibilities. Latte? No. Some type of flavoured cappuccino might be good. What about an expresso? That would put some lead in his pencil at ten in the morning. If he did have a muffin, should it be blueberry, chocolate chip, date, plain, whole-wheat, bran or raisin? Decisions! A bagel might be better. He took a breath and shook his head to clear his chuntering thought processes.

I don't think my processes are processing too well at the moment.

What's he say's the matter with his processes?

What, you hard of hearing as well?

Just wanted to be sure!

He's got a lot on my mind and I'm not sure he could decide what kind of bagel even if the Chief Rabbi of Jerusalem were to ask him.

He should go with the basics.

Won't taste like much then. How about twelve grain and garlic cream cheese?

I was thinking an everything, toasted with butter. He looks as thought he could use some butter right about now.

Our Henry? Not at all. He's fine. We're only talking about a cup of coffee and a snack, for heaven's sake. When did Henry ever have problems making a decision? Carrying them out, mebbee, but making them, not a problem.

No argument there.

Decisions!

Christ!

Henry's teeth hurt. He sipped a plain black coffee and thought about it. It was certainly true that the more life-changing the event, the more important the decision, the less time he generally devoted to making it. His decision to come to Canada was an example.

*

'Eee, our Henry, what's the matter with going to Durham University? It's a good university. It's only a few miles from home.'

'Mam, that's the point. People don't get the benefit of going to college if the college is in their own backyard. What's there to be experienced that's new?'

'Well, then, where would you go? Manchester?'

'Mother! Who would want to live in Manchester? There's hardly a blade of grass within two miles of the city centre.'

'Where then?'

The decision.

'I think I'll go abroad.'

The commotion those words had caused! But there was no denying the decision or him after he made it, and it certainly affected everything that happened in his life from that moment forward. He hadn't thought about it, weighed the pros and cons, or done any of the things that you were supposed to do on such an occasion: consulting soothsayers, examining entrails, weighing the odds. Just made the decision. Decided.

A bit like the decision to lose his virginity.

Henry sipped and smiled.

That had happened not too long after he had decided to go to Canada. On the boat getting there, in fact. Right in the middle of the Atlantic Ocean.

I didn't know that.

Of course, you knew that! You were there!

Well, I'd forgotten.

How could you forget something like that? It wasn't as though he got a hang nail or something. It was his virginity. Not the kind of thing you can find again once you lose it.

I know, I know. I remember it now.

Do you remember her though?

Not someone you'd easy forget, was she?

Henry felt a short sharp nudge, in his ribs.

Thirty if she was a day.

Nymphomaniac eyes.

That's what the steward said she had: nymphomaniac eyes!

They had been standing in the tiny bathroom in Henry's cabin: the steward was running Henry a bath. Henry was half afraid of him. He wasn't much used to people running him baths. More used to his Mam bawling up the stairs to remind him to clean the thing after he had finished using it.

'Our Henry, you make sure you wipe the scum off the sides now. The Vim's in the airing cupboard next to the hot water heater.'

As opposed to the cold water heater, I suppose, Mother.

'Okay, when I'm done. I'm still in it at the moment.'

' . . . the lady in the cabin three doors down. Asking about you, she was. A bit of all right, that one! Couldn't go wrong there. Would be a pity to waste it.'

She had been a bit of all right. He remembered every micro-second, even at this distance.

'Make sure you use your own towel. And hang it over the heater when you've finished. Henry! Do you hear me, Henry?'

' . . . an absolute certainty, she is. Can tell by the eyes. Nymphomaniac eyes, she's got. Those dark smudges underneath. Heavy lids. Want me to tip her the wink?'

A panderer. That's what he'd been. Henry had never thought of it that way until now. A ruddy, bloody pimp. But, oooh, the pleasure.

He hadn't hesitated.

Well, that was a decision that any red-blooded lad would have made.

As I recall, our lad here wasn't very red-blooded by the time the evening was over.

Drained he was.

'Scuse me, I think the correct word is sated.

Henry lifted the coffee cup to his lips again, grinning behind it.

Decisions.

And you've continued the pattern, haven't you?

For good or ill.

How do you mean?

There was your infamous 'for better, for worse' decision. You probably should have thought about that one just a wee bit longer.

Ouch!

You've got him there, alright! What is it they say? Decide in haste, repent at leisure? Well, the poor schmuck is still repenting. Eh, aren't you?

Henry sighed.

It didn't take you long to decide on this, did it?

The coffee?

No, not the coffee! You know! What comes next.

Go on, Henry, admit it. He's right. You decided to do it in a flash. What took the time was the how. The horrible how.

The horrible how, indeed!

28

Just because he had decided on a course of action, got an end in sight, didn't mean he knew how that end was to be accomplished. He had determined on the action, but not on the means. How would he carry his decision out? That was the question. So he had made another list. Thought about it. Weighed it. Put it aside. Came back to it. Eeeny meeny miney and moed it. Rome wasn't built in a day and Henry didn't get everything firmed up all in one fell swoop. He was determined to do it right.

One of his biggest worries was what if he did it wrong. What if he failed and had to hang around afterwards — even literally perhaps, depending on the means — to explain what he had been up to? It would be too embarrassing. The thought of Leah standing at the foot of a hospital bed, peering down at him as he emerged from a euphoric unconsciousness, as he became blearily aware that he hadn't done it right! That it had all gone wrong! Unthinkable! The trouble was, while it was unthinkable he hadn't been able to do anything else but think about it, over and over again, and he had gone back to his search for the correct method with more concentration than Banting and Best discovering whatever it was they had been discovering. Madame Curie was a piker compared to him when it came to reviewing the pitfalls of the how. His list helped him sort it out.

What do you think of hanging?

Wouldn't it hurt an awful lot?

Well, you're not going to get very far if you can't take a little pain, are you?

Yes, but there'd be more than a little, surely. I mean, have you never seen pictures of a hanged man? The tongues stick out and they go all purple.

The tongues?

The faces.

True. And the eyes bug out as well. It must be quite something.

Don't they pee their pants?

I heard that too.

Not very dignified when you think about it, Henry.

What if I were to, you know, soil myself, as well. I wouldn't know where to look.

Where would you do it anyway?

I was thinking of the gazebo in the back garden.

Is it high enough?

Think so. I'd stand on one of Leah's bloody wicker chairs and, you know, kick it away when I was ready.

Might scare Anna Karenina.

Do you know how to tie a noose? Knots can be complicated. You wouldn't want the thing to unravel when you kicked the chair away. All you'd get would be a sore neck.

Henry had given considerable consideration to the different types of knots. Not that he knew many. He was deficient in knot knowledge, and apart from the bow shank and the reef knot, he couldn't tie them very well. They fell apart at the most untrustworthy moments. There were grammatical problems attached to hanging also. When it was all over, for instance, would he have hung himself or would he have been hanged? It all seemed pretty passive whatever the tense. He wanted to go out in a blaze of glory, not in some form of the subjunctive, if that was what it was. Also, 'Henry Hung', as a headline, seemed to beg the question 'what', but then, if you thought about it carefully, so did 'Henry Hanged'. Better keep away from the noose.

Talking about height, how about the Bloor Street bridge? You know, jumping! Over the valley. They go off there by the dozen every year, swan diving to oblivion. You just never hear about it.

For God's sake! They suicide-proofed it. It would be like jumping through a harp.

Okay then, take a taxi up to Millwood. Same difference.

What if he landed on someone? It might kill them too.

It would be a bit of an imposition.

Yes, but from that height at least you'd know you were dead.

Think.

Poison is used quite a bit in those British crime shows on PBS.

Yes, but what kind would work best?

Belladonna!

Deadly nightshade, my Dad called it.

Strychnine?

Cyanide is supposed to be good.

You'd have to be very careful.

Why?

Well, wouldn't it stain? Corrode? Melt your mouth if you got just a couple of drops, even a dribble, on your lips? I mean that's what it does. Rots your gullet.

Should be quite quick though.

Okay, but where would you get it? I mean it won't be just sitting on the shelf, ready for you to put your hand on, otherwise everyone would be picking it up to get rid of their bosses and their wives.

God, you could have disposed of Leah years ago.

I'm think I could get rat poison at the hardware store. No prescription necessary.

Don't you think that's kind of common?

How do you mean?

Well, every Tom, Dick and Harry uses rat poison.

Ah, but not to off themselves! Others, yes, but not for personal consumption.

Perhaps that's because it would taste awful. Anyway, I wouldn't want them saying you had breathed your last like a bunch of rodents. She'd love that.

Well, what about an overdose? You know, thirty pills and go to sleep. No pain. No nothing. Zilch!

Sounds good, but what if it should be thirty-five and I just got woozy?

You? You get woozy from two Tylenol, for Christ's sake.

What if I threw up, vomited all over the bedspread?

What if they pumped him out and brought him back.

I can just see Leah's face.

. . .

So can I!

It's too iffy.

Gas?

The house is electric.

Ahh!

Besides, I'd get nauseous from the smell — which is why I couldn't, you know, do carbon monoxide either.

He doesn't have a garage anyway. Boulevard parking.

That's right, so if he wanted to go the carbon mono route he'd have to tie a hose to the exhaust and lead it in through the back window.

Might take time.

She'd be calling me in to do something. Wash the dishes. Put the trash out. I'd never have long enough alone and anyway, I told you, I'd be throwing up all over the place from the smell. Plus, she'd kill me if I made a mess. That's one reason I don't want to do it inside the house.

Have you thought about a razor?

Hmmm, I hadn't. But it's a thought.

A very manly way to go, I should think. Would suit you.

Swift, too.

Henry nodded his head.

Just a short sharp slice across the neck.

Right across the old windpipe.

Ear to ear.

Oh, I don't know about that. Wouldn't I hear it?

What?

Well, you know, the razor going through the skin, splitting it open like a ripe pear. It sounds a mite grizzly. Fingernails on chalkboard, I should imagine. I couldn't stand that.

I thought you were supposed to be deaf! Isn't that what this is all about? And now we present you with a perfectly reasonable way to go and you complain about the bloody sound. Come on!

I wouldn't be able to hear it out loud, but I'd hear it in my mind. A kind of ripping silk sound.

He shuddered.

Well, what about the wrists? You wouldn't be able to hear it if you did your wrists.

You could hold your arms out. Away from you. Up like this.

He could wear his ear muffs.

Not in the bath! It would look very weird when they found him. Naked in the bath with earmuffs. Jesus, that would be odd!

Why would he be naked and in the bath?

To catch the blood.

Keep Leah quiet.

They say there's no pain if you cut them under the water. Feels like peeling a banana.

Where'd you hear that, Henry?

Dunno, but I read a biography about Marat once. The fellow in the bath from the French Revolution.

He didn't kill himself. Charlotte Corday killed him.

In the bath?

Yeah, see! Women! Every time!

Yes, but it's not the same thing. Killing yourself has to be way different from someone doing it for you.

Anyway, I'm not going to do it if I have to get naked.

Can you imagine a nude Henry at his time of life. Where would be the dignity in that? Charles Atlas, he's not.

Never was, either.

The blood would colour the water. A beautiful rosy red, like Heinz. No one would see.

What about when they decanted him! He'd be, pardon the phrase, a dead weight, so to speak. They'd hoist you out, Henry, and your frilly bits would be flopping all over the linoleum, especially if you bled out.

A sigh and quiet contemplation.

How about a gun?

This is Canada! Where's our Henry going to get a gun?

Only the crooks have guns.

Henry, have you any idea where to find a gun?

He had to admit that he hadn't.

*

When he was growing up, Henry had known exactly where to find a gun. His Dad had one. He kept it in a small mahogany chest on top of the wardrobe in the front bedroom, wrapped in a piece of cloth, the same kind of cloth Henry used to polish his car. It was a revolver and Henry could remember the day he found it, how it shone in the sunlight when he took it to the window. Rummaging further, there had been a packet containing twenty-four bullets — each about the size of an AAA battery — and he was disappointed that there wasn't one missing. Something to indicate to his young mind that his Dad had actually shot someone, or at least shot the gun.

He had been a grown man before he asked about it. His Dad had got it from his friend Reg, but no one knew where Reg got it. Reg had his contacts. After the war Reg had provided them with all kinds of things. Once he had turned up with a van full of cans of fruit — apricots, peaches, pears, all kinds — and vegetables. They had stacked them in the cupboard under the stairs. The trouble was there were no labels on the cans and when his Dad said to him, 'Our Henry, go and get a can from under the stairs. We'll have it with dinner,' they never knew whether they would be opening the main course or dessert. A regular crap shoot, it had been.

After his Dad died, Henry looked in the chest for the gun. It wasn't there.

'What happened to Dad's revolver?' he asked his mother.

'Oh that! I buried it in the garden years ago.'

'What on earth for?'

His mother looked hard at Henry. Her eyes dropped to her lap and she sighed.

'Your Dad used to get depressed sometimes,' she said, 'and when he got depressed, I never knew what he might do.' She glanced up at Henry, perhaps to see how he would take such a piece of news, 'I wanted to make sure he didn't harm himself.'

He had to admit that he wasn't that surprised. His Dad could be moody sometimes.

'It's near the lupins. They were his favourites. I didn't know what else to do with it,' she laughed, shaking her head. 'I couldn't very well put it out with the rubbish.'

'What did you do with the bullets?' asked Henry.

'I dropped them down the grate at the bottom of the street. In the gutter on the corner. Two by two.' She was amused by the memory of it. 'It took several trips. I didn't want to just stand there, plopping them down. Someone might have seen me.'

'Did he notice it was gone?'

'He never said — but I think he must have been relieved if he did. I found him one day, before, polishing it in the front room. Scared me silly it did. He was smiling.'

Henry had thought about his Dad and the gun many times over the years, but he didn't really connect the thought that he might now be, in some way, copying his Dad, mimicking him. After all, his Dad hadn't done anything, had he? Nothing at all really — except clean it. In any case, nothing had defeated his Dad, not for long. He was a soldier and he had soldiered on to the end, while Henry, well, he wasn't as strong, he was only a shadow of his Dad, even if he could feel the echoes of him. The sinews. Inside.

What would his Dad say if he knew what Henry was planning? He certainly knew about the deaf part of it and what that meant, and his Dad had never been able to abide Leah. But then he had Mam, didn't he? He told Henry once just to leave. Get out. Go somewhere and start again: so perhaps he would have understood that part of it as well. He wouldn't have understood about the job though. His Dad would have been only too happy to be pensioned off before his time, given time to do things about the house, dig the garden (Henry always found it strange that his Dad never found the gun — especially since they were under his lupins), go down to the pub, only too happy. Henry wasn't like that. His job was just about all he had, and they had taken it away from him.

*

Perhaps I should get a gun and shoot Rowena with it.
Waste of bullets.
Her kind would probably need a silver bullet anyway.
So you're going to pass on the gun then, Henry?
I think so. Even if I got one, I wouldn't know how to use it.
Just put it in your mouth and pull the trigger.
Yes, but what if it bucked or something? Make a real bloody mess. Blow the top of my head off and brains all over the place.
Put it against your temple then. Click and gone.
What if it shifted? Might just blow his nose off. Terrible eyesore that would be.
Where would I balance my glasses then? Tell me that.
You wouldn't look very classy in your casket either, my lad, not if they had to pick half your head off the bathroom wall.
The bathroom?
That's about the only place you get much privacy in that house — unless you go outside and, if you start shooting outside, you'll scare the birds. They've just flown back North, all worn out, and wouldn't know what the hell was going on.
What about drowning?

Could work.

You thinking of the lake or a river?

Either one really. Plenty of run off swelling the rivers just now, but the current might sweep him back onto the land.

The lake is good and deep.

Aye, lad, take the ferry and, when you get half way to the island, jump.

Tentatively: They say you see your whole life passing before you when you drown.

So they say.

Well then, it wouldn't work. The last thing I want to see is my life paraded in front of me. That's what I want to escape.

For God's sake, Henry, it's only in flipping flashes!

What if I float?

Put rocks in your pockets. Virginia Woolf style. They would keep you down. It'll be over quicker.

Perhaps he could take pills first and kind of do the two together. You know, for insurance.

That's a good point, Henry. What does your insurance say? I mean, is there a suicide provision?

She doesn't get a dime if I do myself in.

Well, there you are then! Just what you want.

But what does he want? He hasn't decided anything yet.

What about jumping under a truck? Or a bus? Would that work?

Henry shuddered.

I couldn't do that. I saw that once. An accident it was, but I saw it.

*

He was out shopping with his Mam. Saturday morning. He was nine. They were downtown, loaded up with groceries and waiting at the traffic lights to cross over the road to Woolworth's. Half the town was with them and it seemed like the other half was facing them. The traffic was heavy, the Great North Road went right through the centre of the town in those days, and the crowd swallowed its exhaust as it roared by. Henry noticed a little girl on the far side of the road. To be precise, he noticed the ice cream cone she was licking. He and his Mam were headed into Woollies to buy him one. The little girl was about four. She was dressed in a pink and white checked dress and her blonde hair was in plaits that stuck out from behind her ears at right angles.

Suddenly, between the traffic — it all happened in a flash — he heard the little girl shout 'Daddy' and wave the ice cream at someone on his side of the road. Then, she dashed forward off the curb. A woman made a grab for her, but she missed. A man just a couple of feet from Henry, on the far side of his Mam, yelled, 'No, pet,

stay there!' but it was too late. The little girl was running towards him, she seemed
to be coming straight to Henry, in the road, oblivious to the passing cars and the
screech of brakes. Then the bus. It didn't see her at all and couldn't have stopped if
it had, but Henry, and everyone else, saw everything. The front mud guard caught
her neck as she ran, slicing through it. It was a good clean slice, as though the branch
of a young tree had been lopped off with an electric saw. Her head made a lazy arc
up into the air while the rest of her disappeared under the tyre. The ice cream
cone followed the head in a smaller arc — Henry would be reminded of the two of
them in geometry class when they were studying the properties of concentric circles
— until the ice-cream and the cone separated and fell back to earth, splashing up
against the side of the bus. Strawberry, it looked like.

He remembered the ice cream more than he did the blood, but he hardly saw
that anyway. His mother yanked his arm and dragged him away before the little girl's
head hit the pavement and bounced into the gutter almost at the feet of her Dad.
His Mam didn't stop until they were out of sight of everything that had happened
and then she led him, running almost, along to his Dad's pub. She handed him over,
put his hand safely into his Dad's big hand, before she went into violent hysterics. At
the time, these frightened Henry more than what he had witnessed. He had never
seen his mother like that before, and he never did again. She wasn't the type.

He was incoherent himself. He babbled on about an ice cream cone and how
he had been going to get one and how it had smeared against the side of the bus
and what a waste it was, but it had been a long time before he had eaten another ice
cream — and never strawberry — and he didn't cross at that crossing again even
when he went back to visit years later.

Sometimes, he wondered what the little girl's life would have been like if she
hadn't seen her Dad standing on the far side of the road that morning, what would
have become of her, what she would have made of herself, but as time went on,
although he remembered everything else about that morning, he found that he
could no longer recall her face. Everything else, but not her face. It worried him
that he could remember the ice cream but not her. It didn't seem right somehow,
and only gradually had he come to realize that this was the way the world was, this
was the way things ended up. The people were less important than the things. All
that remained after the grand essentials were gone were the little things, the bits
and pieces of life.

It was his remembrance of the little girl that finally gave Henry the how, the way,
and in an instant, he saw her again, saw her as clear as day. It was Henry she was
calling out to, not to her Dad, and it was Henry she was running towards. Henry was
the one who would catch the cone. And it was he who would lick it into eternity.

29

At five of eleven, Boney appeared on the other side of the partition, and said, apparently surprised, 'Oh, you're there are you? I've booked a room.' Since Boney had spent the previous half an hour bobbing up and down at three minute intervals, sounding panicked, ready to ululate, asking questions about this project and that one (Henry responded in a binary manner), Henry was sure that where he was was no great mystery.

'They'll be starting to talk if you don't look out!' he replied.

'What?!' Boney's voice was higher than a counter-tenor in an opera by Handel. His face was ashen.

'Well, us two booking a room. Together.' Henry said it straight.

'Oh oh! Ha ha!' Boney's relief was palpable. He practically melted before Henry's eyes. 'Just about ready?'

Henry looked at the screen of his computer. Yes, he supposed he was just about ready. He had spent his time after the wellness meeting deleting personal emails from his computer. After that, he had had the interesting idea of omitting the occasional paragraph from the different reports he was working on. Nothing too obvious and great big whacks of information didn't go missing, just enough to confuse readers and discombobulate their thought processes. At first, Henry had meant to delete entire documents, but that seemed a tad mean, so he cut and pasted them instead. He pasted parts of Executive Summary A into Report B and the conclusions of Proposal C into Working Paper D. Etcetera.

Then, warming to his task, he copied sections of a confidential email from Rowena, in which she implied that the massive losses being suffered by her Mortgage Group were caused as much by employee sloth as criminal intent, into an article that Olaf had written, pseudononymously for Boney, to be published in the Division's e-zine. The subject was the statistical probability of third world hackers breaching the bank's mainframe. He knew for a fact that Boney had only the vaguest idea of what a mainframe was — Olaf had spent half an hour failing to explain it to him — but the article might now get an audience. Henry forwarded it to Olaf for publication bright and early Monday morning.

Getting into the spirit of things, Henry had hopped from the Intranet to the Internet where he entered a porn site using his corporate credit card and obtained a year's subscription for the bank. He purchased a screen saver consisting of a very busty brunette doing unmentionable things to a gentleman's member. He then rearranged some of his desktop icons — Olaf had taught him how — so that the divisional logo appeared on the cusp of her not-so-private parts. He had been sitting there wondering if he had the expertise to superimpose Rowena's head on the brunette when Boney appeared like a jack in the box before him.

'Lead on then, McDuff!' Henry said. 'Oops, sorry. Wrong group of Celts!'

Boney sat with his back to the door, ready perhaps for a quick escape.

'Well, Henry,' he said, 'I'm not sure if you know what this meeting is about.'

'Oh yes,' Henry replied, cheerfully. 'You said you wanted to brief me on the meeting you want me to attend for you. This afternoon. I'll have time to prepare before lunch.' And he added, as though he had just thought of it: 'Perhaps we could have lunch together?'

He was the essence of earnestness, a paragon of professional dedication. His Dad giggled. He was standing behind Henry, hand resting on his shoulder. A big grin was spread across his face. Henry felt the strong engineer's fingers starting to massage his neck. Leaning his head into the pressure of the fingers, he was tempted to place his own hand on top of them.

'Eh?!' said Boney, at sea. 'Meeting? Lunch?'

'Well, I always think it is best to be prepared, don't you?'

His Dad poked him in the back, not in a recriminatory fashion, rather a gentle reminder to be nice.

'Give over, lad,' he said, 'he's only doing his job. He can't help it. And Welsh, didn't you say he was? Let's have a look.' He peered at Boney across the desk to see if he could spot any of the features of Boney's antecedents. 'Looks normal enough. Make him say something.'

Henry laughed, 'But you can't hear him anyway. You're deaf!'

'Aye, lad, but sometimes you can see it in the way they move their mouths.' His Dad put on his glasses, dark old-fashioned horn-rimmed spectacles they were, to examine Boney more closely. 'Nervous enough fellow anyway.'

Boney was busy trying to unglue the back of a tongue that had temporarily adhered itself to the roof of his mouth. He cleared his throat.

'Yes?' said Henry, and with concern, 'You okay, Llewellyn? You're looking a bit pale.'

Dad poked Henry again. 'Be kind now! Definitely Welsh! It's the eyes. Gives them away every time.'

'I'm a, I'm a, I'm ahh fine.'

Henry was all pleasant conversation.

'I see you've still got your taxi chit. Going somewhere?'

Boney slammed his hand down on top of the offending piece of paper. All three men jumped. Far off, somewhere on the floor, someone screamed. Wailed. It was strange that Henry should hear it, it must have been really loud. His Dad reached out and touched the wall absorbing the vibration.

'Another poor sod,' he said. 'Feels like a woman.'

Henry had had enough.

'Dad,' he said, 'Shut up, and let's get this done.'

Boney gave no sign of having heard this, but it was not said in Henry's imagination.

'Okay, son. I'll just take a seat next to you and rest my weary bones awhile.'

'You were saying . . .' said Henry to Boney, throwing him, if not precisely a lifeline, then at least a piece of twine.

Boney grabbed it.

'Well, yes. Well, you know Henry, Rowena was going to have to make some cuts, and you can have no idea how hard it has been for her to make such heavy decisions, because, of course, its not the kind of thing one wants to do, now is it, Henry? I mean, its not her fault.'

'Whose then?' Henry slipped in the words while Boney took a breath. The voice of rational questioning.

'Oh, ah, oh. Not mine! I was all for keeping you but, umm, you know how it is.'

'No, I don't. How is it?'

Henry felt the muscles that were keeping his smile intact quiver and he flexed them. So I was right. It was true all along.

Boney rushed on, a salmon fighting its way up stream determined to spawn. Nothing was going to stop him now: not a weir, not a dam, not a big brown bear leaning over the stream with its paws ready to flick him into the air for breakfast.

'It is good news really. There's a settlement of course, very generous I think you'll find it, and an educational allowance, and and and you're the only one who they're going to bridge to early retirement.'

So there are others.

'No one else receives that,' Boney said it eagerly, gaily almost. 'I insisted on that, Henry. None of the other fifty-six gets that.'

Fifty-six.

It was a massacre, Henry thought. It really was a scream that he'd heard. His Dad had lowered his head so that it rested on his arms. He was weeping. So many! These were people Henry knew. They had obligations. Credit card balances. Many had small children. People who had been willing to come in early and stay late and they were to be let go. Just like that! It really didn't matter about him. He was of an age. He was white, male, well-paid, overqualified and over fifty. He had a bull's eye painted in the middle of his forehead. He had expected it. What did he think? That Boney would recognize who did all the work, and jump on his sword? That Rowena would say, 'If they go, I go,' and accompany the fifty-six — fifty-seven, if he included himself — to the unemployment line?

'But you'll give everyone time to find another position internally?' Henry asked, 'What is it usually? Three months to look?'

'Er, No.'

'But you'll allow me to take the settlement over two calendar years so that I don't get strangled with income tax?'

'Er, No.'

'But what about finishing our projects?'

'No, no no! Everything is effective as of today. Today.' Yelp.

Boney looked at his watch.

'Now Henry, this is no reflection on you.'

No, indeed! It wasn't a reflection, it was a great shining spotlight.

'It has nothing to do with you really.'

Abso-bloody-lutely nothing at all. I just happen to be the poor sod sitting here. Should have stayed home.

'It's a business decision.' Boney seemed to like the phrase and he pounced on it. 'Yes, that's what it is. It's a business decision.'

Henry's Dad stood up. He raised his hands above his head and began to tango around the room, snapping his fingers, singing in a throaty baritone.

'Well, you're certainly giving our Henry the business!'

Boney reached into his jacket pocket, drew out a handkerchief, blew his nose loudly into it and wiped his eyes.

'Definitely, Welsh,' said Henry's Dad. 'A tenor, too.'

Henry reached across the table and snatched the handkerchief away from Boney's face.

'Am I,' he said, 'Am I supposed to feel sympathy for you? Is that it? You silly little man! Do your bloody job and let's get it over with. Then you can crawl away and bawl your eyes out, if you like.'

Henry's Dad hallooed. He jumped onto the table, nearly toppling it over. His work boots tore into the manila envelope, lacerating it, almost shredding the taxi chit. His heels chomped down on Boney's fingers and Boney lifted them high, palms outwards. He was sobbing. Perhaps the stigmata would appear shortly. Pictures at eleven!

Henry threw the handkerchief down on the table. 'Pull your fucking self together!' he said. 'What do we have to do to finish this farce?'

*

Fifteen minutes later, Henry opened the door and let Boney out of the room. The Division was completely silent. All the cubicles were empty. His Dad leading the way, they went back to Henry's desk. Boney drew up the rear. Olaf had disappeared.

'Not Olaf?' asked Henry.

Boney seemed surprised that Henry would ask. 'No,' he said, 'I sent him away.'

Bettina was nowhere in sight. 'Bettina?'

'No, not Bettina either,' said Boney,'

'I shouldn't have thought so. If she went, you wouldn't know how to find your zipper to go to the loo.'

His Dad was doing somersaults over the three high credenza, throwing file folders into the air, but Boney seemed not to notice.

'I. I have to show you out,' he said. His tone was a near to an apology as Henry had heard from him yet.

'Out?' replied Henry.

'Yes. Out. The feeling is that you know too much. We can't allow you to use your computer. Olaf has turned it off. You may try to take information, stuff, with you. You know — the business.'

From the look on his face, Henry could see that Boney did not believe what he was saying, but believe it or not, it was being said. Henry felt as though a long sharp sword had been surgically inserted up his backside. A colonoscopy on his career. Did they really think so little of him, think that he would stoop so low as to steal from them? That he would jettison the loyalty of thirty plus years to thieve from them just because they had stolen his job from him?

Purloin the bank's intellectual property?

Now there's an oxymoron!

It was a moment before he could speak.

'You really are a shit, you know,' he said to Boney. Boney flinched. 'A little shit, but shit for sure, you and the boss you rode in on.'

Henry's Dad had foxtrotted over to Boney's cubicle. When he heard what was being said, he stopped and stood still, looking at his son. He held his hand out towards him, but Henry shook his head. It had been a long time since he had felt very much, but he was overcome with such a tremendous sadness it threatened to break him then and there. His eyes blinked. His knees wanted to buckle.

He said unsteadily, 'So in one short hour I have ceased to exist!'

Boney, misunderstanding, said, 'No. You must leave now.'

He shoved the manila envelope at Henry. 'This is your package. Read everything. You can come back on Friday at three o'clock to pack your personal things. If you have any questions, you can ask me then. Okay? Is that clear?'

Boney was right to ask. Tears glazed Henry's eyes and it was impossible for him to think.

'What?' he asked. 'What did you say?'

Boney pushed him towards the door.

'Read the manual, Henry,' he said. 'Oh, and give me your floor pass.'

Henry was unable to move. It was his Dad who reached inside his coat pocket, took out his wallet and, from it, the small laminated pass. He put it into Boney's hand, careful not to let their fingers touch.

'Here,' said Boney, 'is a taxi chit.'

Henry stood in the foyer. He had handed over part of his identity with his floor pass and he needed to rest his shoulders against the wall. His briefcase stood against his leg. He had no idea how it got there. He rubbed his eyes and felt the building sway slightly, structured steel creaking with a mournful yaw as it sometimes did in a high wind. Today, it is sighing, he thought. It has witnessed murder. In the name of profit.

An elevator dinged its approach but Henry didn't hear. He looked at the taxi slip but hardly knowing what it was, he tore it up. He tore it into tiny pieces. Tore it so that the pieces fell like confetti on the cold marble floor.

'Not a taxi, not today.'

The elevator door opened unbidden and stood empty in front of him. He bent down to pick up his briefcase, not realizing that his overcoat was somehow on his back, his scarf hanging loose around his neck. Then, taking his father's hand in his own, he entered the elevator, and pressed Down.

30

'Splendid, my lad, splendid!' said his Dad. 'Well done! Well handled!'

They were on the subway going North, but not going home. It was the middle of the day after all. Going. Where? Somewhere. Henry found a seat near the door and was clutching his briefcase to his lap. The manila envelope was inside. His Dad had shoved it in while Henry had been searching for his subway tokens. Henry hadn't quite wanted to chuck it out until he read the fine print, the ifs, the ands and the buts. Knowing it was there however, made him feel like a man who was carrying the results of a cancerous biopsy about with him. The verdict was awful, but the outcome was still in doubt. He rubbed the flap of his briefcase with the pad of his thumb, caressing the old leather, warming it to his touch.

There was no room for his Dad to sit down and Henry was about to give him his seat. His Mam always insisted he give up his seat when an older person needed it and he still had the habit. Not like today's kids. His Dad, however, sat down next to him anyway just about squishing an old woman in a faded blue parka. He was almost on top of her. Henry was a bit concerned.

He leaned round his Dad to speak to her.

'I hope he's not too heavy,' he said. 'Old people — like yourself — lose weight when their bones become bleached and brittle. He might break you. Terrible thing really, to get old, but it won't happen to me.'

He winked.

The old woman didn't seem to understand a word he was saying. She was peering at his briefcase.

'You wouldn't want it, I can tell you that,' he said. 'Nothing inside worth having, not for an old lady like you. Not for anyone. You wouldn't even want the golden handshake it came with. You'd never know where the hand had been — customers' pockets, probably.'

He nodded awkwardly to her in the crush of the subway car, the briefcase on his lap.

'Give over, Henry,' said his Dad. 'She's not listening to a word you're saying. Quite comfortable leaning against her though, I must say.' He ran a hand through his silver hair. 'You'd think that such a little bag of bones would be prickly but the parka is well padded even if she isn't.'

He bounced up and down.

'Not bad at all. Perhaps the subway could make it a project. Employ little old ladies, nationality not important, fit them out in padded parkas and park 'em for the comfort of the travelling masses. Not a bad idea, if I do say so myself.'

'Dad,' said Henry, 'I don't think she can breathe.'

'What do you mean?

'Well, her nose is buried in your shoulder. You must be stifling her with your muffler.'

'Rubbish!' his Dad replied, and turning towards the old woman with a wink, he continued, raising the volume with exaggeratedly broad North Country syllables, 'You're alright aren't you, missis? Happen there's plenty of room for't two of us! Happen it's just what we need to keep t'cold out, isn't it, love? A little bit cuddle and we'll all be right as rain.'

*

There had always been that element of embarrassment with his Dad. Beatrice Lillie might not have liked to hear it, but her encounter with him was by no means unique. You never knew when he would yell out, might forget that he was supposed to speak normally, forget that just because he couldn't hear Mam or Edward or Henry himself, it didn't mean that they couldn't hear him. Like Vesuvius, his Dad could suddenly erupt. Mam would shush him of course, put her hand on his arm, shake her head and say, 'Philip!' and he would generally quieten down, but as far as Henry was concerned, ten year old Henry or sixteen year old Henry, the damage was done. People would be staring at them, startled out of their own conversations, pulled out of their own private worlds, looking at them all as though the door had opened and a lunatic had stepped in. A bipolar maniac on day parole. In restaurants, waiters would appear, wringing their hands like a washcloth, hovering. 'Is everything, all right, madam?' Never a mention of his Dad. On the bus, everyone would turn round to see who was creating the disturbance. 'Could you keep it down, please? We don't want to disturb the other passengers, do we?'

A hand on the arm didn't always work.

'What's the matter now, woman?' his Dad might bawl, ramping up the volume to reach the very back pew in the church or the farthest aisle in the supermarket. 'Aren't I allowed to speak?'

It had been a very long time before Henry came to understand that part of that was a game. His Dad was having fun. No, he really didn't know the sound of his own voice, but he was a smart man and he surely knew how to modulate it. He could change the tone of his voice in an instant, when he wanted it to. Henry came to understand that it was a bit of a lark for his Dad to make a spectacle of himself, although the recognition came far too late in Henry's young manhood for it to do him any good. Much too late to avoid the burning red face of adolescence, the embarrassment at being singled out, the fright of knowing it would surely happen again. Then there was the guilt he felt at the hatred that welled up when it did happen. Hatred, he had to admit, was not too strong a word to use sometimes.

The night Henry really twigged what was going on, finally realized clearly what his Dad was up to, was one of the sweetest nights of his life, and one of the saddest.

He had flown over to visit his parents. He did it every spring, leaving Leah behind to look after the girls. She didn't want to go anyway. On that particular evening, his Dad had taken him to his pub. It wasn't really his pub, of course, but he clearly felt it belonged to him: 'my sodality' he called it. That night there were a couple of dozen other putative owners on the premises, and his Dad hadn't been too pleased that his place at the bar, right at the end (so he could sit with his back to the mirror and the horse brasses), was occupied. The barman shook his head.

'They're all in tonight, Phil,' he said. 'I don't know where they come from! Take a pew and I'll bring you one over.' He nodded at Henry. 'Hello, Henry. Your Dad said you'd be visiting. Good to see you. What can I get for you?'

'He won't have a pint, George. Ale's not his tipple. Give him tot of brown rum and sink it in coca-cola. Dreadful stuff. Some crisps as well, if you please. And the dominoes.'

George was 'Mine Host' but his Dad was 'Master of the House'.

George laughed. They went through this every time Henry showed up. Both of them knew their parts cold and Henry's Dad couldn't hear a word anyway. This time, though, they had to shout above the din.

His Dad was on his second pint and clobbering Henry at dominoes when Henry noticed that his Dad kept looking around to see who was there. He was frowning. When he first come to the pub several years ago, they had been part of a group. His Dad had known everyone.

'Hey, Phil. You're late!'

'Got the boy with you? Come sit.'

'George, the usual for Phil.'

'Henry, still drinking that swill?'

All his Dad's friends. They spoke to his Dad the same way they spoke to anyone else, to one another, but if he missed a word or a thought or a sentence, they would mouth the words a little more carefully, and if he still missed it, they'd raise a mock arm or an elbow, and make fun.

'Give over, our Phil. You know exactly what I'm saying.'

And when he didn't, they'd settle down to explain. Act it out. Make faces. Trace the letters in spilled ale, if necessary. Once, Henry remembered, they'd asked George for a pencil and a piece of paper.

That was the night of the shrimp teas.

'Henry wants to go to London to see what? I don't get it.'

The others were roaring with laughter.

He glared at Henry with a look that said, why on earth would you or anyone else want to go to London in the first place.

Henry mouthed the words, 'To see a . . .' No sound. There was no need. He pursed his lips and bared his teeth, sounding out the letters. He must have looked demented.

His Dad shook his head. The frustration showed. He was not one to hide it. One by one, Albert, Reg, Bill, Tommy, Robbie, and even George tried to make him understand.

'Shrimp teas?!' said his Dad. 'He can get a shrimp tea at a café in Northgate, for Pete's sake!'

Everyone, Henry remembered, fell about laughing. Dad was egging them on, yes, but Henry knew he hadn't caught the word, hadn't been able to get it.

'Hey up, enough of this lot,' said Reg, loyal, reliable Reg, 'Get a piece of paper, George. And another round. This is dry work.'

Reg wrote the word on a napkin. He held it in front of his ample belly.

'To see a . . .' he mouthed, and showed the word.

Striptease.

Most of his Dad's friends were dead now, and the one who was left, Robbie, was kept locked up in a back bedroom somewhere. Robbie hadn't been too swift in his younger years and, as his Dad had explained it once over a lachrymose pint, it was either that or put him away entirely, 'and Hilda wouldn't stand for that.' Hilda, Henry presumed, was the woman who kept the key. It was difficult to keep up with the bits of his Dad's life from so far away. Leah couldn't have cared less, of course.

His Dad's mind was clearly not on the game. He didn't try to make the tiles bounce like he usually did when he slammed them down. He didn't even try to cheat.

'You feeling okay?' Henry asked.

'Aye, lad. Fine. Just thinking that your Mam should have come with us.'

Henry laughed. 'That'll be the day when I see our Mam playing dominoes in a pub!'

His Dad shook his head ruefully. 'You're right about that! Not a pub woman at all. Not she. Except the Ladies Lounge sometimes. Likes a small gin and tonic, mind, but prefers it in the privacy of her own house, she does.' He paused, looking at his tiles. 'Still, she never minded me coming out.'

'She's probably glad to get rid of you for a couple of hours.' Henry said it with a grin and his Dad grinned back.

'You're right about that, I say you're right about that. Now how about another?'

It was then that Henry made his mistake.

'Not for me,' he said, with a shake of his head. 'I think I've had enough for tonight.' Even as he said it, he knew it was the wrong thing to say.

'Well, I'll have another.' There was a petulance in the voice and his Dad declaimed the words. Henry should have known; he should have anticipated. His Dad turned away from him, towards the bar to get George's attention, and bellowed, 'George!' The rising baritone cut through the roar of the semi-drunken bonhomie that surrounded them. It bounced off the walls and caused people who were shouting themselves to turn and look.

Henry flinched and said, 'Shhh!' He said it automatically — as he had so often in the past — but his Dad wasn't looking. Didn't want to know.

'George!!'

The roar of the room dimmed, defeated by the blast of the one peremptory word. George was looking over at them and raised his hand, an acknowledgement. He didn't speak, but he was smiling.

'When you have a chance!' Henry's Dad commanded.

'Keep it down, mate,' yelled a man from the next table.

'Yeah, keep it to a dull roar, old man, we're not deaf!

Henry reached out and laid his hand on his father's arm.

'I think he heard you,' he said. A nervous giggle. 'I think they all did.'

His Dad turned to look at him, pulled his arm away, and raised his eyebrows.

'You sure now?' He bawled at Henry with the ferocity of a gale force wind. Henry fancied it roiling towards him. He ducked to shield his eyes from the blast.

It was then that he saw the twinkle. The light finally dawned, after all those years. His Dad knew exactly what he was doing! He knew! He knew what was going on around him and he was saying 'To Hell with the lot of you!' Henry included. He was having his fun. He couldn't hear, his friends were dead, his son had finished drinking with him for the nonce, but, by God, he was here and he was alive and he was as good as the best of them.

You really are a crafty old bugger, thought Henry. He could hardly wait to tell Edward. It's a game! Or part of it's a game, anyway. You know exactly how loud you are and you do it on purpose. In that instant, he relived his whole life. Then he raised a finger, wagged it at his Dad and started to laugh. His Dad turned away, continuing the charade, an all time Academy Award performance. Henry knew that he would not acknowledge either the finger or the laugh, but he could see the slightest twitch at the corner of his Dad's mouth.

'George!!!' Henry had never heard him so loud. 'He won't have one. So you have one on me!'

With that, he looked down at the tiles and began puffing out his cheeks in a whistle of concentration.

Whenever Henry thought about that night afterwards, he loved his Dad more than he ever had. It made him sad that his Dad had had to face the world that way, but it made him happy as well. Most of all, it made him proud, so very proud of his Dad. His Dad had faced the silence, and had continued to shout into it until the very end. At the same time though, Henry knew that he wouldn't, couldn't, fight like that, couldn't keep on going day by day, alone in a silent world with no one to care. That's the difference between thee and me, he said to himself, and he shrugged.

'Fuck it,' said Henry, turning towards his Dad in the crowded subway car, but his Dad was no longer there.

He looked at the old woman next to him, asleep or perhaps even dead, he wasn't sure which, and he knew he was alone. He knew it like a cancer patient must know it, he knew it like someone in free fall towards the concrete forty stories below knows it. He was completely alone.

31

When Henry arrived at the house that evening, after wandering about in a daze for most of the afternoon, it was already dusk. He stood at the bottom of the driveway next to the empty garbage cans she would be expecting him to take round the back and put away under the deck. Well, he thought, one last time won't hurt. He looked up at the big, unlit, bay window, the curtains already drawn to protect them from prying eyes, and he knew exactly what was going on in the house. Today was Wednesday. Okay. One, possibly two, of his daughters (the eldest had married a large, thick Mountie and lived in Northern Manitoba) would be here for dinner. The good thing was it was 'Girls' Night Out'. After dinner Henry would be invited — with a giggle — to leave, to go to the den.

'Well, Henry, why don't you go downstairs now and let us girls have a private conversation?' Leah would say.

He had trained himself not to put too much bounce into his step when he left the room.

'Change your clothes before you clean the kitchen. Don't forget to rinse the dishes before you put them into the dishwasher. And do the pots, Henry.'

The pots were the cleanest pots in the city on a Wednesday night. Henry scoured them within an inch of their lives. Still, he was glad to do it. Anything was better than having to sit in the living room, or, as she insisted on calling it, the lounge. Now there was an irony, thought Henry standing on the edge of the road wondering whether to go on in. No one ever lounged in that room. Not on the ruddy rattan.

About to turn up the driveway, his foot slipped on the sleety ice and he stumbled to steady himself. The stumble took him backward in time and he remembered another winter evening long before when he had been coming home from work late, about eight-thirty. It had been a January night, and the snow had come straight at him until he had had to stop for a moment to get a breath. The only way to get down the street was to follow the tyre treads in the middle of the road. He was making a very slow progress when, misjudging the depth of the snow and forgetting, momentarily, that there was a layer of ice underneath it, his legs flew out from under him and there he was, flat on his back, briefcase thrown aside before he had time to think.

He lay still, not at all hurt, eyes closed, allowing the snow to fall on his face. He liked the snow. There wasn't much of it to be had most winters in England, and, of late, Canada had seemed to be having less and less. Global warming or something, they said. When he first arrived it had been another story. Lying there, blinking the melting snow out of his eyes, he found himself grinning. His first Canadian snowfall had been a joyful thing. Dorcas! Dorcas adored the snow. She spent each November waiting for it to arrive. He could still remember the first time he had seen her in the snow. It was December 6th — he could still remember the date — and his roommate woke him to tell him he had a phone call. She was excited, even more exuberant than usual, and she told him, commanded him really, to look out of the window, look at the snow, to get dressed and come outside.

Fifteen minutes later, they were walking across the campus, kicking the snow in front of them. Dorcas threw great powdery clouds of the stuff at him — packing a snowball was too time consuming for her — and Henry shoved as much as he could manage down the back of her open coat. At a small incline, where banks of flowers were planted in the summer, she threw herself down and lay grinning up at him.

'Let's make angels,' she said. 'Come! I've always wanted to make angels in the snow!'

He fell backwards next to her and they roared with delight.

When he thought about her that evening so many years later, it was the first time in a long time, and somehow the remembrance exhilarated him. He looked up into the night, put his tiredness aside, loosened the buttons of his overcoat, and he made angels one more time.

*

It was quite a few minutes before he began to feel the cold of the night, and before Dorcas began to recede into the comfortable corners of his memory. He didn't want to get up and it was with an effort that he eventually hoisted himself to his feet and gingerly continued his journey. He shook the snow off his overcoat, brushing his gloved hand down his front, caught between his memories and the frigid reality of the night. He saw that the driveway had not been cleared and that the snow lay deep on each of the steps leading up to the front door. The porch light was off.

The thought went through Henry's head that perhaps he should knock on the door, perhaps he should announce himself, but, instead, he tucked his briefcase under his arm, opened the outer screen door and inserted his key in the lock. The only sound he could hear as he stepped into the hall was the sound of the television.

'Hello, I'm home! It's me!' he called out. 'Anybody here?'

'Is that you, Henry?' he heard Leah's voice asking absently.

'No dear, it's the Scarborough Rapist!' he called back, somewhere between amusement and disappointment. 'Who did you think it was?'

No response.

'Did the girls get here alright?" he asked.

No response.

'Girls?'

'Shhh, Daddy, we're playing Scrabble.'

Suddenly, he was on the edge of annoyance.

'It would only take a moment to reply, you know.'

Silence.

'Do you hear me?!'

'Oh, Henry . . .'

'Oh, Daddy . . .'

Leah and the girls were seated on the carpet. The only light was a floor lamp that had been angled to shine on a Scrabble board.

'Well!' he said, 'Bubble, bubble, toil and trouble for someone, I imagine.'

No one was listening.

'Henry, quad is a word, isn't it?' said Leah, asking for confirmation.

'Quadrangle. Not just quad, Mommy,' interjected one of the girls.

'No abbreviations,' warned another.

'No supper?' asked Henry.

'It's in the oven,' his wife said, her mind elsewhere.

'Cold as a dog's nose, I expect,' said Henry.

'Ummm,' said Leah.

'Oh Daddy . . . !'

'Put everything in the dishwasher when you're finished.'

Leah waved in the general direction of the kitchen and her tiles, kept in the palm of her hand for secrecy's sake, flew through the air.

'Oh, Henry, now look what you have done!'

A chorus of high dudgeon 'daddies' followed him out of the room.

*

It was the same January evening that Henry renamed the girls. How it came about, he was never quite certain. Perhaps it began when he opened the fridge.

Any beer, Henry?

I don't think so, but you could ask her?

Who? Leah?

Why not? Nothing to fear from Leah!

Easy for you to say.

It's an interesting name, Leah is.

Waiting for his food to warm, Henry thought about it.

There's a jet, isn't there? A small one.

Not the same spelling, my lad.

Oh, is Lear like the king, then?

Or are you like him?

The thought took flight.

Poor old sod had three daughters too, didn't he?

You're right there, Henry

Can't remember their names though.

Larry, Curly and Moe, wasn't it?

Give over! Let Henry think.

Well, one was Cordelia. I remember that. She was the good one. Another was . . .

He tried to decide which of the girls was most like Cordelia, but for the life of him he couldn't find a pennyworth of difference among them: it would have been a calumny to say that any one of them was more attentive or affectionate than any other. But he had his names! In the end, he never did assign a particular name to a particular girl. They became a moveable feast: whichever one came to mind was applied. Regan. Goneril. What was the difference? It was done with a smidgen of affection, but there was also melancholy ambivalence in what he was doing. Henry knew that somehow he had failed his girls, but the countervailing argument that sometimes ricocheted about in his brain was that they had failed him too.

Of course, the names were his own private joke. He never used them out loud. Well, almost never. In recent months, he would have had to admit, he had slipped occasionally, but the sad thing was it seemed to provide another proof that none of them listened to him anyway. Only once had a comment been made.

'Henry, we are talking about Tiffany's birthday party. What on earth does the President of the United States have to do with anything?' Leah had asked one evening when they were sitting alone in front of the fire. 'Sometimes I think you are losing your mind.'

32

Still not quite ready to go into the house, Henry walked carefully up the drive, along the side of the house and into the back garden. At the far end of a narrow path was what he called a conservatory. What his Dad said, much more prosaically, was a shed. Leah had named it her gazebo. It was made of wood, he had built it himself, lots of lattice in lieu of wicker, about ten feet high at the apex and almost eight feet across. Two steps led up to an outdoor carpet floor on which were placed two chairs (white, rattan) and a small table (also white, wicker). Henry was sure Leah consented to leaving them out in the winter snow for the visual effect.

There was a patina of ice on the chairs and he dabbed at one of them with a gloved hand, stirring a tiny melee of crystals that subsided slowly, twinkling in the early twilight. He put his briefcase by his side and sat down. He knew that he looked smart in his banker's black coat and silk scarf. Only the Walmart rubbers spoilt the picture. It struck him that he must provide quite a contrast against the white paint of the conservatory. He felt more in tune with the dingy grey of the old snow that still covered most of the ground and he turned to look around the garden. It was his garden. Leah had little to do with it — except to suggest that he might like to get outside and do something in it. At this time of year, it was at its worst. The snow was wretched and little patches of confused greenery, the product of the few warmer days they had had, were interspersed with it and the dead foliage he had not got around to raking away in the fall. A frosty February had just about flattened everything, forcing it close to the earth; even the sere stalks of his beloved lupins sagged against the cold. It would take some time for everything to spring back. He wouldn't be around to see it.

Henry had turned his hearing aids off as he walked down his street, and he listened to the silence that surrounded him. He thought of turning them back on, but he became distracted by the sight of his breath in the cold evening air. He could look at it in front of him, rising in front of his eyes, evaporating into the night. He breathed out to see how quickly a part of him could disappear, could vanish in the gloom of the evening. It gave him pause that his breath disappeared so completely. That breath, the essence that made him Henry, went phffft before his eyes and it was comforting to know that his demise would come to pass so easily. There would be no pain.

A squirrel, one of the grey ones with only the memory of a tail, appeared on the low fence of the conservatory, its face angled to stare.

'What are you doing here?' it said, scornfully. 'Get inside and keep warm. This isn't your season. You never come out after the leaves fall. Leave me alone to scrounge for food. Bugger off.'

Henry was about to tell it to get off his land, but he stopped short. He leaned back and lifted his chin so that he could see into the night. No stars, he thought; this is the city. He wiped his eyes with the back of his hand and, when he looked again, the squirrel had gone. He sat down on one of the chairs. It was cold, but he didn't want to get up. To get up would be to begin again, and he wasn't sure he could do that, not sure that he wanted to, pretty sure, in fact, that he didn't want to. So he sat. He wasn't sure what he was thinking about, not much of anything really, which was strange, because he had the kind of mind that was always on the go, active, considering the eventualities, acting out the possibilities, play acting at his own life. He thought again of his father.

'I love you, Dad,' he said.

The words erupted into the night.

'But I'm not as strong as you are. I can't, I can't keep on like you did. We're not the same. You had Mam, and I . . .' He was unable to complete the sentence. 'What do I have?'

Tears dried to rivulets of ice on his face. His ears turned red and his fingers and toes itched from the cold. Gradually, he became calm.

Time passed.

He listened.

'Are you there?' he said, tentatively.

But it was not his Dad to whom he spoke.

There was no answer that he could hear and he wondered whether it would be better if he turned his hearing aids on, but, no, he didn't think so. It shouldn't be necessary, surely.

'Can you hear me?'

He asked the question tentatively, biting his bottom lip after he said the words, hardly breathing.

'I need to hear from you.'

He shrugged his shoulders and, a little hesitantly, continued wryly, 'If you can hear me, you only have to give a sign. I will know. Knock three times on the wood or break off a branch from a tree. Show me a light. Let me see a light!'

Henry shouted this, abruptly shouted it into the night, and was immediately embarrassed. This was not a game! Hanging his head, he took out his handkerchief and blew his nose, the ice in his nostrils shattering under the force of his hand. He mopped his eyes, wiped his face and tried to get a breath. He seemed to have no breath left.

'Please!' he said.

From nowhere, Anna Karenina bounded onto the low table in front of him. She stared up at him, opening her mouth in a long plaintive meow before jumping onto his lap. Henry held her there as she flexed her back and rubbed herself against his coat, purring and looking up into his face. Here was his pleasure. He could see her quite clearly in the dim light, and, for a moment, he thought that he was somehow being given his answer. He buried his face into her fur. He could feel the purring — it had been a long time since he had really heard it — but he knew that she could turn it off in an instant. Cats did that. Even as he thought this, she stopped in mid purr, jumped down, stretched and stalked off into the night. Anna Karenina was only a cat.

'Please,' he repeated the word.

The long vowels of the word drifted away into the night.

'If you are there, I will hear you. If you are there, I will do exactly what you tell me to do. Just let me hear you. One more time.'

He swallowed a shallow breath of damp air.

'What should I do?' he said. 'Should I just go on? Leave the job? There is no job! Let them push me out the door, down the elevator shaft and off into the night? Leave the people I know, work I like, do well at? Try to find something else? How can I, when I won't be able to hear what they say to me? Couldn't answer questions because I wouldn't know what the questions were. Should I go in and tell Leah about it, weep on her shoulder? Wait for sympathy? Should I continue because everyone says you have to continue? Do something else? Find a new solution? But what is wrong with my solution? Would I be wrong to act on it?'

He paused again.

'Or is there too much on your plate? Too much to do in this ramshackle world?'

He felt as though he was running a race and needed a second wind, needed to take huge gulps out of the night air, bites to fill his lungs with its impersonal coldness.

A new thought essayed its way into his brain.

'Are you listening? Can you hear me? Do you hear anyone?'

And another thought, 'Or are you deaf, too?'

Then came words wrenched from him. 'Do you care?'

Henry listened to the silence. The silence of the evening, the silence of his hope, the silence of his life.

He added, not quite an afterthought, 'If you are there.'

33

Henry was weary by the time he finally went upstairs to bed. Anna Karenina had been outside and he lay on the couch, hard as it was, waiting for her to appear at the front window demanding to be let in. Leah was ahead of him, her backside turned towards him, perhaps already asleep. If she was, it was all to the good, but, if not, he could relax in the certainty that the only reason she might speak to him again that night would be if the place was burning down around their ears. Such an eventuality — what was the phrase? — in and of itself, would solve his problems and he eased himself under the covers.

There was no way he was going to sleep. It had been quite the day. Even the expected can be unexpected when it finally happens, when push comes to shove. He began to do what he often did: he recounted his day, went through it, considered it, weighed it. He had been doing this for years. His world might be defined by the commonplace, but Henry had learned that he could embellish it in the half an hour or so before he slipped into sleep. He could set it to music, add trumpets to timpani and orchestrate it. He did this quite consciously, knew what was going on and he enjoyed doing it. It was like his computer. If he went into Tools — Olaf had taught him and he was pretty certain he could do it: he had notes — he would be able to track changes, highlight them, accept them if he wanted to, and even compare versions, lives really, to pick out the better one. Sometimes he made so many changes, he had to lie there figuring out what was the truth and what was fiction. Sometimes, he didn't bother trying.

Let me think, he said to himself, and off he went.

Could he honestly say that he was saddened by the events of the day? For himself, the decision had already been made, but it must have been dreadful for the people with whom he worked. Particularly if they had been dealt with as cavalierly as he was. Boney had said there were fifty-six others and Henry lay there trying to put names and faces to each of them.

When he determined that so and so was one of those to be let go, he led him out into the long corridor that bordered the cubicles and stood him against the wall. He tried to commiserate, but most of the people were not in a frame of mind for comfort. Some of them were shaking: all of them, it seemed, were wailing into the wall and asking why.

'You! Henry!' shouted Rowena, pointing at him. She was standing on top her desk dressed like Calamity Jane, only in polyester. 'Take those strips of cloth from Bettina and put them over their eyes.'

Bettina was on the floor, cross-legged, swathes of fabric spread around her, cursing silently, ripping up the drapes. Henry felt himself move to do Rowe's bidding. It was strange how the beige curtains turned black when he tied the strips of material at the back of a person's head, but he developed a pattern, a rhythm that sped up the process. Put the cloth over the eyes, spin the body round, make a knot behind, whisper in their ear, 'Pax vobiscum', spin the body back and push the poor bastard against the wall.

'Come on, Henry, hurry up, there might be something in it for you, if you do,' bawled Rowe. Henry could almost taste the carrot and he flung the last ten or so so hard against the wall their heads bounced.

'Whee!' he shouted, 'welcome to the bumper cars!'

If he finished quickly enough — he knew this like a child believes in the Easter Bunny — they would let him off, resurrect him, keep him on. He would help with the executions, that's what he would do and that would be the end of it.

'Watch the wall, Henry!' Rowe lifted the business end of her bazooka towards him. 'Watch the fucking wall.'

He looked back and saw that Boney was following along behind him, tying the hands of each person. Henry wiped the corner of his eye with the sleeve of his pyjamas and sniffed quietly into the night.

'Olaf,' called Rowena. 'Do the needful with Henry.'

'Oh no,' Henry moaned. 'I did everything you wanted me to do. Let me go! Let me live!'

'Olaf!' Rowe warned. 'Get moving.'

Olaf stood in front of Henry but wouldn't look him in the face.

'Power to the people!' he muttered. 'Victory for the proletariat.'

'But I'm the proletariat,' said Henry as Olaf spun him round, knotting the blindfold tight at the back of his head. The battery of his left hearing aid started to beep. Beep, beep, beep. Pause. Beep, beep, beep. He would need a new battery in thirty seconds, would have to fish one out of his shirt pocket or he would be decidedly, and lopsidedly, deaf. He tried to get at it in his shirt but Boney grabbed both of his hands, spinning him round again, binding them together with the extension cord from his mouse.

'No extension for you, boyo,' laughed Boney, pushing him up against the wall.

'Llewellyn, please,' yelled Henry, 'I need to hear.'

Beep, beep, beep.

'I can't help that, Earl,' replied Boney, 'Der Rest Ist Schweigen.'

Beep, beep.

Beep.

Henry tried to free himself, but he couldn't do it. He was beginning to panic. He had co-ordinated his hearing aids so that when one battery ran out, the other one would follow suit. They would give up the ghost, as it were, in synch. The right hearing aid was more modern and there would be no warning beep. Just the silence.

'Here it comes!' said Henry to himself as the sudden rush of quietude came towards him, ending his relationship with the world. Ear muffs for the unwanted, he had often thought. He knew that the metaphor — like some of his Dad's — made little sense, but he too liked the sound of words, their cadence, their juxtaposition.

He lay in the bed. He was on his back now, arms to his side, toes pointed upwards, slightly depressed under the heavy blanket.

'Should I go further with this?' he wondered. 'Is it safe? They say if you die in a dream, you die in real life. It might happen.'

So what? I thought the whole idea was to die anyway.

Yes, but not like this. Not standing in a corridor being mowed down by a rampant Rowe.

What are you worrying about anyway? This isn't a dream. It's a reverie. You're just thinking, reorganizing your day. You're not asleep.

Are you sure?

Pinch yourself, if you don't believe me.

Henry slowly lifted his left hand over his stomach and laid it on his right arm.

'If I don't feel anything, what will it mean?'

'Everything set?' Rowena called out.

He turned his head to face the wall, leaning against it for support, sobbing into the fabric, struggling to undo the extension cord behind him.

Strange how I can hear her. I can hear everything that is going on! I can hear the screaming. I can hear her taking the safety off her weapon.

'Stand back, Boney!' yelled Rowena. 'Bettina, get your big ass out of the line of fire, for Christ's sake, if you know what's good for you. Get in line with them, Olaf, if you want to die like a dog with your comrades. This is Tiananmen Square, all over again, you vassal! Watch out.'

Henry opened his eyes, not sure whether he was staring into the dark of the night or into the black of his blindfold. He couldn't see.

Wait a minute, let's think this through. If my batteries didn't work, I couldn't have heard her. Right?

Right!

And, and if I came home, I couldn't very well have been bazookaed to bits, could I?

Do you wear your hearing aids to bed? Think!

Suddenly he could see everything quite clearly all around him.

Rowena was strafing down the line. Bodies hiccupped as the bullets plunged into them and the blood spurted out.

'Whee, watch the wallpaper!' yelled Boney.

'Ah didn't mean to tief dem computer!' came a cry from somewhere in the distance.

A low groan of anguish washed over Henry and he started to shake as Rowe moved towards him.

'For God sake, Henry, what is the matter with you?' Leah pushed his shoulder roughly. 'Keep still.'

*

There was no good reason why he should sleep. After all, what was sleep? Something about ravelled sleeves and care if he remembered right. Not much sense there. Something to recharge his batteries? He really didn't need that. By the end of the week, it would be the end of Henry, and who would care if his batteries were bunny bright and charging along? He began to think about the people who would miss him — 'might miss' might be more appropriate — counting them off on his fingers under the sheets. Would there be enough of them for a decent funeral? He sometimes thought that no one would miss him and he supposed that it really depended on the meaning of the word 'miss'. Not miss in the sense of wanting to see me often, but miss in the sense that they wouldn't mind seeing me one last time. Would want to peer down into the casket and memorize the old physog for future reference.

He had always found it a salutary experience to browse the deceased. They tended to fade away less quickly that way. Not everyone of course, not his Dad or Mam and not ever his dear dead Max — he'd never forget them — but quite a few nevertheless. Looking at a corpse kind of imprinted its face on one's memory. You fasten on just one feature and you commit it to memory. A nose was good, and he also liked lower lips, although he found you had to be careful not to go overboard. It was fine, for example, to fasten on hair with people in their prime, but he had been to a lot of funerals where, heaven knew, they were well past that. The result was he had stockpiled a whole set of comb-overs and couldn't clearly distinguish the faces underneath.

What feature, he wondered, would he want people to remember him by? Henry ran the tip of his tongue over his front teeth as he thought about it. He still had enough hair if he combed it carefully, grey at the side but still quite dark on top. Got the colour from his Mam who had been brown into her eighties. Edward was balder than the proverbial billiard ball: Henry had the hair. On the other hand, he thought wryly, Edward could still hear, so it wasn't all beer and skittles by a long chalk. In fact, sometimes the hair business annoyed him. Quite a few people, at work, at church, even relatives, had asked him in the last couple of years if he had had a dye job. One or two even asked why he had had a dye job. Cheeky buggers. Leah, in her own inimitable way, made matters worse.

'Oh no,' she announced once at a church social, 'Henry doesn't color his hair. It's natural. Why would he go grey? He doesn't have a thing in the world to worry about.'

'Unlike you,' he had replied, 'who doesn't have a natural hair on your head.' The words slipped out before he could stop them.

'Well,' she had laughed, the glint in her eye focusing directly on him, 'Well, Henry made me this way. Heaven knows!'

He paid for it afterwards.

Perhaps it wouldn't be best to be remembered by his hair. It made him look younger than he was, but, lying there in the casket, it was only attached to his scalp by a couple of staples. The nose might be better. He had his Dad's nose, not quite as straight but his Dad's nevertheless. He smiled. You couldn't remember me by the lips, I hardly have any. Got my Mam's lips, and also her eyes. Whenever Henry looked in the mirror it was his Mam he saw staring back at him. Same eyes, they were. Kind eyes, he would have to say. Green. He compressed his lips and blinked to keep back an errant tear. Of course, the best way to remember me would be by my tongue. Henry was proud of his tongue. It was long and thin and he could lick the end of his nose with it. Used to be his party piece, it did, like some people can wiggle their ears or are double jointed. Leah had stopped that.

'It's disgusting,' she had sniffed, 'What will people think?'

She had liked it well enough before they were married. 'Ooh, you remember how Henry used to make us laugh, rolling his tongue about, tying knots in cherry stalks and licking jam off the end of his nose!' She wasn't likely to admit that now. Anyway, there wasn't much point suggesting his tongue to anyone. It wasn't likely the undertaker would let it be seen: Leah would have a closed coffin before she allowed that to happen. Perhaps they could have a photo of him, mouth open, grinning, with his tongue hanging out like Lassie. Not very likely.

Whatever happened though, it was his funeral. They should remember that.

*

I'd kinda like to be there!

You will, my lad, but there is all you'll be.

Perhaps I should write it down. What I want. How I want it to be. You know, the details.

Well, you'd better get a move on. It won't be long now.

You're right about that. Leah won't want to wait. I doubt Edward will be well enough to come over and she has her bridge on Thursdays. She'll want it over before then.

Probably next Tuesday. You're going on Friday and it'll take Saturday to get organized.

Sunday's out. The Koreans are in the church in the afternoon, and it'll give everyone a breather. What about Monday?

Monday is washing day.

Tuesday then.

Have you thought of the hymns and stuff? Who'll do the eulogy and who'll carry you up the aisle? That kind of thing?'

No, I haven't, not in detail anyway. I better get going or I might miss it.

He lay in bed, still, his head slightly angled to the left (his right was his better side, he was sure) and tried to compose himself. Better be composed before you decompose. He nodded to himself. They'll flock to see me when I'm gone.

He wanted to set the stage in his mind's eye, but he couldn't be sure which funeral home she would use. Forrestals was good, the attendants graspingly unctuous, the place well carpeted and suitably sepulchral, but Leah hadn't liked that they kept a coffee urn at the back of the viewing room. She said you could smell the stuff while you were paying your respects to the dearly departed. He had to agree with her about that although his main objection to the place was centred on the neon sign that flashed the temperature in Celsius and Fahrenheit out front, not to mention the twenty-four hour clock. Henry hated twenty-four hour clocks. What did they think they were, French? The trouble with Castellos & Bros. was that the staff looked like mafia men and he had often wondered what they did with the bodies. Christie and Sweeney was said to be excellent all round, but he couldn't imagine anyone English using them: Christie had been a mass murderer and Sweeney fed his clients into a pie machine. Perhaps Leah would go for the Co-operative Funeral Centre, where they would use grey felt and, he suspected, cardboard, but he was sure she would want a better show than that, not for his sake, mind, but to impress the neighbours, and her wide churchified acquaintance.

You could put a word in her ear beforehand, tomorrow. See how it takes.

I'd like mahogany and brass knobs, not to mention an attendant in a top hat to walk in front of the hearse all the way to the cemetery, like they did for our Dad.

That was across the pond though, they wouldn't do that here, it would cause traffic jams all over the place.

Dad must have loved it though. The centre of attention for the very last!

That's for sure! But do you think it would suit you?

Will you be buried from the church or straight from the funeral home, then?

Go for the church. Those homes don't have good organs.

They must be full of organs! Offal and giblets. All kinds of stuff.

Not those kind of organs! Tinny things they are, and the carpets muffle the sound.

It's the music I'm most concerned about.

She would be okay with going from church. You're members and they should give you a good discount. She'll make sure of that.

Even for suicides, do you think? They may not even want to do it.

Heaven's man, you're a blooming Protestant, United Church brand. Not Roman Catholic. They won't even care. They do anything. They're the Heinz of churches.

So what music do you want then?

I've always thought Kris Kristofferson for before the service, when everyone is just settling in.'

Henry warmed to his task.

'Sunday Morning Comin' Down'.

Yes, but it won't be Sunday morning, it'll be Tuesday afternoon.

Well then, 'Me and Bobby McGee'.

Won't everyone wonder who the hell Bobby McGee is?

Perhaps I better go with John Denver. He had a sweet voice.

Leah won't go for either of them.

Well, I don't care. It's my funeral.

Henry pouted but stayed on course.

Also, instead of an anthem, I want 'Di Provenza il mar' from Traviata.

Opera, yet! A bit snobby, don't you think?

And, and, and they will finish with Amazing Grace.

With massed pipes and drums, no doubt!

Why not, she can afford it! What's wrong with that? But just the one solitary piper at the end, remember. Let everyone sit quietly and listen, the melody dying away into the distance at the last. They'll be hearing it all week long, won't be able to get it out of their heads. And I would get to hear it too — for the last time.

Don't get your hopes up! They probably won't put your hearing aids in. Even if they do, do you think they'll turn them on? Wasting the batteries, really, when you think about it. That's what they'll say.

I'll just have to insist. Put my foot down.

Now that might be difficult. Physically, I mean — and you can hardly raise your hand to tell someone to turn them on during the service.

No, I mean in the vestry when everyone is getting organized. Olaf can do it.

Is it going to be an open casket?

I hope so but it kind of depends on whether I make a mess or not. You know, of my face.

They can do a lot with faces these days. Even so, you really will have to try to keep your face out of it. Unblemished, no bruises. You know what I mean.

Hmm, might be more easily said than done.

I'll jump that hurdle when I get to it. Like vault the casket.

Good one, Henry!

Will there be a wake, do you think?

Oh, yes, I'm going to have a wake. People coming to talk about me before I go. There must be a wake. A good long viewing at least.'

34

Anna Karenina was sitting on Henry's stomach, kneading him with her claws, when they opened the double doors of the Chapel of Blessed Rest at Forrestals. Trust Leah to choose there. Another argument lost. She'd found a five percent discount coupon in the Sunday paper and everything was serendipity. A bargain edged out the odour of old coffee. It felt like a Tuesday afternoon. People would be able to drop in on their way home from work. No need to bring them out again in the evening. Leah had spent most of Monday morning — after washing, before ironing — looking for flowers, cheap flowers he suspected, if she could find any. They had been up half the night arguing about the flowers. She had wanted no flowers, just a discreet bouquet on top of the coffin from herself and the girls to show their affection — Henry could imagine how discreet it would be if it was to show that: minimalism personified — with a note in the paper that if people wanted to remember him, they could send a cheque to Heart and Stroke or to the Leprosy Mission.

'But I didn't die of heart or a stroke,' he objected.

'You didn't die of leprosy either, if it comes to that,' she said, adding, just to be nasty, 'People can't very well send cheques to the Suicide Society!'

'What about the Assisted Suicide Society?' Henry wondered, 'That might work.'

'You weren't assisted,' she replied bitterly. 'You did it all by yourself. You could at least have asked for my help. Let everybody see how close we were.'

'I didn't need your help, I had everything in hand, thank you very much.'

'Well, you didn't do a very good job of it, did you! Pieces all over the place, practically. They had to use a shovel. It was embarrassing.'

'Embarrassing for you! What about me? I was the one lying there. I couldn't even find a finger to scratch my nose with. And stick to the subject. I want flowers! Lots and lots of flowers. To heck with giving money for charity: this is my big day.'

Henry suspected that she let him win the battle because, after all, nothing beats back a good display of banked flowers next to the coffin, crammed into an extra hearse and then littered all around the grave. She had quite a wistful look in her eye when she gave in.

'We'll be able to give them to the old folk's home afterwards, I suppose,' she said. 'Don't expect,' she added, twisting the knife, 'that we'll leave them for you to look at when we all go home.'

*

So it came to pass in those days that Henry was ready for the viewing. It had been touch and go whether the casket should be closed, but they had slathered on pounds of industrial strength make-up, and when they fitted his left eyeball back into its socket, he had to say that he looked quite good. In a dim light. He had even persuaded Leah to let him have a hearing aid, although he had had to settle for just the one since the other had disappeared with the right ear when it flew off and hadn't been seen since.

(It had been found by a teenager listening to INXS on his iPod, but Henry hadn't wanted to tell her. The boy had stuffed it in his trouser pocket and forgotten all about it until he went fishing for a condom on Saturday night in the backseat of his mother's car. His girlfriend had shrieked but the boy said, 'Hey, way cool!' and went on about his business. Henry found it embarrassing to have to listen, but, of course, he couldn't turn the blooming thing off. No fingers!)

With the one device, Henry was able to hear just a little bit of what was happening at the viewing, although he had to keep stopping himself from turning his head in the direction of the sound. It tended to frighten the mourners. His main problem lying there was that Leah had instructed the embalmer who dressed him not to bother with shoes. His feet were cold. Still, all in all, he knew he looked good because the family had come in earlier and said so.

Goneril, for reasons completely beyond Henry, had started to cry when she saw him. Her husband, the Mountie, a veteran of suburban marijuana grow-ops and minor corporate malfeasance, had voiced his opinion that Henry was in the top ten percentile in how he looked, had been reconstructed very well, particularly, he said, considering what they had left to play with. This made Goneril weep more. Regan had lifted her youngest up so he could get a good look, and said, 'Don't be afraid, he won't bite. That's your Granddad. Take a good, long, last look.' The child kicked the side of the coffin with his new shoes until Henry bawled, just like his Dad would have, 'Have some respect for the dead, you little heathen!' He said it so loudly everyone jumped. He did himself. 'Now Daddy, behave yourself,' said Cordelia, 'or we'll shut the lid right now, and you wouldn't like that, would you.'

A flotilla of them stood around staring down at him, drinking tea and making idle conversation. Some of it was really idle. Goneril and Cordelia spent more time wondering whether to wear black to the funeral than they did on their memories of dear old Dad. Not that he could really fault them for that: he was more interested in what he would be wearing than in having to hear bogus sob stories about their affection. Cordelia said black made her look sallow, but Henry had news for her. If her skin had been any more yellow, the ancient Egyptians could have written on it. Regan's time was taken up with her boy, except, it seemed to Henry, when she was having a long, eye-batting conversation with the Mountie. This was odd, considering she was always running him down behind Goneril's back, saying things like how his head was as flat as his feet, how he needed a girdle and how could her sister put up with him.

Leah was fixing her face in front of a pocket mirror, plumping up her hair and examining the faltering line of her jaw. She turned to the family.

'Now remember, everyone,' she spoke with a hiss and narrowed eyes, finger pointing, 'he fell. As far as we know, he tripped. Possibly was pushed.' She held up her hand for silence. Several of the group seemed, he thought, to be happy with the idea that he had been pushed. 'He did not jump.'

'Yes, I did,' said Henry sitting up, 'I most certainly did.'

She rounded on him.

'For the last time, you shut up, Henry. You lie there, do you hear me, and don't say a word! Not one word! I've had enough of you to last me a lifetime and if you don't shut up,' Her voice was rising, 'I'll close the damn coffin and let you suffocate.'

She pounded her fist against the side of the casket. Henry shrank back holding onto his eye so that it wouldn't come out. It had already fallen out once and Anna Karenina had had a high old time chasing it round the room.

'Now everybody,' Leah continued, 'take a deep breath and we'll let the people in. Just remember it'll all be over by tomorrow evening. Just keep on smiling. And, whatever you do, don't say a word to the press.'

'What a good idea: to invite the press,' thought Henry looking up at the ceiling, 'I should call someone.'

'What are you going to tell them?'

'I could tell them what I'm going to do and why. Tell them the truth. Tell them about me.'

'They wouldn't want to know. You're not important enough.'

'I'm important enough to me.'

'I'm rather fond of you myself, Henry, but that's only two of us. Let's face it, you couldn't sell a newspaper.'

Inspiration struck. 'I could write my own obit, however. Send it in, so they'd have it on hand, ready to go when they hear. Not a bad idea at all. That would give me the last word, wouldn't it.'

'Do it tomorrow. You've nothing on for tomorrow.'

'I will,' said Henry. 'In the meantime, let's have a look at who's here. Open the doors and let me at them.'

'Okay, they're opening them now, but be still and shut up, or she'll scupper you yet.'

*

It was a good thing they opened the doors when they did. The line was out the front door, down the steps and round the block. The crowd was starting to get ugly and Henry's friends had never been particularly attractive in the first place. Most of them were dropping by on the way home from work and they were hungry. They moved at a fair clip. He would have suspected there was a Leafs' game they didn't want to miss, but it was a Tuesday night so it didn't seem likely. He wished she'd employed someone to keep the crowds back a bit. Some of them were breathing on his face, and they really did need food. He looked at everyone through hooded eyes. Was it an owl that could see when it had its eyes closed? Something to do with more than one set of lids, he remembered, but an owl seemed to fit. He had the wisdom and the damn pussycat was already there, kneading away.

'Mrs. Earl,' he heard a voice say, 'My name is Rowena Filch. I'm here to represent the bank.'

'Oh, how nice of you to come,' said Leah, intent on observing the proprieties.

'Hi, there,' said Henry, 'Sorry I can't get up.'

'Wouldn't have missed it, Henry. You just lie still,' said Rowe reassuringly, patting his prayerfully arranged hands. 'We brought along a few flowers. We got them before we heard about the Heart and Stroke.' Rowe turned to her paramour. 'Trundle them over here, Jacko,' she said, and Jacko rolled in a floral tribute enormous enough to bring out the allergies of a small army. They looked a bit wilted.

'Oooh, aren't they beautiful,' Leah gushed like a Yellowstone geyser. 'Come a little closer and see what they did to him. Mind the hair though, it might come off if you blow too hard. I got them to plump up the lips a bit. Collagen.'

Leah had never liked his lack of lip.

Henry felt the inside of his mouth with his tongue. He had wondered why his lips were swollen and slightly deadened, but he hadn't liked to say anything, given, well, his overall condition. Now it made sense. If he spoke, would he sound slushy, with a little bit of a lisp? He had just about made up his mind that he would say something at the funeral — not the eulogy, mind you — just a few extemporaneous words before they screwed the lid down. And now this! He wasn't about to do anything that would make him look foolish, and if he sounded a little off, he might have to reconsider.

'I was wondering if you would sign this paper, Mrs. E.,' said Rowe, 'Just a little something in triplicate to say that you don't hold the bank in any way responsible for what happened.'

She shrugged her shoulders and held out a thick wad of documents.

'Anybody got a pen,' she asked.

'See if Dad has,' said Regan. 'He usually keeps one in his breast pocket. 'Sometimes he has a whole row of them.' She sniffed.

'Well, I'm sure we don't hold you responsible in any way. Banks are institutions in this country. What would we do without the banks? I ask you that,' said Leah. 'In any case,' she leaned towards Rowe and continued, 'in any case, we're putting the word out that he had a brain tumour.'

'I had a brain tumour!' said Henry in high dudgeon. 'You never told me that!'

It was an intriguing possibility. Here was a man, some would say in his best years, so much left to do, cut down in his prime like a giant redwood.

'That one across the river looks good,' said the lumberjack to Rowe's husband.

'Tall, strong, good smooth bark. Handsome, I'd say. Take at least an hour to get it down. Bring in the heavy equipment while I use the facilities.'

Jacko swung the axe.

Rowe leaned over the side of the casket staring intently at Henry's face.

'Hmmph, Henry,' she said, 'I always did fancy you. A fine figure of a fellow I found you.'

A single tear fell from her eye landing on Henry's forehead.

'Oops!' She took out her hankie and dabbed at it, bringing the makeup and a smidgen of flesh away with it. His hair came askew when she tried to put it right.

'Give over, for God's sake,' said Henry, 'Let Leah do it. She's a dab hand at that kind of thing.'

'Hello well, Henry,' said Boney. He had come up behind Rowe and was peering over her shoulder. 'Sorry mess you're looking, boyo. Couldn't they do better than that?'

'I was looking fine until you people came along. What are you here for anyway? You're the lot that killed me.'

'Now, Henry, no hard feelings,' said Boney, 'and anyway, you know that's not true. You did that yourself. Wouldn't stand up in court, to say we did it. In any case, it was Rowe's decision. She's the one you should blame. Think about it for a moment. She's the boss.'

He moved over to whisper in Regan's ear, shaking his head, 'And no more conscience than a cartload of monkeys.'

Regan batted her eyes.

'Oh Mr. Bonnet, you do say such things!'

And after a pause, 'We were going to ask you to be one of Daddy's pallbearers.'

'Oh I couldn't!' replied Boney. 'Its against my religion, you see. I'm a Druid.'

'You're Welsh, is what you are!' A voice rolled over from the back of the room.

Henry opened his eyes. It sounded like his Dad and he sat bolt upright to make sure, but there were so many people nearby, it was hard to see beyond the first three rows. In any case, Bettina was blocking much of his view. She had combed out her dreadlocks for the occasion and a huge curly halo surrounded her head. She was crying softly into a small lace handkerchief. Henry patted her hand to comfort her.

'Who's that woman, Mommy?' asked Cordelia, 'Is that the one?'

'No, no I don't think so. Not as dark as I remember her,' Leah replied. 'Mind you, there may have been more than one. Many more than one, over the years.'

'Oh, Mom, I wouldn't have thought so,' said Goneril dubiously, weighing the thought and finding it wanting.

Henry hadn't heard such nonsense in his life, but he liked the idea of it. 'Yeah, team,' he yelled, but everyone shushed him.

It was then that he began to hear the crying. Actually hear it. He had been aware for a while that there was a certain dampness in the air. He was reminded of the underside of a snaggled rock near a fast moving brook deep in the woods and it took time to realize that it was all caused by lachrymosity. The tears of a multitude. If I open my eyes, I will see them. Bunches of women mewing in their grief, old Italian dames in black, bunches of toothless Greek ladies, keening curry Indians, even a few damp-eyed Canadians, all on their uppers, desolated. I'm gone, he wanted to shout, but the grief was so thick around him that it felt impenetrable. And all for him! Finally, he preened, they see me for what I am, who I am, and they're sorry that I'm gone.

This feels so good. They're so sad for what they've done, allowed to happen, that they've come to pay their respects, by God.

To me!

This is the life, he thought, static electricity shooting through his fingertips.

I could even come back.

Or not go?

'Pray silence for Her Majesty The Queen.' A loud voice called out from over where Henry had thought he heard his Dad.

The crowd shushed immediately, separating to let majesty by. A woman who looked exactly like his Mam made her way through it, shaking goldfish out of her hair, flicking minnows off her frock. So many tears. Water spurted out of her handbag.

'Our Henry, is it really you?' she peered down at him. His Mam had become increasingly short sighted in her later years, as, indeed, had Henry himself.

She waved a white-gloved hand at him.

Henry lay in his bed and frowned. His mother didn't resemble the Queen, the Queen Mum a bit, but not the Queen herself. Was it really likely that the Queen would come to his funeral? It seemed a little much, everything considered. (On the other hand, his Dad was Philip.) He had only seen the woman once. Coming out of Buckingham Palace it was. Standing with the girls, he'd been. A bit of a mob scene, just like this one, come to think of it. To confirm where he was, Henry reached out with his fingers, trying to feel the side of the casket, to run them up against the plush of the silk, to confirm that he was there. He closed his eyes tight, willing himself to get it right, not quite daring to open them in either the dark of the night or in the finality of the coffin.

Then he had another thought. It wasn't a comforting one but since it came to him, willy-nilly, he could hardly just shove it away disregarded.

I mean, I have to take it into consideration. Or else people will think I'm not rational. Off my head.

He weighed the thought carefully, trying to orient himself to it as if it held the secrets of the universe: 'If Mam died five years ago, how come she's coming to my funeral?'

'It's not your Mam, it's the Queen. Her blooming Britannic Majesty.'

'No, I'm sure it's not. It's our Mam. The Queen would never call me Henry.'

'Ah, but what about as in, "Rise, Sir Henry". She might be here for that. They might be doing it posthumously. You never can tell.'

Henry opened his eyes and peered about in the dark. He would have liked it to be so, how he would have liked it, but he knew in his heart that it wasn't. If I close my eyes again, he wondered, will it all still be there? Can I go on with my dream? He pressed his eyes tightly shut and, turning on his side, tried to recall the scene in his mind, but it had evaporated. All he could see was greyness and regret. And when he opened his eyes again, he saw the same.

35

Henry had never had much truck with Thursday. Left to its own devices it might have been alright, but it was the longest day of the week, its interminable hours dog-paddling along, ho hum, a pause before the swift backstroke of Friday. Today would be no different, would be worse in fact, for the general salvation of Thursday was work. It got you through. Having none of that to do, he would have to invent the day.

There was nothing for it but to be out and, supposedly, about as usual. He didn't think Leah would have noticed if he had left the house stark naked under a red kimono, but he was certain she would have noticed if he didn't leave at all. Getting underfoot, she would have called it. 'What are you doing? Why are you here?' He wasn't going to get into that, that was for sure; she'd find out soon enough and her ignorance was his bliss. He decided to do some of his favourite things, not big things, but things he liked to do, surrounded by the anonymity of the city he had loved so well. A little bit of planning would not come amiss either, he thought as he set off, as banker-dressed as he usually was.

As to that, however, he didn't know why he bothered. Most bankers dressed no differently from anybody else these days. The days of the suit, never mind the three-piece, French-cuffed accessories, were long gone. 'Business-casual' they called it now with more emphasis on the 'casual' than the 'business'. It was a wonder that the entire necktie trade hadn't declared bankruptcy. White shirts were an endangered species. No dress code at all seemed to exist for Friday. Women wore tighter pants than hookers on a holiday weekend, and with not dissimilar results he suspected. Everything was in the name of increased productivity, of course. If we let them dress comfortably, the idea was that they would work harder. In Henry's opinion, there was a point at which slovenly took over, depressing the mind and infecting the output. He hated to see people in a branch these days, the men five o'clock shadowed or unshaven, the women so snugly packed into their tank tops that you could tell at a glance which of them had forgotten to put on a bra. The women chomped on their gum, the men walked around with sweat stains in their armpits. Management was no better, it could just afford better labels. Long ago, Henry had settled for clean and neat — and a suit. He tried hard not to offend anyone's visual or olfactory senses.

He remembered how smart his Mam and Dad had been: straight, with better posture than he ever had. His Mam was probably the last woman in Britain to wear a corset, he didn't know how she did it, but she did look great. He had a picture of her. (Leah wouldn't let him hang it: too old-fashioned, she said.) She was in a long blue dress, from the thirties, bobbed hair, beads down to her waist. She had a silk shawl over one arm, its tassels dangling down almost to her ankles. His Dad must have picked it up on his travels. Henry still liked to look at the picture. It was hidden in the back of his wardrobe and he determined to have one last look tonight. His Mam had been a bobby-dazzler in that picture. Why didn't I get someone like that, he wondered? They say a man looks for a woman like his mother to marry, but it hadn't been true in Henry's case. And God help Henry if he, in any way, shape or unfortunate form, resembled Leah's father — not that he had ever heard that the saying worked that way round.

'She's a bonny enough lass,' his Dad had said cautiously after he met her, although he had to be asked. 'Nothing like your mother now, but a bonny lass.' Henry could almost hear the words sticking in his Dad's craw as he said them. After a pause, his Dad had asked, 'What's the matter with the mother?'

You may well ask, thought Henry, although he had only shrugged and said, 'They think it's the change of life.'

His Dad gurgled up from his belly, quietly but not without sympathy, 'Well, I should hope she hasn't been like that all her life!'

The truth was Henry had had to cope with Leah's mother all of his married life. It may have been an early onset something or other, but an onset it was. His mother-in-law had kept them home when they should have been out building a marriage. Leah had diapered four babies and eventually she diapered her mother. 'I can't be expected to leave Mummy, Henry,' became her refrain. You could have set it to music. All his plans to travel and to see the world evaporated. The woman's husband was no help at all. He couldn't be expected to do the nasty things, the personal things, his daughter had to do. 'Poppy is too sensitive,' Leah had sighed, 'and too busy. His own health isn't good enough for him to be able to cope with hers.' The day his mother-in-law died, Henry had wanted to put the flags out, but she was hardly cold before Leah was making plans for her father to move in with them.

'He can have Bonnie's room, the girls can bunk up a bit. He'll be company for you, Henry, you'll like that, won't you?' she said, although it was not up for discussion.

'Isn't he allergic to rattan?' Henry had wondered, although he didn't ask the question out loud. He sighed instead.

This way perdition lies, he thought now. Dwell on memories like this and the next thing you know you'll be cutting your throat.

Pre-empting yourself, eh?

Robbing yourself of the finale.

Cheating yourself out of the last act.

Your denouement.

Your big finish.

Let's go and see some places. What do you say?

Quite right, Henry. The next thing you know, you'll be talking to yourself like her mother did.

Yes, and answering myself, too.

In the best family tradition.

He chortled.

*

So Henry set off. He set off out into the city he loved, into the byways of his knowledge of it. Into the byways of his mind too, but he was determined that it should be a good day, and he tried to keep the memories that were stirred up happy ones. He wanted them to gambol into his consciousness and he chased them when they hid out of reach, like a sheepdog snapping at their heels, bringing them back, leading them home.

He passed the branch where it all began. And he remembered.

He had been in training, a teller, and one evening, after five it was, on a still formal Friday, a woman, brunette and eye-shadowed, appeared at his wicket to take some money from her account. She wrote a cheque to cash. Alarm bells went off in Henry's head. Fraud, they shouted. He knew whose account it was: a man's, a young man's. He usually came in at lunch and he was quite friendly. Someone was robbing him. Henry looked at the smiling woman standing in front of him. Was she flirting with him, just a little?

'I won't be a minute,' he said, closing his cash drawer, 'Just got to get authorization.'

He walked over to his supervisor and whispered in her ear. 'There's a woman trying to cash a cheque. She signed it in front of me, but I know whose account it is. It's a man's account. I know him.'

Henry and his supervisor looked over at his wicket. The customer waved.

His supervisor waved back. 'Don't worry, Henry. It's Friday. He becomes a she after five.' She laughed. 'You could probably get a date if you wanted one!'

The same branch introduced him to The Scotch Tape Lady. She asked him for scotch tape and taped six inches of it over each eye. Henry stood there not having a clue what to do next. The rest of the staff roared with laughter.

He got his revenge when he was selling old Mrs. Selig a term deposit. She had dumped the contents of her purse onto the counter trying to find her passbook. The contents included a revolver that she used to ward off the homeless that roamed the streets round the branch and the ghosts that roamed the nearer reaches of her mind. Mrs. Selig was harmless and Henry had seen the gun before when she had rummaged through her purse in search of a cough lozenge.

'What the hell is that?' he had blurted.

'That?' she replied with her usual charming vagueness. 'That's Lorenzo. I keep him for good luck.' She had added, 'Don't worry, he's not loaded.'

Henry held the revolver chest high and turned to face his fellow members of staff, pointing it at them one by one. 'Look everyone,' he called out. 'Have you guys met Lorenzo?'

Each one of them ducked, and his supervisor screamed.

He was called to the manager's carpet afterwards, but he enjoyed the commotion and the manager had a definite twinkle in his eye by the time he had finished dressing him down. He commented on Henry's lack of banking gravitas, not to mention scaring the girls half to death, but the twinkle was there nevertheless. 'Watch out, Henry,' he said, when Henry had his hand on the doorknob ready to leave, 'they'll get their revenge, particularly that little spitfire, Marisa.'

Marisa was his supervisor, a feisty Sicilian who loved to laugh but who was as precise as a pin when it came to her job.

Marisa's revenge came when the Audit was at the branch. Henry was the loans' officer by then and the Inspector asked for his credit files. He handed them over in batches of ten. The Inspector sent for him first thing next morning. He was a thin man with false teeth that clattered in his mouth whenever he tried to use a word with a hard consonant.

'Mr. Earl,' he said, chomping away, 'Would you care to explain this?'

He opened a file and took out the photograph of a Sunshine girl in all her semi-naked glory. She peered up at Henry as if to say, 'Howdy, Henry!'

'And this?' The Inspector opened another file.

'And how about this?' Another.

Henry could not but laugh.

'This is not a laughing matter!' The Inspector said, continuing to open further files. He held each photograph gingerly. Something might be catching.

Henry had been confused how the pictures came to be there but the woman in the last photograph had the word 'Marisa' written in magic-marker across her abdomen. He guffawed in the Inspector's face. Marisa owned up and flashed her eyes at the Inspector. He took her out to lunch.

'By God, you two,' said the manager afterwards, 'if you ever do anything like that again, either of you, you'll be out the bloody door so fast . . .' But the relief of a clean audit trumped everything else in his world. The whole staff went out for dinner and drinks. Henry planted a big wet kiss on the top of Marisa's head, but he was wise enough to go no further. She was more than five women put together. He wouldn't have been able to handle her, and he wouldn't have wanted to stop. They remained friends for years afterwards until she died of kidney failure. He saw her last in a hospital bed, tiny, wasted, eyes still shining. Her hand reached out to pull him towards her. 'Those were the days, Henry. We worked hard, but we played hard as well.' It was a cliché but it was true. Good days, great days.

It was Marisa who taught him that branch banking was a game, a huge complicated, highly organized game. The object was to balance. The tellers balance. Ins balance outs. Debits, credits. Balance the books. Roll up the General Ledger. Run an enormous tape. Come to zero outstanding. And do the same thing again, with all the myriad possible permutations and combinations, tomorrow.

The manager got his revenge at half year end.

*

On April 30, of each year, the banks close their books and then, having carried out this task successfully, open them again. Every branch in the system does it and Head Office does it, too. The same thing happens on October 31, at the financial year end, when every branch General Ledger is balanced, closed, rolled up into the Bank's GL and begun anew. Henry, on his accelerated management course, had been a Savings Supervisor in October but Marisa asked him if he wanted to stay and watch them close the books. Three of them did it. He was fascinated by the precision with which they worked, the checking and the double checking, the running of tapes and the transferring of figures from one column to another: Suspense and Memo Accounts, Currency Trading, and the completion of the F613. Marisa was a little general, a petite feminine Mussolini, in charge of everything and Henry soon found himself co-opted into the process. 'Run me a tape, Henry,' and 'Make some more coffee,' meshed quite well with 'Explain to Henry what you are doing,' and 'Are you getting it, Henry? Is it going in?' Remarkably it did.

The following April, Marisa arranged for him to go on a two day course on closing the half-year books, and Henry learned the theory behind the whole process and got a better understanding of the long form, literally two inch wide and two feet long — why it was called the F613 he never did know — onto which every final figure had to be transcribed. In the middle of the month, she told him not to make plans for the thirtieth. Henry was looking forward to being a cog in Marisa's machine again when she came down with the flu. He was certain that her two assistants would close the books instead, but the Manager refused to pay them overtime and they declared that they would be unable to work that late anyway. With Marisa not around, where would the fun be, said one of them shrugging her shoulders? Henry assumed that the Manager would take over and that he would assist him. Being in management training, he wouldn't be paid overtime anyway.

By five o'clock in the afternoon, most of the staff had left for the day, and Henry was excited. He had reviewed his course notes over lunch, taking out the package of forms Head Office had dispatched to the branch. He placed the famed F613 on top of the wide counter he had cleared as a workplace. He made a new pot of coffee, Henry had always liked his coffee, and, for good measure, he put out a plate of cookies for both of them to munch on. It would be a long evening. He doubted they would get out of there before ten. Everything had to be completed correctly. If the numbers didn't add up, you had to go back and find out why. And do it all again. He was growing impatient for the Manager to come out of his office so they could get started. It would be fun. 'Treat it,' Marisa always said, 'as a game: a huge, complicated, very serious game.'

At ten after five, the Manager's door opened. He came out dressed in his overcoat and scarf, said, 'Good night, Henry' and let himself out of the branch. Henry heard the words, 'See you in the a.m.' as the door closed behind him. Afterwards, Henry wondered if this hadn't been when his scorn for management first began. True, he would admit, this Manager was not particularly senior, but he was senior to Henry and like all managers in those days he could act as though he was a direct descendant of the Lord God Almighty himself. Henry sank slowly onto his chair.

'Jesus,' he said to the adding machine that sat silently in front of him. 'Shit.'

There had been a revolution in Henry's language since he had joined the bank. Bankers, Henry had learned, swear. A lot. And not very inventively. Unimaginative Chaucerian four letter words. They do it casually, almost as punctuation. Henry fought the good fight, but eventually he had joined in. It had appalled Leah, but he expected that, and that wasn't going to stop him. In any case, bankers had a lot to swear about. All beer and skittles, it wasn't.

'Holy fuck, Marisa, where are you now when I need you?'

Henry said this as he looked at the telephone on his desk. On cue, it rang.

'Hi!' He heard a croak on the other end of the line. 'It's me. Did he leave yet?'

'I can't believe it. He just walked out. Not so much as a by your leave!'

'Well,' she replied hoarsely, 'what else did you expect?'

'What am I going to do?' Henry was near panic, standing almost on its edge.

'Calm down, for one thing. You can do it. Get yourself organized and take it slowly. Use your notes. Think. Just remember what I always tell you, dummy.' Henry felt himself begin to relax, hearing Marisa's usual term of endearment. 'Treat it as a game!'

'What do I do if I get it wrong?'

She was not a woman known for her patience.

'Henry, if you get it wrong, you won't balance, so you'll have to start again. Just backtrack to where you went wrong. Do everything in pencil until you're sure.'

Henry moaned into the phone.

'And Henry,' he could almost see her wagging her finger at him, 'don't call me unless you absolutely have to. I feel lousy and am going to sleep. You won't need to call me.'

Henry didn't call her. He took a deep breath, opened his notes and followed the instructions, spare though they were, that came with the F613. By eight o'clock, he was beginning to enjoy himself. An hour later, his stomach lurched when he realized he had forgotten two lines in the ledger and had to go halfway back and begin again. At one point, he went off to the stationery room to find a new eraser — the first one was covered in sweat — but somewhere during the evening he knew he could do it and it became fun. Henry could play the game.

Leah called at nine wondering where he was. When the telephone rang, he had hoped it was Marisa checking up, seeing how it was going, but he should have known it wouldn't be. Instead, he listened to what Leah had done with her day, how well she had done it and how hard put upon she was in having to do it. (She had had four ladies over for tea to discuss the social evening she had volunteered to organize at church.) She wanted to know when he would be home but had little interest in his crisis. He didn't bother to go into detail, couldn't get a word in in any case, and eventually put the phone down with the excuse that supper had just arrived and they were all going to eat. Chinese, he said. He went back to work with a solitary sigh. Ah so!

Henry finished balancing the books at ten to twelve. It would have been sooner, but at eleven o'clock the police had rapped on the window to see if he was all right and he lost his train of thought. By that hour of night, he was beginning to run out of steam, anyway. When he was finished, he put the completed form on the manager's desk, watched it lie there long and thin like a snake, and he hoped it would jump up and bite the bastard in the morning. Then he packed everything away, called downtown to tell them he was going to close the vault, and left. He decided to walk home. He felt marvellous. It was quite an accomplishment. There was no doubt about it. He walked along with that six-inches-above-the-ground lightness, that twitching with the electricity of his happiness, that he always felt when he was enjoying life in Canada.

He remembered the feeling now, and he tensed to see if he could recreate it, conjure it up once again, bring it back, but it was no longer there. It had evaporated somewhere along the years.

*

Henry pressed on with his journey. Street to street, branch to branch. Or was it only in his mind. Am I really moving or is the city moving around me? He steadied himself against the wall of a building. It was cold to the touch, its stone had seen little sun since the fall. He took off his gloves to trace his fingers over the roughness of the surface and turned to look at the bleak greyness all around. There is no warmth here, he thought. Just winter in the city. Just sleet and snow and winter in the city. He had arrived in the summer. The city he loved wasn't a winter city at all. For him it was a city of sun, its warmth had embraced him and he had immediately and forever embraced it back. He looked around and saw he was not far from where his life here began.

36

Henry had crossed an ocean and travelled by train to go to university. He arrived in Canada with a trunk, a suitcase and his 'cello. What had happened to the 'cello, he wondered now, but he couldn't remember — firewood for someone, probably. Why had he ever brought it? He had been eighteen and too foolish to realize what he was doing with the 'cello and everything else, but, he was young and, oh, he did enjoy the adventure. Everything had been an adventure in those days. Finding a skycap to help him with the luggage, locating the taxi stand (his Dad never used taxis), counting out the coinage and figuring a tip — every last thing was an adventure. It energized him. All of it. Watching the people hustle and bustle in the big city, the gigantic cars, the accents, the confidence of everybody as they went about their business, everyone seemed tanned, the cleanliness of the station, you could have eaten cake off the floor, he was sure. The taxi driver really did say, 'Where to, Bud?' just like in a Hollywood movie. Henry had been enchanted from day one. Enchanted even as he had been nervous as hell.

After all, he hadn't known where he was going. He had applied to a foreign university on a whim so it was only when he was accepted that he realized there was a dilemma: he had applied to the University of Toronto, but the letterhead was from the Victoria University.

'Where's Victoria?' Henry asked.

'Somewhere near the Pacific,' his Dad replied. 'On an island, I think, lad.' He said it cautiously, perhaps not certain himself or not wanting to deflate Henry's balloon. 'The far end of the place.'

'Where is Toronto exactly, anyway?' Henry's Mam asked. She began to laugh. 'We don't know much, do we!'

'Come on, our Henry, get the map out.'

Henry raced upstairs to get his school atlas and nearly tripped racing back down trying to find Canada. They spread North America out in front of them. It was only then that Henry realized that he didn't know the first thing about the continent.

'There's New York.'

'Canada's above that.'

'Big place!'

'Hold on a minute. Let's see if we can find Victoria.'

Henry's Dad ran his finger up and down the west coast.

'There it is,' he shouted. 'Just where I said it was.'

'Shhh,' said Mam, 'no need to shout,' but she wasn't looking at him. She was peering at the map. 'Where's Toronto then?'

It took them a minute or two to find it. They found St. Louis, and Montreal, and Winnipeg and Chicago easily enough but Toronto eluded them until Henry's Dad, triumphant, bawled, 'There it is. Just right of the Great Lakes. On top of Lake Ontario.'

Even when Henry boarded the ship a month later there was some doubt where exactly he was going. He had sent a letter asking, but hadn't received a reply. He carried a railway ticket from Montreal to Toronto with him, and, in the strange currency of Canada, a bit like Monopoly money it was, enough cash to get him from Toronto to Victoria. They had looked at the distance on the map with awe and his Mam began to cry.

'It's so far away,' she sobbed.

'Cheer up lass,' his Dad had said, hugging her to his chest, 'It'll be the making of the lad.'

It had certainly been an adventure. Henry had loved his life in those days.

The taxi at Union Station took him to the Y. He would spend the night and make inquiries about his final destination next day. Whenever he looked back on that day, Henry was amazed at how innocent he had been, but he always exulted in what had happened. He loved to tell the story and he never thought that it made him appear foolish. He was doing something that most people would never have dared to do. Not even in those more innocent times. The pity of it was that, somewhere along the line, he had stopped daring. Only the remembering gave him a lift now. That was all he had left.

*

He got out of bed that first morning, eager for a new beginning, eager to see the city that he could hear all around him. He came out the front door of the Y and was amazed as a streetcar, huge like everything else, clanged by. Should he turn left or right? He turned right. It seemed more hopeful. More positive somehow. A short walk brought him to a wide avenue, wider than any he had ever seen at home, six or eight lanes it was when he was used to two. Even London mostly had four. He looked at the street sign: University Avenue. What luck, so early after setting out!

Should he turn left or should he turn right? Right again, he decided, and off he went. He followed the curving road around an imposing pile of a building, red and ugly and flags flying. He examined it from across the street, but was not about to get himself killed crossing over to find out what it was. Maybe later. Walking on, he came upon a sign saying Loretto College, and wondered whether he should go in to ask them for help — a college was a college, after all — but he knew he wouldn't. It would be too embarrassing to have to explain.

He walked on again towards a monstrosity of a building as red and as heavy as the one he had just passed. He was almost up to it when he saw the sign. A big brass sign. A gorgeous, shiny, big brass sign: 'Victoria University'. Henry gawped. Whenever he thought about it afterwards, he knew that that was the right word. Gawped. The sign was gone now, but standing there once again, he gazed affectionately at the building. The redness had turned into a rusty warmth over the years and the heaviness was solemnity, weight, worth. No longer a monster, this was a friendly giant. He leaned against the iron fence and recalled that first day.

He ran, actually ran, along the walkway and bolted up the wide front steps. The large wooden doors wouldn't budge. He thought they were locked. It took Henry years to learn that doors in Canada had to be pulled out rather than pushed in. Once inside, however, he made a complete idiot of himself with his breathless questioning. They tried to calm him down, laughed at his evident joy at being there, and plonked him down in a big armchair while they arranged for him to go into residence that very day. He grinned at the memory.

He had spent four years living not a hundred yards from where he was standing. He could see the house in the courtyard across the way, stone grey and full of memories, and he considered walking over to it. Perhaps he could ring the bell and ask to see his old room, but he knew he wouldn't. What would be the point? They would think he was crazy and they might be correct. No, it would be better to take his memories with him and keep moving on his journey through the city. They weren't all happy memories anyway.

This, after all, was where he had met Leah.

37

Leah walked into a sock hop at the beginning of his senior year. Bells didn't chime and lights didn't blind him, but he was lonely for a girlfriend, with his last one gone for over a year, and she seemed pleasant enough. Henry had found Canadian girls rather more than he was able to handle and until the demise of his relationship with Dorcas he hadn't needed to cope with them that way anyway. Most of them seemed intent on casting off whatever inhibitions they had, now that they were at college in the big city. They may have come from small Ontario towns he had never heard of, but it was not long before they were dusting themselves down and adopting the sophistication of Bloor Street.

Looking back of course, he realized that most of these young women were not that much different from him — tentative, eager and, at the same time, scared; but they did not appear that way then. One girl he rather liked changed her hair colour with the semester. He could cope with the brunette, adored the blonde from a distance, but stuttered at the brass of the redhead. Another had been a beauty queen: that fact itself made certain that they would never go out together. She was a touch above. When he did go out in his junior year, he dated not girls from his own college but girls from Trinity, the shy ones, serious bluestocking types with their own hoity-toity accents that were not that much different from his. He related to them better.

That first evening of his last year, however, Henry was feeling his oats. Leah had a peaches and cream complexion (although perhaps the peaches were already a tad overripe) and she knew how to bat her eyes. Later he decided that the word should have been 'swat' — he the fly — but at the time it seemed charming. If she had a slight stoop, surely not a slouch, it was easy to forgive and it was not long before she was saying 'O Henry' in a most tantalizing manner.

She had her limits, and very far from the homestead they turned out to be, but to Henry it was, at least initially, all giddy freedom. Home on the range. That kind of thing. It was years before he realized that she had played him like a fine fiddle. She loved his accent and the whole Brit thing, but she was one of those who was there for her Mrs. and apparently quite determined to obtain it. That first night, however, she was a suppliant. She wanted to know which courses to take, who the best profs were, where was good to eat. He took her to Peter Palmers' for the best apple pie in

the whole wide world. She declared it to be yummy. By the end of the evening, he
was beginning to think that he was the most intelligent individual he had ever been
privileged to meet.

   His friends in residence tried to warn him not to get too close. Even a couple of
the girls hinted that, perhaps, he would be better to watch out, but Henry was happy.
Not exactly besotted — she simpered a little too much for that — but that year he
had her on his arm at all the big events, went to her formal and was taken home for
Thanksgiving. Just as a foreign student, mind you. Nothing serious so soon. Not to
meet the folks or anything as drastic as that: just to make sure that he got a good hot
meal with all the trimmings. Looking back, Henry knew that he should have known
better. The giveaway, if nothing else, was the beginning of a lifelong aversion to her
pumpkin pie. They had forced it on him, tied him down almost, and forked it down
his throat. Great gobs of it. The colour and texture of shit and the consistency of
sodden cardboard. He didn't like cranberries either. That should have been a signal
too, but he had stayed on and loved — Oh God, should he use that word? — being
in someone's home.

                                            *

   Henry was beginning to tire. He still wanted to see the city, savour and taste it
one last time, but his legs were feeling weak and his concentration was beginning
to go. He had been lucky in some ways, he couldn't deny it: some people his age
already had knee and even hip replacements. Some had already keeled over with
coronaries. No warning. Gone. Just like that. There was Ted, a fellow from church,
whose waistline had been growing rather precipitously. He told Henry he had
decided to do something about it and he bought a pair of running shoes, sweats
and a headband. Got all nikied up. Hauled himself out of bed at six in the morning
to go for a first run before going to work. A lawyer he was. Kissed his wife and told
her to rise, shine and put the coffee on. He didn't make it to the end of the second
block. His son found him under a hedge on his way to school an hour later. Tongue
out, purple in the face, grasping at the peonies, Ted had keeled over defunct. His
son almost did likewise. The wife was in the breakfast nook reading the morning
paper when the paramedics knocked on the front door wanting to know if her son
was on any medication before they gave him any.
   Then there was the big C. It was beginning to take people too. Women mainly.
Breasts and plumbing. In their forties even. But men as well: prostrate, colon, lung
and brain. He heard about them all. Not too many at the bank, but that was not to be
expected. The Bank disposed of its middle-aged white men in its own inimitable way.
Rather the husbands of Leah's cronies, men from the neighbourhood, churchies,
people in the paper.

Henry couldn't remember when he first began reading the obituaries. He had always laughed at people who did.

'Did you see that so and so died?'

'No, really? I didn't know you knew him.'

'Oh I didn't. Saw it in the paper. Quite a write-up there was.'

'Don't read the obits, myself.'

'Neither do I. Was just skimming and saw it.'

'Umm.'

His quarterly alumni magazine was also required reading to find out what had happened to the people from college. Awarded the Order of Canada. Published his sixth book on mediaeval riddles in the Latin language. Opened an eco — B and B in Costa Rica with his third wife, Consuela. Dead at fifty-three. Leah was as avid a reader as he was. The university made it easy for them since it never cross-checked its lists and realized they were married. Two copies of everything arrived simultaneously.

'Did you see that Clive Banning was appointed a director of the CBC?'

'Er, no. Which one was he?'

'You know. That nice curly headed fellow from Middle House. Tall and handsome.'

'The one with the rabbit teeth?'

'Rubbish! He had lovely straight teeth.'

'Plenty of them, if I remember correctly.'

'Just because he could have any girl with a flick of his fingers . . .'

'I wouldn't have thought it was a girl that he was flicking them for.'

'Why Henry, what a thing to say!'

Silence.

'Why couldn't you have been a director at the CBC?'

Henry would have loved to be a director of the CBC. He would have loved to be the director of anything, come to think of it. Traffic, even. There had been a time when he had been ambitious enough for it, too. For a long time he told himself that the reason something like that didn't happen to him was because he was an immigrant, someone who lacked friends in high places, lacked relatives who could put in a word, but, over the years, he had come to doubt it.

38

Henry's career hadn't exactly been breaking land speed records when he was transferred into the city and installed as manager of a branch in the middle of what, in later years, would become known as the gay village. The move didn't help his home life. The girls were too young to understand their mother's horror at the appointment, but her instructions when he arrived home from work must have upset and confused them. 'As soon as you get in, I want you washed. You never know what kind of germs you will be bringing home with you. The girls could be contaminated.' A vein palpitated in her throat when she said this, but it was the early days of AIDS, and, to tell the truth, Henry was almost as anxious and ignorant as she was. Leah laid down rules beyond the statutory ablutory requirements as well. He was not to tell anyone — neighbours, people at church, her relatives, grocery store assistants — anyone at all — where he was working. Should he be asked, he was to mumble the phrase 'a few blocks away from Maple Leaf Gardens' and, presumably, bodycheck any further conversation as speedily as he could. She, she stressed, had no intention of telling people that he had been transferred and, as far as everyone was concerned, he was still employed in the wilds of Scarborough.

Henry spent the first week in his new branch in a fog. He had been thrust into a new world. His accountant, an incipiently moustachioed woman of imposing circumference, took it upon herself to educate him in the infinite variety of his clientele. It was an education indeed. He exited Friday evening far more bamboozled than he had entered Monday morning. Not to mention more apprehensive.

There were the homosexuals, the lesbians, and the transvestites (some professional, some part-time, and neither necessarily to be confused with the trannies or the common or garden drag queens). 'Fag hags': a phenomenon of whose existence he had previously been completely unaware. Transsexuals were mostly pre-op in those days. Eighty-five percent of them, for reasons it took Henry a while to figure out, were called Christine. Those who had gone all the way, the posties, were few and very far between, and generally treated with awe and a quick shudder by their neighbours. In the teller line, people moved away, afraid that they might be catching. Then there were the bisexuals and those individuals who were just plain sexually confused. Few were more confused than Henry and it took him quite a while to realize that each one might have to be treated differently when it came to their business relationship with the bank. Head Office didn't offer a how-to course either.

Contrary to his expectations, there were many business relationships. The neighbourhood was expanding rapidly. Closets were being emptied with aplomb and an out, outed and outing marketplace wanted to be catered to. One of Henry's credit-related jobs, in addition to reading financial statements and monitoring lists of receivables, was to check inventory when he made an operating loan to a business, and his customers had some fairly hair-raising businesses.

His first visit to a sex emporium brought moisture to places on his body that had never known moisture. The fact that the proprietor was what his accountant described as 'a flaming queen' did not help. This individual greeted him at the door of his establishment in a waistcoat and black leather chaps. He appeared to be wearing precious little else however, except, that is, what Henry could only describe as a codpiece. He had had to ransack the swashbuckling juvenilia of his mind to come up with the word, and he found that he couldn't take his eyes off it. Mr. Queen (Henry had a lifelong and sometimes unfortunate habit of ascribing nicknames to people on first sight) didn't mind a bit.

He proceeded to show Henry the great variety of his merchandise, frequently fondling it — the merchandise, that is — in the process, offering demonstrations of usage and capacity. Henry was appalled. His mind was as stretched taut as the rubber band on a child's toy. It might have snapped hadn't a customer interrupted with an inquiry about a dildo and something called poppers. Henry sought the cocoon of his office. He was pursued there half an hour later by Mr. Queen, desperate to find out in what way he had offended his bank manager. He had no wish, he said this at least ten times, to do so. Henry sat safe behind his desk, the codpiece at eye level, while he said it.

There was no one at the branch with whom he could gossip or talk. Banks were hierarchical. The sole possible exception was his accountant but, Henry's knowledge growing by leaps and bounds, he had come to the conclusion that she was some kind of a — now what was the term? — dyke. Latent, possibly; bull, probably; and butch, absolutely. To be fair, he had to doubt whether she realized it. Soon, however, Henry began to relax and he found that he enjoyed his customers. They had a spry sense of humour, they said what was on their minds — a little too floridly, he sometimes thought — and they were what one of his aunts back home would have called 'jolly'. Not all of them of course, but a great many more than the somewhat spastic heterosexual entrepreneurs he had dealt with previously.

Admittedly, the first time he took a client to lunch it had been a disaster.

*

Peter Lacey owned a small bookshop, the front portion of which catered, as far as Henry could make out as he fled past the shelves, to bizarre sexual proclivities beyond the farthest reaches of his imagination. Henry's imagination was certainly active — as we have seen — but it lacked the earthy and hyperbolic assurance of the type of reading material Mr. Lacey stocked for his customers, always slamming up against the bourgeois barricades of his background. Mr. Lacey, however, was willing to put up with what he described as 'the junk at the front' for the sake of the lovingly maintained literary first editions he displayed at the back. This part of his store was a feast for the bibliophile, although Henry had to wonder how anyone felt having to run the gauntlet to get at these treasures. The response when he asked, was an arch 'you'd be surprised', and, indeed, one day he had seen a very maiden lady, eyes to the floor, rubbing a gloved palm down the spine of an extremely old book bound in black leather. Not the bound-in-black-leather the village was used to either. Her ecstasy was of an entirely different kind.

Lunch might have gone better had Mr. Lacey not mentioned in passing, before Henry had even spread the napkin on his lap, that he had AIDS. Henry, vaguely aware that the disease was passed by way of bodily fluids, spent the rest of the hour trying to protect his meal from any errant saliva his guest might expectorate. Particularly, on his soup. Mr. Lacey had a lisp and was slightly sibilant. Only when Henry returned to the sanctuary to his office did he calm down and wonder what the gentle bookseller must have thought of him. It was a while before he realized that Peter Lacey was, in all probability, fully aware of Henry's discomfort. The fact that he had neither encouraged it nor tried to free Henry from it, Henry ultimately found admirable but, at the same time, it was all most unsettling.

Henry was dimly aware, even in those days, how uncomfortable he was in his own skin, and that his flights of fancy, his imaginings — humdrum though, it now appeared, they might be — were probably symptomatic of something unsatisfactory in himself. A malaise. A need. At the very least, a lack. He began to compare himself to the bookseller. Here was a man, he realised, so entirely comfortable with who he was that he could be at ease with a disease that would destroy not only his skin but his very being. And do it very quickly as well.

How does he manage? Henry wondered. How does he do it? How does he survive? How can he be so at peace with himself?

Oh, you're not like him. He's queer.
What has that got to do with it?
Gay people are more arty. Self aware. All that stuff.
You're crazy. You know that? You're buying into stereotypes.
No, I'm not. Go home to your wife if you want to see a stereotype!

He attended Peter Lacey's funeral nine months later. He suggested to Leah that it would be proper if she attended with him, but she refused to hear of it and told him he wasn't to go either. He was just the bank manager and shouldn't get involved.

It was too dangerous. 'Remember: don't go anywhere near the open casket, or don't come home tonight. How could you like a person like that anyway?'

Henry cried at the graveside. He had lost a friend.

Henry's horizons grew during the approximately four years he was at the branch. One skin was shed and another Henry gradually emerged. Sometimes it seemed to him that he imagined less, had less time for it, less inclination. He became involved in other people's lives. The dissatisfactions of his own could be put aside — temporarily — while the living went on all around him. It could be embarrassing to be hailed on the subway — 'Halloo, Mister Bank Manager, dahling' — by a female with a five o'clock shadow, but the accompanying wink made him part of the conspiracy. Only occasionally did it occur to Henry that such playacting could be dangerous, that it could go wrong, or that the ordinary might ultimately prove irretrievable.

*

Henry had been at the branch for three years when, late one afternoon, Dr. Raymond pushed open the front door and came in. He was there to apply for a loan. A short, stocky man in his forties, the doctor introduced himself and told Henry that he was a psychiatrist, newly appointed to the Mental Health Facility on Queen Street and that he needed the loan to upgrade office equipment. Henry completed the paperwork, chatted, and told the doctor it would take a week or so to carry out credit checks and have the application approved by Head Office.

The following afternoon, just as the branch was about to close, Dr. Raymond came back into the branch and began to repot all the plants in the banking hall. Henry sat in his office and watched. The good Doctor watered, took cuttings, stripped away dead leaves and supported neglected flora with bamboo sticks. Most of the staff had left by the time Henry approached him to suggest he also might like to leave as they were about to close the vault. He escorted the doctor out of the door.

Two days later, the doctor came back. He sat down in the banking hall next to the table that held the deposit slips and began to empty a pillowcase that he had brought with him slung over his shoulder. It was a large pillowcase. From it, he withdrew an extravagant quantity of toiletries. Toothbrush, face cloth, razor, comb, Neet, a hand mirror. All these things and many others were removed and placed side by side, precisely, on the table. Then the doctor held the pillowcase between his knees, reached in, and began to extract a variety of clothes. A flowered dress with a scalloped white collar came first. It was followed by a man's striped tie and a large pocket handkerchief. Then a pair of men's shoes, size twelve from the look of them. A ladies' petticoat, satin and shiny, appeared next. Then black high heeled pumps. Also size twelve, or so they seemed. And a pair of trousers. On it went. When there was nothing left to put on the table, the items, one by one, went back into the pillowcase. When all were in, the process began again.

The tellers giggled, but soon they turned their heads away.

Henry watched. Eventually, he approached the doctor and asked if there was anything he could do for him. Dr. Raymond smiled and said, no, he was just taking stock of his belongings, and didn't require any help, thank you so much.

'Unless, perhaps, you know whether my loan has been approved.'

'No, not yet,' said Henry, 'Nothing in from Head Office yet, I'm afraid.'

'Ah, too soon, I imagine, to expect a response. It's just that,' Dr Raymond smiled, 'I'd like to get organized.'

He began to unpack the pillowcase once more. He was the most organized man Henry had ever seen.

'Do you have any toothpaste I might borrow? This is almost finished.' He held out a full tube of Crest, forcing Henry to take hold of it.

Henry shook his head. 'No, I'm sorry, I don't, but this one should last you a few more days.'

'I'm not sure. Do you think so? Really?' The doctor looked up at Henry as though seeking reassurance. 'I must have clean teeth. Must have.'

He began to mumble to himself and soon Henry could not make out anything he was saying, nothing that made sense anyway. He leaned towards the doctor and took him by the shoulder.

'I think you should be on your way now,' he said gently. 'It's time to go.'

'Yes, yes of course.' The doctor pulled himself up and shook his head as if clearing the cobwebs from it, but then immediately slumped down again. Tears filled his eyes.

'I couldn't maintain the charade, you see,' he said, adding, both surprised and forlorn, 'She left me. I couldn't do it any more. It was too wearisome.'

After Henry and his accountant failed to coax the doctor out the door, Henry felt obliged to call the police. He didn't like doing it, but the man was scaring his staff — they weren't saying anything but Henry could see it in their eyes. Not least, the man scared Henry. He had been so believable that first day. Believable even when he pruned the plants. Believable — almost — when he placed his possessions neatly in rows for inspection and then, with quiet courtesy, tried to explain the conundrum of his life. But not when he wouldn't leave.

The next day the doctor's application came back approved.

There was a certain amount of flack when Henry wrote back to say that the loan would not be drawn down. Really, he should not have tried to explain why, but he did. He didn't do it very well and, in the fullness of bank time, a memo appeared commenting that Henry might have been expected to notice that the man must have been mad from the outset. Henry didn't agree. It was true that the doctor was not a medical doctor at all, but he was a Pd. D., and until he became a patient, he had been the head of the institution's Personnel Department. Married, with children. Perhaps his mind came and went, a tide ebbing and flowing on the shore, as Henry knew his own was sometimes capable of doing. Even at the end, even as the man was being led away, Henry thought he had seen a reality there. But what was the man's reality and what — it really did make Henry think — was his own?

The incident didn't do much for Henry's reputation with the mucky mucks and he knew that they would have much preferred to forget they had approved the loan. The history of Robbery Central didn't help either, but it was the teller-line defalcation in which he finally did play the role of super hero that completely sank his career in the branch system he loved so much.

39

'L'Affaire avec Pot' was Henry's name for what happened on the worst day of his working life. He had never tried to quantify exactly where it stood among the most miserable of his whole existence, but it would certainly be up there amongst those as well. The name marked the day that nature, matrimony and business all joined together to conspire against him and they succeeded beyond anything they could have imagined or hoped for.

He had been in the Inspection Division of the bank for a couple of years, learning how to audit in the outer reaches of Ontario, enjoying it quite well thank you very much. He was away from home, gaining confidence every day and out of sight of the Head Office denizens and dimwits, except when the team returned to Toronto to write its reports. The camaraderie of his fellow auditors, their increasing reliance on his precision and dedication to the task at hand, and their willingness to put up with the fact that they had to remember to speak up, shout even, when they were talking to him, made getting out of bed in the morning something to look forward to.

If his hearing was declining exponentially — he was still a one hearing-aid man at this point — worrying about it remained something that could be shunted aside or joked about. He knew very well that there are only a limited number of ways a person can say, 'Sorry, I didn't hear what you said,' but if he made fun of himself in the process, the embarrassment was eased. The worst time was when he was in a crowded room and all the noise came at him at once, unfiltered and unadorned, but on the audit circuit the crowded room was usually a tavern after hours and the rosy glow he could induce with the assistance of a glass or two of good merlot made his infirmity more acceptable, both to himself and to his companions.

Then he got promoted. The call to be a Senior Audit Inspector back in Toronto was telephoned to his motel in Wawa in the middle of a blizzard, and he had accepted the position before he thought about the implications. The hive of congratulations from the team when he told them next morning further lulled him into a benign belief that acceptance had been the right thing and it was only when he arrived at his own good front door the following Friday evening that doubt began to raise its hoary head.

Leah, however, seemed reasonably content to have him back and, with one daughter married and the other two away at college, he settled into his new life without too much regret. Fate was lying in wait, however, and Henry should have known it. It began with a telephone call from Inez Morganthau. She informed him that she had made a long-delayed appointment at a downtown hospital for a series of tests on his mastoid bone to make certain that everything was in order with that aspect of his hearing. He should have had the tests some time ago, said Inez, but now that he was back, there was no time like the present. Henry had replied with his own cliché, something to the effect that they might as well strike while the iron was hot, and booked the morning of the appointment off work.

The evening before the appointment two things happened. He was called in by his boss and informed that, as a result of a bout of influenza, the Inspector who was scheduled to begin an audit of Staff Banking at Head Office would not be able to work and Henry was to take over the team. Auditing Staff Banking was regarded as a plum, and Henry was pleased. The job was downtown, all the equipment was first class, and one could assume that it would be a clean audit, in that the branch was a training ground for the up, the coming and the connected. It was generally acknowledged that the people who worked there were among the most presentable and, not to put too fine a point on it, the best looking the bank hired. Particularly the females. It was true that Henry would have to be a little cautious of the politics of the place since the percentage of nieces and nephews of mucky mucks on staff was said to be a statistical improbability, but he was sure he could cope with that. He didn't put much mind to a warning from a friend who reminded him that the manager, a large blonde lady, was the concubine of an Executive Vice President.

Henry should have paid attention, if only because the rumoured EVP in question was Kotex Clark. The large blonde lady had been known for years as Kotex's Confucian secretary (she was, as they say, permanent and had been screwed on his desk) but age was sidling up to her and Kotex had taken the dicey step of promoting her to a managerial position to get her, metaphorically, off his back, while, at the same time, keeping her close enough to ensure her occasional availability for what his Dad would have called 'a little bit of slap and tickle'. Nudge, nudge. The excellence of her staff ensured that the large blonde lady would not require a great deal of banking experience and her monumental dearth of knowledge could be supplemented by a quick call for assistance to one of Kotex's minions.

The other thing that happened the evening before Henry's mastoid examination was that, out of the blue, while sitting there watching television on the rattan, Leah had announced that, since she would be downtown having afternoon tea in the Arcadian Room at The Bay the next afternoon, she and the minister's wife would drop in to see him at his office. Henry was so stunned by these words he had to ask Leah to repeat them. Twice. She had never been to his office, had never evinced the slightest degree of interest in seeing any of his offices, and he could not understand why she should want to start now.

'Henry,' she said, 'you're at Head Office now. I should know where you work. Mrs. Abercrombie was asking me about it.'

Mrs. Abercrombie was the minister's wife. The sine qua non of Leah's snobbery.

'But I'll be working!' Henry replied. He really didn't know what to say.

'Well, Henry, it's not as though we'll be there all day. Don't you want me to see where you work?'

There was a very short answer to that question, but in the end Henry made an accommodation. If Leah and Mrs. Abercrombie found themselves in the building at a quarter to five, he would be there to show them his desk, his computer and what constituted his office. With a little bit of luck everyone would either still be out on a job or gone home for the day.

Henry should have known better than to rely on his luck.

*

The next morning Henry went straight to the hospital. The hour of his appointment passed, but he didn't particularly mind since it gave him time to read through the report of Staff Banking's last audit. Everything had gone swimmingly (at that juncture the manager had been a sister of the Chairman of the Board) and he did not envision that he would find much wrong now. The job should be finished in a couple of days and it would be clean. By the time the nurse came to take him into the examination room it was almost noon. He was hungry and thirsty and no longer in the best of tempers. He had telephoned his assistant to tell him that he wasn't sure what time he would get in, but that they should aim to arrive at Staff Banking at five to four just as the branch was closing. His assistant — a political being down to the high shine of his black oxfords — asked whether Henry was going to phone the large blonde lady to give her a heads up on what was about to happen. Henry, being Henry, demurred. In those days branches were never given notice of what was to descend on them: to be forewarned would very definitely be to be forearmed and he was pretty sure that the Chief Inspector would have his head if he told anyone — the Lord God Almighty included — that they were coming.

In the examination room, Henry was put to lie down on a flat vinyl-covered table and told to wait a few minutes. Forty-nine of them — he consulted his watch — had sped by before the nurse, all breezy apology, wheeled in a large machine the shape and size of a small refrigerator which she positioned at the head of the table, just out of his line of sight. The machine was humming gently.

'I'm just going to attach the machine behind your right ear,' the nurse explained. 'Could you turn your head to the left, please.'

Henry did as he was told and a plastic cup-like attachment was placed behind the ear. It was held there with a clamp that went over his head, the other (sharp) end already beginning to dig into his left temple.

'Comfy?' the nurse asked. She added, at a velocity that precluded the possibility of an answer, 'I've just got to put this pad underneath you.'

The pad, an inch high and two inches wide, was a piece of unvarnished wood.

She inserted it between his backbone and the table just below Henry's shoulder blades. The effect was to raise his spine off the table, flatten his diaphragm and stick his stomach out.

'Ouch!' he said summarily. It was not that the pad hurt, but it was immediately uncomfortable.

The nurse took no notice.

'Now,' she continued, 'I want you to lie still. Keep you head steady — we don't want the machine to come undone — and whatever you do, don't move. Any questions?' Again, there was no possibility of a response before she added, 'I'm going to turn the machine on now and then I'll leave you for a few minutes. Okay?'

She had turned the machine on and the door was closing behind her before Henry could open his mouth to speak. What happened next, however, removed his power of speech. The machine that had been humming quietly to itself during the nurse's preparations erupted. A crashing of waves pounded into his head. The noise could have been no more intense if two choleric oceans were to meet on some distant shore and begin to fight each other for domination. He tried to define the sound, but so awful and constant was the noise that he soon gave up and tried to concentrate on merely surviving it. Every crevice in his head was being assaulted. A loose filling in one of his back teeth began to shake (Henry was filled with dread), and his jawbone seemed to be in the process of separating itself from the rest of his skull. He closed his eyes, grimaced mightily, and breathed slowly out trying to eject every last drop of air from his lungs in the hope that if he could, he would somehow be able to begin life anew when he breathed in again. The effect of breathing out, however, was to press downward on the portion of his spine that rested on the wooden pad. An intense pain shuttled through his body and the confluence of oceans pulverized his brain.

'Aaaaayeeeahh!' Henry howled, forcing back a sob.

Not daring to move, he could, nevertheless, not bear to lie still. He began to utter spare rhythmic grunts from the back of his throat in the vain hope that such a ritual might appease the evil spirits which were attacking each atom of his being. His second hope was that the nurse would return in every consecutive instant and release him. This hope too was vain. It was thirty minutes before the door opened.

'Here we are then!' the nurse said, 'Everything alright?'

Henry could not speak. His clothing was drenched in sweat, every muscle in his body seemed to have seized and even when the machine was turned off, his head throbbed with anguish. The best he could do was swallow some of the saliva that was threatening to slop over and drown him.

The four words that Henry heard next were the most fearsome he had ever heard. He heard them dimly but he heard them nevertheless.

'Now the next ear,' said the nurse, quickly readjusting the wiring and the head attachments, and moving a nimble hand to check on the spine pad. 'Still in place, is it?' she asked.

'Bloody fucking hell!'

Henry whimpered the words as the door swung closed again and left him the next best thing to knackered. When the nurse returned the requisite thirty minutes later, he wondered whether she noticed the tears that were flooding down his cheeks, running in rivulets along his neck and soaking the front of one of his best white shirts. He suspected not. In any case, he could not have cared less. Released from the machine, he turned on his side, yanked free the pad and lay foetally on the table for ten minutes before he was able even to consider hauling himself upright, focusing on the door and getting out of the place.

*

The audit team was waiting for him, bags packed and raring to go, when Henry finally arrived at the office. It was almost four o'clock and they had just enough time to take the elevator down to Staff Banking. First, however, Henry had to sit down. He had been having to sit down every five minutes since he left the hospital. If they were late, so what? He was much more interested in what he could do to rid his head — and his neck, his shoulders and the small of his back — from a pain that still threatened to crush him. A quick beheading seemed a likely solution. Instead, he reached inside his desk drawer and took out a bottle of aspirin. Just a few, he commanded himself, immediately chewing six to a fine powder. For insurance, he swallowed six more. One aspirin had escaped and rolled across his blotting paper. He grabbed it, 'A baker's dozen!' he said to no one in particular.

'About ready then, Henry?' shouted his assistant through the open door. 'We should be off.'

'Just give me a few more minutes.' Henry snapped at the man. 'I've got a bad headache.'

'Should we go on ahead?'

'No, I'll be with you soon.'

'They'll have closed the branch when we get there.'

'I know they'll have closed the branch! They'll just have to open the doors again to let us in.'

Henry's assistant decided to push the matter. 'The tellers will have finished counting their cash.'

'Well, they'll just have to count it again, won't they!' said Henry, carefully resting his forehead on his hands.

The audit team arrived at Staff Banking's closed glass doors at twenty past four. When they rang the bell, a shocked and clearly dismayed individual approached the door from the inside. He turned out to be the branch accountant, and it was evident that he was not happy to see them. The element of surprise was considered an important aspect of an audit, but traditionally the team arrived at closing time, not when everyone was well into the work that allowed them to pack up and go home. Tellers were being balanced, ledger keepers were totting up rows of figures, loan officers readying documentation to be sent to the Credit Department and so on. Even if an audit was expected, it was a reasonable assumption that if it did not arrive by five minutes after closing, it would not be coming.

The accountant, a likely young fellow still in his twenties, put his head through the door. 'What do you lot want?'

'Guess!' replied Henry's assistant, rather nastily.

'I've already got three of the tellers balanced and locked up. Their blotters are finished.' A blotter is where the teller records the work of the day and shows that everything is in order.

'Are you going to let us in or not?' asked Henry, more crabbily than was his wont. He wanted to sit down. His head was throbbing and the whooshing sound of rushing water would not go away.

The accountant was sweating slightly but he opened the door to let them through. He had no choice in the matter.

40

Henry had been on the audit circuit long enough to get a feel for a branch in the first thirty seconds of being there. An inspector's intuition, it was called. It might be that the atmosphere becomes just a little more tense than an audit's appearance usually induces; that smiles disappear (or reappear) a mite too abruptly; or that the staff becomes just that much too intent on what they are doing at their desks, but Henry's intuition was a good thermometer that something might be awry. Not that outright thievery was necessarily going on, but that something was out of whack and would need looking into. Perhaps it would only be that the staff had been taking shortcuts or that the work was not as up to date as it should have been, that safes had been left ajar to save time now the branch was closed and customers were no longer wandering about.

Henry couldn't put his finger on it yet — and his headache didn't help — but the hair on the back of his neck was standing up, which was usually a dead giveaway. Something was amiss. He walked down the main banking hall towards the Manager's office, letter of introduction in hand. In his peripheral vision, he noticed that one of the ledger supervisors was issuing frowned instructions to her juniors. Nothing unusual there, he thought, she wants a good audit. Further on, one of the loans' officers waved to him.

'Oh God, Mr. Earl, not today for pity's sake. I've a pile of work to do,' she laughed, 'Come back next week.'

Henry waved back, smiling as much as his head would allow. He had known the woman for years, and however much work she had, he knew it would be accurate and neat and her credit decisions would be unimpeachable. He walked on and, as he did so, he glanced to his left. Three tellers, smart young women all, were whispering among themselves. One of them had a hand over her mouth. She appeared nervous. That, of course, was not unusual. It might be her first audit, but somehow Henry didn't think it was that and, as he passed by, he saw that the three of them were holding (somewhat awkwardly, he reckoned) their locked cash bags in front of them. This meant that their cashes had been counted by amount and denomination and everything noted on their blotters. They were balanced and, essentially, their work was over for the day.

Having made a mental note of all this, Henry entered the office of the large blonde lady, introduced himself, handed her his letter and sat down. She did not appear to be impressed. Evidently the importance of the inspection function had not been covered while canoodling with Kotex. She greeted Henry as though he was an unwelcome, but not at all important, housefly that had somehow gotten into her room and was buzzing around her head.

'No one told me you were coming,' she said.

Henry, cranium still awash like a running toilet that would not turn itself off, tried to make a joke of it. 'That's the idea, I imagine!'

She was not amused.

'Well, I don't have to stay, do I?' she said, pouting attractively. 'I've things to do.'

Henry was reminded of a grown up Glynis from his Scarborough days. No, 'grown up' was wrong, he thought. She was pushing forty, but something about her seemed childish, unfinished.

'You don't have to be here, no, it's not absolutely necessary.' Henry said this as though giving considerable thought to the subject. 'But,' he continued, a light going on, 'you might want to stay and support your staff. It's always a good thing for the general to be with his troops at a time like this, don't you think?'

Whatever her response was, Henry didn't hear it. He could see the three tellers through the open door. They had been joined by the accountant who leaned into the group, pushing a large red handbag at the young woman who had had her hand in front of her mouth just minutes before.

'Who is your accountant? Do I know him?' he asked.

'Vincent Perigrine's son. Nice boy. Did you know Vince? He's retired. He used to be EVP West. We see him at the club.'

'Umm,' said Henry.

A couple more minutes of stilted chit-chat and Henry excused himself. There was work to be done. His audit team had dispersed and was already hard at it. His assistant was in charge of the cash counts and had begun to count the tellers who had not completed their work. The counted cashes would be dealt with in due course: the keys to those cash bags were in his assistant's pocket. The teller with the red handbag looked peculiarly uncomfortable and it went through Henry's mind that her two friends were endeavouring to shield her from view. The accountant was nowhere in sight.

Henry called out, 'Let's finish counting the tellers and they will be able to get out of here.' And almost as an afterthought, 'Give me the keys to the counted bags and I can get on with those while you finish the rest of the line.'

Keys in hand, all bonhomie and beatitude, he approached the three young women.

'Who wants to go first then? How about you?' He took the cash bag from the woman with the handbag, adding, 'Do you have your blotter? Should we put your handbag under the counter out of the way while we count your cash?' It might have sounded like one, but it was not a question.

With the cash out of the bag and back into her drawer, Henry checked her blotter. It did not take more than a glance to see that a bundle of twenties was missing. He could feel the shallow breathing of the teller behind him.

'Who counted your cash?' Henry turned to her. Her face was paper-white and she refused to look at him.

'The accountant did.'

'Hmm, there's two thousand I can't see. That's a great deal of money for the two of you to have made a mistake over. Very strange.'

It would not do to accuse anyone too soon.

Henry was aware that the accountant had been watching what was going on and he called him over.

'Everything alright?' asked the accountant, a bit bleakly Henry thought.

'She seems to be short a bundle of twenties.'

'She can't be. I counted them myself.'

'Do you want to do a recount?'

Tears had begun to run down the teller's face. Henry turned to her and said gently, 'No need to be upset yet, my dear. If I miscounted, I'm sure we'll find it. Come on, let's get a handkerchief out of your purse and wipe those tears away.'

He reached under the counter and pulled out the handbag. She refused to take hold of it, however, and it dropped to the floor.

'It was him!' she cried, pointing to the accountant, 'and them, too!' She turned to the other two tellers and started to sob, 'They made me do it!'

*

In the melee that followed, accusations were flung hither and yon. It turned out that the cash had not been so much stolen as borrowed. On a weekly basis the three tellers took turns giving two thousand of the bank's cash to the junior Peregrine who bought marijuana with it wholesale and, before the evening was out, sold it retail up and down Yonge Street. The base capital was returned next morning. Each of the three tellers received five percent of the profits and Mr. Peregrine's youngest pocketed the rest. Capitalism at work. Of course, Henry did not garner this information in efficiently parsed sentences or precisely defined bullet points for easy understanding. It came out in dribs and drabs and accusations and counteraccusations, and the getting of it took time.

The accountant turned out to be a more than usually nasty piece of work. He complained to the large blonde lady that he was being set up to take a fall. She, evidently believing that the son of a retired Executive Vice President, an Executive

Vice President who was, indeed, himself the buddy of her inamorato, was more to be relied on than a mere bank Inspector, told Henry that he was wrong — she did not say how she knew this — and that it was all nonsense. Henry's head was percolating quietly by this time, but the ache was still there and he was in no mood to listen to a floozy, whether large and blonde or of any other variety if it came to that. They had found the bundle in the handbag. The large blonde lady refused to accept what she could see with her own two eyes.

Eventually coming to dimly realize, however, that a defalcation found during the course of an audit might be an unsightly blot on her hithertofor immaculate career (the word 'immaculate' was only to be applied to her career, mind you) the large blonde lady at length became hysterical, disappeared into her office and called her boyfriend whose office was some forty stories above her own still pretty but now heated head. Five minutes later, Kotex Clark appeared at the door of Staff Banking suited up as pristinely as Henry remembered him from his days at Robbery Central, but, at the same time, appearing to be extremely perturbed.

'What's going on here?' he demanded.

The large blonde lady endeavoured to fling herself into his arms, but if she was willing to throw her career down the drain with such public displays of what he had always hoped would remain a hidden liaison, Kotex was apparently not. He must have been aware too that the whole of the branch staff and all of Henry's auditors were crowding round agog at the events that were unfolding. He fended her off and turned to Henry for an explanation. Henry was in the middle of giving it — and Kotex clearly did not like what he was hearing — when a loud rapping began on the glass doors of the branch.

Henry's wife was not in the habit of being stood up and when she and the minister's wife had waited upstairs for his appearance ten minutes beyond the appointed time, she had had enough. She demanded to be told where he was. Against all protocol, the receptionist, a junior and practically alone in the place, not only told her, but proffered directions on how to get there. When Leah peered through the door of the branch, she could see Henry at the centre of a couple of dozen people and she waved to catch his, or anyone else's, attention. Since no one took any notice, however, she then banged on the door with a black leather encased fist.

'Henry!' she shouted.

It was Kotex who saw her.

'Who the hell is that woman?' he demanded, 'What does she want? Doesn't she know the damn place is closed?'

Henry looked up and saw his career slipping away before his eyes.

'Aaarrgh!' he said.

'I know that woman from somewhere,' said Kotex.

'I don't know what he's talking about,' declaimed the accountant.

'He forced me into it,' cried the teller.

'Oh, sweetie, what are we going to do now?' said the large blonde woman.

'We weren't involved at all,' bawled the other two tellers practically in unison.

'Jesus Christ Almighty!' muttered Henry's assistant.

'Henry, where were you? I told you we'd be there at a quarter to five!' said Leah advancing rapidly towards him down the banking hall.

'Shit! Shit! Shit!' quoth Henry evermore.

41

In the years after L'Affaire avec Pot, Henry gradually came to realize that the best that the bank would ever permit him to be was competent. He had wanted to be so much more. There had been a time when he had been hot to trot to become visible, 'out there' in his profession, but somewhere along the way, such ambition curdled and circumstance hadn't helped. Somewhere on the journey, he ran out of energy, too. Ambition faltered. His hearing was a hindrance, and Leah, well, she was never much assistance either. Not actively a hindrance, not purposely, but when he compiled a list of the pros and the cons of his career, where was he more likely to put her?

Through it all, he managed to maintain his love of the ridiculous. His sense of humour, a bit bizarre at the outset perhaps, became increasingly unkind over the years, but his Dad had always said that you can make a joke about anything, that nothing was out of bounds. His Dad had loved to ruminate on grand topics, particularly after his second pint.

'Laugh at the lot, my lad,' he would say 'You can laugh at it all. The only thing to do with politics these days is have a good laugh anyway. Religion? Organized religion is the biggest joke of all! Yes, at marriage, too. Life? Hold a mirror up to life, my lad, and you'll be roaring with laughter.' Henry would nod, partly in agreement, partly at his enjoyment of the performance. 'Even . . . ?' a pause and several nods of a serious head, 'Even, yes, at death!'. Henry had loved the tone of pontification more than the message. 'But always, my lad,' his Dad would conclude, 'Always remember that the most important thing is, you've got to be able to laugh at yourself first.'

Henry couldn't do that, not any longer.

*

He spent the rest of his day wandering through the city, strolling about in his memory, meandering in his imagination. He hopped over the slush in Kensington Market, rode the streetcar to his graduation ceremony along with his Dad and his Mam visiting from England, and he sledded, red-faced in the icy wind with Max, colliding with a snowman in the ravine on St. Clair. He passed by the church in which he had been blown away listening to Mozart's Requiem and he wept again remembering the magnificence of the music and mourning that he would never hear it again.

He was weary as he boarded the subway to go back to his house. He had to wait three stops before he could find a seat. So much for this generation standing up for the aged. As he looked around, he was surprised to see his Dad seated opposite reading the football results. He waved to him, and his Dad must have seen the movement, for he looked up and waved back. They sat grinning at each other across the aisle all the way North until it was time to transfer to the trolley bus, but when Henry looked for him in the crowd that surged out the door, he no longer seemed to be around.

Henry was already late when he reached the house, but he walked round the back for a final look at the garden. He felt old and his limbs were aching, but he knew that he still had far to go. The questions that he had been asking himself all day hung unanswered in the frigid April air. They wound themselves around the branches of the blue spruce and attached themselves to the brittle, dry stems of the hollyhocks against the North fence. If there were answers, he was unable to hear them. He pushed at the earth with his overshoe, turning up snow and dry frosted leaves, trying to decide if spring was about due or whether there would be another two weeks of winter. Not that it mattered to him, but it would have been nice to know, just the same. He paused, and an all-enveloping sadness seemed to pull at the hem of his overcoat, weighing him down. He did not know why, perhaps it was the general anomie of the world. He felt that he should want to pray, but he knew that there would be no point. No one was listening. God had more important things on his mind, more important stuff to do than to hear Henry. And, and Henry almost chuckled at the thought, perhaps God was deaf, too.

The thought cheered him a little and he began to feel better. All in all it had been a good day. In some ways, it had been a good life: he had to admit it. Still, nothing in the day, no thought, no sight, no remembrance, made him want to change his mind, to alter the course of what he intended to do. His life had gone on long enough. He would enter the house for one last last supper, quite sure, quite at ease, that his decision was correct and that he could go ahead.

Tomorrow, it would be over.

Wouldn't they be surprised!

42

When the elevator doors opened at Henry's floor on that final Friday afternoon, he fished, as usual, in his pocket for his swipe card only to find that the pocket appeared to be empty. His nails trawled the bottom, catching onto little bits of unexpected algae, but it was clear there was nothing there. As he fished, he moved forward, wading walking straight forward until he stopped almost at the elevator door on the other side of the foyer. His feet were sodden and heavy. He felt totally unable to turn the requisite ninety degrees towards the entrance doors. It didn't even matter which ninety degrees. There was a door to his left and a door to his right, and while the one on the left would lead directly to his desk, the other one would let him in just as well.

Panic! What if the elevator in front of him opened? Anglers would have to splash by him, or treat him as a stepping stone in the stream, and he could not take anyone jumping on his head just now. He had been pummelled enough, thank you very much.

Where was the damn card anyway? It was true that he was early, but that shouldn't have made any difference, should it? Perhaps the card only appeared when it was time for it to be used. Perhaps a big fish fighting its way up stream to spawn had swallowed it, or another fisherman had stolen it from his tackle box and was swiping it somewhere else right now on another floor, another access point. Henry inclined his head towards the bank of the river but he was uncertain whether he would be able to wade through the swirling bloody waters. They didn't appear to be deep but he had reason to know how treacherous they were.

He was wondering what to do next when Boney walked by on the other side of the glass door and saw him.

'Henry,' he said, opening the door a fraction and manoeuvring his head through it, 'you're early. It's not time yet.'

When Henry looked at his watch, he saw that Boney was correct.

'I say,' he said, 'what a good thing this watch is waterproof. It would have stopped by now if it hadn't been, and then where would we be? Or, what is more important, where would I be? Not here, I bet! Or late, at any rate.'

'You can't come in yet.' Boney sounded annoyed. 'You're supposed to be here at three.' It was a quarter of. He was peering over Henry's shoulder, keeping the door ajar only as far as was absolutely necessary, and whispering.

'That's okay, don't worry about it,' Henry said. 'If you could just give me a hand out of this deep bit, I'll sit on the bank and dry off until you are ready for me.' He laughed. 'I should have worn my wellies.'

Boney frowned. He was opening his mouth to reply when the security alarm went off. The door had been open too long. Henry gazed up and around, towards the ceiling.

'Birds!' he said, 'I have always loved birds.'

This certainly wasn't true. Henry had grown up with his Dad's view of birds, a gardener's view. They were filthy little creatures that picked and pecked at his seedlings, and shat all over his driveway. Henry had agreed so well with this sentiment that he had arranged scarecrows among his veggies and stretched chicken wire across his azaleas. But then he changed. His late but total affection for the species came about abruptly. It was the day he came home from having his first hearing aid fitted. He sat out in the back garden and there they were chirping their fool heads off as though their lives depended on it. He hadn't heard a bird in years, and suddenly there they were. Lice infested they might be, but being able to hear them, he could forgive them anything. He was enchanted. He had come to genuinely worship the carillon of the cardinal and to anticipate the symphony of small birds that arranged themselves in rows on the branches of the old trees that surrounded his property.

'What a lovely sound,' he said, 'I wonder what kind they are.'

'Oh, for God's sake, come inside,' said Boney, evidently not quite knowing what to do. The shrillness of the bell continued to bounce off the marble walls: a submarine's pinging radar searching for the bottom. 'Be quiet about it.'

Henry waded to shore.

'I must have forgotten my pass,' he said, as he hauled himself onto the dry bank. 'Sorry about that.'

Boney looked at him, 'You gave it in to me on Wednesday. You surrendered it when you left. Everyone had to.'

Henry could see the heads of people above the level of the cubicles, looking up to see what the commotion was about. There seemed to be fewer of them than he remembered. Most of them glanced away when they saw him, their eyes returning to the greys and blues of their computer screens.

'You were supposed to come in at three.' Boney hissed the words at Henry, a reproach. 'We told everyone here they could go home early. So they wouldn't be here. So they wouldn't see you.' Anxiety was leaking out. 'They haven't gone yet! We didn't want you to be embarrassed.'

Henry wondered what it was he was supposed to be embarrassed about but was interrupted when Olaf stood up in his cubicle across the way and called out in his usual Slavic bark, 'Henry, my friend, how's you doing?'

Boney flinched.

Olaf came towards Henry at a gallop. He raised his hands to welcome him, head listing to one side and his face an essay in tragedy. 'There, there!' he crooned as he wrapped his arms around his erstwhile boss, taking hold of the back of Henry's head in the palm of a massive hand and clasping him against the harsh Baltic wool of his pullover. He clung to Henry, cooing at him, rocking him sideways slightly, as if he were a baby. 'Shhh, shhh,' he said. 'The bastards!.'

Henry could barely breathe. His nose was lodged under Olaf's armpit and he felt the thick weave of the pullover imprinting itself against his cheek. He struggled to come up for air. He had no intention of being smothered to death by a large Lithuanian at this stage. Not even in the name of solidarity.

'Off!' he bleated, 'Get off me!' He pushed back as hard as he could, but Olaf was six inches taller, fifty pounds of flab heavier, and in the grip of a powerful emotion. Henry remained in the grip of Olaf.

'Olaf!' said Boney sharply. 'Leave Henry alone. Put him down. And none of your Marxist ranting, look you!'

Olaf, however, lifted Henry clear off the ground and carried him back to his old cubicle. Henry inhaled the pullover desperately searching for pockets of air. What he got were the vapours of the alcoholic beverage Olaf had consumed with his lunch. Henry had given Olaf his job against some stiff competition and Olaf had always been grateful. There was no need for gratitude: he had been the best man available.

'All power to the bloody fucking people,' Olaf muttered, raising a fist in the air and, in the process, clamping Henry ever more firmly against him. He could feel Olaf's suspender digging into his nose. This was not the way he intended to go. Not at all. What would the papers say? 'Henry smothered by techie's winter woollie'? He began to wriggle. He pushed his face downwards until he could make out Olaf's belly and launched his head as far backward as he could. Henry Houdini, the human cannonball.

'Aaaaaahh!' he yelled, coming up for air. 'Arrrrghh!'

He swung into his cubicle and slumped down on his chair. Olaf, all concern, followed him in and knelt like a suppliant before him, untucking the bottom of his pullover to wipe Henry's brow.

'There, there,' he said once more.

Boney seemed to be in a dilemma. Henry imagined him speaking to his wife about it later over a dry sherry. Should he have entered the cubicle or should he have stayed back?

'Henry,' he coughed, 'since you are already here, perhaps you should get down to business and then you can get out of here.' His voice had a skip in it when he added, 'To begin your new life!'

Henry moved backward away from Olaf, the rollers on his chair going from first to fourth in less than a second. He took a deep breath, looked around and waved Olaf to his feet.

'Oh,' he said, 'I shouldn't be long. Just want to pack up my personal belongings.' He laughed, wondering if they could hear the edge of the hysteria he was feeling. 'When you work in a place as long as I've worked here, you do accumulate stuff.'

He looked around at the bric a brac that lay like a heavy dew on all the available surfaces of his cubicle. 'I certainly have been a pack rat,' he said.

He had to admit he liked his cubicle. It wasn't much and it wasn't very big, but it was his. Still would have been if they hadn't thrown him out, tossed him aside like a used tissue. His cubicle was his home away from home, and really he preferred to be away from home. All his personal things were here. A Rubik cube, his pet rock, a kooz ball, three globe paperweights, a minute, teeny tiny dictionary. The mementoes, the keepsakes and the fad items. They were all here.

This was the place he came to to get away from Leah. Everything was here except photographs. Not even one of Max. The boy was his secret. But she was not far behind. One day someone had asked him if he was married. Henry, deep in the womb of his workspace, snuggled by security, had had to think for a moment. Was he? He sometimes worried that they might think he was gay, a man his age seemingly unattached, no significant other who popped up for social events or was moaned about at the water cooler. He had considered putting a four by six on his credenza, but the thought was not a happy one and, in the end, he decided they could think what they bloody well liked.

'I got you some boxes, Henry,' said Olaf, 'I'll help you pack.' He looked at Boney with defiance.

The unassembled brown packing cases were leaning against the wall of the cubicle, several of them stacked together. Olaf reached for one and brought it over his head, threatening to decapitate Boney as it swung in a wide arc before landing on the carpet. Boney flinched but remained standing. Henry, panting slightly, was still out of breath. He and Boney watched Olaf as he worked, twisting and inserting the flaps to assemble the box, getting it wrong like everyone always does the first time and having to start over again. Henry reached down to help him, but Olaf waved him off, swatted at his hand and commanded, 'Stay!'

Henry did not know whether to bark or wag his tail. He sat quietly, running his hands along the edge of his desk and across its surfaces, letting his fingers trace the contours of his mouse, caressing the metallic coolness of his keyboard. Henry liked surfaces. They were, he imagined, like braille. They told you quite a lot but they didn't ruffle you; they didn't threaten as much as they informed. They were erotic, too. Whether it was the fluted edge of a piece of cardboard or the inside of a woman's thigh — not that he could recall one of those very well — surfaces go far beyond the surface. They can be deep.

He pulled his chair forward, away from Olaf, so that he was seated properly at his empty desk. Dictionaries stood straight and proud to his right, his computer on the left. For some reason, it was turned off. Here it was nearly the middle of the afternoon and his computer was turned off. It didn't make sense. He looked at the monitor's screen and saw that it was covered by a film of dust. So much for the cleaners, he thought, reaching out to rub the cuff of his jacket sleeve against it.

Olaf handed an empty box to Henry.

'Why don't you start on this one while I get another one ready, yah?' he said. 'As for you,' he turned to Boney, 'you could go away.'

It was not said unkindly or impudently, but as an afterthought, a coda, to someone of supreme unimportance. Boney had been standing absently picking with his thumb at the fabric of the cubicle wall where it joined the metal upright, but he stopped, smoothed it back down, and turned away. Then he turned back.

'Henry,' he said, 'remember, before you go, there's one or two things I want to ask you, just to clarify the things you were working on, so give me a head's up when you're ready.' A nervous laugh. 'Olaf can't help me!'

Henry peered up at him but the words didn't register properly. He closed his eyes for a moment; he needed to rest them. Then he rubbed his hands over his face and stood, wondering what he should pack. It was funny really, he thought. What do I want to take with me?

You can't take it with you anyway.

And — he glanced at his watch — I'll be going soon. I'm not going to leave stuff for Boney to pick through though, although he's probably done that already.

What a dreadful sentence.

But it's true.

I'm not so sure. Olaf wouldn't let him take much. He would guard the door.

Olaf would set the dogs on him, if he tried anything.

Perhaps Olaf might like some of my stuff. God knows a dictionary or two would come in handy. Dialectical Materialism to English would be good.

And he can have your pens.

The man already has more pens in his breast pocket than a peacock has feathers, but you can give him yours as well, I suppose.

Henry began to put items that he thought might be useful for Olaf into the box. Then he began to fill another box with personal stuff. A third box was given over to textbooks and a fourth and fifth to binders from courses he had attended over the years.

Suddenly it was important to leave nothing behind.

I'm taking the lot.

How will you carry it?

We'll get a dolly and roll it down to the parking area and load everything into a taxi or two. A fucking fleet of taxis if we have to.

Watch your language.

Nothing stays behind.

Where will you send the taxi?

You'll find out!

*

Henry opened his credenza. No doubt about it, he was a bit of a pack rat. Two unopened boxes of tissues stood next to a roll of toilet paper — 'butt tissue' Olaf always insisted on calling it. Why he had that there he did not know, but there it was, the end trailing down, trapped under a box of large paperclips. Behind a broken desk lamp he could see a pair of his summer shoes. A plaque was wedged into one of them. He had won it for one of his research projects. He deserved that plaque. His findings had saved a VP's bacon and the porker hadn't hesitated to say so — until the crisis was over and he began to think that it was not the best thing to be beholden to anyone. So he arranged the plaque for Henry and got himself sent to the Harvard Business School on an intensive six months executive management course. Henry never saw him again. He heard about him, of course — his upward rise, the speech he gave to the Empire Club and his swift, sudden dismissal when one of his product launches fell flat, costing the bank millions. He might have got away with it — what's a few mill between execs? — but the press got wind of the story and the shareholders began to ask questions.

Henry hefted the plaque. It was beginning to tarnish and he threw it in the trash.

Olaf had finished his boxes and was hovering.

'How's about a cup of coffee?' he said.

Henry shook his head. He couldn't speak.

'Come on, yah? Your mug's right here.'

Boney's voice came over the top of the partition.

'He's not allowed to leave his cubicle.'

Olaf raised his left index finger and thrust it towards the voice.

'I'll bring one,' he said, mouthing Baltic obscenities in the same direction, and off he went.

'Henry,' said a voice nervously. 'I just wanted to say how sorry I was to hear that you are leaving.'

Standing at the door was a young man whose name Henry should have known, but didn't, at least not today he didn't. They had worked together on a couple of projects. His visitor glanced over towards where Boney was sitting, but quickly looked away.

'I wanted to tell you,' he continued slowly and deliberately, 'how useful, how valuable, I found your expertise and your willingness to share it. It helped me a lot. I appreciated your taking time to explain things. Most people wouldn't have bothered.' He leaned toward Henry, modulating his voice to a conspiratorial mutter, 'They're crazy. They don't know what they're doing, firing you!'

Henry knew how good he was, dammit, but it was still good to hear it.

'You'll do well,' he replied. 'Work hard and you'll do well.'

His visitor came into the cubicle and leaned forward awkwardly to embrace Henry. Then he turned away and was gone.

When Olaf returned with the coffee, he was trailed by three marketing people from the other side of the floor. They all looked shell-shocked. Their smiles appeared etched in ice. They kept looking around, Henry thought, to see if anyone was watching them.

'Hi, Henry, sorry that you're going.' A slight stammer.

'We'll miss you, Henry, take care of yourself.' Uneven braggadocio.

'Oh, Henry, don't worry! You'll find something easily. You're a great worker!' Tentative defiance.

The three stood at the door of the cubicle, but they didn't step inside. Henry honoured their bravery, foolhardy as it undoubtedly was, but he knew how right they were to be afraid. Perhaps, he thought, the air in his designated space had been polluted and the powers that be had determined to fumigate it — and him with it — in case a lethal toxin somehow began to spread out beyond his eight by eight piece of real estate. He breathed in to see if he could detect something, something odiferous perhaps, anything that might cause him to reassess what he knew very well had happened, but he was quite certain that the only smelly thing here, the only thing rotten, was ensconced on the other side of the partition.

'Don't worry about me,' he said in a slightly raised voice, 'I'm just glad to see that they didn't screw you as well.'

The trio shuffled their feet, skittish like young horses and Henry regretted what he had said. Bravery should be rewarded. He had no right to turn the spotlight on these people any further than they themselves already had in coming by. It wasn't too late for them to be popped off one by one, added to the body count, if Boney got his sights on them. Nothing said that ethnic cleansing had to stop at fifty-seven.

No one responded, and Henry heard Boney clear his throat.

'I thought you were told you could leave early today.' His disembodied voice came from the other side of the partition.

Pop.

'We're just saying goodbye to the people who got fired,' said one of the three, putting her tongue out in the direction of Boney's voice.

Boney shot to his feet.

'No one was fired! People were made redundant! It was a business decision!'

Pop pop.

'Strange,' said Henry, 'it felt as though I was fired.'

'And you, Henry, you were given early retirement.' He repeated this to the people at the door of Henry's cubicle. 'Henry was given early retirement.'

Pop pop pop.

'Fuck your early retirement!' muttered Olaf under his breath, leaning against Henry's desk. 'That's the height of shite!' Olaf had a number of mellifluous sayings that Henry found continually fascinating. Most of them, he wouldn't have chosen to say out loud, but sometimes he found that he was uttering them silently, just for fun. This one was a keeper.

Henry waved his hand in the air in front of him and smiled at his visitors. It was not a good smile, not steady, the muscles of his face not entirely at his command, but he tried it nevertheless.

'Go home, folks,' he said, 'don't look such a gift horse in the mouth! It'll be a new world on Monday morning.' His voice strove to be upbeat but settled for composed. That was difficult enough. 'Take care of yourselves.'

He shook hands with each of the three and they took themselves off to join the resistance, to fight another day.

Between sips of coffee, Olaf and Henry continued to pack.

'So much stuff,' said Olaf with a laugh. 'Where does all of it come from?'

They heard Boney clear his throat and he said in a halting way, 'Don't forget, you can't take any project files with you Henry. They belong to the bank.'

Henry lobbed back his answer. 'Don't worry, I'll put them through the shredder before I leave.'

A yelp. 'No! You can't do that!' Boney sounded as though some good soul was throttling him. I wish, thought Henry. 'The work will still go on. Which reminds me, don't forget there are a few questions I have about some of the files I've been reviewing. When you're ready, of course. No hurry.'

Henry did not answer. Instead, he acted out wringing Boney's neck for Olaf, who grinned widely and mimed spitting on the carpet. They continued emptying drawers, sifting through Henry's stuff, putting some of it into boxes, the rest into the trash can.

After a while, Henry called out to Boney, 'I'm just going into my computer to get a couple of things.' He said it almost gaily, 'Then I'll be ready for you.'

Boney shot to his feet again. 'No,' he smarmed, 'you can't do that. We can't let you use your computer.'

'Oh, I won't be more than a minute or two.' Henry replied, playing the innocent. 'I just have a couple of personal files that I'll copy to take home — my Last Will and Testament and, oh, a genealogical table I brought in to put on PowerPoint.' Henry's will — a document that would, in due course, surprise everyone who read it — was locked away in a safety deposit box and the family tree was pure invention, but both of them sounded good and if Boney had a shred of decency, Henry thought, they might give him pause. Olaf, after all, could look over his shoulder. Boney could too, if it came to that. Not that Henry really wanted to get in to his computer. Why should he? There wasn't anything there worth having. It wasn't even the principle of the thing. What it was, was he wanted to make Boney squirm.

Boney obliged.

'You can't,' he wheedled, 'You're not allowed. I've already changed the password.' Boney couldn't have changed the password if his life depended on it. 'Rowena made me do it! It's a rule.'

Henry looked at Olaf sitting on his haunches closing the last box. Olaf nodded. There didn't seem to be anything more to say. Henry closed his eyes. He could feel the rise and fall of his chest and he became aware that he was breathing with his mouth open. He could feel the air going in and out. It was laboured like the air going through an old pair of bellows, one that hadn't been used for a while and wasn't quite used to the effort of it.

'Olaf,' he said, 'I'll need some help to carry these boxes out.'

'Don't worry about that,' replied Olaf, 'Bettina is bringing a dolly at four o'clock. She's already arranged it with Stationery Department.' He looked at his watch. 'She should be here soon. It's five to, now.'

As if on cue, Henry heard squeaks coming down the corridor and Bettina cursing, 'What kinda focking ting dis is, man? Ent go straight fuh anyting! Wher dih arse yuh goin? Keep straight, a 'tall!'

The squeaking grew louder. His funeral procession was assembling.

43

Henry wasn't sure how they were going to manage so many containers on such a small dolly, but he did know that he wouldn't be much help. Perhaps Olaf had been wrong to dismember him and to pack his body into so many different boxes, even if each one had been correctly labelled on the side in black magic marker so that he could be reassembled — or not — later in a less hostile environment (He hesitated to use the word resurrected: it might be a mite presumptuous). Olaf was about to close the last box, and Henry couldn't see what he had written on it. He thought the box contained the last of his manuals along with his left thigh and part of his pelvis, but he had become distracted listening to Boney while the lid was closing and he couldn't be sure. Not to worry, he'd lay out all the pieces eventually and, as long as they were all there, everything would be fine.

There would be a problem, however, if even one box was to get lost. How would all the king's horses ever put Henry together again? What if his life's blood were to seep through the bottom of the cardboard and thus diminish him! Where would he get a transfusion? Did the Red Cross do that kind of thing these days? And what if bits fell out, his contents tumbling onto the ground somewhere, into, say, the nether regions of the trunk of a taxi! What then?

Well, wouldn't I still be okay, as long as it's an unimportant bit.

What bit would that be, though? I'm very fond of all your bits. Surely your pieces are as important to you as your peace of mind.

I haven't had much of that lately!

It's coming, Henry, it's coming.

Plus, I don't see why I should leave anything lying around for Boney to throw in the trash.

Steady on, boyo, no way he would do that. I'm sure he's very fond of your bits and pieces. In his own way, of course.

And you! You keep your hands to yourself, don't you put a finger on me — unless you find one lying on the carpet.

'There you are, Henry. Bettina's here.' Henry heard Olaf afar off. 'Let's get you loaded up.'

'Oooh, 'Enery! What av dey don tuh you?' Henry felt himself being lifted out of his chair and squeezed until what air was left in his chest cavity began to rattle. He felt like a filleted fish.

A salmon, perhaps.

Why would I think of a fish?

'Holaf, man. I go 'elp yuh.'

Watch my head! If you squash that I won't be able to replace it. It's not as though I've a spare lying around.

Don't worry, Olaf will do it scientifically. It's the kind of thing his lot are good at. Order. Precision. He'll put your torso on the bottom, that's the heaviest part, along with some of your statistical analyses. They're heavy enough in all conscience.

He could use my thesauruses for ballast.

Thesauri.

Whatever! They're full of words, aren't they? They'll be just the thing to absorb most of the blood.

A literary sponge, if you like!

What about the long intestine? What if it jumps around like a jack-in-the-box and flips out?

They'll look after all that too, Henry. Relax.

What about my bile?

They better leave that alone. You'll want your bile for yourself. There shouldn't be a shortage anyway. You've been full of it recently.

Well, I'm going to use every last drop before I'm finished.

Christ, Henry, is that your thumb sticking out of that box in the middle of the pile? Not very well packed, if you don't mind my saying so.

Say what you fucking well like, it couldn't be helped. We didn't want to start another box so we were jamming things in, spleen and pancreas and all kind of giblety things. They're in there with my digits.

'That it, then?' Henry asked aloud. 'Am I done?'

A voice. 'Henry, what about our talk?'

Boney stood in front of the cubicle door, blocking the egress of the cortege.

'You'll want to take your plants with you,' said Olaf, placing one of Henry's fici on top of the boxes and walking round to pull the dolly out into the corridor.

'Move!' he commanded Boney, 'he hasn't got time for you now.'

'Llewellyn, my friend,' said Henry, lifting his shoulders in mock resignation. 'I can't stop now. Why don't you call me at home on Monday? I'll be in touch with you at the beginning of the week anyway when I'm supposed to sign the documents. We can talk then.'

It'll depend, of course, on whether the old windpipe manages to remain in one piece, but I wouldn't like to let you down.

Unless it were into a shallow grave.

'And thanks for everything you've ever done for me.'

Not that it was much, mind. I've been carrying you for the past five years.

'Here, take my card then,' said Boney. 'It has my phone number on it.'

Henry gently pushed Boney aside and laughed. How could he not know Boney's phone number? It was engraved on his brain — not to mention his liver, bowel and bladder. He had been calling the thing for years, but Boney had a fetish for giving out his card whenever he had the slightest opportunity. Perhaps, in his mind, it justified his existence. More like, however, Boney had ordered too many and was just trying to use them up so that he could order the new embossed kind. Henry took the card and shoved it into his breast pocket.

He turned in the doorway for a last look back.

'Bye,' he said. 'Nice knowing you.'

*

No great emotion smote him. Lightning did not strike. Tears did not win the day, and he turned again, this time to stand behind the cortege. It was going to be a struggle to get the hearse down the corridor, cornering would be particularly difficult, but if anyone could do it it would be Olaf. He possessed the plodding persistence of his breed. Bettina was standing pressed against the wall to let them past. She was sobbing into a handkerchief and as Henry came up she blew her nose. He noticed that there were other people there as well, lining the walls, blocking out the blood, now dry and rusty, that had scarred them earlier in the week.

Everyone was wearing black and, as Henry came up, they took off their top hats, doffed 'em and dipped 'em towards the boxes on the dolly. He could hear music beginning in the background. The thin skirl of a solitary piper it was, or possibly the solitary skirl of a thin piper, he couldn't be sure which and he couldn't make out the melody either.

The largest ficus wobbled precariously. Henry wondered whether the container underneath it should be straightened. It would diminish the dignity of the moment if the boxes came down ass over teakettle showering the crowd with his innards or even his outtards, and, whatever else, he had no wish to make a fool of himself. This was serious business. He willed himself to steady the boxes, to lie there prone, in whichever boxes he was, remaining calm and, above all, balanced. He spoke to each of his body parts in turn, like a transcendental guru patiently instructing his devotees to relax and be at ease.

Easy for you to say.

'Henry, I'm sorry to see you go.' It was Rowena. She had emerged from her lair and was standing with the rest of the crowd on the edge of the sidewalk waving a Union Jack.

V J Day.

'Well, then,' Henry replied, 'Don't look.'

He walked past the hand she held out.

'It was a matter of numbers. We had no choice.' Her voice trailed him down the corridor.

Henry turned to face her. Priscilla Brace was peeping round her hip, a look of something like satisfaction on her face.

'You,' he said to Rowena, 'are a liar and a very stupid woman. You cannot help being either, but do you even realize that you are going to pay me the same amount to leave as you would have paid me if I had stayed on and worked until I retired? A bit more, in fact.'

He was gaining momentum.

'Halt!' he called out to Olaf, mortuary attendant extraordinary. 'Put the dolly into neutral for a moment. I have something I want to say.'

He turned towards the crowd that was lining the sidewalk far into the distance.

'You can't say anything.'

Was that Olaf hissing to get his attention?

'You're in the boxes and I'd have to get the one with your head in out. I'm not sure which one it is.'

'If you can hear me though,' Henry objected, 'why wouldn't they be able to?'

'I can hear you because we're friends. I think Rowena can hear you because she's a bit like you.'

'Rowe! Like me?'

'Well, yes. You're going to die and her soul is already dead.'

'You mean I may see her in my afterlife?'

'I wouldn't know about that, I'm an atheist and proud of it. Good Stalinists gave up on God. I thought you knew that.'

Henry was preoccupied with the image of bumping into Rowe somewhere in the great beyond and the thought rankled.

'If her soul is already dead, won't she go to the other place?'

Rowena interrupted him triumphantly. 'That's where suicides go anyway. Everybody knows that!'

Her hand remained out, still ready to shake his. Everyone had disappeared and only Bettina and Boney stood next to her by the wall. Henry managed a watery wink in the general direction of Bettina, but he turned his back on Rowena. Olaf kept the foyer door open with his foot and began to manoeuvre the dolly through. The door began to close behind Henry.

'You'll be hearing from me very soon,' he said, into the diminishing space.

Sooner than you think.

'I'll help you down to Parking and we'll get you a taxi, yah?' said Olaf, 'Are you alright?'

*

Henry gazed round at the swirling river. He couldn't fathom why there was no greenery, no flora at the edge of it. Marble rock, pale beige, appeared all impersonal. And why were there doors? It didn't make sense. He felt weak at the knees and leaned against one of the boxes causing the dolly to skew to the left, to bump against the river bank and splash water against it.

'Sorry,' he said. 'Don't want to wake the corpse!'

Olaf put a heavy arm around his shoulder but he didn't speak. Henry did not have the energy to pull away. Olaf had always been a toucher. It had nearly cost him the job before Henry even hired him.

'Press the button,' Henry said, 'we have to go down.'

'Yah,' Olaf replied with a nod, moving away and turning the dolly so that it faced the elevator doors. 'What you bet? It will be the other side that comes. It is always the other side.'

Olaf was wrong. The light above the doors nearest the dolly lit up and the ding of the approaching elevator warned them to be ready. As he invariably did when he was leaving work, he patted his pockets — trouser, jacket and shirt — to make sure that everything was in its appointed place.

Hmm, seems right. Everything's shipshape.

He felt the outline of something small and flat in the breast pocket of his shirt.

What's this? he wondered. He reached inside and ran the ball of his thumb along the edge of a small object, feeling the sharp point of a corner.

*

'What's this, then?' his Dad asked, picking up the card the man had left on the edge of the table, next to their coffee. Henry, his Mam and his Dad were in Tim Horton's having a bite. Henry's Mam loved dutchies and his Dad was very partial to lemon donuts. They came to Tim's every time they visited Toronto. It was part of their ritual.

'The man's deaf,' Henry explained. The words came out before it occurred to him to think about them.

'What do you mean, he's deaf?' His Dad took out his glasses and read the words that were typed on the card.

'You've got to be kidding!' His Dad's voice was rising, and this time there was no acting in it. 'He's deaf — so he's begging?!'

'Shhh, our Phil,' said Henry's Mam, patting her husband's hand nervously as she looked around to see who was watching. Like Henry, she knew her husband.

Henry shrugged.

'What happens next?' asked his Dad, in a dull roar.

Henry did not know what to say.

'Well, he'll,' he tried to clear his throat, glancing round the restaurant to see where the man was. 'He'll come back to pick the card up and,' he coughed cautiously, 'and see if you will give him some money. Change or a dollar or two.'

Henry tried to make it sound like a trifling thing, an event of no importance, but his Dad took flight.

'You mean to say he's asking for a handout? Just because he's deaf!?' People were staring at them. 'Don't be daft, lad, that's ridiculous.' He began to shred the card. 'I'm deaf! I'm deaf and I've worked every damn day of my life. I've never begged from anyone!'

He threw the pieces of the card into the air.

Henry didn't dare move. If he shrugged, it might seem to his Dad that he was sympathizing with the man, taking his side.

'I know.' He mouthed the words, lips moving as they had when he was a boy, just learning that his Dad would be able to follow them. 'I know, Dad,' he said sadly, but somehow he felt too ashamed to look him in the eye when he said them.

His Dad's face was a livid red below the white mane of his hair and his eyes were watering. Henry had never seen him like this. It frightened him, although at the same time he was thrilled at the vitality, the magnitude of the indignation and his father's need to express it.

'He's an absolute bloody disgrace, he is!'

Everyone in the restaurant was looking at them. People on the far side were standing to see what all the commotion was about. The kitchen staff were peering round the door. The only person who didn't look was the man who was still delivering his cards, plying his flatulent con. It flashed through Henry's mind on the wings of giggling hysteria that he wouldn't be coming back here soon. God, no!

'Up!!' His Dad roared the word. 'You two! We're out of here! Now! Come on!'

*

'Down,' said Henry. He said the word far louder than he intended to, startling Olaf who was still manoeuvring the dolly for a quick entry into the elevator. 'We're out of here; it's time to go. Now! Come on!'

He took a deep breath.

'Then I'll be free.'

The elevator doors opened. Olaf pulled the dolly forward. Henry stood outside, watching as the wheels cleared the rim of the door.

Olaf was struggling to stop the large ficus from falling and did not hear.

'He was right to act like that. To shout and roar and leave. You have to do what you believe in. Have to shout from the balcony. You can't rely on anyone else to do it. You have to do it yourself. You have to make a decision and you have to do what you have to do.'

There was a spring in Henry's step as he entered the elevator.

And me, I'll be dead in an hour. Ninety minutes tops. Let's get this show on the road.

'Going down!' said Olaf.

'All the way,' said Henry.

44

He was thirsty again. He decided to stop for a drink when he left the building. He was feeling shaky but it didn't seem wise to put more caffeine into his bloodstream, to add more jump to his jitters. Alcohol wasn't an option either, although there was a tavern right next door. A clear mind was crucial. In honour of his mother, he decided on a rare cup of tea. It was true that tea had caffeine, but his mouth was parched and he had to slake his thirst with something.

The temperature had been next to freezing all day, but he elected to sit outside, virtually on the sidewalk. It was one of those poncey coffee shops that normally he would have passed with scorn: three bucks for a beverage that was no better than it ought to be and a lot more perfumed than he would have wished. He hated these places with their little iron tables that forced pedestrians to hop and skip into the gutter to get round them. In another month or so, the awnings would be up and flags would be strung all atwitter around the doorway, as though the shop itself was a cause for celebration. There ought to be a law. Today, however, he needed the air. He needed to calm his nerves, to breathe the chill of the city into his lungs and reorder his senses. Get back to the plan.

He had thanked Olaf for his help even before the big man had loaded the last of the boxes onto the back seat of the taxi, telling him that he should go now, that he, Henry, would look after closing the doors. No, Olaf had insisted, he would stay and wave Henry off. It was inspiration that made Henry suggest that it might be better if Olaf took the dolly back upstairs so that other people would be able to move their belongings. Olaf grabbed Henry again, one arm under his armpit, the other over his shoulder, squeezing him like the Soviet bear might have squeezed a recalcitrant member of the bourgeoisie, but eventually he let him loose and took himself off, not looking back — but not looking forward either since he tripped on the step leading to the elevators. The last thing Henry heard from him was an oath, an anti-imperialist imprecation, delivered in his lusty baritone.

When Olaf was safely out of sight, Henry slammed the door of the taxi and leaned in at the front passenger window.

'Take these boxes,' he said, 'and drop them on the sidewalk outside the Toronto Sun. It's on King Street East.'

'I know where the Sun is, buddy, but who's going to unload 'em?' said the burly taxi driver. 'I don't do no heavy lifting.'

Henry took out two fifty dollar bills from his wallet. The old kind with the Newfie firing squad.

'Here is something for your trouble,' he said, adding 'and twenty for the fare. Keep the change.'

Henry winked, but the man remained fish-eyed.

'Oh, and when everything is unloaded, take this letter inside and leave it at the front desk.' Henry withdrew a white business envelope from his pocket. 'When you've given it to them, don't hang around. Leave.'

Henry had thought long and hard about what to do with all the trappings of his working life. He didn't expect the newspaper to use them of course, but he did think that there would be enough of them to call attention to themselves, sitting there on the doorstep of the city's tabloid newspaper, blocking the way in and causing people to ask what the hell was going on when they came out. In case that message was somehow missed, the envelope said it all. 'Here lie all my worldly goods,' he had written on the outside, 'Handle with care.' The letter inside was addressed to the Editor. Henry was not sure whether the Sun would be the best repository for his final thoughts — he really did not approve of the tabloid format — but the other morning papers were not likely to take notice of his boxes or the life they contained and even less were they likely to give him the coverage he was seeking.

Even if he ended up on an inside page facing the nearly naked lady, it would be better than the Obit section of the Star or — it hardly bore thinking about — anywhere at all in the Globular Male, 'the nation's newspaper'. Both of these had politics antithetical to his own and, not that he knew a great deal about it, he figured their front pages would already have been chiselled in stone and stereotype for the following morning. The Sun might still be able to sort it all out before it was, what was the phrase, put to bed.

It would not, he hoped, take much sorting. Suicide was not something the press leapt to report but the boxes would help and the letter very briefly went over the facts of the case. He had given his life to his bank — the Sun hated the banks, his more than the others, he thought — and here he had been thrown aside like so much flotsam. Or possibly jetsam: he wasn't exactly sure which word he had used and he wasn't about to pry the envelope open to find out. He had written that ending it this way would be a far, far better thing than he had ever done, and, by Christ, he was going to do it. The wording had given him pause. He had no wish to go out on a wave of plagiarism, but he had always liked the tragic romance of the thought and, in any case, he was pretty sure that only about two percent of the population would know the reference and those who did probably wouldn't be reading the Sun. He had concluded the letter with the hope that his passing would not be an inconvenience to anyone, but that, all in all, it was much better this way. This was an arrant lie, and Henry had twisted his mouth when he wrote it. He was hoping to inconvenience everyone — he would have done it in the middle of the night otherwise.

He had enclosed the best photograph of himself he could find. It had not been easy. Henry did not photograph often and he didn't photograph well. He had, however, found a head and shoulders shot, taken about ten years ago, that didn't look half bad. And if his hair and his lips were a little too thick, they would balance the fact that his chin was a little too firm and his jaw line a little too tight. He felt that he was recognizable, even if it was better to squint your eyes when you looked. A short bullet-point biography was also enclosed. He had watched the number of words he used, knowing that space was likely to be at a premium, but he managed to mention his Dad and his Mam, and Max. Leah was consigned to the mention of 'a wife'. Goneril, Regan and Cordelia were nowhere at all. He was very quite proud of it. On the back of each page, and on the reverse of the photograph, he had written the word 'Scoop' in block capitals. He had felt a bit like Clark Kent when he wrote that.

Henry was reasonably content with how everything was working out. After the taxi had disappeared up the out ramp, he had taken the stairs into the daylight and ambled along the chilly sidewalk. Now he sipped his tea as he decided what to do next. Come to think of it, it was all already done. He was nothing if not organized.

*

His tea was getting cold and the milk had begun to congeal. He blew into the cup and watched the little whirlpool it created. Looking around, he saw that people were walking briskly by on their journey home, or getting ready for a Friday evening on the town. Even at the end of the day, at the end of a business week in the city, many of them still had a spring in their step and he could tell that they were going somewhere. He peered into the passing faces trying to discern in what way he differed from them, but there was nothing that was apparent, nothing that came immediately to mind.

They were men and women: people. Nothing special, nothing to shatter the world or to rock it. Like him. Once or twice he thought that they were looking at him as they passed by — he was sure one woman smiled — but they kept on threading their way along the sidewalk, bodies slightly bent forward in the cold April evening. A couple of young lovers wove by arm in arm. He could see their breath in the air between them. They made him sad. On the far side of the road, a middle-aged man in a three-piece suit stepped into the street to hail a taxi. Was he another Henry? It seemed to Henry that they did resemble each other. 'Is your life as empty as mine?' he wanted to ask. It didn't seem possible that it could be, but what was possible these days? Everything and nothing, it seemed. You had to learn to expect anything, everything — and nothing — all the while factoring in the unexpected.

And that was what Henry was going to do! The unexpected! He was going to bring the city to its knees. Well, if not quite to its knees, he was going to make it stumble. Cause a hiccup in its hurry. Bring people to a stop — mostly people he knew but others as well, if he had to be a hundred percent honest about it. And inconvenience a great many of them. He looked at his watch. Time was passing, ticking inexorably on. Tocking away the minutes to the height of rush hour. He had to be ahead of the train Rowena would take, so that when the system was brought to a screaming halt, she would be stuck on the platform with wall-to-wall people waiting until they cleared the tracks. Henry knew he wasn't being very nice and part of him had been rueful about this aspect of his plan but she, at least, deserved the inconvenience, the bother — and, as for the rest of them, they were going to pay attention to him, this one last time.

When he stood up, it seemed as though the earth trembled a little on its axis. He reached out and steadied himself against the plate glass of the coffee shop's window. A woman sitting inside frowned, as though afraid the window might shatter and shower her with shards of the glass, but nothing happened and Henry turned away, moved out onto the sidewalk, into the steady stream of persons going North. He didn't want to get on the subway at King, he had to get ahead of Rowena, and he set off up Yonge Street towards Dundas.

He saw a man, silver hair combed straight back slightly ruffled by the wind, coming towards him, hand in hand with a young boy. They were talking, laughing with each other about something — Henry couldn't hear what it was — enjoying the late afternoon. They might be going to the Hockey Hall of Fame, he thought, or perhaps they were hurrying to Union Station to catch a train home to the suburbs. As they walked — they were nearly abreast of Henry now — the boy leaned over and flung both arms around the man's waist and squeezed, a wide grin on his face. Henry could smell the fabric of the man's overcoat as they passed by. The boy brushed against Henry's side, hardly touching him at all really, doing no harm, but Henry stumbled sideways. Neither the man nor the boy noticed. They went on their way, disappearing in the gloom of the early evening. Henry wanted to cry.

He looked back, the habit of years, to see if he had forgotten anything. The woman inside the coffee shop was still staring at him. Still frowning. He raised a hand and essayed a brief wave of reassurance. Then, fumbling, he turned off the hearing aid in his left ear. The noise of the traffic dimmed. Next, with the experience of years, he twisted the hearing aid completely out of his right ear and the world turned to silence. The tiny device slipped out of his fingers. It came to a stop underneath the table, but Henry walked away.

*

Not much longer now.
Soon be there.
Soon be over.

Watch where you're walking! Don't stand on the cracks.

Clicketty clack.

Break the devil's back.

Stop for the light. Always wait for the light and then walk.

Don't run.

Ice cream for everyone if you take your time.

Not strawberry though; never strawberry!

Careful how you hold it or up it goes.

Into the sky.

Up, up and away, and I will go with you, let us go then into the sky. Like a patient. Last look.

Now, down, down the stairs.

Into the earth.

Ashes to ashes and into the earth.

Are those footsteps? Don't think so.

Used to be footsteps, but not now. Only echoes.

The walls were cold and the mock marble surrounded him.

Why are they yellow, he wondered? Too much of a cheerful colour for my entrance into the underworld.

Beneath him, he could hear the rumble of the trains.

His Dad had always insisted on calling it the Tube, but this was his subway and that was its name.

The escalator was out of order, so he went down the slick wet stairs.

A large puddle straddled the bottom step. People were jumping over it, landing safe and dry on the other side, but Henry splashed on through. A man coming in the other direction, against the traffic, skipped out of his way, cursing at him, flattening himself against the wall, but Henry moved forward unrepentant. He took a token, his last token — told you he was organized — from his trouser pocket and slotted it into the turnstile, coming onto the crowded platform, the crowded backs of the commuters all before him.

Move.

Move. I'm going forward.

All the way. Forward.

Let me through.

I'm through.

Let me to the front.

Excuse me. Let me pass!

Soon after I've passed you by, my future will be past.

I'll be passé.

Like tyrannosaurus rex or the dodo bird.

Or things not quite remembered, but not completely forgotten.

You'll be at rest, Henry, that's what you'll be. You'll be sitting on a star, swimming in the milky way, pub crawling with the angels. I wish I were you.

But you are me! You all are. We're on our way.

Is that it? Do you hear it coming down the track?

Yes, my lad, that's it now. Coming through the tunnel, punching the cold air before it, eating the ice cream. Won't have to hang about much longer.

Here it comes! What do you think? This one, or do you want to wait for the next one? They come every five minutes in rush hour.

No, it has to be now! Rowena's coming down the steps at King.

Clicketty clack, down the track.

Henry remembered taking the subway back to work after he had been fitted with his first hearing aid. The noise was a revelation and it had buoyed him up, made him laugh out loud, made him want to begin to live again. Now it was only a vague rumble under his feet, the vibration of a world going away. He threaded his way through the crowd, edging towards the green light at the far end of the platform. He was surrounded by the suits of the city. Every sort of person was there. The young and the old, the hopeful and the hopeless, the sweet and the sour. Women as ancient and as bitter-looking as his Gran elbowed their way by, trying to find a space at the very edge of the platform.

Give one of them a push, Henry.

Which one though? It wouldn't be fair if it wasn't my Gran.

Well, you can't have everything, you know.

Look over there. That woman with the red handbag, what a bobby dazzler she is.

Looks like your pal Lola, fifteen years on. I wonder what happened to her.

Sometimes you lose touch with people. No reason. There's usually no reason. It just happens that way.

I'm like my Dad, I guess. All my friends have gone.

Your future's in your past.

Cheer up, laddy, you'll be gone too in half a mo.

Think who you'll see! Marisa! Dorcas! And your Mam! And Max!

Whoa, don't walk too far. No point if the train is almost at a standstill when it gets to you, is there?

Just far enough to shoulder your way through the people, to be able to see into the tunnel.

Easy does it.

Soon there.

He could see the train!

It was almost to the station. Its lights came closer each time he blinked. The platform itself was beginning to throb, to pulse with the life he so wanted to give up. The crowd surged around him, unconnected and impersonal, pushing itself forward. Was that Anna Karenina weaving her way among the feet of the city? She had better look out! He thought he caught a glimpse of his friend David in his duffle coat, still young and diffident but smiling at him from a distance, his eyes as bright and as sad as ever they'd been, but then a teenager with a backpack tried to elbow her way by him, eager to be in front, eager to get somewhere else, eager to show she was alive, and David was gone. The girl popped bubble gum in Henry's face but she didn't see him. Not as a person anyway. Not as Henry. Just an entity, something that was in her way.

'You're just like everybody else,' he said aloud.

This train?

Yes, this one.

At last!

Steady on, Henry. Count to five.

One.

It's almost here. I can make out the driver.

Is Max there, will he be looking out of the front window to see me? Will I see him?

Two.

Think of the chaos you'll cause! No one will be home on time tonight.

She won't even wonder where I am at first, but then she'll find out.

Three.

Now remember, just before it reaches you, step right out.

Like the little girl?

No, no! On purpose! Launch yourself! Fly you to the moon! Get ready to sit upon the stars.

Four.

Any last words, my lovely boy? Oh, my sad son!

What's left to say, Dad?

Five.

And jump.

Feci quod potui, faciant meliora potentes.

Edwards Brothers,Inc!
Thorofare, NJ 08086
14 June, 2010
BA2010165